THE MEMORY
OF
RORY-BEAG

The Memory of Rory-Beag

a novel

Prue Phillipson

**KNOX ROBINSON
PUBLISHING**
London & New York

KNOX ROBINSON
PUBLISHING

34 New House
67-68 Hatton Garden
London, EC1N 8JY
&
244 5th Avenue, Suite 1861
New York, New York 10001

First published in Great Britain and the United States in 2014 by Knox
Robinson Publishing

Copyright © Prue Phillipson 2014

A CIP catalogue record for this book is available from the British Library.

ISBN HC 978-1-910282-12-0
ISBN PB 978-1-910282-26-7

Typeset in Adobe Caslon Pro

Printed in the United States of America and the United Kingdom

This is a work of fiction. Names, characters, places and incidents are either
the product of the author's imagination or used fictitiously.

www.knoxrobinsonpublishing.com

Dedicated to my daughter Claire

who died in 2004

The Memory of
Rory-Beag

1

—

Rory-Beag remembered everything but could communicate nothing. In these days of May 1819 there was almost too much to remember. Fire and water. Burning and drowning.

The first sign of disaster was the thud of a club on the door of Annie Matheson's house at the foot of the glen. She had given birth to a baby boy the day before but there was no man to protect her. Her husband was dead. Rory-Beag had been a witness on that October day when the Factor's man brought the news that the sheep were coming to their glen in the spring. Roderick Matheson had sworn at him and received a blow on the head for his pains. Annie had been angry with him for losing his temper but a few days later he died in the night. She was stricken then for he had left her pregnant. Rory-Beag was unable to tell the Factor what his man had done and Annie's pleas for help went unheeded.

The shout of "Everyone out" cut into the clear air and reverberated round the hills. Rory-Beag peeped from the doorway of the next house and saw Annie walk from her home cradling her baby, her face set like stone. The man with the flaring torch could not meet her eye but Rory-Beag sprang out with hands raised to hold him off for a few moments. He dived into Annie's house, bundled all he could carry into a blanket and tied the ends together. He dragged it out even as the man applied his torch to the heather thatch.

Alistair and Mary Gunn had been gathering their goods together and emerged now as the warning yells leapt up the glen from house to house. The little piles of furniture, bedding and clothes grew like mushrooms. Everyone knew this was coming. It had happened in so many places already but the hope had lived on like a tiny spark that they might still be spared. And now the spark was fire and it was here.

From higher up the glen there were screams and Rory-Beag ran to see what he could do. The old were not quick enough for the Factor's men and the children were so bewildered they could emit only breathless shrieks of panic. The burning began the moment the houses were empty. Rory-Beag was almost trapped when a flaming roof fell in as he dragged out the precious bedding for an old woman who would surely die without it. Nights could be cold still when the north wind swept down from the mountains. His crop of dark curls was singed but he was happy.

Rory-Beag at eleven was still a child in age but mature in upheavals. He could see he would be moving again. It had happened first when he was four years old and his parents had died of small-pox. The people of his glen said it was a pity he hadn't gone too. God had afflicted him, the minister said, and it would have been well for Him to have taken him.

So at four years old Rory-Beag wandered away over the hill and found himself starving in the next glen. Someone gave him two spoonfuls of porridge and asked his name. He tried to say "Angus" but as usual only a sound like a rutting stag came out. A well-dressed man laughed and said, "We'll call him Rory for all he can do is roar." This was spoken in the strange English tongue but he answered to Rory-Beag, Little Rory, from then on.

There had been two more glens since then. No one wanted him since he could only make wild sounds but no one was willing to let him starve. He slept where he could, by peat stacks, under the heather-covered eaves of cottages, wrapped in plaids so frayed and worn they'd been thrown out. He survived. He listened to everyone and in his head he could speak Gaelic fluently and some English from the few well-dressed people that sometimes came to the glens. It was his curse from the devil for the sins of his ancestors that he could not frame words with his distorted mouth.

Finally in Kildonan Glen he had found Alistair Gunn or rather Alistair Gunn had found him, tearing with his teeth at the flesh of a dead grouse. Alistair had asked his name. He answered, "Rory-Beag", but the sound was like the barking of a dog.

"How old are you?" Alistair said then. He'd never been asked that because people gave up too quickly. Alistair Gunn didn't give up. Rory-Beag knew how old he was because he had heard his mother say to his father before they died, "Who will care for Angus the way he is? He cannot survive at only four years old." "You mean we should put him out of his misery," his father said. But they had died before they could do anything and he had run away to find some way to stay alive. He had counted the winters and summers so he was able to answer Alistair Gunn. He held up five fingers of one hand and four of the other.

"Nine years old and no bigger than a six year old! We must fatten you up. I believe I have heard of you from the minister of Strathnaver. You are the one they call Rory-Beag. They say you are the devil's child."

He nodded at the name Rory-Beag but shook his head vigorously at devil's child.

"Why I believe you are a bright wee lad but the good Lord has afflicted you to test the mettle o' the rest o' us. Stay with me, Rory-Beag. I am minded to marry Mary Munro if I'm allowed to and I'm sure she will be good to you or she's not the lass I take her for."

Alistair Gunn had taken him by the hand and led him to his cottage. It took a year but Alistair was given permission by the landowner to marry Mary and she accepted Rory-Beag into their home. By then Glen Kildonan had grown used to him. He would do any task he was given and "the blessedness of him," said the minister, "is that he can never answer back." He grew taller and stronger with Mary Gunn's cooking, sparse as the diet was for everyone in Glen Kildonan. So now at eleven years of age he could drag out tables and chairs before the Factor's men got to work with their torches.

It was a pity that he had to move again but this time he had a family – Alistair and Mary. She was great with child like the Mary in the Bible the minister read in the chapel. Now she huddled with Annie Matheson and her baby while Rory-Beag ran up and down helping wherever he could and Alistair held counsel with the other men about where they were to go.

When all the houses were well alight and the Factor's men and the constables armed with cudgels had departed, Rory-Beag hung about at the fringe of the group of men to listen to their debate. Most of them were old because so many younger men had had to leave home to find work. They were admonishing Alistair as to his duty.

"You're young, Alistair Gunn, and should take a piece of the land they're offering on the coast."

"I hear it's bare rock or with soil no thicker than a cow's hide."

"You could learn fishing. We are too old for that. We're for walking overland to Thurso for the emigrant ship to Canada. We can but die at sea or make our fortunes there. Your Mary is near her term. You can't make her or Annie Matheson wi' her new babe walk all that way. It's your duty to take her poor Roderick's place and be a brother to her. Offer your services to the new owners. They'll surely need hands for the sheep rearing."

Rory-Beag saw Alistair lift his head and stare round at them all. He was a tall man and strong with hair the colour of ripe oats and a bronzed fine-chiselled face. Rory-Beag pictured the archangel Gabriel would look like that. He spoke out now in a voice only a little roughened by the smoke still drifting down the glen.

"I will indeed care for Annie Matheson and her babe if she'll come with us. She and Mary shall be as sisters but I will not bring our bairn into this world of evil men. Nor will I offer my services to men who drive us out of the valley where our ancestors lived and destroy our homes before our eyes. I hid a barrow in the ditch yonder for I knew this day would come. Rory-Beag will help me push it down to Helmsdale carrying Mary and Annie and the babe by turns. There's a man there will take us by sea to Thurso for the Canada ship. If Mary gives birth at Helmsdale there are folks there can help her. I believe the whole glen can start a new life in the new world where there are no cheats, liars nor cruel tyrants. We will meet you at Thurso and trust ourselves to God and the wide ocean."

Rory-Beag had never seen Alistair so inspired. He couldn't help jumping up and down and cheering, though the noise made everyone's head turn.

"Hold your whist, Rory-Beag," said one of the old men, and added, "but I'm thinking we would all be happier if we were like him and didn't understand the trouble we're in."

Rory-Beag kept his counsel. Without speech you were an idiot even when you obeyed orders to perfection.

When Alistair had hauled the barrow up out of the ditch Rory-Beag helped to pad it with the bedding they'd saved. Annie, sitting on her three-legged stool, fed her baby and Rory-Beag saw a tear drop on the tiny face as she watched him suck. Mary was crouched by her, dry-eyed. Her lips were parted, her brows drawn together as she stared at their two burning houses, her hands resting on her swollen belly.

Rory-Beag had first seen her as Alistair's chosen one, small and dainty of face and figure, swift of movement but serene as an angel, with a thick plait, the colour and sheen of a doe's back, reaching to her waist. He turned his eyes from her so that he wouldn't shame himself with tears.

They didn't wait for the procession from the rest of the glen to form itself up. There were many hours of daylight left and litters for the old and sick were being constructed from some of the saved furniture. Rory-Beag saw people so dazed they just sat on the ground and watched their lives reduced to ashes.

He himself gladly shouldered Annie Matheson's bundle as Alistair lifted her into the barrow. Mary, who had held the baby briefly, placed him in her arms. Rory-Beag could see from the way Mary handled him that she was thinking of her own child she would soon be cradling.

They piled what they could round Annie and filled the peat basket with clothes and provisions for Alistair to carry but there were still possessions left in a little heap. Alistair said, "I'll walk back for them with the empty barrow if we can find Mary and Annie a lodging for tonight. But God knows what we can take on Robert Mackay's wee boat from Helmsdale."

He set off pushing the heavy barrow with the peat basket on his back. No one waved them off. No more words were spoken.

2

Rory-Beag trudged along a few paces behind and from time to time Mary put her hand on his shoulder to steady herself when the way was rough. He thought how tough it was to be a woman and carry all that weight in front.

After three miles Annie insisted on getting down and letting Mary ride. Mary looked very happy to hold the baby. He slept. Rory-Beag had noticed that new-born babies did a deal of sleeping. He wished he could remember being a baby before his parents knew that he would never be able to talk like other people. But they had taken the trouble to have him christened Angus and he never forgot that was his baptismal name though he had been Rory-Beag for seven years now.

Helmsdale was a cluster of houses round a harbour. He had seen it before and the closeness of the houses always surprised him. In Kildonan they were scattered up the glen. Here they clung onto each other as if seeking protection from all that water out there. Alistair sought out the man called Robert Mackay while Rory and the women waited on the waterfront.

Mary pointed. "Is that the boat will take us to Thurso? It's a sloop I believe."

Rory-Beag saw a vessel with a mast and two rolled up sails. It had a half-deck so you could go below and be dry if it rained. Its name was painted on the side. Mary told him it was *Gannet* and a gannet was a seabird. He yearned to step on board and be carried out to sea. The waves were only little and would not toss Mary about too much.

Robert Mackay was a solid man with a walk like a bull when he came towards them with Alistair.

"I'll no take ye myself, Alistair Gunn," he was saying. "Brother Jamie does the sailing now and I mind the business at home." He shouted out, "Captain Jamie!" and a florid man in a sailor's hat stuck his head out of the cabin and grinned at the little party.

"He likes to be called Captain Jamie. You'll please him by addressing him as such, for he is a captain when he's in charge o' a ship, is he not?"

Alistair acknowledged this with a nod. He laid one hand on his chest and encompassed his little family with a wave of the other. "You see what we are – a man, a boy and two women. We only want to go to Thurso for the emigrant ship. What will you charge?"

"You have a babe as well and like to be another soon I reckon."

"They take no room. We have little baggage, though if you're not for sailing today I might go back for what I had to leave behind."

"Ay, well the evening's drawing in and the tide would be better at first light. If I give you all a bed and a supper the night and Jamie sets sail wi' you tomorrow well-provisioned for the voyage to Thurso I'd be wanting five pounds."

"Five pounds! They are only charging ten pounds to cross the ocean."

"You were let off your rents for the sheep coming."

"I can give you a pound and ten shillings if you can feed us a dish of porridge too in the morning."

While they were bargaining Rory-Beag saw Captain Jamie come up out of the sloop and pull on his brother's sleeve. He smelt of whisky and was fat and wobbly, whereas his brother was fat and muscled.

"I canna make her ready for sea by morn." He whispered it but Rory Beag's ears were sharp. "There's seams to caulk."

"Do your best, man," Robert Mackay muttered and then in a jovial voice, grinning sideways at Alistair, "Gunn here and the boy can crew for you."

"Nay, I'm no sailor," Alistair protested.

"You're strong and you can do as he tells you."

Rory-Beag shouted, "So can I!" The roar that came out startled both brothers.

Captain Jamie recoiled. "I'm no sailing wi' him aboard. He has the devil's curse on him."

Robert Mackay laughed. "Nay, I've heard of him. He's harmless and he's handy too. He'll wait on the two women."

"Women!" Captain Jamie looked at them with even more horror. "Are they coming?"

"They're all for the Canada ship at Thurso."

"She'll be dropping her bairn soon, that one."

Mary shook her head. "Two more weeks I reckon. We'll be safe aboard the big ship where there'll be room enough and plenty of help."

Robert Mackay made a dismissive gesture towards his brother. "Enough talk. Make ready to sail at first light. Come away in, Alistair Gunn, and we'll get your womenfolk food and rest for they looks in sore need o' it."

He spoke kindly and Rory-Beag was sure he must be a good man at heart. Had he not referred to him, Rory-Beag, the butt of so much suspicion, as 'harmless and handy'?

He wished Robert was taking them to sea rather than Jamie. He looked a man of more purpose and capability. All the same venturing on the water was going to be a great adventure and it was hard to have to wait a whole night for it to happen.

In the morning the sea was an eerily flat calm and the air heavy with heat. It had built up in the night in the cramped room under the eaves of Robert Mackay's house which they had all shared. Annie's baby was fretful and none of them had slept well.

Meg Mackay, a spare, ageing woman gave them porridge with an ill grace, but there was plenty of it and Rory-Beag ate all he could cram in. He was ready to walk back up the glen for the goods they had left behind but Alistair had decided against returning.

"Captain Jamie has loaded a keg of whisky and a barrel of fresh water. The sloop is too small to take more than we've already got and I'm told we're to be given houses in Canada with the furnishings needed for life there. Besides, I have no wish to see the ruins of our homes again. We mustn't look back. The future is everything now, Rory-Beag."

Rory-Beag nodded. Now that morning was here he would have liked to ask Captain Jamie if he had caulked the seams, whatever that meant, and he wanted to tell Alistair what he had overheard but the luxury of communication was denied him. Robert Mackay came to the harbour wall to see them off.

One thing was plain to all of them: Captain Jamie had been drinking. When he held out a hand to help Mary aboard she was steadier than he.

"Are you in a fit state to take charge o' the boat?" Alistair asked him.

"Ay, man, let me just get her out in the open sea and I'll be in my element."

Rory-Beag, waiting on the quay with Annie's bundle, saw one of the many boatmen who were busy about the harbour, sidle up to Robert Mackay. "Ay, Mr Mackay, your brother needed whisky courage to sail in that thing."

Mackay glared at him and then seeing Rory-Beag watching them he laughed.

"He sails better with a dram inside him. They're only going to Thurso."

Rory-Beag could see the man screwing up his courage to say more. "I just have a thought that this heat will turn into a storm later today, Mr Mackay."

"Man, as long as you take my wages you can keep your thoughts to yourself. Get to work on *Seagull*. The duke's agent is hiring her to take him and a party to Leith in a few days."

The man touched his hat and stepped over the sea wall onto a smart two-masted sailing ship where another man was already at work with a mop and bucket. Rory-Beag edged close to hear what they said.

"You see how it is," the first man said behind his hand to his mate. "Robert Mackay would no grieve if he never saw brother Jamie or *Gannet* again. Their father left them four other boats between them and Robert will have the lot. *Gannet* isn't worth the money it'ud take to put her in good shape."

His mate shrugged his shoulders and went on mopping. The first man growled, "Ay well, I wouldn't want women and children on *my* conscience." He went below.

Rory-Beag battled with confused impressions. Robert Mackay had been greedy when he wanted five pounds payment. Then he had acted kindly towards Annie and Mary and he had been a jovial host compared with his dour wife. Now it seemed greed and heartlessness were foremost again.

How could he warn Alistair? Alistair was calling him. The women and the baby were aboard. He ran to him and tugged at his sleeve and pointed towards *Seagull* alongside the quay, but the man with the conscience was not visible.

"Why, Rory-Beag, you're no wanting the great big boat? See how still the water is. We'll be fine in *Gannet*. And Captain Jamie says there's enough breeze beginning to stir to get us out of harbour and we'll pick up a wind there. This is the start of our big adventure, our new life. Tomorrow we should be aboard the great ship that will take us across the ocean. That will be a sight." He was chivvying Rory-Beag on board as he spoke. If he bent down Rory-Beag could spy Mary and Annie and the sleeping baby snug below deck, padded around with bedding.

He could feel the hopefulness of them all. Confidence seeped into him. Alistair was certain they were on their way to Canada. He stepped in, handed Annie's bundle down to her and stood braced by the wooden side, ready to perform any task demanded of him.

Captain Jamie was cheerful too. He explained the terms mainsail and jib-sail to Alistair as he let them loose and Rory-Beag logged them in his memory.

"Ay, we'll do very well." Captain Jamie looked up at his brother on the quay. "You can cast off, Robert." Then there were more lessons about the ropes and how you could manoeuvre the sails to catch the slight breeze and how the wooden thing at the back called the tiller guided the sloop this way and that.

"I'll be letting you take the tiller presently, Alistair Gunn," Captain Jamie said, "so you can feel the wind in the jib-sail. When you've sailed as long as I have you and your ship breathe as one."

When he said that, Rory-Beag had to believe that Captain Jamie knew what he was doing even if he had been drinking whisky already. He clasped his arms about his body to hold in his excitement as the sloop moved away from the quay and the little breeze wafted them out of the harbour.

Now he could see water stretching both ways along the coast and way out to a straight line where the sea met the sky. Alistair Gunn had told him many things and he remembered them all. The earth they were all living on together was a ball and the sky went all the way round it. This was hard to believe but if Alistair said it then it was so.

There was *no* steady wind out here, after all, only fitful gusts, but Captain Jamie showed Alistair how he could use the jib-sail to keep some movement going. Rory-Beag heard the word 'tacking.' He studied what they did with the ropes and wanted to help but no one asked him to.

"Ay, I wanted a good south-easterly," Captain Jamie said, "to drive us up the coast. I was reckoning to make Thurso before nightfall."

"Will you have to anchor for the night if we don't get there?" Alistair asked.

"Well, it's light till late and if it's clear there's stars. I know my way up the Caithness coast. There's no sailor like Captain Jamie Mackay in these parts."

This was good, Rory-Beag thought. What was not so good as the morning wore on was seeing Mary place her hands on her swollen belly, drawing her brows together and compressing her lips. Alistair hadn't noticed. He was too busy learning about sailing from Captain Jamie.

Rory-Beag stepped down from the half deck and crouched in front of the women in their snug covered space. Mary gave him a little smile but went on speaking softly to Annie. He thought, even *she* forgets I can understand all they say. I can't speak so she forgets I can listen.

"Annie," she was saying, "surely it can't be the real thing this time. You know I've had false pains for the past twelve days or more but they passed off and old Morag said I would go at least two more weeks."

Rory-Beag looked at Annie's face and decided she was worried.

"Have they just started again, Mary?" she asked.

"No, they began in the night, small things, nothing. There was some bleeding but I didn't tell Alistair because it dried up and I didn't want to worry him. I wanted nothing to stop us going away but now it's strong."

"Mary, we must turn back."

Mary shook her head most emphatically. "We are skimming along quite merrily. We'll soon be there. Thurso is a proper place and the babe can be born there. The big ship will sail when our people come overland. We will all go aboard together and be comfortable. But if we turn back now we will surely miss the sailing. I beg you if you love me say nothing to Alistair."

Annie lifted her brows and shrugged her shoulders. Her own baby stirred and gave a tiny wail so she put him to her breast.

"I don't like the boy staring so," she said, so Rory-Beag clambered back up and took his place beside Alistair with the enquiring look which said, "Can I help?"

Alistair gazed up at the sun. "It must be about noon. You can hand out the cheese and oatcakes Robert's wife gave us and a mug of water each from the barrel." When he'd said it he looked up at the sun again. "There's a haze creeping over it and that's a strange hot wind flapping the sails." He looked back the way they'd come. The sloop was making an interesting pattern in the water Rory-Beag noticed. But Alistair was looking at the sky. A dirty yellowness had replaced the blueness. The line between sea and sky was blurring. They could still see land over to their left. It had been there all the way so far, green and happy-looking but really blackened and desolate, Rory-Beag knew. It was a land he had left with joy and hope. He didn't like to see an anxious face on Alistair. He didn't like the women to be worried.

Only Captain Jamie with his hand on the tiller and his eyes on the sails seemed happy. He was singing and there was a pewter mug wedged down by his feet. As Rory-Beag looked he refilled it from the keg of whisky which was also snugly placed within reach. Rory-Beag wanted to do so much, to be in control of things, but all he could do was hand round the rations as Alistair had told him.

3

It was mid-afternoon when Mary uttered her first cry. It was more a cry of fear than a shriek of sharp pain but Alistair was down by her side in a moment. Rory-Beag heard him say, "Sweet Jesus, is it the baby?"

Annie said, "She's been in labour since last night and said nothing. It could be near now. What are we to do? Put in to shore?"

Mary was shaking her head. "I can hold back till we get to Thurso."

"We may not reach Thurso till tomorrow with this uncertain wind." Alistair was clasping his head with both hands, the fingers lost in his thick curls. He leapt back up to Captain Jamie and demanded, "Do you know where we are? Can we put ashore?"

Captain Jamie threw back his head and laughed. "We're opposite fifty foot cliffs. Is it your wife? Well, we've not had a babe born on *Gannet* before but if it wants to come you'll no stop it. T'other woman can help her. She's just had her own bairn so she knows all about it. I'm not putting ashore anywhere but Thurso. By the Lord, I knew women and babies would be trouble."

"There must be somewhere you could land when we pass the cliffs." Alistair's voice had a note of panic which Rory-Beag didn't like to hear.

Captain Jamie just shook his head.

In the next hour Mary struggled with what was engulfing her body, the tough business of expelling a baby. Rory-Beag had seen it often, though if the women saw him peering in they chased him away. There was talk of the evil eye but he was only curious. He had seen dogs have puppies with less effort. The minister said it was the curse on Eve that made it hard work for womankind. It was sad though to see Mary go through it, especially when Alistair was casting worried looks at the sky.

Sudden sharp spurts of wind from all quarters began to slap at the sails. Captain Jamie, unsteady on his feet, fought with the ropes and called Alistair to help him. The water around them was whipped into points when before it had been flat.

This must be a storm at sea, Rory-Beag thought. He had heard folk speak of such things and of ships lost. He looked in at the women and saw Annie had wrapped her baby up so that he lay between two folds of a rug in the place where she had been sitting and she was now crouched between Mary's legs and encouraging her to push down. He turned his head away. He wanted to help Alistair. The boat was rocking and Captain Jamie had fallen over laughing. The mainsail swung across and Rory-Beag ducked. Alistair was wrestling with the ropes.

Rory-Beag felt life was going wrong as it had so often done before. But this time the steadfast folk that had seen him safe through the last two years were themselves in trouble. Shouts came from Annie to keep the boat still but how could that be. The wind and the sea had a different plan. They were doing their best to overturn the boat altogether. Captain Jamie had got to his feet again and he and Alistair had somehow reduced the sails but the boat was still rolling.

There came a huge squawk of effort from Mary, a shriek of joy from Annie and an answering baby cry.

Alistair left Captain Jamie to manage and jumped down to see.

Annie yelled at him to keep out of the way for now and he shrank back. Mary had fallen back on her cushion exhausted but Annie was urging her, "Let's have the after-birth, then I can give her to you. She's a perfect wee babe."

Captain Jamie shouted, "Boy, hang on to that rope." And Rory-Beag, thrilled that a live baby had been born, was thankful to have something useful to do. Perhaps God was not angry and would still the wind and the waves as Jesus did on the Sea of Galilee.

Captain Jamie was muttering, "A girl! That's three females aboard and only two men, a crazy lad and a baby boy to balance them. It's unlucky, that's what it is."

From his position Rory-Beag could peer down at the women below and now there seemed no reason not to look. Annie had found scissors in the old leather bag they had kept close by them at all times. Rory-Beag knew it held all the necessities for babies, clean rags, knitted shawls, little home-made caps. She had now cut the cord. He knew you had to sever mother from baby but it didn't hurt anyone. She had pulled down Mary's skirt and was holding a swathed bundle towards her. Mary looked as if someone had picked her up and wrung the life out of her but she took the baby and the smile of an angel lit her face. Alistair had got himself down beside her now and the wild wind and rising waves were all forgotten in that moment. Rory-Beag thought the gaze that passed between them was a glimpse of what heaven must be like.

The rope was ripped from his hand. Captain Jamie cursed, the boat dipped to one side and a wave washed over the bow and sprayed those below.

Annie shouted up, "Watch what you're doing, Rory-Beag."

The noise of sorrow that broke out of him was lost in a rolling growl of distant thunder. Lightning played on the horizon behind them.

Captain Jamie yelled, "That's it, we're cursed. I knew we'd be cursed if the bairn was a girl." He abandoned the tiller to drain the last of the whisky in his mug.

Alistair clambered back to him and seized the tiller. "How do I get this boat to land? Where is the land?"

Rory-Beag had grabbed his rope again as it snaked over the deck but Alistair's question made him look about. There was no land visible. All day they had been aware of the coast of Caithness and that they were making some progress northwards but daylight was fading with the storm. About them was nothing but a troubled sea and the lurid sky touching the masthead. Rory-Beag, for the first time, was truly afraid. If Alistair was at a loss maybe they were all going to die.

Captain Jamie, slumped against the side, lifted his head. "Man, you don't seek land in a storm. You ride it out in the open sea. The land is out there somewhere" – he waved his hand – "and now the wind's settling in yon quarter" – he waved his hand the other way – "we'd be driven ashore if we sought land and smashed to bits." His voice ended in a slurred croak. "We need to make nor'west."

Alistair slapped him across the face with his free hand. "So how do we do that? Tell me what to do. God help us, we trusted our lives to you."

"It's night now. We must ride it out as best we can. I can lash the ropes and hope the wind stays this way." He hauled himself upright using Alistair's arm. "We'll see where we are when dawn comes." Rory-Beag saw him tie some knots. He wanted to understand why they were important.

Then Captain Jamie sank down again and fell asleep. The thunder rolled nearer and rain began to fall out of a coal-black sky.

The sea was playing games with the boat. Alistair held onto the tiller. Rory-Beag supposed he was trying to keep the waves from breaking over the side.

Annie called up, "Mary took a bang at that last lurch. She had her arms about the babe and couldn't save her head from striking that chest. We need a lantern down here. I fear she's bruised. Are we ever going to come out of this, Alistair Gunn?"

"Can you pad the blankets round her?"

"I have. Oh Alistair, we must say our prayers. Can it be that these two babes will have their lives snapped off when they have barely lived? The minister baptised mine – Roderick, after his father. You should baptise yours. You know any Christian soul may do it when life is at stake. What will you call her?"

"What does Mary say?"

But Mary didn't answer.

Alistair told Rory-Beag to hold the tiller that way if he could. Rory-Beag fought with it as Alistair got down below, soaking wet as he was.

"Mary," he called to her, "we must baptise our wee girl. What name shall we have?"

Rory-Beag couldn't see what was going on now. He could only

16

hear Alistair's grunts of effort. He must be struggling not to crush the women or the babies in the dark. He must be bending over Mary, perhaps touching her face to rouse her.

There came a great yell from him. "She's cold. Annie, she's cold. There's no breath coming from her."

"Mind where you're stepping, man. The two babes are here between us. O' course she's cold. We were splashed when the spray came over."

"Nay, it's not that. I've got hold of her hand that was in the blankets. It's cold and limp. Annie, there's no pulse. Oh God, Mary."

Annie shrieked, "What are you doing? Mind the bairns."

"Did not Elijah stretch himself on the dead boy and he lived?"

"She cannot be dead. She cannot have died just like that. What, when she hit her head?"

Rory-Beag began to feel sick in his stomach. The boat had lurched when he left go of the rope. Had *he* killed Mary?

He could hear Alistair's wrenching sobs. "She's all wet below. Not water. It's sticky. She's been bleeding. She's been bleeding her life away and we didn't know. I've kissed her mouth and there's nothing. She's all cold. Oh Mary, Mary how could you leave me?"

It wasn't me, thought Rory-Beag. Women often lost blood and died when babies were born. But for it to happen to Mary! And now Alistair, his rock, was all broken to pieces. In the rush of the wind and rain, in the wild rocking of the boat, he could hear Alistair pleading with God to take them all too. Where was the point of living? This was the end of all their hopes. They had better all drown.

Then he heard Annie speaking up. "Nay, Alistair Gunn. I lost my Roderick but I didn't give up. I lived for his wee son. We may come through this night and still get to Thurso and the Canada ship. You must live for your daughter. Call her Mary. You still have a Mary. Be a man. Would *she* have wanted you to give up?"

And then the two babies set up a wailing.

Rory-Beag could hear shuffling about below and then Annie's voice again.

"Oh for some light here! The lightning would have helped but that's gone. You shift away and let me sit up."

Alistair, choking with grief, cried, "Our baby won't live without her mother."

"That's what I'm trying to do, you fool, put them both to my breasts at once. If I'd borne twins I'd have had to. God sends the milk a woman needs."

"Annie, you shame me, but do not speak of God. He has laid his hands on us all in judgment. I know not why. Here, here's one of the babes."

"That's wee Mary. Give her to me. Roderick's already feasting. There, my pretty, have a drink there. You'll never know it's not your own mother's breast."

The noise of wailing stopped.

Rory-Beag's hands were wet and stiff with cold. To stop himself from losing hold of the rope he got it under his body, twined about his wrists and lay on top of it. The wind was gentler now that the storm had turned to rain. He could feel the huge bulk of Captain Jamie beside him, snoring and heaving about in his sleep. The boat was moving but where he had no idea.

4

Rory-Beag never knew when he fell asleep. Someone, Alistair he supposed, must have found where lanterns were stored because he became aware of a flickering light and that he was no longer clutching the tiller rope but lying wrapped in a blanket below and looking up at the light. He lifted his head and could make out the dim round of Annie's face, eyes shut, mouth a little open. She was propped up on her own bundle and some cushions and the two white wrapped shapes lay on her chest. He could hear her breathing but beside her was a covered dark shape he didn't want to think about.

The boat was creaking and groaning. He could hear water sloshing about under the planks below him. That was a different sound from the slap of the waves and the flapping of the sails. But the rain had stopped.

He scrambled to his feet and poked his head out over the half-deck. Alistair sat at the tiller. It seemed the knots had been undone but Captain Jamie was stretched out asleep against the side.

Alistair said, "Rory-Beag? You're awake. Did you know that Mary died in the night?"

Rory-Beag nodded vigorously.

"God took her. Why I can never know. I wanted to die too but Annie has shown me I must live for the baby. I want her baptised Mary."

Rory-Beag nodded again with a big approving smile. Alistair was himself again. People died around you all the time, as his own parents had died when he was only four, but if you were given time to go on living you had to find something to do and looking after baby Mary was a very big and important thing. If he, Rory-Beag, was allowed to

19

help he could see a deal of happiness coming his way.

"You can blow out the lantern," Alistair said presently. "The sky is lightening yonder but it's a wild grey day and the wind is rising with the dawn."

Captain Jamie stirred as if the words had penetrated his brain. He sat up, rubbing his head. "What's to do? Is the day come at last?"

"Where are we?" Alistair asked him.

Captain Jamie looked all round the horizon and then shook his head.

"Not enough light yet to see where the land is."

"Surely it should be to the west of us. There's the dawn light in the east. We're still drifting northwards. Rory-Beag had the tiller for a while and I've had it the rest of the night. I have to tell you my Mary died after the baby was born."

"Died, eh? That's bad. I won't have a corpse on board. I knew it was ill luck bringing a woman near her time and the devil boy. I never in my life had a cargo like that."

Rory-Beag could feel the heat of Alistair's anger but his face in the growing light showed only exhaustion. He said softly, "Are you a Christian man, Captain Jamie?"

"Course I am, what else would I be? Maybe the boy's not so bad."

"This is not about the boy. If you're a Christian man I want you to baptise my baby Mary and marry me to Annie Matheson."

Rory-Beag, crouched on the half-deck, started and stared up at Alistair. Even Captain Jamie was so astonished he got to his feet, unsteadily and faced Alistair.

"You want me to do *what*? I'm no a minister. You must seek one in Thurso."

Alistair went on talking as if he hadn't spoken. "I've been thinking all night. I've put it to God that He brought us through that storm with two babies still alive. Does He mean them to live? I'm not getting a word from Him as to that but I came to see that if we ever get to Thurso in time for the sailing then Annie and I and the babies must be a family – with Rory-Beag of course. No one but Annie can keep my wee Mary alive and Annie will need a man if she gets to Canada.

It follows plain as can be that I must be her husband. For if I'm not married to her how will I bring up my wee Mary as I want her brought up. And wee Roderick will need a father too."

"Ay ay ay. But all that can be done when we land at Thurso." Captain Jamie looked all round the horizon as if he hoped Thurso would appear before him out of the gloom.

It was much lighter now and Alistair still held the tiller and Rory-Beag had learnt enough now to feel the wind in the jib sail pulling them along but not a sign of land lay to the west of them.

Alistair looked fixedly at Captain Jamie. "We may never get to Thurso. There could be another storm brewing. You as a Christian man may baptise a baby in an emergency and as the captain of a ship you are by law authorised to marry a couple. Rory-Beag, wake Annie."

Rory-Beag slithered down below and crept beside the sleeping Annie very carefully so as not to disturb the babies. But how to wake her without her rousing herself and rolling the babies off? He began to pick up one of them in his own arms, not sure which one it was, when her eyes flew open and she cried out, "What?" And then seeing him, "Rory-Beag, what are you doing?"

Both babies' mouths opened and little cries came out. Rory-Beag pointed up to Alistair and Captain Jamie holding on but both rocking with the boat. The water sloshing below was deeper he could see, closer to the planks. This couldn't be good, he knew, but how to tell Alistair whose mind was set on being married now and having baby Mary baptised? Rory-Beag had much experience of life but this was altogether new and strange.

Alistair shoved the tiller rope into Captain Jamie's hands and stepped down as Annie struggled to sit up and loosen her bodice so the babies could both suck.

Rory-Beag snatched at his hand and pointed at the water below.

Alistair just nodded. "Annie," he said, "we are in great danger. The boat is taking in water and riding sluggishly. I felt the difference before but I see why it is now. We cannot see land though it may be there but the clouds are low and the wind rising. Baby Mary must be baptised and there is no one to do it but Jamie. You and I must be the parents and make the vows for her, and if you and I are to bring up her and Roderick – should God spare us – we must be married. Will you consent to that? I own I cannot love you yet as I did Mary but I know you for a good woman and if the Lord brings us to a life in Canada you will need a man. I will be true and faithful to you and love young Roderick as a son."

Annie stared back at him over the babies' heads. A wave slapped the side and spray came over. A moment of terror showed in her eyes but when it had passed her face changed and her eyes and mouth were wide with joyful surprise.

"Marry you! It may be the last thing I do but it'll be the best."

She stared at him a little longer, laughing now and shaking her head. Rory-Beag forgot the danger they were in. Annie was happy.

"Did you not know," she said at last, "that I always loved you, Alistair Gunn? I took Roderick Matheson because you were pledged to Mary and Roderick was a fine man and loved me. Can it be done? Afterwards we can have a minister pray over us."

Rory-Beag saw hope shining in her eyes. She wasn't as beautiful as Mary but it was a lovely sight. He turned his head to Alistair and saw his eyes were bright too.

"The babies must be cleaned up," she said. "They are both wet. There should be some dry rags in the leather bag." She reached for it.

The boat lurched again. "There isn't time," Alistair said. He drew from the pocket of his coat the Bible which was the first thing he had saved from their house. Rory-Beag loved to fondle the silky ribbon that could be used to mark a place in it and he could see that Alistair was opening it now where the ribbon was.

"Annie," he said, "after I lit the lantern in the night I found the place where the Apostle Peter baptised some people. All we need are the words they used then. I will tell Captain Jamie what to say. Can you stand and hold Mary up? Rory-Beag will take Roderick for a few minutes."

Roderick was not happy to be eased off the breast but Rory-Beag took him and gave him the knuckle of his little finger to suck. Annie got to her feet with Mary still at her breast supported by her left arm.

With her right hand she clung to the edge of the half deck. Alistair had already lifted off the lid of the water barrel and beckoned Captain Jamie to stand beside it. He lashed the tiller rope and came, shaking his head and grinning, as Rory-Beag could tell, at the madness of it all.

Alistair lifted Mary gently from Annie. It was the first time, Rory-Beag knew, that he had held his baby. The little head lolled.

"Captain Jamie, say, 'Do you two repent for her?'"

"D'you repent? My God, this is the craziest thing I ever did."

"We do repent."

Annie echoed it.

"Now scoop your hand in the water and say, 'I baptise thee Mary in the name of the Father, the Son and the Holy Ghost.'"

Captain Jamie gabbled the words and splashed the baby's head. She squawked.

"Not in her mouth you fool," Annie snapped.

Alistair held up his hand. "Annie and I promise to bring her up in the fear of the Lord. Now, Captain, marry us. Say 'Alistair Gunn will you have this woman, Annie Mattheson for your wedded wife?'"

The boat swayed and rocked.

"I must see to the ship."

"Say it first." Alistair's voice was imperious.

Captain Jamie rushed through the words and scarcely waiting for Alistair's 'I will' he gabbled on "Annie Matheson wilt thou have this man, Alistair Gunn, for your husband."

"That I will," she said sturdily and Rory-Beag could feel her joy through the swish of her skirt as it brushed his cheek.

"Then you're man and wife afore God and if we ever get out of this alive I want a fee for doing it." He leapt back to the tiller, released the rope and called Alistair to help him reduce the sails still more. They were tugging this way and that as the wind swirled around them.

"The boy must bail out," Captain Jamie said then.

Annie had settled down under the half-deck and was attending to the babies. She looked at Rory-Beag and pointed to a metal scoop and a gap between planks.

"Get the water out." She grinned suddenly at him. "I'm Mrs Gunn now. You're my boy. I can give you orders."

Rory-Beag was gloriously happy to obey. He saw at once what he had to do. The words 'not finished caulking the seams' came back into his mind. That must be why the water was coming in. Could he keep pace with it?

Alistair had sat down on the deck above with his back to the mast and was writing in his Bible with a stub of pencil.

"Can you read and write, Captain Jamie?" He shouted it over the noise of the wind and the waves.

"Ay."

"I've written here on the blank page at the front, 'I have this day in May 1819 married Alistair Gunn to Annie Matheson on board the Sloop *Gannet* of Helmsdale. Can you sign this 'Captain James Mackay'?"

"There's land to the sou'west!" was his reply to that.

They all turned. A grey shape loomed out of the sea. They were being driven towards it as the gale seemed now to be concentrated from the north east.

"We are saved," Annie squealed out.

"Saved!" yelled Captain Jamie. "More like to be driven to our deaths."

"Then sign this – there." Alistair pushed the pencil at him and he made some sort of scrawl on the page.

Rory-Beag looked at the shape of the land they could see. It had formed itself into a looming cliff and there was other land further back.

"Keep bailing, boy," Captain Jamie screamed at him and got down himself making Annie draw up her knees to snuggle the babes between them and her breasts. Rory-Beag couldn't think what Captain Jamie meant to do as he bent over and grabbed at the blanket-wrapped body of Mary.

"This goes overboard."

He had raised her in his arms when Alistair shouted, "No!" and leapt down too, the boat rocking wildly. "We will make land. She shall have Christian burial."

Annie squealed as the men seemed about to fight for the body.

"Stop it! You'll trample the bairns to death and me too. For God's sake! You'll overturn the boat. Alistair, she's *dead*. Her soul's in heaven."

A stronger gust spun the boat and a wave washed over it.

Rory-Beag bailed but the water was now level with the lower deck planks.

"We must lighten ship," Captain Jamie said, as Alistair, swaying, was still trying to get hold of Mary's body. "I give the orders. She's going over."

"Then I'll do it." Alistair was choking with grief, Rory-Beag could see. He climbed back up to the half-deck and reached for her.

Captain Jamie let him have her, her feet dangling out of the blanket and with a great cry Alistair let her slip into a wave as it rushed past. He crouched there for a moment with his hands over his face unable to watch her vanish out of sight.

Captain Jamie was now watching the cliff drawing nearer. "This is not the Caithness coast. I believe we have past Duncansby Point in the night and should have been heading due west for Thurso. We may have strayed nor'east o' one of the islands – it could be Stroma. There's a good harbour on the south of it but I'm thinking this here might be Swilkie Point. There's a terrible whirlpool about here. We must head south."

Alistair came to life again. "I'll do anything. What can I do?"

Captain Jamie had climbed up again, moving quite fast, Rory-Beag thought, for a man of his bulk. That meant their situation was bad but with a wee speck of hope in it. He was already breaking out the mainsail. He thrust a rope into Alistair's hand.

"Haul on that."

Rory-Beag's hand and arm were numb. His eyes were on the canvas as it billowed out and the boat swung, letting a fresh wave over the top. Then to his astonishment he saw a gash open up in the sail and the next moment the gale had torn it to shreds. At the same time he felt the water below surge over the planks soaking his legs.

Annie screamed, "We're sinking. The babies!"

Rory-Beag looked towards the land. The cliff was nearer but it was like a wedge of cheese. Beyond the sheer fall of it at the highest point he could see it sloped back downwards but the waves were so wild and high he could make out no sort of shore that way. Rather he was transfixed by the huge white plumes they made when they struck the cliff.

Without sail the sloop was entirely at the mercy of the sea. Captain Jamie struggled to his whisky keg and filled his pewter mug and drank it off.

"Take some, man, and die happy." He filled it again and drank it.

The keg was empty. He lurched towards Alistair waving the mug but his foot slipped on the wet deck and he toppled like a huge falling tree.

Below him Annie had just inserted the babies onto the shelf in the deepest corner of the lower deck in the bow of the ship where it was still dry. She was now on her hands and knees gathering up the leather bag and her bundle when the weight of Captain Jamie crashed down on top of her. There came a sickening crack and Rory-Beag in the stern let out a horrified yell. Alistair was down in a second trying to roll the heavy body off her. Rory-Beag abandoned the bailer and scrambled to help. He knew it was no good. Her neck had broken.

Captain Jamie was winded and gasping as they hauled him to one side and looked at the limp crumpled body. Rory-Beag peered into Alistair's face. It was a mask of disbelief as he gently turned her over and her head flopped to one side, eyes and mouth open, aghast at her sudden end.

"Oh no no no," he cried and the sounds went to Rory-Beag's heart.

Fury followed. "You killed her!" He put his hands to Captain Jamie's throat. "You'll die for that."

"Nay, you pushed me," he croaked out. "God damme, you've lost two wives in twenty-four hours." And he began to laugh and choke at the same time.

Rory-Beag didn't want to see Alistair commit murder. He tried to pull his hands from the man's fat neck, looking up into Alistair's distorted face and shaking his head violently.

Alistair straightened up. Captain Jamie drew a gasping breath and then seemed to subside in a drunken stupor. But Rory-Beag looked at him again and saw his eyes were half open watching Alistair's movements warily.

Alistair was looking at the cliff still some way off. "He'll drown anyway. We're all going to drown. Look at that. The babies cannot live without Annie. This is the end, Rory-Beag. We will all meet in heaven. But I would wish our family and friends from the glen to know what happened." His eyes were on the water barrel. "Our bodies may be washed ashore somewhere but I would like a record to go with them. Take your last drink, Rory-Beag, and then I will empty that and put in it the record of my marriage to Annie and fasten the lid and it may float ashore."

Rory-Beag dipped the pewter mug in and drank, but as he did it his mind was working fast. It was terrible to him that Alistair had given up, just because Annie and Mary were dead. He, Rory-Beag, was not going to let his life be snatched away or that of the wee babes who had only just begun to live. They were asleep where Annie had put them but the water would reach them soon even if the boat didn't overturn. He scrambled past Alistair and drew out very carefully the first bundle. Then he turned about and pointed to the water barrel which Alistair was emptying over the side. He made sounds to attract his attention. Alistair looked round.

"What, put the babies in the barrel?"

Rory-Beag nodded, smiling happily at being understood. He handed a dry cushion first. Alistair hesitated but Rory-Beag was insistent. The barrel was lowered on its side into the space and rested against Annie's body. Alistair wiped it inside with a rag from his pocket and laid the cushion in. One baby and then the other were inserted and nestled down onto the cushion. Then he took out his Bible and looked at the first page. "I will add some words. 'I married Annie to bring up our children lawfully before God and men.'" He was writing the words as he spoke. Then he tore out the page and laid it on top of the babies in the barrel. "God be with them. I fear we are all doomed and no one will find them, but it is done."

He had picked up the lid and, sobbing, inserted it firmly. "How to seal it up and how long can they breathe?" He turned the lid by its handle to tighten it. With his fingers he smeared round the rim some tar from the tar barrel used to caulk seams.

The boat was wallowing now, the water inside lapping within inches of the half-deck. She would go down any moment.

"You can swim, Rory-Beag?" Alistair was poised with the barrel.

Rory-Beag nodded, grinning. He exulted that Alistair had done the deed. Now he would swim ashore pushing the barrel and the babies would live.

Neither of them had seen Captain Jamie rear up behind them till Rory-Beag realised out of the corner of his eye that his arm was raised with an iron crow aimed at Alistair's head.

He gave a great squawk but too late. The blow fell and Alistair tumbled into the sea, the barrel pushed in front of him.

Rory-Beag saw the body and the barrel float away. Alistair was face down. He was stunned. He would drown.

"Now you, Devil Boy!" Captain Jamie brandished the iron crow. "I'll get *Gannet* to land without this cursed crew."

Rory-Beag ducked and dived into the water just as a wave swept over her and she keeled to one side tipping Captain Jamie in even as he spoke the words.

Rory-Beag didn't wait to see his struggles. Among the waves he could still see the barrel bobbing. Despite the shock of the coldness of the water he swam after it. All the rest were gone to God but he and the babies would live.

A current washed him past the face of the cliff but he heard a grating sound. Was that *Gannet* smashing against it? A howl rose over the noise of the surf. Had Captain Jamie been crushed between the boat and the rock? If it were so he was well punished. He had killed Alistair who had been Rory-Beag's rock for two precious years of his life.

"God," Rory-Beag's mind was shouting, "I am alone again but I am alive and it is I must save the babies."

5

The barrel was being carried away from him and the wave dragging him refused to let him swim after it. He was caught in the wave and it was breaking round him in a mass of foam. How was this? It flung him down and sucked him back. There was a shelving shore beneath his feet. He stretched out his arms and legs and let the wave carry him forward again. It scraped him over a rock. He clung to the rock as the wave tried to tear him off. But now he could leap and run before the next came. He could dig his hands into the shingle and the water went away from him and he saw before him a scrawny bit of shore with tumbled rocks leading to a wall of cliff. Somehow he had missed the sheer face that fell into the sea and he was alive. He had been right to hope. God meant him to live.

But where was the barrel?

To his astonishment he began to hear shouts and looking away along the shore to his left he saw how it widened and the cliff was only a steep grassy bank over there and people were running down it and pointing at something bouncing in the water. Oh joy of joys! He could see what they were looking at. Now they were surrounding it as a wave rolled it in. It must be. It was, the barrel!

They hadn't seen him, here on this narrow strip of land against the dark cliff. He wanted to yell, "Have a care of it!" but only strange noises came out that didn't penetrate above the roar of the surf. He began to run and only then did he realise the agony of his legs. He looked down. His old homespun kilt had been ripped off him and the skin of his legs was torn and dripping with blood.

He staggered at the shock of it but kept moving, waving his arms and yelling. Someone looked up. They had rolled the barrel clear of the waves but had stood it upright. What would the poor little babes be like, tumbled together in the bottom? Rory-Beag felt a cold fear that they must be dead and only he had survived the storm.

These were strange people. Captain Jamie had said it was not the Caithness coast. It might be a foreign island far from anywhere. They might speak a language he didn't know and they would all believe him to be an idiot. The word 'Stroma' stayed in his mind. His memory held onto everything he had ever been told.

His pace slowed as some of the people approached him warily.

Then a woman made a rush at him, crying, "Oh! Look at the poor lad. Look at his legs and arms. Has he come from the wreck?"

With huge relief he heard the Gaelic tongue. He nodded his head several times, but now his whole thought was for the babies. He pointed past the woman to the barrel and tried to tell her what was in it. The word 'Babies' came out as his usual roar. But his urgency conveyed itself to her.

She laughed. "He's after the whisky." She and the others with her now returned to the barrel, Rory-Beag desperately struggling after them. Someone was attacking the lid with an iron bar.

Rory-Beag pushed among them and grabbed the man's arm. He peered into his face and shook his head.

"What is he saying? He wants the whisky all for himself?"

And then the man held back his hand and listened, horror-struck.

Everyone shrank back. The barrel had uttered a wailing cry.

Now Rory-Beag gave a dance of glee despite his legs. He nodded at them all and made baby-cradling motions with his poor bleeding arms.

"God in heaven!" cried the woman who had shown him compassion. "Is there a child in there?"

Rory-Beag nodded harder than ever and held up two fingers.

The man with the iron bar had come near again and fitted the bar through the handle and turned it with all his force. The lid was loosened. It came away. Rory-Beag was motioning them to lay the barrel down. They understood him and were all down on their knees in a semi-circle as the woman pushed the man on one side and inserted her arms. One tousled bundle was drawn out and then another. A gust of wind caught a paper but a man grabbed at it as it was whirled up.

Rory-Beag's eyes followed it and he saw a gentleman in the black coat of a minister descending the hill. He held out his hand for the paper and it was yielded to him. He looked at it and put it carefully in his pocket. Alistair's message was safe.

Words were flying about over Rory-Beag's head but now he had no attention for anything but the babies.

Both bundles were squirming and tiny fists appeared among the cloths and blankets they were wrapped in. Busy hands soon exposed the little faces, identically red, creased and wailing.

"Oh the poor little things." "Twins!" "Scarce a day or two old." "They are so hungry." "We must get them to the village."

Rory-Beag saw them picked up, saw the minister giving orders and that he himself was forgotten for the moment. It didn't matter. The babies had survived. He took a step to follow the procession up the grassy slope but his legs buckled, the pain of them was too great, a moan came from him and he sank forward, sprawling into a strange buzzing darkness.

He came to himself in a box-bed like his own in the house of Alistair and Mary Gunn. But the pain he was feeling was like nothing he had ever felt before.

A voice was saying, "Keep still, don't squirm."

A woman was leaning over him in the small cupboard-like space and doing things to his legs. He bit his lip and held back the scream. Only babies screamed.

Babies? Where were the babies? Alistair, Annie, Mary – they had all gone from him. He was amongst strangers and the strangers had taken the babies. He couldn't ask what had happened to them. The pain of his legs was nothing to that pain. He began to shake with sobs.

"There, there, now. All done," the woman said presently. "You're a sturdy lad. You'll heal." She withdrew her head and turned to someone in the room behind.

"You wished to question him, Minister?"

"Ay, if he's calm enough now."

Rory-Beag took a gasping breath and raised his head. The gentleman in the black coat was peering in to him and had drawn up a stool to sit by the opening. He had alarming eyebrows like grey furry caterpillars but Rory-Beag was thrilled to see him holding a paper in his hand. Surely it was the page from Alistair's Bible. Please God he was going to hear about the babies now.

"What's your name then, laddie?"

He made sounds that were the nearest he could get to 'Rory-Beag'.

"He must have had a blow on his face," the minister said. "His lips and teeth don't meet properly. I'll wait till he's better."

He got up but Rory-Beag made a grab at his wrist. The minister must ask him things to which he could nod or shake his head. He must be made to understand that he wanted to know where he was and, above all, where were the babies?

His eyes pleaded at the man's face, shifted to the paper and back again.

"You've seen this paper before?"

Nod, nod with great emphasis.

"It's a bit smudged and damp and hard to read but these people are known to you? I fear that you and two babies are the only survivors of the wreck."

More nods.

"The man Gunn. Was he your father?"

Shake, but a sad shake. He wished Alistair had been his father but that was no good. He'd gone for ever.

"Alistair and Annie? They were the parents of the children?"

He had to nod to that. It was true. Alistair was Mary's father and Annie was Roderick's mother.

The minister turned and looked at the woman in the room. He seemed to be smiling a little. "It seems they feared their end was nigh and they wished to make the children legitimate by getting the captain to marry them. Well, we will not judge the dead." He turned back to Rory-Beag who memorised his words even if he only half understood them.

"Was the captain your father?"

Shake, shake with heavy frowning.

"Had you *any* family on the ship?"

It had to be another shake. Of course Alistair and Mary had been a family to him but he had not forgotten that he had been baptised 'Angus' and left orphaned at four years old. He could never tell anyone that but it was there, locked in his memory.

Again the minister turned back to the woman. "He doesn't seem to belong to anyone. I fear there will be no more clues. Anything washed ashore from the sloop will be pounce upon by the villagers. The cushion and the barrel itself disappeared fast enough. Thank God this paper was saved. When I return to the mainland I can send word to Helmsdale of the loss of *Gannet* and find out where they were heading. It was likely Thurso for the Canada sailing."

Rory-Beag tugged his sleeve and nodded.

"The boy understands all we're saying. I wonder if he has *ever* been able to speak. There are no marks of recent blows or bruises about his mouth, now I come to look at him. He's no idiot though. He may be dumb but he's not deaf."

Rory-Beag grinned and nodded.

The minister smiled back. His eyes peeping out from under the eyebrows were a lively glowing red-brown like two coals alight in a cave. "Well, I may find out his name. But he's not fit to be shifted from here till those legs heal. The Canada boat will sail in a few days. I'm afraid they'll not wait for him. Can you care for him, Martha, for a wee while? I find I'm interested in his case and am minded to come back here when I've learnt something of his origins. If we can restore him to any relations we must do so even if we send him to Canada on a later sailing."

No, thought Rory-Beag. It would have been bad enough to go to Canada without Alistair and Mary but at least there would have been the others he knew in Glen Kildonan. They tolerated him though none but Alistair had gone so far as to invite him to live with them. But to go on a boat knowing no one, to a strange country! No, this minister had quickly found out he was not an idiot. This minister had smile lines at the corner of his eyes and was interested in him. If the minister went to Helmsdale himself he would find out his name from Meg Mackay who had heard Alistair call him Rory-Beag. He might learn more too from the man with the conscience on *Seagull* if that ship hadn't sailed yet with the duke's agent on board. He might learn that *Gannet* was a sloop that should have had its seams caulked and new sails that wouldn't rip in a gale. He might get Robert Mackay punished for sending them to sea in such a boat. Then the minister would come back and tell him everything and take him into his home and he would work for him every hour of the day to earn that sweet twinkling smile.

The minister seemed to want to move again but he pulled on his hand and then, as he had on the shore, he made the motion of cradling a baby in his arms. He tried to make a baby face and squeaked a thin little sound.

"Of course. He wants to know the babies are safe."

Rory-Beag made a joyful grin of relief and the minister's smile answered him.

"There's a young woman in the village whose wee bairn died of a fever yesterday. She has milk and is feeding the babies. She has no husband but says she is happy to nurse them till we can find someone to adopt them and bring them up."

Rory-Beag nodded and tapped his own chest.

The minister smiled and shook his head. "You're no but a wee lad still. You can be sure they'll be well cared for and given every chance in life. Now you rest. I leave you in Martha Sinclair's good hands, but I will return and you shall hear all I have found out."

He patted Rory-Beag's hand and withdrew into the room. Rory-Beag heard a door close. The woman was seeing the minister out.

All the pain of his limbs came flooding back. He was not to be the one who watched over the babies and saw them grow up. Dry sobs shook him till he heard the woman Martha coming back.

"Well!" She peered in at him. "You and I are stuck with each other till those limbs of yours have healed." She bustled about the room clearing away some mugs and plates. Perhaps she had given the minister some refreshment. She talked as she worked. "The whole village is down on the shore collecting every scrap of the wreck that's come in. What's too smashed up to make shelves or stools is good firewood. And all I get is a lad that can't talk and needs nursing and feeding. I reckon no-good Bet Moray has the easier job with the babies. Minister was right to say she has no husband. She never did have. It was a sailor got her into trouble but they say she was ready to go with any man. You needn't fret that she'll have the bringing up of those wee bairns. She'll keep them till they're weaned, that's all." She came back and looked in on him again. "But then they're no kin o' yours, is that right?"

He nodded sadly.

"Well, well, I'll bring you a bite to eat in a wee while. The minister'll not get away to the mainland till the morrow when the sea's gone down. He comes four times a year and we're lucky it was the time for his visit just now. Stroma's a fine place to live but we lack all they have on the mainland and the sea can be wild as you know only too well."

She trotted through to the living space, calling over her shoulder, "Get yourself back to sleep, laddie. The body heals quickest when it's asleep."

The house must be a but and ben just like Alistair's and Mary's and he could hear her stirring up the fire in the but end, perhaps to make him some porridge. He was hungry and he didn't think he would sleep but he took note of what she had said. There was that name Stroma again. So he *was* on an island. And the minister only visited it four times a year but he would make an exception. He'd promised.

He lay as still as he could. But in his head he was hearing and seeing the waves that separated him from Caithness where the minister might go tomorrow if the storm had passed. Caithness was the only place he had ever known with its long green glens, soon to be covered entirely with sheep, its people driven to the coast and from there miles and miles to Canada on the other side of the world.

It was hard to contemplate the things that had happened in what must be only two or three days. Annie had had her baby on the eve of the day of the burnings. Mary's had come only the day after. Now Mary, Annie and Alistair were all dead and the people of Kildonan would have reached Thurso and perhaps be already on board the big ship. Every detail of these crowded days was clear in his head, all the words that had been spoken, the message that Alistair had written, the dying yell of Captain Jamie, and the tugging of that strange current that had dragged him, Rory-Beag, past the rock face to throw him onto the shore among the tumbling waves.

There must be a purpose in him being still alive and the tiny babes surviving too. It struck him then that the babies were still on the island with a despised woman called Bet Moray. He would find out where and go and see them. He began to thrust a leg out of bed but the agony defeated him. He lay back, gritting his teeth. His legs must heal. He had always run about all his life. He couldn't speak but he could run. He thought of old Morag in the glen. She spoke all the time but she couldn't move from her bed without help. He had always been sorry for her. Yes, it was what the Kildonan minister always said: "Reckon up what the Lord has done for you and be thankful."

He closed his eyes. Kildonan and its people and the leaving of it were locked up in his memory. Nothing could take these images from his brain.

A chicken feather sticking through the pillow tickled his face. He drew it out and held it near his mouth and blew it away. Maybe it was true what Martha had said. "The body heals quickest in sleep." His legs were raw but if he didn't move he could bear them. He settled his head again and let slumber creep up on him and wash over him without the fear of it drowning him like the fearsome waves.

Martha found him asleep, gave a grunt of annoyance and then ate up the porridge herself.

6

Clara Reid sat at her hotel window with her looking-glass in her hand. She was studying her face but from time to time would peer out of the window at the activity in Leith harbour. There was no sign of the steamboat returning with Ridley on board and their manservant Tom who had accompanied him. Without Ridley at her side she was lost in this unfamiliar place. Yet when he was there his restlessness and impulsiveness wore her out.

She couldn't fathom what he wanted from this journey away from home. To escape from the coal business? Ridley had never really wanted to be in coal. Yet he had seemed to agree with his father that it would be a great thing to create a wealthy dynasty like the Ridleys of Northumberland after whom he had been named. But the Ridley she had married was a dreamer too, a lover of nature. He had told her they would move out of Newcastle when he made his fortune and raise a family in the country. But no family had come.

It should not surprise her that his love had faded. The features she was looking at were too buried between the plump cheeks and the double chin. The nose was too small, the forehead too low, the blue eyes lethargic. Beside her on the window seat was a dish of sweetmeats. She looked round at Jane who was as spare as she was fat and as energetic as she was lazy.

"I was called pretty six years ago when we married, wasn't I, Jane?"

"And you still are." Clara knew Jane secretly laughed at her but would always say and do the correct thing.

Clara sighed, laid down the mirror, took a little cake topped with marzipan and looked out of the window again.

"The master and Tom will soon be back," Jane said. "Then we'll all be cheerful again."

"Not if he plunges into another of his great ideas. Steamboats if you please! He talks of buying one for the transport of coal – as far as London one day he says."

"Well, it's the new thing, ain't it? Already the *Perseverance* takes passengers down the Tyne to North Shields. Another ten years and there won't be a sail in sight anywhere."

"Would *you* travel on one of those noisy smelly things?"

"If I had a day off and it was cheap enough."

Jane never had days off. She had no relations. She had belonged with Clara's family since her childhood, endeavouring to teach her cooking, sewing and general housewifery and had come with Clara on her marriage. "You must have a lady's maid," her mother had said. "Then I'll have Jane." But in the handsome stone terraced house Ridley Reid had rented as their first home in Newcastle, Jane did everything the mistress should do. She supervised the cook and the skivvy, managed the shopping, the laundry and household accounts as well as Clara's clothes. Clara was left to produce children. Ridley never alluded to that nowadays, a silence which was as disturbing as everything else about him.

"You say sails will disappear?" Clara's eyes had been caught by a handsome two-masted ship gliding into the harbour. "Look at that beauty?" She picked up the spy-glass Ridley had left for her entertainment while he took his trip to Bo'ness. "I can read the name, *Seagull.* Is not that charming? It has all the grace and beauty of a gull. See how it glides to the quayside and furls its sails just like a gull folding its wings."

Jane chuckled. "And see the big ugly passenger coming off her."

"You can't tell from here that he's ugly." She peered at him through the spyglass. "Well, he is, but there are more coming out of the cabin. Some well dressed gentlemen and a woman carrying a basket. A sailor is bringing her small sea-chest. She's just a peasant in a bonnet with a shawl round her. But she's holding the basket very carefully as she steps onto the quay. Oh she's with the big ugly man. He's taken her box from the sailor and set it by her. She's lifting something from the basket. Why, it's a baby!" She opened the window. "I think I can hear it crying. She's patting its back. Oh Jane!"

Clara dropped the spyglass and turned and buried her face in Jane's apron.

"I can't look."

"You really mustn't take on so every time you see a baby. It don't do no good." She was looking over Clara's shoulder at the scene below. "The ugly man's escorting the gentlemen to the next door hotel. He's abandoned the woman. Well, I never! She's sat herself on her sea-chest and is feeding the baby under her shawl."

Clara had to pick up the spyglass again and look. Yes, there was the woman with the bustle of quayside activity going on around her, ignoring her. She looked alone and friendless.

"Jane, she shouldn't have to do that in the public street. Run down and bring her up here. She shall have privacy. The porter will bring her box into the hallway and she can fetch it away later wherever she's going. Maybe someone was to come and meet her. The porter can watch out and tell them where she is."

"Are you sure?" Jane's eyebrows spoke more than the rest of her phlegmatic face.

"Yes, be quick."

Clara looked round the room when she'd gone. That low chair in the corner would do for a nursing mother. She could put it in the dressing-room to avoid Ridley seeing the poor woman when he came back. But he shouldn't be angry. He claimed to be an enthusiast for the poor. His mother had encouraged him to join a reform society when unemployment increased after the war, but he had seemed too distracted lately to attend their meetings, though two bad winters and failed harvests had provoked bread riots throughout the country. He needed reminding that the poor were still about. Perhaps this woman was coming here to throw herself and her child into the care of the authorities.

She watched from the window and saw Jane come out and descend the six stone steps that led down to the street from the hotel portico. She saw her cross to the quayside and speak to the woman.

The woman seemed to be laughing and shaking her head but Jane took her arm and picked up the basket in her other hand. Jane seemed startled by something as she did so. Clara looked through the spyglass. Something was moving in the basket. What, another baby? Had the woman put it back? No, she was still cradling one on her arm. She was coming now willingly enough it seemed, but she looked back at the chest she'd been sitting on. Jane was beckoning. The porter was running down the steps and picking up the box and following them up. It was all happening as Clara had suggested.

Now her heart was pounding. Were there *two* babies, double the agony of seeing them in another woman's care? She swallowed hard and went to the room door and opened it. The hotel was a tall narrow building, chosen by Ridley for its modest price, but the floors were carpeted and there were pilasters at the head of the stairs with an archway and a decorative cornice all the way round the first floor landing. Clara saw Jane leading the way up and yes, there was a baby in the basket she was carrying. The woman under the bonnet was young, perhaps barely twenty, with a pert little face and excited eyes darting about. She carried the other baby whose lips were seeking the nipple that had been tucked away.

Jane grinned at Clara as they reached the landing. "Two babies and the girl is a foreigner. Leastways she doesn't understand English. But she seemed happy enough to come in when I pointed out the hotel."

Now Clara had eyes only for the babies. They were very small but it was their smallness that wrenched her heart. The one in the basket was wailing. Clara pointed to the chair in the corner of the room and the girl nodded and went over to it and sat down, looking quite at home. She beckoned Jane to set the basket down by her and, propping one baby on her lap lifted the other out too and promptly produced both her large breasts. Spreading her legs in her rough skirt she nestled each baby in the crook of her arms so it could suck. The sound of their avid lips was almost more than Clara could bear.

Jane's eyebrows were saying, "Well, it's what you asked for."

The girl was speaking words and pointing her finger.

"She wants a drink," Jane said. There was a jug of water on the side-table.

"Give her some of course."

The girl drank thirstily and handed back the glass so she could support the right-hand baby who was grimly hanging onto her nipple.

"How can we ask her where she is from and where she is going?" Clara asked.

"The ship came from Helmsdale," Jane said, "but I have no notion where that is. I could make enquiries I suppose."

"Yes, yes please." Clara went to the window and looked down. The big ugly man had returned to the spot and was looking about with a puzzled air. "Oh Jane, speak to him. Bring him in if you have to. I believe he is seeking her after all."

Jane grinned, shrugged her shoulders and left the room.

Clara sat down heavily on the window-seat. She was alone with the mother of twins, too embarrassed to watch her feeding them and afraid of her own urge to snatch one of the babies from her and cuddle it. Instead she watched Jane reappear below and accost the man. It was obvious from his relief and eager following of her into the hotel that he was concerned with this little family. Could he be the father? Or the girl's father? She would soon know.

He came lumbering into the room and glanced at the girl before turning to Clara and holding out a large rough hand. She rose and took it warily.

"Robert Mackay at your service, Ma'am." Well, at least he could speak English. "Good of you to bring her in off the street. There's no one as far south as this speaks the Gaelic tongue. But she's bright enough. She'll pick up English quickly and find work when she's weaned the babes and got them off her hands."

"Off her hands, Mr Mackay! Will she not want to bring her children up herself?"

"Och, they're no hers. They survived a shipwreck and there's not one of their family left. She's wet-nursing them, that's all, for her own bairn only lived a few hours."

Clara sat down abruptly, then remembered to motion the man to a seat too. There was an upholstered sofa in the room facing the window and he perched on it.

Jane had withdrawn into the dressing-room where her own bed had been set up but she left the door slightly ajar. Clara knew she would listen to every word spoken.

"Let me understand you, Mr Mackay. You say she speaks only Gaelic. May I ask what language that is? Where is she from?"

"A wee Scottish island, Ma'am. But Gaelic is widely spoken all over the highlands. I speak it myself at home but I'm a business man and I'd get nowhere without the English in these enterprising times."

"And your interest in –?" She looked at the girl.

"She's called Bet Moray. Nay, I've no interest as such except to oblige a minister o' the kirk. He heard I was sending one of my ships to Leith and it struck him that there's more places in a big city like Edinburgh where she could be cared for with the babes while they're young than there is in a wee fishing village like Helmsdale. There's terrible poverty in the highlands and he told me he hoped they could be placed with a family of some wealth and status."

"You mean adopted?" Clara croaked out.

"Ay well, why not? I wasn't going to travel myself. I have crews working for me but I thought I'd better see her safe." He looked down between his great knees and grinned. "I may not look it, Ma'am, but I'm soft-hearted where bairns are concerned and the poor lass needed someone to speak up for her."

"And are you going to take her to Edinburgh yourself?"

"Ay, if I don't find anyone here in Leith prepared to take her on with the babies." He lifted his head and looked her in the eye.

The upheaval going on in Clara's mind must be visible on her face. Two babies had dropped from heaven. She looked over at Bet Moray and saw she had finished feeding them and was spreading a blanket on the carpet and laying their squirming little bodies side by side on it. She said something in Gaelic to the man.

"She wants to know if she can have a basin of water," he said.

Clara called Jane and her needs were quickly supplied. When she was given soap she picked it up with delight and smelt it.

As she washed the babies and changed their very plain little gowns Clara got down on her knees to watch, her pulse racing, the words she dared not say hovering on her lips. The babies were a boy and a girl, both with a smudge of fairish hair, their tiny limbs perfect but moving wildly without co-ordination.

She looked up at Mr Mackay who was watching the scene with amusement.

"What are their names?"

"Nay, I don't know that they have any. The mother must have given birth on the boat and they put the babies in a water barrel to save them from the shipwreck but she and her husband and another woman and her child must all be dead. The minister said no one else but an idiot boy was saved who can't speak. Just these twin babes."

"What about the parents' names?"

"Ay well there was a paper put in the barrel but it's blurred with wet and written in the Gaelic. The minister gave it me. I'm to pass it on to the right authorities who take the babies."

Clara sat back on her heels and the words came out. "Give it to me. We'll adopt the babies."

She couldn't believe she'd said it.

"You will, will you?" The man was chortling quietly to himself. "And you'll take Bet to feed them?"

She nodded. Of course she would have to. They would starve else. Later she could get rid of her for there was an impudent assurance about her that told her Bet Moray would be too many for her if she kept her on. But what had she done? She had never bought an item of furniture without Ridley's agreement and these were two little human beings that would grow up. He would have to father someone else's children when he had longed to start a dynasty of his own like the great Ridleys. These waifs could never fulfil Ridley Reid's dreams. His father, George Reid, both magistrate and coal merchant, aspired to Newcastle's highest social circles. "Peasant children from remote Scotland!" she could hear him exclaim. It couldn't happen.

She stood up, shaking. "Of course I shall have to consult my husband."

Mr Mackay got up too, clutching his hat in his hand. "And where would *he* be?" His grin had gone.

"Oh he should be here very soon. He took the excursion to Bo'ness on the new steamboat. He thought of buying such a vessel to employ on the River Tyne. He works in his father's coal business but he wants to branch into something new. We have been several weeks travelling about from home so he could inquire into many schemes. In Edinburgh he learnt that a steamboat operated from this harbour so we came here to see if Leith to Bo'ness was a profitable enterprise." She was babbling in her anxiety. "Oh tell me, are you absolutely certain no one will claim these babies?"

He shook his head. "Not a chance."

Jane had gone to the window, hearing an unusual sound outside.

"It's the steamboat back. The master will be here in a few minutes." Her eyebrows were telling Clara, "You're in for it now."

Clara looked to see what Bet was doing. She had wrapped the babies up, making them into little white tubes, and was preparing to lay them in the basket.

"No," Clara exclaimed. "Give me one." She held out her arms and Bet picked one up and handed it over as if it was nothing more than a loaf of bread.

Clara knew it was the boy because she had observed his head was slightly larger than the girl's. She stood clasping him in her arms, fixing her eyes on his small features, wanting passionately to be allowed to love him. And then he opened his eyes. Suddenly a human soul was looking out. She was overwhelmed. She couldn't move, just went on gazing back at him, till the door opened and Ridley walked in and saw her.

He stood transfixed, apparently seeing no one else, his mouth and eyes wide. Gradually he became aware of the bulk of the man who had risen from the sofa at his entrance. And then, hearing a tiny cry, he looked the other way and saw the girl rocking the basket on her arm.

"What – what is this? What has happened?"

"Oh Ridley," she said. "No one wants these babies. I thought we could adopt them." She couldn't read his face. It was thin and mobile and his moods were generally well etched upon it. Beside the florid, bull-like Mackay he was a slight figure, insignificant, of moderate height, pale with thinning brown hair. His mouth remained slightly open and his eyes staring.

"Who is this man?"

"Robert Mackay at your service, sir." He stepped forward and held out his hand. "I haven't the honour of knowing your name yet, sir. Your lady wife is quite taken with these twins but of course she was awaiting your return."

"Twins?" Ridley repeated the words stupidly.

"A boy and a girl. Orphaned. No family. The lassie here is not the mother, but the wet nurse."

Bet, still swaying the basket, gave a little bob of a curtsey.

Ridley met Clara's eyes again. "How did they all come here?"

As she didn't answer at once Robert Mackay broke in eagerly, "Your good lady's kindness brought us all here. I own that fine ship *Seagull* at the quayside. You may have noticed her. She is but one of my little fleet of vessels that are available to hire." He seemed to expand as he said it but Ridley was still gazing at him in utter bewilderment. Mackay went on. "I transported the babies from their homeland of Caithness to find them a new family. It was at the request of a minister who rescued them from a wreck washed up on the shore of Stroma Island. The parents drowned. The wee bairns are quite abandoned for all the people in their glen have already taken ship for Canada. If there was any distant kin to these children among them they are long gone, believing no one survived the wreck."

Ridley looked from Clara, still holding one baby, to Bet with the other. Then he seemed to absorb the last point Mackay had made and his mind fastened on that.

"Gracious heaven, man! Why would a whole community depart like that?"

Mackay shrugged his shoulders. "They were given notice to quit, sir. The landowners are all going over to sheep. Seems there's money in it and all the little crofts brought in a pittance in rent."

Ridley looked back at Clara and some light came into his eyes.

"I read of that in the newspapers. I thought it was all over. 'Clearing the highlands' they called it. Shameful business it seemed to us in England. Of course *our* borderlands are all given over to sheep now but we didn't burn people from their homes to bring in the flocks."

"It was nothing to do with me, sir. But that's how these poor wee bairns come to be abandoned."

"I beg your pardon." Ridley was coming to himself, Clara could see, but she was still far from knowing what the outcome would be. Had he grasped yet what she was asking of him?

He now stepped forward and peered at the child in her arms. Then he looked up into her face. Her eyes filled with tears. "Please!" was all she could murmur.

He turned to Mr Mackay. "Would you leave us, sir, for a little while? Pray go downstairs and request some refreshment to be charged to my bill. Reid is the name. Jane, will you take the young woman too and see that she is looked after in the kitchen. Leave the babies."

When they had gone out he shut the door and came to Clara and drew her down on the sofa and sat beside her. The baby girl in the basket seemed to have gone to sleep. Clara sat trembling with the baby boy lying on her lap gazing about him.

Ridley just touched the soft cheek, then withdrew his finger and covered his face with both hands. His shoulders shook. He was sobbing.

She was horrified. "My dearest –"

It was a few minutes before he could speak. "I thought – I don't know what I thought, seeing you standing there holding a child. It was a sight I believed I would never see. And I thought – I really thought for a moment that you had given birth while I was away. You put on weight recently. I thought, she hasn't told me because she was afraid it wouldn't happen, something would go wrong and there you were holding a tiny baby."

"Oh Ridley. I wish it had been like that but could we not – would it matter – they would truly be ours. They are so small. This is the boy. Is he not looking at you and seeing his father for the first time?"

Ridley was nodding slowly. Tears were still running down his cheeks. He didn't speak for two whole minutes. Then he looked into her face. "He *is* ours. You *have* given birth."

She was beginning to hope now. "And the little girl. Bring her here too." He got up and brought the basket. She pleaded, "Is she not beautiful too? A son and a daughter."

"A son and a daughter. You had twins. No wonder you put on weight. We must delay our return to give you time to recover. What a joy and surprise for our parents! Will your mother be hurt that you kept her in the dark? Surely not. She is such an anxious being. She will realise you were sparing her weeks of worry. *My* mother will understand that you feared a miscarriage. She lost two babies between me and my young brothers. My father will be happy to have an heir to the business. And yours? *He* certainly noticed your bulk because he told me you would soon be matching his girth and he was chuckling about it. Now he'll know the reason for it."

Clara stared at him. "What are you saying?" His eyes were shining with excitement. "You are willing for us to adopt them?"

"No no no, not adopt. They *are* ours. We have a son and a daughter. And how lovely they are! My darling, this is the happiest day of my life."

Clara sat still. The man beside her was not the withdrawn, restless, impatient, wayward husband that he had become these last few years. Had he returned to the idealist, the dreamer that she had first fallen in love with? One thing, the only thing that mattered was that they were to have the babies, but where was he taking her with these mad words? Was he truly suggesting that they should pretend the babies had been born to them, during this time away from home? How could that be? Jane knew, this Robert Mackay knew, the girl Bet knew, everyone in this hotel knew.

"What are you saying?" she asked him again.

For answer he got abruptly to his feet.

"I must speak to that man again."

She rose too, clutching the baby to her bosom. "Oh yes, I forgot. He has a paper found with the babies. Something about their origins."

"We'll take it and destroy it. I must know no one will ever seek the babies again. He knows the name Reid but not where we live. We will tell him nothing more."

"It can't be done, Ridley. Jane – the girl, Bet –"

"Jane depends on us utterly. As for the girl we can pay her off when she is no longer needed."

"But adopting abandoned children is perfectly respectable. We will love and raise them as we would our own. They cannot be more than a week old. We will be the only influences in their lives."

"They have to be ours. I will not have them unless they are."

"You will not have them –?"

"Not with any vestige of their past. I will go and speak with that man. I will make all safe. Stay here."

He was stepping to the door when he turned back and again laid a finger on the baby boy's cheek. "My son." Then he lifted the basket and set it on the sofa. He touched the girl's cheek. "Oh God, my little daughter." He was almost breaking into tears again but he controlled himself and abruptly made for the door.

"Ridley!" she called out. "What happened on the steamboat?"

"Steamboat? Oh nothing. I thought I might buy one. They are building them here. I told Tom I would, but now – no nothing. Not important." He went out and shut the door.

Clara sank back onto the sofa. Asking him that question had been a test. She supposed he had been disillusioned with his great project and this sudden appearance of babies was a relief. But that wasn't the case. The babies had superseded it entirely. He said it was the happiest day of his life. He had wept. When was the last time she had seen him weep?

She had not believed he could want a child so desperately. That was wonderful to know, for she had been terrified of his anger at her acting alone. But to impose so impossible a condition! How could they live a lie for the rest of their lives? It was still hard to believe what he was asking of her. Had she understood him? Had he thought of all the implications? It was not possible that he could have in so short a time. The whole situation had rushed upon him and he had spoken in the passion of the moment.

She drew a long breath. He would realise the folly of his first reaction. Talking to that Mr Mackay, who seemed a commonsense sort of fellow, he would know it was a generous, benevolent act to take in and raise two poor orphans. Her pulse slowed.

Now, looking about she realised that for the first time she was alone with the babies. Both were asleep now. Very slowly and gently she inserted the boy into the basket beside his sister and then sat looking at the two little heads facing each other. Their sleep was an act of complete trust. Someone was feeding and caring for them and that was all they needed just now. I think, she told herself with a fresh surge of joy, that Mr Robert Mackay will be happy for us to take them off his hands straight away. We can hire a carriage to take us all the way to Newcastle. We can't expose such tiny babies to the rigours of stage coach travel. I shan't worry about the folk at home yet. I wonder how often babies need feeding and what spare gowns has Bet got packed in their basket or her box? Oh we must buy new and beautiful gowns and shawls and little baby caps. Perhaps Jane will know what to get.

She was suddenly frightened at how little she knew about babies. What if they both wakened and cried now before anyone came to help. What a long time Ridley was taking? Why didn't Jane bring the girl back? Why didn't she come herself?

She got up carefully so as not to dislodge the basket and stepped over to the window seat where her dish of sweetmeats lay. She brought it back and sat with it on her lap, dipping into it for comfort while she waited.

Ridley walked in, saw what she was doing and, grabbing the dish, he went to the window and threw the contents into the street.

"What – why?" She was aghast.

"You are to be slim again of course, after the birth. I shall watch what you eat." He smiled at her discomfiture, then rubbed his hands together, drew himself up and announced, "Well, it is all settled. I have the paper and Mr Mackay translated the Gaelic for me. The people named in it are dead. The babies start their life here and now with us. We will remove to a hotel in Edinburgh where you will have a suitable lying-in period. Bet knows what is expected of her. Mackay explained in her own tongue and she is very happy to be paid what English ladies would pay a wet nurse. I think the way her eyes opened it was more than she has ever earned in her life. We will teach her English too of course. Jane is very pleased that we have at last produced a family and she can be a nursemaid as she once was to you."

Clara knew she was staring at him with her mouth open. When he stopped speaking she closed it and compressed her lips tight. She felt sobs rising in her throat.

"You can't expect –" she began and couldn't go on. She was going to have to say no to this mad plan and risk losing the babies altogether.

Her tears welled out and dropped onto the hand he had put round her waist. His tenderness overwhelmed her.

"My darling one," he said. "These are natural tears. I shall not worry about them. I am told ladies often have bouts of weeping after giving birth. Let us think of something cheerful. We will have our twins baptised when we get home. What shall we call them?"

There was a tap on the door and Jane came in followed by Bet.

Jane was chuckling. "Well, she put away a bowl of broth, two eggs and a plateful of bread and butter and a mug of ale. She's learnt the words for them too. She seems quick enough but she's made signs she's sleepy now. Will I put her some cushions by my bed in your dressing-room, ma'am, and we'll bring the babies in so she can feed them when they wake in the night. I don't mind. Master says we're moving somewhere with a bit more space in the morning. Where we're not known," she added with a wink.

"Jane –" Clara began, but Ridley took charge.

"Bed for you too, my precious."

"But it's only early evening."

"And you know what you've been through today."

She looked pleadingly at Jane gathering cushions from round the room.

"Best do as the master says." More nods and winks as she passed the sofa. Did Jane think they were indulging some strange whim of the master for the time being? But it looked as if the babies were theirs to keep. This was the miracle she must cling to. Surely there could be no giving them back now if Robert Mackay was going away and leaving them.

As Ridley put a hand firmly under her elbow and propelled her towards the door of their bedroom, she turned her head and looked into his eyes. They were shining with an unearthly brilliance. Those were tears of joy in them. She couldn't argue now. She felt suddenly very tired as if she had truly given birth that day. She kissed the air above the basket and allowed him to escort her into their bedroom.

7

Rory-Beag was awake early one morning. When he lifted the curtain of his box-bed he could see a streak of sunlight across the wooden planks of the floor. He put his feet over the partition, holding back a squawk of pain. The bandages Martha had renewed the night before pulled at his skin but he padded across into the but end and heard her snoring behind her curtain. As quietly as he could he clicked open the latch of the outer door and looked out. The treeless landscape was scattered with little crofts here and there, picked out sharply by the early light with pools of shade beside them. A calm sea lay to the east.

He knew that Stroma was to the north of Glen Kildonan so the summer nights were even shorter here. It was one of the many interesting things Alistair had told him. But that meant it was probably too early to go visiting to find the babies.

The air was sharp but there was warmth when he turned his face to the sun. Not a soul was stirring anywhere. He knew suddenly how alone he was.

Grief for the loss of Alistair swelled inside him. He leant his head against the doorpost and rare tears broke from him. He watched them fall into the dry earth.

"Eh now!" said Martha's voice behind him. She had risen and come to him in her flannel bed-gown with a bit of plaid round her shoulders. "Those legs are still hurting. You shouldn't be walking on them yet. The minister will say I'm not looking after you properly."

He brushed his hand across his eyes and looked round at her and shook his head.

"Dear me, it's uncanny not being able to talk with you like a Christian soul. I cannot tell what you want or what you're thinking of."

He made the motions of cradling a baby and pointed in several directions from the door, cocking his head on one side and lifting his eyebrows.

"Ah, you want to know where the babies are. Well don't you fret. They're safe enough. The minister thought it best to take Bet and the babies with him when he went back to the mainland. 'For if I find any relations,' says he, 'however distant, it makes sense to have the poor wee babes with me and save a journey for them later.' He was minded to go to Helmsdale himself if that was where *Gannet* had sailed from. The broken bit o' timber with its name on came ashore. But he'll be back and if you're fit to walk about, lad, you can take out that bucket and feed my chickens."

She had babbled on not noticing the desolation that he knew must be plain on his face. The babies were gone from the island. Would he never see them again? He had thought it was to be his task to care for them and play with them as they grew up. Why else had God saved him and not their parents? In a lifetime of blows it was one of the hardest.

Martha had set down the bucket of scraps by the door. He picked it up and followed the sound of sleepy cluckings round the house to the coop built against the wall at the back. It must be an earlier hour than the chickens were used to but one beak poked out and then they were all running about him as he emptied the bucket. The sight cheered him a little. At least the minister would come back and tell him where he had taken the babies. One day he would go there and find them again.

Soon Martha was able to take the bandages off his legs for good. They were puckered and scarred but she said, "Och, they'll clear up fine as you grow." She fed him and spoke quite kindly from time to time, calling him 'lad' or 'laddie' but she seemed to want to keep him from the sight of other people, shooing him into his bed behind his curtain if neighbours came to see her. And she didn't tell him things as Alistair had. He wanted to know all about the island and how the people lived. He knew its name, Stroma, and that Captain Jamie should have headed *Gannet* westward from it if he wanted to reach Thurso, that mysterious place from which great ships went to a land called Canada. But that was all he knew. He could peep from the cottage and see that the crofts had vegetable patches as Martha had and that there were fishing vessels on the sea and men came up from some spot below with catches of fish and sometimes one would come to the door and give Martha a fish and she would give him eggs or a basin of the healing paste she had mixed for his own legs. He soon realised she was looked upon as the healer or wise woman. The man would bring the basin back later and tell her his boil or his bruise had cleared up fine.

One or two asked if she still had the idiot boy with her and she would answer, "Ay, till the minister's back for him."

If they said, "Can I see him then? It's not the evil eye he has, is it?" she snapped, "Nay, he's harmless but I won't let him loose to frighten folks, especially the children."

"Must have been cursed at birth," was a common remark which he had often heard in his days of wandering the glens.

One woman said, "Can you no heal him yourself, Martha Sinclair?"

"Nay, he's beyond human skill. Just let him be. The Reverend Mackenzie will come for him soon."

And then one noontide of summer heat and calm sea Rory-Beag heard the minister's voice outside calling, "Are you at home then, Martha? And is Rory-Beag with you?"

Rory-Beag! The minister had discovered his name! Oh he had his old identity back! He ran to the door and flung it open and clasped the minister about his waist, as Martha came round the house with three eggs in her cupped hands.

"What? Is that what he's called?" she asked. "Well come away in, Minister, and have a mug o' beer. It's a thirsty day."

Rory-Beag shyly detached himself and retreated to his three-legged stool in the corner and gazed at the friendly furry caterpillars and those twinkly smile lines at the corner of the minister's eyes.

When he had had a few words with Martha and she had sat him down in the best chair and poured him a drink the minister beckoned him over and putting his arm round Rory-Beag's shoulders he looked at his arms and legs and commented how well they had healed.

"I brought some clothes, Martha, for I knew you'd be hard put to dress him."

Martha had in fact cut a piece off an old plaid that she used as a blanket on her bed and made him a short kilt. This and a patched vest too big for him were all he had worn day after day.

Rory-Beag was not bothered about clothes. He looked into the minister's eyes and made the baby rocking motion and put on his pleading face for an answer.

"Ay, well, I'll tell you how it was, Rory-Beag. I went in person to Helmsdale, taking Bet and the twins with me. There I inquired after the owner of *Gannet* and was directed to the office of a Mr Robert Mackay which was in the front room of his quite substantial house near the quayside."

Rory-Beag was nodding vigorously. It might have looked a substantial house but all their little party had been crowded into the stifling attic room.

Martha had taken up her knitting to sit and listen.

"Well, Rory-Beag, he was very sorrowful about the loss of life on *Gannet* which he said was his brother's sloop. He feared his brother had not cared for her as he should have done but I assured him that in a severe storm the best of ships can be lost. When I told him about the boy that was saved he remembered you and was able to tell me he had heard you called Rory-Beag and that you were known in those parts as a poor afflicted lad. But as for the glen you came from he had to tell me there was not a soul left there. I already knew there had been a sailing for Canada from Thurso for my parish of Canisbay is close by. So he assured me there was no one at all to take charge of you or the twin babes who were also miraculously preserved."

Rory-Beag longed to tell the minister that Roderick and Mary were not twins, but how to convey that by signs? Perhaps it was unimportant now. What mattered was where they were. Evidently the minister hadn't brought them back here to Stroma.

"Well, to cut a long story short, Rory-Beag, this kindly man offered to transport Bet and the babies to Leith as he had a ship sailing there that day."

Seagull, Rory-Beag remembered. The duke's agent hired it. I saw the men making it clean and shiny but it seems the minister never spoke with them, only with Robert Mackay and he's too good himself to see that Mackay is a bad man to entrust with my precious babies.

The minister went on, "I told him that in big cities there are religious houses and charities that would care for Bet and the babes till they could be found good people to adopt them. Leith is the port of Edinburgh, Rory-Beag, which you may know is the capital city of Scotland."

He raised his eyebrows questioningly at Rory-Beag who nodded, pleased that this one of the many things Alistair had taught him.

"My parish duties kept me from going myself to Leith but I asked him to send me word when he returned to Helmsdale. And now I have his news. He met with a well-to-do lady and gentleman only moments after he landed at Leith. They were childless and took pity on the babies and were pleased to take them into their home with Bet Moray as their nurse. I must say," he looked at Martha as he said it, "that I see the hand of God in this. Those babes will receive loving care and a good education."

Rory-Beag bounced up and down, bursting to ask where they were being taken. The minister looked at him, puzzled.

"You're pleased, Rory-Beag?"

Rory-Beag put his head on one side and wrinkled his forehead.

"Ah you want to know where these people live? Well, Mr Mackay said they didn't want praise or thanks for what they were doing and he wasn't going to give me their names at first but when I pressed him he said he thought it was no harm since it was I who had brought them to him. They are a Mr and Mrs Johnson of Carlisle."

Rory-Beag grinned happily, touched his chest and pointed to the outer door.

The minister laughed. "You'll go there, will you?"

He nodded vehemently.

Martha asked, "Where is it? I never heard of it before."

"It's way over the border into England."

"England! That's a mighty long way, is it not?"

"It is indeed. Rory-Beag and I will be happy to go as far as my Manse in Canisbay as soon as he's dressed in his new clothes. That will be quite far enough for today." He patted Rory-Beag's shoulder. "Are you content to come and live with me, Rory-Beag? You can keep my little garden tidy."

Rory-Beag nodded so hard he made himself quite dizzy. The minister handed him a bundle of clothes and told him to get dressed quickly because the boat that brought him would be leaving soon.

Rory-Beag found he had been given trews which he had never worn before and which felt hot on his legs when he pulled them on. A cotton shirt was a great luxury and shoes were strange when he was so used to going barefoot.

Martha said he could keep the plaid she had made for him and she gave him two of her oat cakes for the journey. He wanted to give her a hug as a thank-you for looking after him but she just shooed him out of the door after the minister.

"Away with you, laddie. I canna say I'll miss you for it's been mighty strange having you, but he's always done what I've asked him, minister."

The minister put an arm round his shoulders as they went out and gave him a squeeze.

They followed the track Rory-Beag had often looked out at and wondered where it went. A few of the women stood at their cottage doors and watched them pass, pushing their young children out of sight behind their skirts.

"This little place is Nethertown," the minister said, "and in the south of the island is Uppertown. There are about forty families on the island and they have their own little ways. You mustn't mind them. Now we are descending to the seaside and the sea is very calm. You won't be frightened to take the short journey to Caithness, will you?"

Rory-Beag shook his head. A little boat with a mast and furled sail as well as oars, much smaller than *Gannet*, was moored at a short pier with two men sitting smoking pipes on a stone bench. They looked curiously at Rory-Beag so he gave them a hopeful smile which made them look away quickly. He had often noticed that his smile had that effect on people.

He looked about at the surroundings and saw the ruins of what must have been a grand house behind a stone wall close to the shore.

"That belonged to a rich man who owned the island in days gone by," the minister said. "He kept a fine herb garden and many of the plants still grow there. That's where Martha picks the leaves that she pounds into a paste with oat flour and water. And that's what healed your legs."

Rory-Beag smiled up at him and nodded. It was wonderful to be talked to and told things but how he longed to be able to reply and ask the thousand questions that always crowded into his mind. What had the minister done with Alistair's paper? How far was Carlisle? And he wished he could have told him that Robert Mackay was not a man to be trusted. He told lies. He, not his brother, had sent *Gannet* to sea in poor condition. He was not a kind helpful man and he must have agreed to take Bet and the babies on *Seagull* to make money. The minister would give him something for his trouble and he would set a high price on the babies if the Johnsons were childless and really wanted them. One day, he thought, I *will* go to Carlisle in England if I have to walk all the way. And then it struck him that when he found the babies he wouldn't be able to tell them who he was and what he knew about Alistair and Mary Gunn and Roderick and Annie and Glen Kildonan, their homeland. He was very thoughtful as one of the men in charge of the boat held out his hand for him to step down into it.

The minister sat with him on the bench. "I wonder what you're thinking, Rory-Beag. Your eyes are sad. Are you remembering your friends who drowned?"

Rory-Beag nodded.

"You're starting a new life now. I think we can be happy and I'm wondering if I can teach you to read and write. And then you know you can communicate with me. You can write down everything you want to say."

Rory-Beag stared at him. Could that ever happen? Reading and writing were wonderful mysterious things which many of the men in his glen could do but no one had ever suggested it could happen to him. He put his hands up to his face, saw the minister nodding and twinkling at him and let out a great whoop of joy.

"Damme, what ails the boy?" exclaimed one of the men, casting off and jumping into the boat to take the other pair of oars. It was too calm to set the sail, Rory-Beag realised.

"Nothing ails him," the minister said. "He's just happy."

The men shrugged their shoulders and grinned at each other. Then they set their bronzed arms to tug at the oars and the little boat slid away from the Island of Stroma.

Rory-Beag clasped his arms across his chest to hold in his excitement. He had had several new starts in his life but this, if it brought him a means of communication, would be the best.

8

Unable to sleep Clara lay listening to Ridley in their sitting-room talking with the hotel owner. He must be making arrangements for their departure in the morning. She heard the clink of glasses as they had a drink together.

The summer night was still light and she noticed his outer coat tossed on the bed within reach of her hand. She drew it towards her and felt in his pockets and found the crumpled paper Mr Mackay had given him. Fearful that he might come in at any moment she took it to the table in the window where there were pens and an inkstand. Tense with guilt because he had been so loving to her, she drew from her reticule her pocket diary with the embossed flowers on the front and the jewelled clasp. Painstakingly she copied all the letters of these unknown words onto a back page. There was a date 1819 and names – Alistair Gunn and Annie something. There were smudges and what must be a signature was indecipherable. But below it were more words in the same hand as the first writing but shaky. If it was written during a storm she could understand that.

As soon as the paper was copied she returned it to his pocket, fastened the clasp of her diary and tucked it to the bottom of her reticule. Then she slid quickly under the coverlet and hoped she could sleep before he came in. But her mind was now engaged with the paper, so fragile a thing but so momentous in its contents and mysterious in its unknown language. Who were these drowned people? A woman had given birth to twins on board ship in a storm. Someone, her husband probably, had written this so that the babies would have an identity if they were saved and if everyone else perished. Maybe there had been no time to baptise the babies. What were those last dreadful moments like?

She must have fallen asleep because it was dark when she felt Ridley creeping in slow stages into the four poster bed beside her. Never in their lives had he shown so much consideration. He had been tender when they were first married but that had worn to a toleration, almost an indifference, and lately this desperate restlessness.

Was all this going to change? Were there really two babies in the next room who were to be theirs for the rest of their lives? She turned over towards him and he instantly had his arms round her.

"Ah, you are not asleep," he said. "I have been thinking of names. My father's second name is Kenneth and your mother is Ida Katherine. It would please both sides of the family if our twins were Kenneth and Kate. What do you think, my darling?"

He was caressing her, approaching his lips to hers.

She murmured, "They are lovely names." She was just going to add, "But they may have been baptised already," when he closed his lips on hers in a kiss so fervent she couldn't speak for several minutes. This was love again. She was in ecstasy.

When he released her he spoke first. "I am so happy that you like the names, dearest one. We must agree on everything. We must hide nothing of what we are feeling. This is truly the beginning of a new life for us and our children. Does not that sound wonderful, 'our children'?"

It did and she wanted to get up and peep through the connecting door to the dressing-room and make sure those little beings were still there. When we get home, she thought, it will be the time to tell our families how we came by them. I shan't write to my mother for we can be home as quickly as the post. If only this wondrous new love of Ridley's will survive the telling.

He was still stroking her, her cheek, her neck, sliding his hand down her arm but it was he who was being soothed to sleep. She saw his eyes closing while there was still a smile on his face. He was happy but weary. His hand came to a stop on her wrist and lay there heavily.

It was too painful now to dwell on those last minutes of a ship succumbing to the waves. She must think not of what the babies had lost but what they might gain now as Kenneth and Kate Reid. Even if the parents were rough peasants the children would be refined by their upbringing and would not be despised by society. Her fear had been that Ridley would say "We know not from what stock they have come? It is too great a risk." Or was this why he wanted to pass them off as their own offspring? No one would dare say they were foundlings of unknown origin.

Clara's head ached. Why had Jane behaved so oddly? She had whispered to Clara as she helped her to bed, "It will all look right in the morning, my pet." She hadn't called her that since her marriage.

She wriggled out from under the weight of his arm and her last thought as she finally slipped into sleep again was, "I must talk to Jane." There had always been comfort in such a thought and with Ridley so quiet beside her she slept dreamlessly till daylight peeped between the heavy velvet curtains and a mewling baby cry came from the next room. It was truly happening – the first morning of life with children.

She began to put her feet out of bed. Ridley was instantly alert.

"Stay still and rest." It was a tone that had to be obeyed. "One of our children is crying. I will go and see whether it is Kenneth or Kate." He seemed to be chortling with glee as he inserted his feet into his slippers and approached the door to the dressing-room, indifferent to his bed-gown and night-cap.

Clara raised herself on her elbow and listened. "Whichever it was it must be suckling now. The crying has stopped."

"And that does not stop me from looking at our babies. I will tell Jane to see that you are served breakfast in bed."

"I would prefer to be up."

He smiled sweetly as he shook his head and opened the door and went in.

Tears of frustration burned the back of her eyes. She lay down, biting her lips till, to her great relief, Jane peeped round the door and, seeing her awake, walked in.

"Oh Jane! Come and sit by me. He says I must stay in bed for breakfast. I'm hungry. I want to sit at the table and have some of that good porridge and those delicious fish they served yesterday."

Jane laughed. "You're to have one lightly boiled egg and a dish of tea and I'm to lace you so tight you won't want to eat."

Clara grabbed her hand as she sat down on the bedside chair. "Jane, you are not going to go with this madness of his?"

"I don't see why not. The people here will soon forget us and we're not likely to see that Mr Mackay again. The master says we'll spend a month or two in Edinburgh for you to recover before we go home. He was up late writing letters to the families and they were despatched by the post-boy first thing this morning."

"What!" Clara sat up and clasped her hands over her open mouth. "What has he told them? You mean he has written to his parents and mine!"

"I didn't see the letters but he told me he was going to suggest they might have guessed your condition before we came away – you *did* put on weight. He would say you had been afraid to speak in case of a mishap. But now he could announce the joyful news – words to that effect anyway." Jane finished with her eyebrows raised.

"How dare he –?"

Jane laid her finger on her lips, nodding her head at the door. "Why be angry, pet? I've never seen the master so happy and where's the harm? He wants the babes to be properly your children. They're very new and small. No one will think anything after a few more weeks. And eh, my, it'll be good to have some baby Reids at last. We don't need keep that Bet Moray when they're weaned. And why should she talk to anyone once the master's found her a good place and paid her handsomely?"

Clara shook her head in despair. Scenes chased each other before her eyes: her mother asking her about the birth, her father wagging his finger and pronouncing that the babies favoured the Stokoe family not the Reids, and her sister Adelaide peering into her eyes, Adelaide whose boast was never to have told a lie in her whole life. She could never deceive Adelaide. Adelaide was jealous of her for being the pretty one who had early secured a husband. Adelaide was slyly pleased when no family came and would be mortified at the production of twins. *If* she believed it!

Then there was the rector of their parish. Would he not have to put 'date and place of birth' in the baptismal record when he christened the babies Kenneth and Katherine? And Ridley's parents! His mother, Ann Reid, was large-hearted, and straight-talking. It would be appalling to lie to her. And with George Reid Clara had always been nervous. He was wiry and tough, thin-faced like Ridley, but tight-lipped till his emotions broke out suddenly. Was it because of his father that Ridley was taking this extraordinary step? No, he had wept last night. It sprang from his emotions, not his reason. But it was too late. The letters had gone!

"Oh Jane, are you sure the letters will be at the posting-house by now? Will they be on the mail-coach? Can we not send after them and get them back?"

Jane laughed again, softly. "Would *you* like to suggest that to the master?"

Ridley came back into the room with the babies in their basket covered with a blanket. He said, "Leave us, Jane."

She jumped up and scurried from the room.

He set the basket on the low table at his side of the bed and reached over to pull the bedcover off Clara. She watched him, puzzled. Was he going to get in beside her? No, he drew back the babies' blanket and Clara saw they were naked. He picked up the boy and ordered Clara to pull up her nightgown.

"Why? What are you going to do?"

"My darling one, you must experience the sensation." Laying the baby on his pillow he pulled her nightgown up himself and placed the boy between her thighs. "Feel him there." The little shape squirmed and thrashed out with all his limbs.

Clara squealed and thrust her legs wider. "He scratched."

"Good, some pain." He drew the child forth as if he had just been born. "Look, my darling, a son." He placed him on her breast and opening the ribbons of her nightgown laid the baby's face close to her nipple. The lips fastened on it and tugged at it but, finding nothing, they pouted and parted in a cry of disappointment.

Clara struggled to sit up and clasp him to her. "Oh Ridley, how could you –"

He eased the child from her and laid him howling on the pillow and picked up the girl.

"No, please."

"Nay, push again, Mrs Reid, I believe there is another. You are to have twins."

He repeated the performance with the little girl. "Look, look, a daughter. Oh what fine healthy babies and hark at their crying at once. That is the best sign that they will live and flourish."

Both babies *were* crying now. The girl burped and dribbled milk on Clara's breast. Clara held her to her shoulder as she had seen mothers do and patted her back. She couldn't believe what the feel of their bare bodies was doing to her.

Ridley stepped to the door and called, "Bet!"

Clara hastily drew up the coverlet leaving only the babies' faces exposed.

"They must be swaddled," he said to her. "Nurse will bring them back to you."

Bet came in, wearing a homespun shift in which her breasts flopped low. Her fair hair which had been hidden under her bonnet now fell about her pert little face in tousled curls. Clara felt a stab of jealousy. The babies were fair. Was it possible Bet really was the mother? That must not be. The babies were hers.

Bet put them both in the basket, grinning at Clara as if – woman to woman – they were amused at the eccentricities of men.

"Take care! Gently!" cried Ridley as their uncoordinated limbs thrashed at each other. Clara thought, she cannot be their mother. No one else survived the storm. I want the babies back to feel them again but the boy, Kenneth – my little Kenneth – scratched me. One of his toe-nails or a finger-nail must be quite sharp.

She lifted her nightgown and saw a red mark on the inside of her thigh. Aware that Ridley had closed the door on Bet and was coming back to her she quickly adjusted herself and lay back on the pillow. What could she say to him? Was the hasty simulated birth an act of brutality or love? For the moment it had smothered her fury about the letters. It had been strange, frightening, miraculous.

She gazed up at him as at a new and incomprehensible being.

He sat on the bed and took her into his arms. "You beautiful, wonderful, clever wife. You have made me the happiest man in the world."

She yearned to feel the same happiness but she had to draw back her face and murmur, "The letters? You wrote letters."

"Yes, indeed." His voice was hearty, his face all smiles. "You would wish our families to know the marvellous news as soon as possible." He poked forward his lips and pressed a kiss on hers. Then he bounced upright and announced, "I shall send Jane out into the town before we leave for Edinburgh. She can buy all that our babies need and a decent outfit for the girl Bet. We must present ourselves in fine array at our new hotel. The babies have just been born and you must have special care."

As she opened her mouth to protest he bent over and implanted another kiss and was then withdrawing from the room when she called out in desperation, "Ridley, is all this done in fear of your father and his friendship with important people."

He stopped at the door. "What! What an extraordinary thing to say!"

She sat up and scrambled across the bed to see round the bedpost. His face was distorted with angry astonishment.

"Well," she blustered, "you might think people like the Ridleys would scorn our children if they thought they came from some lowly highland cottage –"

"If *they* thought! I don't care a fig for the Ridleys' thoughts. *Who* will think? No one will think *anything*. Everyone will know the truth. *Our* children." He took a deep breath and tried to smooth out the lines of anger. In a lower voice but with genuine puzzlement he asked, "And when have I ever been afraid of my father?"

When I first knew you, she thought, and he was driving you into the coal business against your inclinations.

He took a few steps towards her and held her gaze for a moment.

"We must be clear. We must be at one in this. Now that I am a father and you a mother nothing else matters. Our parents are the old generation. I wrote to them out of courtesy as we will be away longer than we expected. Of course they will be proud to have grandchildren but it is we who are a family now. We four. I am minded to quit Newcastle and find a place in the country to bring up Kenneth and Katherine. The air will be better."

"Oh!" Here was an old longing resurrected. "But the business?" Her voice faltered.

"My father will be happy to carry on till my brothers are old enough to come in. We – you and I – have our work now, the most important work God could give us. Now get back under those covers. You must keep warm and I'll see your breakfast is sent in. We want you to get back your lovely figure as soon as possible."

He finished by taking her face in his hands and implanting a kiss on her forehead. His anger had vanished when he spoke the babies' names and as he backed out there was that beaming, encouraging smile again.

A few minutes later Jane came in with the dish of tea and a boiled egg.

"Tom is coming with me when I go shopping," she said, "for there will be so many parcels to carry." She rubbed her hands. "I'm going to enjoy this."

"And what does Tom say about the babies coming?"

"Why, what does he know about babies? He has learnt that of course the mistress knew she was expecting but they came sooner than she or the master thought, or else, as he told Tom, he wouldn't have dreamt of leaving you yesterday."

"So Tom believes – Oh Jane! What can I do?"

"Enjoy being a mother at last! Now a carriage is coming at noon so I must away to make my purchases. I've had my porridge and fish and bannocks and honey."

Jane trotted out, laughing.

This was cruelty on top of cruelty. Clara was so choked with tears she could scarcely swallow the egg. When she had put the tray down on the little table she flung herself face down and sobbed into her pillow. She had often felt alone in her marriage but Jane had always been buzzing about and she had never doubted her loyalty to herself rather than 'the master'. If Jane had deserted her she was truly alone. Ridley's sudden show of love must only be to bring her to heel. It was a delight to have his kisses and hear him utter endearments but if she couldn't live out his lie they would vanish like smoke.

Then she sat up. I am not alone, she said out loud. I have my babies. She threw a shawl round her shoulders and crossed to the dressing-room door and peeped in.

The babies were quiet in their basket and Bet Moray was sprawled on the cushions on the floor beside them, her limbs flung wide, her mouth open, fast asleep.

I mustn't be cross, she thought. She will have had a broken night with them, but they are my babies and I will have them on the bed with me.

At first she thought of lifting them out but when she inserted her arms and got her hands round the little boy his eyes flew open and he looked at her. It was such a wise knowing look that she was utterly taken aback. How could he have lived but a few days in this world and look as if he carried the wisdom of ages in his little head?

She took the basket in and set it on the bed and climbed in beside it and continued to gaze at him. "Dear God," she murmured, "will I manage him as he grows up? The girl will be so biddable. I will make a real companion of a daughter but a son! Will Ridley be strict with him? Oh when I saw him touch his cheek!" She touched it herself as she spoke and the baby's eyes came round to her again. She was moved to address him direct. "Surely, Kenneth, he will never take a cane to you as his father did to him. He made light of that, saying 'all fathers do'. But, Kenneth, I'm afraid he is quite mad now, your father. He has told your four grandparents that I have given birth to you and oh when I had you naked between my legs and you scratched me – how can I forget that? You *are* mine. And you, little Kate, so peaceful!"

Ridley opened the door and walked in. "I heard you speaking and I see it is our children you are talking too. Good. Ah, look at the intelligence in that little face!"

"There is, isn't there!" Their eyes met and she felt their joy together as one emotion. She must cling to this. It was too precious to lose.

He sat on the bed and wriggled over to her with the basket in front of them. His arm was round her shoulders in a moment, holding her and looking from her to the babies and back again. She knew her eyes were filling with tears and that he had seen them. She waited for a remark about ladies' lying-in but all he did was weep too, shaking his head and smiling, even laughing as the tears fell. If his love was faked there was nothing false about his joy.

"Clara, my dear love, have we ever been as happy as we are now? I believe I am a new man. I have never lived till this moment."

"*We*," she said, "*we*. And, oh look! Kate's eyes are open now. So blue, lighter than Kenneth's."

"Your colour, exactly," he said.

She nodded. "And Mamma said I was very fair as a baby."

They sat locked together until the little faces simultaneously puckered up and a hungry cry rose from both.

The dressing-room door opened and Bet walked in, yawning and running her hands through her hair.

She leaned over and casually picked up the basket and walked out again. Clara gave a little gulp and hugged Ridley for comfort.

"When they're weaned," he said. "Patience till they're weaned."

"Yes," she said. "You are right. Patience. But I want them back quickly."

He squeezed her shoulders.

"To be wholly ours."

She repeated it. "Wholly ours."

He was kissing her again. "I love you, I love you, Clara."

She thought, oh let me hold onto that too.

9

Ridley wrote home with their new address in Edinburgh and a letter came for Clara from her mother. *'How could you do this to me, Clara?'* she wrote. *'Everyone thinks it so strange that I knew nothing of it. Ridley said in his letter that if you had proclaimed it from the housetops you feared tragedy might follow. I understand – but not to tell your own mother!'*

When she showed it to Ridley he said, "*She* would have told everyone. But see, further on, how delighted she is and my parents are too."

Clara murmured, "They want us to come home."

"All in good time."

She was dreading the homecoming but longing for it to be over. Her sister Adelaide had written one line of congratulation at the bottom of their mother's letter. Was her prying nature already suspicious? The babies *are* wholly ours, Clara told herself over and over again. If we could remove swiftly to the country we would be among new people who would accept us without query as the birth parents.

While he still kept her in bed for breakfast in the new hotel he was very tender to her but fatherhood engrossed him even more. Bet Moray showed her astonishment when he took Kenneth in his arms and talked to him and exclaimed at the first signs of what he claimed was a responding smile.

He showed no interest in the newspapers although he had them delivered to their rooms. Clara began to look at them herself in some alarm. There were reports of bread riots and attacks on machinery. In Newcastle, Clara pointed out to him, the keelmen were smashing up the new 'spouts' that had been installed on the quayside to speed up the loading of coal.

"Your father will expect you home if there's trouble."

"He can deal with it. It will all settle down."

"But this is our livelihood – coal. How can we afford to spend any longer here? Surely you wish to go home?"

He looked her up and down then. "You are getting your lovely slender figure back, my darling. We will go soon."

"Jane is making me wear an old-fashioned corset. I can hardly breathe."

He smiled. "I told her to lace tightly. And you are so much prettier than you were. Kate will be a lovely girl. Everyone will say 'Like mother, like daughter.'"

It was true that Clara was beginning to look with pleasure in the cheval glass in their hotel bedroom. Her face would always be round but it was no longer podgy. Her father, fat and lazy, wrote a few lines saying he was glad to be a grandfather but he supposed he would be amongst skinny women again. '*Your mother keeps thin by worrying about other people's opinions and Adelaide by a Spartan diet that she believes fits her for sainthood. Your funny old papa prefers to be stout and happy.*'

The words brought her benign father and anxious mother vividly back to her and she felt a pang of homesickness. In Newcastle she had always been able to walk up to Brandling Village where both her parents and Ridley's lived on the prosperous northern edge of the town. She would miss that if they moved away but perhaps being a mother herself would free her from her need of their love and petting. And she would feel safer away from Adelaide.

"We will invite Adelaide to be godmother."

Ridley startled her with this on the first morning that he allowed her to get up for breakfast. "She reads her Bible daily which is qualification enough. I won't ask either of my brothers to be godfather. They are too young. My cousin, Cuthbert, the vicar of that little village in Durham, will do. We will not let them influence the children as they grow up. You and I will be both parents and godparents."

Clara couldn't help saying, "But *Adelaide*! I thought you would have wanted a Ridley or someone who could help them on in life."

"*We* will help them, not godparents or grandparents."

"Oh!" Clara knew her mother would be a fussy grandmother and her father too indulgent but Anne Reid would be a blessing with her independent mind, great capability and abundant good will. Clara knew herself deficient in all those qualities yet Anne never criticised her. She wrote her one of her warm, humorous letters.

'My dear girl, George and I rejoice with you and he is happy that his second name of Kenneth has been chosen for your son. He wanted to have the bells of the city churches rung to proclaim the birth but I told him that was too ostentatious. 'Well,' says he 'when the Ridleys' son and heir was born they had the bells rung.' I told him we are not the Ridleys, but suggested that we might host the baptismal gathering. To this he has agreed so we trust you will soon give us the date of your return. Our boys want to be home from school for the occasion. They are mightily looking forward to playing uncles. Kenneth and Kate are going to be the centre of much celebration.'

Clara's heart quailed when she read that. Anne Reid would invite the whole of Brandling Village and reign over them all, unruffled and gracious, managing George in a way Clara had never learnt to manage Ridley. How can I face her, Clara thought, and tell her lies?

Jane brought her a new concern. "Bet Moray is learning English fast and she won't leave Tom alone. She sidles up behind him in the hotel kitchen and puts her arms round his neck and whispers at his ear, 'You like me, yes?' I tell him to say, 'No' but he's too shy to say anything. He just grins at her."

"Does she talk about – about where she comes from – and the babies?"

"She hasn't enough English for that."

"But will she ever tell?"

"Bless you no. But what is there to tell? Tom *knows* they were born while he and the master were on the steamboat. And I'll wager the families have put an announcement in the *Newcastle Chronicle*."

"Oh Jane!"

But Jane would only raise her eyebrows and smile at her. "Now look, pet, I've my orders. The better we all keep to 'em the easier it'll get. The churching and the christening will make everything comfortable." And she trotted out, leaving her alone.

Churching! Thanking for safe delivery! 'God is not mocked,' Clara recalled with terror. *He* knows. And so does Bet. If she could read she could explain the paper I have in my reticule. I saw Ridley burn the original in the hearth of our bedroom at Leith. I alone hold the knowledge but cannot unlock it myself. Maybe I ought to tear it out of my diary and burn it. But, dear God, that wouldn't make the truth go away.

At last Ridley announced the day of their departure. "I believe you are quite fit to travel now, my darling. I have written to my mother that she can plan the baptism celebrations. There will be the churching first of course. Under our circumstance it couldn't be done at forty days but it will take place immediately before the baptism. My mother has settled it all with the rector."

"Oh Ridley, must I? I am so dreading seeing all these people. They will bombard us with questions we cannot answer."

"Cannot, why? Tell them how the birth pains came on suddenly but you let me go on the steamboat trip believing they might come to nothing. You were mistaken, that's all. Can you not picture the moment I returned and saw you holding our son?"

She could and could also feel the little naked bodies between her thighs. She had renewed that sensation of handling their squirming shapes by participating in their bath times now with Bet's help. She was gaining confidence as a mother. But to go among the families at home . . .

She looked into his face and received his encouraging loving smile.

She bit her lip and forced herself to speak in a strong brave voice. "I know they are our babies. There is no one else on earth they can belong to."

He took her in his arms and gave her a prolonged kiss.

They arrived in Newcastle on a Friday and the baptism was arranged for the Sunday. Clara had no time to fall into a panic. Strangely the churching ceremony and the baptismal service brought her the sense of security Jane had predicted. God has sanctioned our parenthood, she told herself. We have promised to bring up Kenneth and Katherine in the faith.

Ridley's cousin Cuthbert took his godparent duties with brisk loud-voiced professionalism and said he had to get back to his parish at once, but Adelaide looked becomingly devout and never uttered a word of scepticism.

Finding everyone talking about the babies and accepting the story of the birth gave it validity in Clara's mind. George Reid declared, "Young Kenneth will be a great man. Under that little cap I detect a high forehead – abundant brain power."

Her own father said, "They're both fair like the Stokoes," and her mother babbled to anyone who would listen, "Kate is the *image* of Clara as a baby."

At the Reid family home for the christening feast, Anne Reid kept at bay the ladies of Brandling Village who wanted to know how Clara had hidden her condition so successfully. She put an arm round Clara. "It showed great strength of will."

"It was Ridley's idea," Clara murmured back. "He hoped a change of scene and the country air would be good for me."

"Well, it was one of my son's cleverer ideas then. We grandparents were spared all the worry we would have endured."

Ida Stokoe burst in with, "My grandmother *died* giving birth to twins. I would have been in my grave with worry. But of course I should have been at the birth. I can't get her to say much about it so I think it must have been very dreadful. I know she missed having her mother at her side."

Clara sniffled, but her fears were melting away. "Oh I did, Mamma."

George Reid rose at that point to propose the health of the twins. "Kenneth, *my* name, an excellent name, and Katherine after the good lady there, a name I believe we are happy to shorten to Kate. Raise your glasses to Kenneth and Kate Reid. May they have long and happy lives."

After the guests had left Ridley told the parents that they were moving to the country and again it was Anne Reid who soothed the heat out of the protests.

"George," she said, "you know Ridley's heart was never in coal. He can buy a bit of land and farm it in the country if that is what he wants." She folded her arms across her broad bosom and concluded, "We can put money down for him."

"He should *earn* it," cried his father. "What happened to his ideas for new ventures – the reason for his travels we were told – steam traction and refining the new metal tracks for coal wagons." He glared at Ridley. "Steam*boats* you were investigating when the babies were born. You must *work* now you have a family."

Clara watched Ridley's chin go up and his eyes blaze. This was what his own fatherhood had done for him. "I want no work that will keep me away from my family. If it is too much for you now, sir, a manager could take over the business."

Anne Reid intervened as George looked ready to explode. "*I* can sell some jewels and give Ridley enough to buy a farm. He is not afraid of work but his new task is fatherhood and he wants a source of income that will keep him in the home."

Clara's father broke in. "The babes are Stokoes as much as Reids. I have properties in Newcastle that bring me in a canny rent. Ida and I were planning to hand over a thousand pounds to mark this great day. I doubt if you can match that."

Clara saw Adelaide's head shoot up. She glared at their mother who seemed just as surprised. Clara was sure it was the first either of them had heard of it. Anne had noticed too. She smiled across at her husband who had gone very red and fierce.

"I can give them *two* thousand with no trouble," he snapped, "but I expect my sons to work. Take note you two" – glancing at the schoolboys, Peter and Martin – "I expect you to add to the fortune *I* have built up through hard grit. What do you know of *farming*, Ridley?"

There was a tap on the door and Jane and Bet brought in the babies who were awake and lively. Over two months old now they could smile and gurgle in response to happy faces. Clara held out her arms and took them both onto her lap. Love and joy overwhelmed her. They looked up at her, smiling.

Her mother burst into tears. "You can't take the darlings away from us into the country. That would be cruel."

"We won't go far."

"We'll go where I can earn a living," Ridley said. "I am indeed mighty grateful for what has been so generously offered to us." He got up and shook his father-in-law's hand.

When he moved to his father George Reid growled out, "You can have two thousand in *trust* for the children. I didn't build up the coal business for you to desert it when it's going well. Farming has hardly recovered from the bad times after the war – long winters, failed harvests and riots everywhere about the price of bread. For God's sake stick with coal which we can always sell. This country could still go the way of France. The rabble is teetering on the edge of revolution."

Clara looked at Anne for reassurance. She had no idea that these poor little babes were to grow up in such a horrific world.

Anne leant over and tickled Kate under the chin. "Your grandfather Reid is a prophet of doom, my precious. England will *not* go the way of France. We have some liberal minds in parliament. We never ground down the populace as France did. I hope, my son," looking up at Ridley, "you will not bury yourself in the country and forget you joined a reform society for the welfare of the poor."

Ridley inclined his head. He still stood in front of his father. "I thank you, sir, on behalf of our twins." Clara thought, he'll take the money but not allow influence. I see trouble ahead. Can I ever know this man? Everyone here wants to love the babies and now that I'm more comfortable I'd rather stay among our own families.

Ridley was now telling Jane and Bet to take them out before they became excited with too much attention. "I will give orders for Tom to bring the carriage round to be ready to take us home."

"We'll go too," Clara's mother said. "We're only round the corner but I walk in the street as little as possible in these uncertain times. Come along, Mr Stokoe."

Clara saw her father heave his bulk reluctantly from his armchair. Adelaide, whose presence was hardly noticed by anyone, rose too. She gave a little bob to Anne.

"Thank you, Mrs Reid, for a delightful party."

"Bless you, my dear. Life *is* delightful if the men don't lock horns at awkward times. Not you, Mr Stokoe. You are a nice comfortable man. Goodnight to you all."

As they went out, her mother whispered to Clara, "We'll follow you to the country. If so much unrest persists in the town I would feel safer there. Then I can help you with the babies, you know, for I worry that that foreign girl is no better than she should be. Did you see the way she eyed Ridley's good-looking young brothers when she came into the room?"

Ridley, bustling ahead, did not hear this but to Clara he said the minute they were alone, "I want to be away from all of them as soon as possible" and he began studying advertisements for country properties the very next morning.

"Do you know *how* to farm?" she dared to ask.

"I intend to employ returning soldiers and sailors who worked on farms before they enlisted. Don't bother your head. This is not woman's business. When Kenneth is older he will share all such burdens with me."

She was crushed. Was this the end of his tenderness?

In the next few weeks his time was divided between visiting properties and talking to the babies about their duties in life. So Clara devoted herself to the babies when he was out. He hardly seemed to notice how little they were seeing of each other. And then on a bright August morning he called her to his study after breakfast and laid before her an advertisement showing a drawing of a solid square house.

"This is the one. I am writing to Lord Allendale's agent to confirm acceptance of the lease. We will be in it before winter."

She was flattered to be shown it and bitterly hurt that she was to have no share in the choosing. "It's very – plain." She feared his anger but before he could speak they both became aware of a figure waving at the window. The study which adjoined the front hallway looked straight onto the street.

She exclaimed gladly, "Your mother's here."

He grimaced. "You see, there's no peace till we get away."

That 'we' was a little comforting.

Sarah, their general maid, showed his mother in. She had walked in the heat and wasted no time in greetings.

"Leave that for now," she said, pointing to the advertisement. "Have you not heard the news?" He gave her a blank stare. "Why, Ridley, all the reform societies are planning a great protest. I trust you will play your part." He spread his hands and lifted his shoulders to his ears. "What," she cried, "do you not even know that a peaceful march in Manchester has been violently suppressed? I didn't believe it could happen in England. We must show your father that this country will not tolerate hussars on the streets drawing their sabres against civilians."

Ridley pointedly folded up the advertisement. "Mother, Kenneth has had a little cold this week which has affected his breathing. I have not been reading the papers." Clara had seen the headlines but had read no further. Manchester, she thought, was a long way away.

His mother cast her eyes upward. "When Kenneth is a man I believe the reforms demanded now will have come in. If I live that long I hope I can tell him his father spoke up bravely in the year of his birth and carried a banner proclaiming justice for all." Ridley's brow puckered up and his eyes narrowed as if he was peering into the distant future. "Well," she concluded, "I've said what I came for. If I may look at my grandchildren first I will take my leave. See what you can do with him, Clara." And up the stairs she went to the nursery to see the babies.

Clara expected an outburst but he only stroked his narrow chin.

"She is right," he said at last. "I must do this for Kenneth. He may be in parliament one day. I will write my letter but I will call in the society's office when I take it to the post and see what is afoot. This business of our future home has been absorbing me to the exclusion of all else."

Clara took heart from this. Perhaps it was a tentative apology. He laid the advertisement out and while she studied it he wrote his brief letter.

This is where we are to go, she thought, to this stone box in a wild empty country. The name is pretty enough – Allenbrae – but there is little joy in a name.

He had sealed the letter and hearing his mother coming downstairs he intercepted her in the hallway.

"I will walk a little way with you, Mamma, as far as the society's office and tender my services in any capacity they wish."

She clapped him on the back. "That's my boy." Seeing Clara in the doorway of the study she added, "Has he found you a farm then, my dear?" Clara nodded. "I will hear all about it soon but just now I am rousing our liberal troops."

Ridley took his hat and cane and they set out together, a broad woman in a large hat and a stick-like man prancing beside her with that purposeful bounce which told Clara he was all set for a new goal.

He returned fired with zeal. "I have offered to carry the banner. They are planning the greatest march ever held. Clara, when the day comes you must go among the crowd on the Town Moor so you can tell Kenneth about it when he is older. There were many killed in Manchester. They are calling it the Peterloo Massacre."

"Oh but then you will be in danger!"

He preened his head like a peacock. "No matter. This is for our children's future."

When his father learnt of his intention he was shocked. "My son to align himself with revolutionaries and I a magistrate! I absolutely forbid it."

Clara pleaded, "Surely you won't go against your father? You are a father yourself now. What about paternal authority?"

Ridley laughed. "*My* rule will be so wise and benevolent that Kenneth will not *wish* to cross me. My father has been harsh and arbitrary. I will *nurture* Kenneth's dreams, guide them gently into right channels. I will be an inspiration to him."

"And are we still moving to Allenbrae?"

"Yes, yes. The lease commences at Michaelmas but I will set improvements in train so that we can be in by November. We must get the children into the good air before winter. Kenneth is better but the smoky conditions here are not good."

She thought, surely the internal decorations are a woman's business but she dared not say it. His mind was on the great march which would take place in October.

Clara read every word she could find about the Manchester event. A wicked thought stabbed her brain. If Ridley is shot I will not go to Allenbrae.

The day took on a different air when her mother-in-law called for her on the morning with extra shawls and a picnic in a basket. Anne sought a place on rising ground where they could see over the heads of the crowd and watch for the procession coming. When it began to wend its way onto the Town Moor Clara didn't know whether to laugh or cry. She had never imagined so many people could feel so deeply about anything that they would subject themselves to this. They marched in solemn silence, all the northern reform societies, behind a Union Jack, flown at half mast, and a great wagon draped in black cloth and bearing the words 'Truth! Order! Justice!' Every person in the procession was clad entirely in black.

"There he is," cried Anne Reid and Clara picked out Ridley marching stiffly, holding his banner erect and gazing straight ahead. She was afraid he looked just a little comical.

Tedious speeches calling for universal suffrage were now bawled through loud-speakers. Clara's legs ached but she daren't sit down on the grass and cover her ears. Anne was applauding enthusiastically.

"His father doesn't know I've come," she said in one of the pauses. "He told me the town is heading for anarchy. He will be surprised to learn what an immense crowd has gathered and all orderly and disciplined. The constables scattered among them have had nothing to do. Well, I am very pleased Ridley has taken part." Then she looked down at Clara from her broad height and added with a twinkle, "whatever his motives." She began to gather up their things. "A good day for England anyway."

"Ridley does throw himself into things with great feeling," Clara murmured. "It was nearly steamboats."

Anne laughed. "At least his father is happy now that he's moving out of town. He's an embarrassment to him. But be assured we'll visit you when you are settled."

Clara gulped. Would Ridley permit it? She followed Anne down the slope with heavy steps.

Despite the peacefulness of the occasion, she heard later, the magistrates were disturbed by the vast numbers and a Volunteer Corps of Cavalry was set up and a troop of Dismounted Yeomanry to keep order on the streets of Newcastle.

"*That*'s where you should offer your services," George told Ridley. "I heard that many of your *mob* carried concealed weapons."

"That was an untrue rumour, sir. I support law and order and when I am established in our new home I may enter local politics if paternal duties permit."

"Have you found a new home then? With Stokoe money eh?"

"I have bid for the lease of a farmhouse and land south of the market town of Hexham. It is known as Allenbrae. Stokoe generosity has helped but I have always been abstemious and accumulated my own savings. My energies will now be absorbed in making a home appropriate for a healthy life for our children."

"I am glad to hear it." And his father had no more words with him before the mild November day when their little family with Jane, Tom, Bet and Sarah, set off to travel twenty-five miles from Newcastle. Clara's mother wept and Clara had to fight back her own tears. Her father, whose strongest quality was his inertia, had refused to think of leaving their comfortable home. He said it was no distance and Ridley and Clara could bring the children to see them as often as they liked.

Clara was a little cheered by the small market town of Hexham which they passed through. There were shops and an abbey and some houses that might contain gentry. At only three miles away Allenbrae was not as remote as she had feared. The road south from Hexham was little more than a dirt track but the fields looked well cared for and there were sheep and cattle grazing. Away to the north were faint blue hills which Ridley declared were the Cheviots on the border of Scotland. He was twisting this way and that, his eyes shining, his lips parted in excitement.

They breasted a hill and the house in the advertisement was there, planted in the landscape. A cowshed loomed beside it and fresh gravel was spread all round. No greenery anywhere. Jane and Bet lifted up the babies to see it.

"Your new home, my pretties," Jane said. She worked her eyebrows at Clara. They were saying "You have to like it. There's no going back."

Stark as a prison, Clara thought, when Ridley jumped down and took out a big key and unlocked the front door. Then all at once he was at her side again. He seized her in his arms and, staggering with her weight, carried her over the threshold and set her down in a wide hallway from which a gracious stairway rose to the upper rooms.

"My darling girl," he cried, tears in his eyes, "our dream has come true."

10

In the minister's study at Canisbay Rory-Beag always sat at the desk with his back to the mirror above the fireplace. Here he learnt to read and write. The mirror had been a terrible shock to him the first time he had seen it. The hideous face with twisted mouth and jaw and tangle of wild hair made him yell out when his eye caught it as the minister showed him round.

"Oh no, my dear boy. It's all right. Give him your best smile."

So Rory-Beag smiled and the face grimaced back at him and he knew. He touched the smooth, shiny surface and remembered that Mary had had one with a wooden handle which she looked in sometimes but never left lying about. Now he knew why. He understood all the people who recoiled or screamed when they saw him and he was sorry that he had ever nursed anger in his heart towards them. Now he would be patient with the minister's congregation who took a long time to grow used to seeing him working in the Manse garden or out running messages for him.

He plunged with zest into learning his letters.

"I have hardly enough hours in the day to keep up with your enthusiasm," the minister said and wrote the letters on the slate so he could practise them on his own.

It had puzzled the minister at first what language he should teach him.

"You want to travel, don't you, Rory-Beag? I'm thinking you are better to have the English. You understand Gaelic and a little English but once you are south of the highlands it is English that is mainly spoken. Most books are printed in English and you are a clever boy who will gain much pleasure from reading as you grow up."

Rory-Beag held up two fingers.

"You want to learn to read and write in *both* languages?"

Rory-Beag nodded vigorously.

"It will take a long time but I suppose you have many hours before you are a man when you might think about journeying as far as Carlisle. Is that still in your mind? You want to trace those little babies?"

More nods and happy smiles.

"You must not forget that they will grow up too. You will always be eleven years older than they but your coming to them must not upset their lives. They have their new parents who may not tell them they are adopted. We must think whether it is wise for you to do this thing. I could not let you travel alone and I am not so young as I was. You will be a young man in ten years but I will be nearing seventy."

Rory-Beag put on his sad face. What the minister didn't know was that he had no intention of waiting till he was a man. He wanted to see the babies while they were still little and he very much wanted to explain to everybody, including the minister himself, that they were not twins, nor even brother and sister. It was essential then that he learnt to read and write very soon. He would write in Gaelic for the first part of his journey so that he could ask directions but later it would have to be English. He must earn his bread too as he went so he must be able to write down work that he could do.

The minister had said he was clever so he entered on his task with confidence, progressing from printing letters to copying the names of common objects. He would point to the table, the Bible, the fireplace, a tree, a flower and the minister grasped that he wanted the words for all these things written down in both Gaelic and English. Once learnt it was impossible for Rory-Beag to forget them. He wiped them off the slate but they piled up in his memory.

It was easy to convey to the minister the objects he wanted to name in writing but phrases were more difficult. "Where is Carlisle? How far is it?" After a while he began to connect similar sounding words with the letters he wrote down and realised he would be able to build up words himself. 'Carlisle' began like 'cart' which he had learnt and then there was the sound which started the word 'light' so one day he wrote on the slate 'Carlil' and fetched the minister to look at it.

"Ah, I see what's in your mind. You are nearly there but some words have more letters than they need, especially in the Gaelic which sounds quite differently from the English. Luckily place names can be recognised in both languages." And he showed him out to write it.

This was a landmark moment for Rory-Beag.

By the spring of 1821 when he assumed he must be thirteen years of age he was armed with what he believed would be enough knowledge of both languages. He stood in the Manse garden and looked across the sound at the dark cliffs of Orkney. Between lay the low green island of Stroma where the minister had gone on his quarterly visit. Behind him in the house he could hear Beathag the housekeeper pounding the washing. Beathag was jealous of him, he knew, jealous of the time the minister spent with him "which keeps the good man from his duties," she said often.

Well, I will be away some time, Rory-Beag thought, for I know not how long the journey will take or what will happen at the end of it. And then I must come back and report that I have been wise as he said and not upset anyone's lives.

The minister had given him an old knapsack to carry his gardening tools in. He emptied them out and stored them in the shed and brushed out the bag, shaking it over the soil. From the attic where he slept he took his spare trews and two shirts and the plaid Martha had given him and an old fisherman's jersey.

It was a fine wild day with clouds racing across the sun. He had grown taller and thickened up from the skinny boy he had been at eleven and the cool wind was nothing to him. He stuffed the clothes in the knapsack and then, most precious of all, his notebook and a pencil. He had already written in it many phrases he might need. "Can you direct me to –?" "Thank you, good sir/lady." "May I help you with that?" "I am hungry." "Can I ride in your cart?" It would be so laborious to write things down while people stood about impatiently. Now he could point to the appropriate phrase.

He knew he would meet many people, especially women, who

could neither read nor write. He was adept at signs but had developed many which only the minister understood. Beathag had no time for his signs, but pointing to his mouth and rubbing his stomach conveyed hunger anywhere. Resting one cheek on his hands signified a place to sleep. Oh, I will do very well, he told himself, as he took from the larder the hunk of bread and piece of cheese that would have been his lunch. He knew from his early wanderings that the highlands provided plenty of streams so he would not take a flask of which the minister had several.

Beathag was still in the washhouse. He could hear the creak of the mangle. He could leave now while the day was still young but he must not worry the minister by simply disappearing. He slipped into the study, wiped his slate clean and chalked three words in English, "Gone to Carlisle. RB". Beathag wouldn't understand it if she came in to clean the room while the minister was on Stroma.

Satisfied and happy he walked out of the house and followed the dirt road south that would take him by the coast first to Wick. He knew that was about fourteen miles and he resolved to cover that before he ate his bread and cheese. Some of the way he ran spurred by the thought that he was heading for the babies, Roderick's and Annie's boy, little Roderick, and Alistair's and Mary's girl, little Mary. Roderick-Beag and Mary-Beag in Gaelic. They will be toddling about now, he told himself, but still only babies. I shouldn't be Rory-Beag any more – he laughed aloud – I will soon be Rory-Mor. My father was a big man, I remember. And my real name is Angus and one day I will write down all I can recall of my first four years of life and I will ask the minister to call me Angus. But I must be even better at reading and writing than I am now. I will also write of my wandering life and how Alistair Gunn found me and gave me a home and then – he shook his head as he jogged along – there was the day of burning and another of drowning and I lost all my friends but the babies. They were so small and miserable when they were taken out of the barrel and I have not seen them since that moment. Oh to set eyes on them again! He quickened his pace.

He sat down on a wall above the river to rest when he reached

Wick and gobbled up his bread and cheese. The town behind him had seemed huge to his eyes but he was staring across to what seemed like another town on the south bank, a town with a big harbour and many fishing boats.

A voice behind him said, "Ay, they call that Pulteneytown. None of that was there when I was a boy your age and they're planning a big distillery too. Changes, changes, changes. But it's brought work to the folks put out o' their homes for the sheep. Are you a stranger here, lad?"

Rory-Beag, excited by his last remark, made the mistake of turning round to nod to the man. He just glimpsed a bearded old face before the man gasped and hobbled away on his stick. Rory-Beag was sorry because it was the first encounter he had had that day. There had been a few riders and some pedestrians on the road but they had ignored him as he trotted along. Two driving carts had turned to offer him a lift but had whipped up their donkeys when they saw his face. It was going to be hard to find anyone to stop and let him show his notebook.

He crossed the bridge and headed on south, past Pulteneytown, which was so new it wasn't even on the map of Scotland the minister had showed him. He knew he had to keep going south because England was a long way below Scotland. This was different country from the glens he had wandered in as a small boy. It was flat and green reaching to the cliffs which fell to the sea on the east. There were streams but not bubbling among rocks. They had weeds and floating vegetation but they would have to serve. In Wick he had found a street fountain from which he had drunk long and deeply.

Soon he was tired and hungry again. He came to a line of scattered cottages and by the side of one he saw a woman struggling to bring in her washing which was blowing wildly. She was unpegging a shawl when a gust snatched it from her grasp. Rory-Beag caught it and, holding it so that it covered the lower part of his face, he brought it to her.

"Thank you, laddie. That was well done."

She took it and bent over her basket and stuffed it in. Rory-Beag turned to the clothes line and brought down all the rest. She had gone in to empty the basket and when she came back he hid behind the pile of clothes in his arms. She took them without glancing up. He saw she was quite old so he put his hands to the basket handles before she could do it herself and carried it into the but end of the little house and set it on the kitchen table.

Now she did look at him. "Eh, lad, what you been doing to your poor face?"

He covered his mouth leaving his eyes smiling at her. With his other hand he rubbed his middle.

"Hungry eh?" He nodded. "Well I reckon you've earned a bite."

He could smell a pan of broth simmering on the hob. She set a wooden bowl on the table beside the basket and scooped out a ladleful. "Sit ye down." She sat down herself on the other chair.

He was about to take a spoonful when a shaggy-haired man appeared at the open door and exclaimed, "Mother! Who the devil's that?"

"Just a lad saved my shawl from being blown into the sea and brought in the rest o' the washing, a thing I've never seen you do in your whole life."

"What's the matter with him?" He glowered at Rory-Beag. "Where are you from eh?"

Rory-Beag had managed to gulp down a few mouthfuls. If he wanted to answer he would have to take off his knapsack, extract his notebook and point to the words on the front page. 'Rory-Beag from Canisbay going to Carlisle.' But he must finish every last morsel of this broth.

"I reckon he's deaf and dumb," the woman said. "Fancy being out on his own! Where can he be heading?"

"I don't like the look of him. And he's sitting in my chair. Where's *my* supper? Get this basket off the table and set the bread crock out."

She got up stiffly but Rory-Beag was quicker. He was up and lifting the basket into a space under a broad shelf where he saw the other washing lying. Then he looked round for the bread crock, spotted it and set it on the table before the woman's son. He pointed to the chair he had occupied and whisked the bowl from under the man's nose and finished it standing.

"My," cried the woman. "He can hear fine. I'll cut him a hunk o' bread for that."

"You'll cut one for me first and fill *my* bowl," the man said, sitting down.

Rory-Beag waited while she did and then she put a thick slice into his hand.

"And now get you gone." The man was half-rising with his knife raised.

Rory-Beag wanted to produce his notebook and point to the words, 'Thank you' in Gaelic but perhaps neither of them could read. He made a little bow to the woman and scurried out.

He ran along the road till he passed all the cottages. Then he sat down on a grassy bank and put the bread in his knapsack. That would be his breakfast in the morning. He took out the plaid Martha had given him and carried it over his shoulder as he trudged on till the long daylight was fading and he could walk no more.

The strong west wind was still blowing so he left the road and thought he might find a hollow to curl up in below the top of the cliff. When he came to where he could look down towards the sea he saw there were not rocky cliffs here but scrubby slopes leading to a shelving shore. He went a little way down, wrapped his plaid round him and snuggled between two bushes with his head on his knapsack. In a minute he was fast asleep.

Next day, footsore and weary he reached Helmsdale in the late evening. He was amazed to see that it hadn't changed. So much had happened to him that it seemed impossible that the harbour should look the same and *Seagull* was even moored in the same spot as before. He drew closer and could see down onto her deck and there were the two men who had worked for Robert Mackay touching up her paint. They looked up and saw him and stared open-mouthed.

The one Rory-Beag thought of as the man with a conscience shouted out, "We thought you were drowned on *Gannet*." He looked at his mate. "Ewen, didn't Mr Mackay say no one else survived – you remember when he took the babes to Leith?"

Ewen, the one Rory-Beag recalled as silent and grumpy, shrugged his shoulders. "We cannot ask him now, Calum." And he went on with his painting.

Calum beckoned Rory-Beag to descend the iron steps set in the harbour wall.

"What you come back for, lad?"

Rory-Beag was down in a moment. It was a delight to see faces he recognised and here was a chance to try holding a conversation. He lowered the knapsack from his back. Calum watched him curiously.

"I forgot. You can't speak, can you? It's no good you coming here to make trouble for Mr Mackay about *Gannet* for he's been dead these past two months, of an apoplexy. But *I* knew she should never have gone to sea."

Ewen glared round at him. "You'd best keep silent about that."

Calum just grinned. "He can't tell anyone." He turned back to Rory-Beag. "Mrs Mackay's the boss now and she's tough as nails. There was no inquiry into the wreck for there *was* a bad storm and any ship might have died in it."

Rory-Beag nodded. He had mixed feelings about Robert Mackay's death. God had punished him which was good but he had hoped to see him and if possible learn more from him about the Johnsons.

He took out his notebook, opened it and put his finger first on the opening words, holding it so Calum could see it.

The man's pleasant, open face flushed up. "It's a canny while since I was at school, lad. Let me see. Is that your name?"

Rory-Beag nodded and pointed to the words 'From Canisbay.'

Ewen laid down his brush and came over. "Give it here. 'Rory-Beag from Canisbay, going to Carlisle.' Where the devil's that?"

Rory-Beag found the place where he had written 'North-west of England.' The minister had told him few people would have heard of the place.

"That's a mighty long way away then," Calum said when Ewen had interpreted it for him. "Why do you want to go there?"

Rory-Beag pointed to the word 'Babies.'

When he read that, Ewen laughed, "The ones that survived the wreck?"

Rory-Beag nodded.

Calum said, "We sailed *Seagull* to Leith when Mr Mackay took the babies with that wee lass who couldn't keep her eyes off anyone in trews. As it happens we're taking *Seagull* to Leith in the morn but if you want the west of England that's no use to you. The family must have took them to this Carlisle place."

"Anyway we can't take extra passengers," Ewen snapped. "We'd be in trouble. Especially not that one. We saw the ill luck he brought to *Gannet*."

Calum patted Rory-Beag's shoulder. "Don't take that to heart, lad. He doesn't mean it. How old are you now. You've grown a sight bigger in nigh on two years."

Rory-Beag held up both hands and then three fingers.

"Thirteen eh? You're a strapping lad for thirteen but is it not too great a journey for you to be undertaking on your own? Have you any money?"

Rory-Beag shook his head.

Turning so that Ewen, who had resumed painting, couldn't see, he took some coins from his pocket and pressed them into Rory-Beag's hand.

This time Rory-Beag did point to the words 'Thank you' before putting his notebook away. Whether Calum understood or not he wasn't sure. He just said, "Ay, Ewen's more for the reading than I. Mrs Mackay always leaves her messages for him, but you're a real scholar, Rory-Beag, if you've written all those words in your book."

Rory-Beag saw Calum's face change as a figure appeared on the quay peering down at them. It was Mrs Mackay, the dour landlady, who had squashed them all into her hot attic room.

She pointed her finger at Rory-Beag. "Where's he come from? What's he doing here? Why are you talking to him? Why aren't you working, Calum MacNeill?"

Rory-Beag put away his notebook and hoisted his knapsack on his shoulder. She was looming above the iron steps but there was no other way up. As he climbed she stepped aside and took a swipe at his head.

"You're not wanted here. Clear off."

He would have liked to turn back and wave to Calum but feared he had already got him into trouble so he just ran, following the coastal road up the hill and heading out of the village. It seemed that wherever he met kindness it ended up with him running away. He slowed down panting at last and a pang of longing for the safety of the Manse and the minister's kindness made him gulp. There was so much further to go and if it were all like this . . . He breathed deeply, remembered he had money in his pocket and pressed on more cheerfully looking out for a place to sleep with the thought that he could buy food and maybe a lift on a cart in the morning.

11

Anne Reid looked round the door of her husband's study. "I think we should visit our grandchildren next week on their second birthday."

George didn't even look up. "You go if you want to." It was the answer Anne was hoping for. She had chosen her moment deliberately. He was immersed in a report on the latest methods of ventilating deep mines.

"Very well, my dear," she said. "I'll take Ida Stokoe for company. She is sure to want to go. They have a guest room so we can stay overnight and rest the carriage horses."

He looked up then and grunted, "Humph."

It would be a more peaceful visit without him and she would be free to reproach Ridley for his failure to attend any more meetings of the Reform Society. George had already pronounced the clamour for reform as dead. There had been two years' good harvests. "Men with full bellies are not troubled about votes," he said, "so you can stop pestering Ridley about that nonsense. Marching with banners! He may be free of my business but he's still my son and I want no more shame of that sort." He was angry too that Ridley had found a capable farm manager and was prospering.

So when the day arrived Anne took the carriage round to the Stokoe house where Ida was waiting with many packages to be stowed away under the seats.

"I didn't know what to bring," she murmured as she clambered in. "I wouldn't wish to insult Ridley as if I thought him unable to support his family."

Anne patted the seat beside her. "Sit down and don't fret. If it's clothes for the twins he'll scarcely look at them. Women's business."

Ida settled and the coachman whipped up the horses. "I'm sure you're right," she said as they clattered out of Brandling Village, "but Ridley is much more engaged with the children, especially Kenneth, than fathers usually are. Mr Stokoe hardly saw Adelaide and Clara when they were babies."

Anne thought, she's observed that, has she? Or has Clara written her the same letter she wrote to me? That Ridley is trying to train Kenneth up to be a noble citizen when the poor child has scarce learnt to walk or talk. He harangues him in a solemn voice, frowning at his baby misdemeanours and crowing over his achievements. Clara says she wonders if she should try his method with Kate but Kate is either sweetly loving or wild and fretful. Ridley recoils from her tantrums with horror and says if that is how a girl behaves she's best left with the women.

"Of course there's only Jane now to make the children's clothes," Ida was babbling on. "Clara was always hopeless with her needle. Did you know that the wet nurse has married their manservant Tom? Clara said she pestered him till he gave way. I'm afraid it was a matter of necessity for she had a baby within a few months of the wedding. They're living in a tumbledown cottage – at least Tom has repaired it. Tom is all right. He still works for the family and drives the carriage but the girl isn't allowed near the twins now for which I'm quite thankful. I never fancied her at all. They found her in Leith I understand." She stopped to draw breath.

The spirit of mischief that sometimes seized Anne Reid since she had reached middle-age and grown more independent of her husband grabbed her now. Ida was the last person to whom she should voice her fleeting suspicions but she found herself saying, "I did wonder once whether Bet Moray was more than the wet nurse."

"Whatever do you mean?"

"Whether she was in fact the mother."

The carriage was rattling out westward now, leaving the town behind.

Ida looked at her without comprehension. "She *is* a mother now, that's what I'm saying. She's had Tom's child. And she'd had a baby before, out of wedlock I believe, which was how she could serve as wet nurse."

"Clara could have fed the babies. I fed my boys myself. We are not aristocracy – though I know George would like us to be."

Ida was flurried. "*I* had a little trouble with my milk coming down. Clara is like me in that. And Kate will be like her. She has such a look of Clara as a baby."

Anne said no more, but Ida was unnaturally quiet for the next five miles. Anne remarked on the new spring foliage, the freshness of the green, the blueness of the Tyne across the water meadows.

"What did you mean," Ida broke in suddenly, "when you said 'whether she was in fact the mother?'"

Anne immediately regretted her rash words but she was too honest to prevaricate.

"Well, my dear, at first I found it hard to believe Clara had been with child – unknown to any of us – so when I saw Bet Moray I wondered for a moment –"

Ida threw up her hands. "No no no. How could you *think* such a thing?"

Anne patted her arm. "No, as you say, no."

"It was *your son* made her keep silent. I told her it was a cruel thing to do."

"Ridley can be secretive, especially from his father. George never handled him well, the eldest, you know. He has been better with Peter and Martin and they are eager to go into the business with him. Ridley is trying to be a humane father. Pray have no fear for Clara and the twins. I believe he has found domestic bliss at last."

"I hope for her sake he has." Ida had become tight-lipped and conversation was heavy-going for the last part of the journey.

Anne castigated herself. She knew she should keep Ida placid and contented. She hoped the sight of the children would prove a happy distraction.

Clara was looking out for them as they drove up the gravelled track to Allenbrae. She greeted them with excited looks.

"Oh you dear grandmothers, do come and see what is going on in the garden. Just peep from the French windows in the dining-room. Ridley is playing with Kenneth *and* Kate. *Truly* playing. It never happened before and they are so happy!"

Anne loved the distant views from the back of the house but today the nearer view was more fascinating. Ridley was rolling coloured balls down the sloping lawn below the terrace and the twins were chasing them down, shrieking with glee. As they toddled up again they threw the balls for him to collect and roll back down. The balls were tightly bound pieces of rag, and their wild arms couldn't propel them far but Ridley patiently collected them up and sent them on their way again.

"How they can run now!" murmured Ida.

"Ah but see, Kate is smaller and more agile than Kenneth," Anne said. "He still has his baby chubbiness. She's quicker coming back up."

The French window was slightly open and they could hear Ridley exclaiming, "Hurry, Kenneth. You don't want to be beaten by your sister."

"Me won," shouted Kate.

"I think you're both tired now and it's time for your dinners." Ridley produced the wooden box the balls had been in. "What do we do now, Kenneth?"

Clara whispered, "Watch this now. This is always the conclusion of his play with Kenneth. Nothing must be left lying about."

"In box," Kenneth said and began to gather the balls up. Kate immediately started throwing them down the slope again.

"Oh dear!" Clara jumped up. "Ridley will blame me for not training Kate to do the same. I'd better go out and prevent trouble. Mother, pray find Sarah in the kitchen and get her to bring in some refreshment."

Anne peeped round the curtain and saw Kenneth copy Kate and tip out the balls he had already collected. Ridley stood hands on hips aghast at this flagrant disobedience.

"Kenneth!" he roared.

Kenneth was enjoying himself. He rolled a ball away and rolled after it himself. Kate did the same. Both were wearing white dresses with pinafores on top and were becoming happily grubby.

Anne watched Clara blunder down the lawn and grab Kate. "No, Kate, dirty, spoil your dress. Naughty Kate." Kate kicked and screamed in her arms as she struggled back to the house with her.

Ridley was glaring at her. "That child is not under discipline. Take her to the nursery without her dinner."

Kenneth heard this and flew about the garden gathering the balls and returning them to their box.

"Good boy. But you did wrong before. What do we say when we do wrong?"

"Sorry," said Kenneth.

Kate was looking back over Clara's shoulder.

"Want dinner," she said.

"Papa said no."

"Me sorry."

Clara couldn't carry her any more and set her down. She turned and trotted back to meet her father coming up with Kenneth and the box. She stood in front of him and now they were all quite near the dining-room French windows. Anne saw the pretty little show that Kate was putting on for her father, head on one side, fair curls all tousled, eyes uplifted to him, wide and pleading, her lips half smiling.

"Me sorry. Have dinner?"

Oh my son, you can't resist her, can you, Anne chuckled to herself.

He couldn't. He picked her up and gave her a kiss. Then he hugged her little form to him tightly and gave her another. Her arms went round his neck and she snuggled her face into his.

Anne stood up at the window and waved. Ridley's face showed surprise and embarrassment. He set Kate down and the twins took hands and came running in together.

"Gammama Reid!" said Kate lifting up her arms to her. Ida came back from the kitchen. "Gammama Stokoe!"

Kenneth hid behind his father's legs and put his thumb in his mouth.

Clara said, "I told them you were coming."

"And she knows which of us is which," Anne said.

"Oh they have grown so much," Ida cried "I'm not sure the clothes will fit."

Ridley said, "I had no idea the time of your arrival was near."

Anne gave him a peck on the cheek. "You were having a good time, son."

From now on, she thought, he is Kate's slave. I hope it doesn't turn her head.

After a pleasant luncheon she found an opportunity to talk to Ridley on his own while the children were having an afternoon rest and Clara was closeted with her mother. They walked down the garden to the stone wall and he pointed out this year's herd of young bullocks in the field beyond.

"Have you given up support for parliamentary reform?" she asked him.

He was taken aback. "Is there much demand at present?"

"If you want Kenneth to stand for parliament would you not wish for a system untainted by corruption and representative of a wider electorate?"

"Of course, of course. We'll have to see which way his talents lie, won't we?"

"So it is a personal matter not one of principle? What were you thinking when you carried a banner on the Town Moor?"

He looked about as if they might be overheard. "Here in the country if I am to make my mark I would prefer that not to be mentioned. They have very conservative views here. Reform is all very well, Mother, but it must come in slow stages."

It was the best she could get from him. At least I have kept it before his eyes, she thought. Now what has Ida said to Clara that has made her look askance at me.

They were approaching from the house and Clara's face was red and her eyes frightened. Anne greeted her with her usual straightforward warmth.

"What a delightful place you have here, my dear. The children have come on wonderfully since we last saw them. They are a credit to both of you."

Clara smiled but when Anne and Ida shared the four-poster bed in the guest bedroom that night Ida, after fiddling with the strings of her nightcap, broke out, "I must say this, Anne, but it is not to be mentioned again. I told Clara your unworthy suspicion that Bet Moray – well, I don't need to say the words. She nearly fainted away on the spot. But she recovered and assured me solemnly it was not so. Bet Moray was, as they said, the wet nurse they hired in Leith when the twins were born."

"I am delighted to hear it. I should never have spoken the thought. Pray let us remain friends. We share two very fine grandchildren."

Ida nodded. Anne told herself, Clara would not lie barefacedly to her mother. But if it wasn't Bet Moray of course it could have been somebody else. Women don't faint from indignation but they might from being found out. Well, we will see how the children grow up and maybe the good Lord doesn't mind where they came from as long as they are loved, so why should I?

Clara dared not tell Ridley what had passed between their mothers. She lay sleepless beside him wondering who else had such suspicions. Anne had always been the one she feared deceiving. Adelaide perhaps, but she saw little of Adelaide who showed no interest in her godchild. Anne was on a grand scale in both body and mind and seemed to have a God-like knowledge of everything that went on around her. Clara kept telling herself, Mother promised to put her right about Bet Moray, Mother was quite angry with her but has it sowed a seed of worry in Mother's head?

She slept at last and lay so late that Ridley and even the grandmothers were up before her. When she did present herself in flustered haste at the breakfast table Anne could not have been kinder.

"My dear, young mothers must sleep when they can. Two is a tiresome age with small children. At least I had mine one at a time. Twins are exhausting."

Ridley said with great solemnity, "That is so, Mother. And I fear I have not been paying proper attention to Kate. Kate is a different temperament from Kenneth and Clara has found her difficult. Of course Kenneth's education must be my special task but the character-training of Kate is equally important. I have had her on my lap in the nursery this morning and she played with my watch chain very contentedly."

There were no more upsets and the visit ended pleasantly after luncheon with the whole family waving off the carriage as it headed home to Newcastle.

Ridley turned back into the house. "I trust they don't intend to do this every birthday. One is left with a sense of being inspected. And I couldn't help noticing that your mother managed to upset you yesterday afternoon. We are very tranquil as long as we are left alone as a family. What did she say?"

Jane came along the hall to take the children for their afternoon rest.

Clara thought she could escape with a murmur of "Oh nothing much" and a wave of her hand but Ridley drew her aside into the room by the back door which was really his study which he had grandly labelled, 'The Estate Office.'

He shut the door and faced her in the small space between his desk and the fireplace. "I repeat my question. What did she say?"

The May sun was sending dazzling beams into the room. Clara shut her eyes and exclaimed, "She told me what *your* mother had said to her – on the way here – that she suspected Bet Moray was the twins' mother."

Ridley's face darkened with fury. She put out a hand to touch his breast. "No no, she only thought it for a moment, not any more I'm sure. I wasn't going to say anything about it. Mother said she would tell her that was nonsense. I know she did and your mother accepted it, so it's over. I didn't *want* to tell you. I knew you'd be angry. But we can't help people having *thoughts,* can we?"

He took several deep breaths. "One's own mother! To dare to harbour such a thought even for a moment. You should have told me. I would have spoken my mind to her."

"No, please let it alone. It's best left alone, isn't it?"

He nodded slowly. "Why yes, I believe it is." Clara was thrilled to have her opinion for once taken as right. But he added, "The truth is as plain as can be and yet people presume to question it! You say we can't control their *thoughts*. But she *spoke* it. My mother spoke it! I find it hard to forgive that. And your mother crushed it you say, for certain."

"Oh yes, absolutely."

He stamped his foot and made several jerks of his head and twitches of his mouth as if ridding himself of an unpleasant taste. Then he impulsively seized her in his arms and planted a kiss on her lips. "At least we know the truth. We do, my darling." He released her, clapped her cheeks between his hands and said, "I must go and talk to Foster about the calves."

12

On a mild, wild Spring day when cleaning fever was at Beathag's fingertips the Reverend Josiah Mackenzie, Minister of Canisbay, opened the seldom used bottom drawer of his desk and uttered a little moan of dismay.

"Ah Rory-Beag, Rory-Beag." He drew out the slate which he had felt unable to wipe clean. 'Gone to Carlisle RB'.

Beathag looked over his shoulder, the duster in her hand. "Now what did you want to keep that for, Reverend? If I clean out that drawer you've somewhere to put that pile o' sermons I have to move every time I sweep up in here."

"I think about that poor lad every day. I wish you'd been able to stop him going off like that."

"Nay, I wouldn't have stopped him if I could. We're better without him."

The minister straightened up and shook his head at her. "That's not a Christian thing to say, woman. But I still wonder, if he died on his wanderings, why no word ever reached me. He had this place named in his precious notebook. Would you not expect someone to seek on his person for identification if they found his body in a ditch?"

She snorted. "Nay, they'd take one look and bury him quick I'd say."

He sighed, laid the slate on his desk and stood back so she could clean out the drawer. She got down on her knees and drew it right out and banged it on the worn rug. A beetle scuttled away.

"Will you hand me the sermons, Minister?" She slid them in, patted them down and pushed the drawer shut. Clutching the top of the desk she hauled herself to her feet, grunting. "I'd have put them for kindling. You've preached everyone a dozen times at least."

"Which is why I won't take them out again for at least another five years if I live that long."

She picked up the slate. "They could use this at the school" and her hand with the duster hovered over it.

"No!" he said. "Come May it will be a year since he went away. I'll not wipe off his message till then." And he propped it up on his desk behind the inkstand.

Beathag went out muttering, "Ay, cluttering up the place just when I've cleared it."

She went to the back door to shake her duster. The minister heard the click of it opening and then a scream of horror and it was slammed shut again.

She came running to him, white-faced. "It's the devil's own work. That slate! It's brought him back. I should have wiped it. He's out there or the ghost of him."

"What, Rory-Beag?"

He was at the door pulling it open with shaking hands. The garden gate was ajar and the body of a curly-haired boy was slumped in the opening as if the effort of unlatching it had drained the last of his energy.

"Bring water," he yelled at Beathag and stumbled down the path of sea-pebbles to the inert shape.

He lifted the head onto his knee and the eyes opened at once and there was his dear boy smiling at him.

"Oh thank God, thank God. Beathag, the water." She came running now, the water sloshing out of the earthenware jug.

"My, he's dirty but it's himself all right. I thought it was the devil taken his shape."

A few gulps of water and some splashed on his head and he was able to stand holding onto the stone gate post. He drank some more then and gave what the minister knew was his best grin. Then he rubbed his middle.

"Of course he's hungry," she said. "Come back to eat us out of house and home again I warrant." She ran back and brought a hunk of bannock as the minister began helping him forward. He tore at it with his teeth and nodded at her grinning again. They got him into the house and into the basket chair in the minister's study, though Beathag was protesting that she'd just cleaned the place.

She went back to the kitchen and put the pan of broth for the minister's supper on the fire. The minister had managed to peel the old knapsack from Rory-Beag's shoulders and set it on the desk. He pointed to the slate.

"I wasn't going to wipe it till you came home, Rory-Beag, but oh my heart was nigh broken when I came back and found you gone."

Rory-Beag's face went very sad.

"Did you – did you find the babies?" The minister hesitated to ask the all-important question.

Now Rory-Beag's head sank lower and waved from side to side.

"Surely you couldn't have reached Carlisle?"

He looked up then and nodded. He was stretching a hand out to his knapsack. He wants his notebook, the minister thought, but he must eat first. He is exhausted and his rags hang on him like a scarecrow. Time enough for me to learn his story when he is stronger.

It took many days for Rory-beag to tell the Reverend Josiah the story of his travels. He remembered everything so clearly, day after day, but he soon realised he must shorten and summarise or the telling would never be done. He tried putting down a few words and the minister made guesses and asked questions so he could nod or shake his head.

In this way, a little at a time for they both soon tired, he managed to convey that he had made his way to Carlisle, mostly on foot, occasionally by cart and once by water when he got work for several weeks digging the great canal that was being built to link the two seas. The mainly Irish labourers tolerated him. There had been an outbreak of fever among them and when enough were recovered to leave him unwanted the foreman gave him passage to the southern end and he found himself at last on the west coast where he knew he ought to be to reach Carlisle. It was still a long long way and often he couldn't move on till he had found other work and had a little money for food. He had many rebuffs and most people never gave him time to show his writing skills.

In Carlisle he got into trouble with the law. He picked up an apple fallen from a market stall and the holder saw him running away with it and shouted for a passing constable to catch him. He was brought before a magistrate and heard him referred to as Mr Johnson J.P. His excitement made the magistrate curious and when he was handed Rory-Beag's notebook which they thought he had stolen he gave Rory-Beag pen and paper to see if he could write like the writing in there. The name Johnson was written in the notebook and Rory-Beag was closely questioned about it. It was too long a tale for Rory-Beag to write down but he pointed to the words, 'the Johnsons of Carlisle adopted two babies in May eighteen-nineteen in the town of Leith.'

The magistrate took him to his house and fed him a great meal of beef and vegetables and an apple tart while he summoned his own relatives to make sure none of them had so increased their families without his knowledge. Failing in this he put out notices for anyone else of the Johnson name in the neighbourhood to report to him. An aged couple turned up alarmed that they had somehow offended against the law but they were allowed to go home after questioning. Rory-Beag showed the minister how old they were by holding up both his hands eight times. The incident gave them a laugh together as the tale unfolded.

The magistrate could do nothing more for him. If these babies were no relation of his, which Rory-Beag had admitted, he would do well to forget about them and go home. Rory-Beag wore his saddest face to show the minister his sorrow at the failure of his mission, but he wrote down that the magistrate had given him money for a stage coach ticket as far as Glasgow and a thick cloak for his back. Then in Glasgow he was attacked by a gang of youths who dragged him into an alleyway, tore his cloak from him and were trying to pull off his knapsack when he made such a roaring that they fled in horror.

He was not anxious to recall the hardships of the winter that followed though the minister would keep asking how he survived without his cloak. He continued to head northwards, sometimes begging, sometimes working, often starving.

The minister asked more questions than he could possibly write answers to so he did what he could with gestures. He clasped his hands in prayer and then indicated galloping, with his arms round someone's waist.

"You prayed and an angel in human form gave you a ride behind him on a horse?" Rory-Beag nodded, pleased. So little by little and spread over several weeks of the slow spring much of what had happened to him was made known.

He heard the Reverend Josiah comment to Beathag, "God must have preserved him for a purpose. His spirit is unbroken. He is eager as ever to improve his reading and writing. He has gained much in the English from his travels."

"What help is that to me?" she grumbled.

"Nay but we will build him up till he recovers his strength and then he'll save you much heavy work. My vegetable plot will be tended again and he'll be bringing you kail and potatoes and turnips for the pot."

"Ay and he'll eat twice what he did as he grows to man size."

All this set Rory-Beag thinking hard as he grew daily stronger, filling up his notebook with sentences from the Bible, and digging the ground as soon as the minister let him wield a spade.

It was a wet day in May, three years from the time of *Gannet*'s wrecking on Stroma, when the post brought a small parcel to the Manse door.

"Good, it's come." The grey caterpillars were active as Reverend Josiah winked at Rory-beag. "This is for you, my boy. I sent to Thurso for a new one." He took off the wrappings and handed Rory-Beag a book with a leather cover on it.

Handling it reverently Rory-Beag turned back the cover. The book was full of pure white pages. It was not something for him to read. It was space, acres of it, for him to fill with writing. The minister was smiling up at his awe-struck face. He could only gaze back, eyes and mouth wide, cheeks crinkling into a great grin of delight.

"What will be the first sentences you put in it, eh, Rory-Beag?"

Rory-Beag laid the book on the desk and rested his fingertips on the cover. Thoughts and plans were crowding into his head. There was something portentous about all the whiteness within. It was waiting for words of special significance. He could see that a new stage in his life had come.

He lifted his eyes to the small window and saw how the rain had dimmed the outline of Orkney to a faint line beyond the low green back of Stroma washed with a tumble of waves in the foreground. There would be no outside work today.

He itched to begin. With a few slow nods up and down to the Reverend Josiah he picked up the book and backed out till he could turn and scamper up the stairs to his room in the loft space.

Here he hunched on his bed with the precious leather bound book on his stool. From the shelf above he took down the wooden box he kept his pencils in and selected one carefully.

Then to his astonishment he heard slow footsteps on the stair and the minister's head peered round the door.

"Ah, I thought so," he said, "you need a desk or a little table the right height for your stool if you are to do fair writing. You shall make a start at my desk today and I will get Diarmad, the village carpenter, to knock you up something for here so you can work undisturbed."

Rory-Beag wasn't sure he wanted a moment's delay. Words were ready to pour out of his mind. But the minister seemed to have more to say. He sat down on the other end of the bed.

"You were going to start on a great work, eh Rory-Beag? Your life story?"

Rory-Beag shook his head.

"The history of the babies?"

Rory-Beag nodded hard. The day for the great revelation about those 'twins' had arrived.

"Then I must tell you what I was holding back because I didn't want to disappoint you further." The words sounded ominous in Rory-Beag's ears. Had he received news? Were the babies dead?

"I must tell you what I did after I came back from Stroma and found your message on the slate. You had many days start of me for I had stayed longer on Stroma than usual because poor old Martha who cared for you had fallen ill and I spent some time praying with her and then, alas, having to conduct her funeral. But when I did return here I set out at once for Helmsdale to see if I could trace your movements. I made inquiries and Mrs Mackay told me she had seen you with two of her men. She wasn't pleased about it. That was plain from her manner and she professed complete ignorance of where you had gone from there. I did however find out where her men lived and unknown to her visited them each at home. The man Ewen was unco-operative but Calum told me your coming had made him curious too about the fate of the babies and when they docked at Leith on their next visit he chatted to some of the workers on the quayside there and found one who remembered the young woman with two babies in a basket being taken into a hotel. Calum boldly went in and talked to the porter and even the hotel manager. He was certain they remembered all about it but pretended not to. His words to me were, 'I'll wager they'd been well paid to act dumb if any inquiries were made.' I fear, Rory-Beag, that whoever did adopt the babies was determined to keep it a secret."

Rory-Beag listened to this very solemnly. But then he gave a great sigh of relief. The disappointment was only that there was no news and the minister thought that was the end of the road. But that must not be for the truth must be told which only he, Rory-Beag, knew: that the babies were not twins at all. Not brother and sister but born two days apart to different parents.

Reverend Josiah was peering at him, expecting his sad face. He looked at him with bright, excited eyes.

This is what he must write down and then find a way of tracing the family who took them. Calum was just a rough deckhand. No one at the hotel would be willing to speak to him. But if the minister himself went –?

Reverend Josiah was puzzled. "You still think you would like to write their history. What history? They were only a day or two old when they were found. Do you mean their parentage? Have you forgotten that frail paper that was in the barrel? I gave it to Robert

Mackay. He told me he had translated it for the gentleman – the one he called Johnson. Did it not say that the man called Alistair Gunn and the woman Annie were the parents? Did it not have the testimony of the captain that he had married them on the ship? Is there any further history that you could write that would be important to anyone now?" He picked up the leather bound book. "I was hoping to learn your own story Rory-Beag. When you are strong enough. A little at a time?"

He cocked his head on one side and the grey caterpillars went expectantly up and down and the fan of smile lines deepened.

Rory-Beag gave him back his biggest smile but shook his head and made a baby-rocking motion and a squeaky baby noise. He held out his hand for the book and picked up his chosen pencil. The minister handed over the book and stood up.

"In my study then. In comfort."

Rory-Beag would rather have been alone to write but he followed him down the stair. The rain and wind was not so loud in the study and the minister sat himself in his basket chair and took up the Bible.

That was good. Rory-Beag sat at the desk, opened his new book and contemplated the white page. There must be a title.

He wrote 'Roderick and Mary' in his best writing and started a new line.

He was thinking of a moment when he would show this to important people, educated ladies and gentlemen. It was hard for his hand not to tremble as he shaped each letter. It would take a long time unless he began with bald statements of the most significant facts. This was what he wrote.

'Roderick Matheson was married to Annie. He died in October 1818.

Annie had a baby boy baptised Roderick in May 1819, the day before the clearing of Glen Kildonan.

Alistair Gunn was married to Mary Munro. She had a baby girl the day after the clearing. They were all on the sloop *Gannet* sailing to Thurso.

Mary died. Captain Robert Mackay baptised the baby Mary.

He married Alistair Gunn to Annie Matheson.

Annie died. Alistair died. The Captain died.

The babies were put in a barrel and lived.

I swam ashore and know all this is true.'

He considered whether to say Robert Mackay killed Annie and Alistair. Of course if he was asked how it all happened he could write it down but the stark facts had taken him fifteen minutes of painstaking writing.

He sat back, flexed his fingers and with a look of relief and triumph he turned round and handed the notebook to the minister. It was a triumphant moment for Rory-Beag. He watched the minister's face. He saw his grey caterpillar eyebrows shoot up.

He exclaimed, "What! The babies were not twins at all, Rory-Beag, not even brother and sister!"

Rory-Beag made a great shaking of his head. At last communication had become possible to him and this troubling secret had been revealed.

"Well well! We all – everyone on Stroma – assumed they were twins. And that was the word passed on by me to Robert Mackay and by him we must suppose to the family who took them and gave employment to Bet Moray. What was written on that paper did not make it plain. They must now be three years old and talking English we presume. They will grow up believing they are twins. You must have felt so frustrated, Rory-Beag, that you could not explain this to anyone." Rory-Beag nodded. "But you must sign it with your name. This is a testimony." He handed him the book.

Rory-Beag took it. He scratched his head. He sucked the end of his pencil. When the minister signed letters he wrote Josiah Mackenzie, minister of Canisbay.

What could *he* write? Rory-Beag knew his true name was Angus but he had no knowledge of a surname. He printed clearly 'Angus,' and showed it to the minister.

"Angus? Not Rory? I supposed Rory-Beag was a nickname. But not even Rory? You want me to call you Angus?"

Rory-Beag nodded and then laughed and shrugged his shoulders.

"Take a fresh page and begin your own history," the minister said.

"Not now because your fingers are tired. When you get to the time of the wreck on Stroma you can show me what happened on *Gannet*. I am curious about Alistair Gunn's marriage following the death of his wife. But all in good time. When you just want to say a few words we will use the slate for I think you would like to keep this book for special writing."

Rory-Beag nodded and taking the chalk that rested in a groove of the slate he scrawled, 'I get work. Earn money. You and I go to Leith.'

"You think I can persuade the hotel people to talk? The Kirk will not let me be away from my parish so long."

Rory-Beag rubbed out those words and wrote 'Must tell them not twins.'

The Reverend Josiah scratched his balding head. "I have heard what is sometimes done when lawyers wish to trace people. They put advertisements in the newspapers about it. We will see."

Rory-Beag clapped his hands and jumped up. He wanted this done at once.

Josiah held up his hand. "We must remember this will be a settled family. The children will call those who have brought them up Father and Mother even if they know they were adopted. They will look on themselves as brother and sister too."

Rory-Beag wrote 'I want to see Roderick and Mary.'

The minister nodded sadly "Ah that is the truth of it, isn't it? Well, Angus, you have been patient with your sad trouble for many years. Now I am asking you to be patient again. You will grow big and strong and earn a living and your learning will increase mightily when you have read every book in this house. You will be able to write letters to lawyers and sheriffs. If you write your own life story it may be published for many people to read. But I beg you not to be in a hurry, not to go off again on your own. I was sorely troubled. I thought I had lost you for ever."

Rory-Beag bowed himself at Josiah's feet uttering cries of sorrow. He felt the minister's hand patting his thick mat of hair and his arms raising him up.

He turned to the slate again and wrote, "I be patient. Write story."

From that day Rory-Beag's room in the roof space with bed, chest and stool, became his writing place. The minister asked Diarmad, the carpenter, to make him a small table at a suitable height for his stool. If he was directly below the skylight he could see well enough in the daytime and Josiah said he must have a candle at night and on dark winter mornings. Beathag grumbled, "He'll knock it over."

"If you observe him," the minister pointed out, "Rory-Beag is not clumsy. Unless he is excited for some reason his movements are quiet and controlled."

"Ay, but he's going to grow into a big man and then that room will be too small for him and you'll have to give him *my* room and send *me* up there."

"Now Beathag, sufficient unto the day is the evil – or the trouble or even the delights – thereof. I will see he has the means to write and there's an end for now."

When Rory-Beag was presented with his table he jumped up and down like a small child and the house shook. He disappeared up the little stair on wet days and when the sun shone and he had completed his outdoor work he took his notebook outside and sat on the garden seat. His eyes often filled with tears when he pictured Mary, so slight and slim when he first knew her, with her heart-shaped face and the long plait down her back and the dimple when she smiled.

Once he broke down in sobs when his mind's eye showed him Alistair Gunn addressing the men of Kildonan with his hopes for their future in Canada. He could see him standing there, the wind that had fanned the flames of the burning houses, stirring his bronze curls. What would their child, little Mary, be like now? What would young Roderick be doing this moment in an English home? Rory-Beag yearned to tell him how his father Roderick Matheson had stood up to the factor who broke the news that they must leave the glen come spring just when Annie's baby would be born. Roderick was dark-haired, strong and swarthy of face. Annie's hair was coarse, the colour of wet sand, her face broad. She would have made a good solid wife to Alistair in Canada but she had nothing of Mary's sweet, ethereal nature.

When he shed tears he turned to let them drop on his bed, not on his precious book. Sometimes he looked back to read from the beginning. He had begun to borrow books from the minister's shelves and it amazed him that he was writing one himself which people might read. I must not grow proud, he told himself. I must work and earn money. Roderick and Mary are growing up and one day I will find them.

Reverend Josiah let it be known in the parish that the boy's baptismal name was Angus but Rory-Beag stuck in folk's minds and Beathag would never use anything else. She was right about his growth. Rory-Beag not only made great strides in his studies but grew taller and broader till at sixteen he was indeed man-size. He could heave a sack of peats like a feather pillow. His stride was nearer two yards than one and the minister felt like a little old man looking up at him. The loft room was now too low for him but Rory-Beag laughed when Josiah said he couldn't be expected to manage in it any longer. He wrote on his slate, "I do not write standing up and I always sleep lying down. The room is good."

Diarmad, the carpenter, was growing old and at the same time the displaced crofters who had made a success of life on the coast were improving their homes. Some were putting deal panelling on their walls and needing more furniture. Diarmad said to the minister, "Yon lad you call Angus now could be a help to me, Reverend. I cannot heave logs the way I did or comb the shore for wrecks. He has good hands on him to wield tools. He shouldn't be wasting time with tiddly pencils, now should he?"

The minister smiled. "He could do both, Diarmad. There are many hours in the day. Can you pay him a fair wage?"

"If I get through the work quicker wi' him he can have the extra. At least he doesn't waste time talking."

Rory-Beag thus acquired his first job outside the Manse. "Jesus was a carpenter," he wrote on his slate. "I am very happy."

13

Clara stood at the nursery window of Allenbrae looking south east towards the road and beyond to the vibrant green of the Hexhamshire woods and pastures. The May morning was serene. I ought to be serene, she thought, all is well in my little world. The cherry trees we planted are in blossom. The twins are quiet at their lessons.

Two figures on horseback, a gentleman and his groom, were approaching. They would not turn in to Allenbrae she was sure. Although the family had now lived here four and a half years their acquaintances were few. Ridley was not disliked by neighbouring farmers. He had learnt from them and they trusted Foster, his farm manager, who was a local man, but Ridley did not frequent public houses and that set him apart. Besides he refused to send his children to the tiny village school.

Clara looked round at them. Kenneth and Kate were sitting at miniature desks performing the tasks Ridley had set them after breakfast. Kate had already declared several times that she had finished while Kenneth sat on copying letters into his book. He was quite a big boy and Clara was embarrassed that he was still in a dress like his sister. Ridley had read that boys should be breeched at age five and their birthday was in two days' time. Tom had driven them in the pony cart to Hexham and she had bought the breeches and little shirts and two sailors' jackets which she was told were popular for little boys. Today, she thought, is probably their birthday but it has to be kept on the 'true' anniversary. Ridley insists.

Kate saw her mother watching her and jumped up to join her at the window.

"I've really finished now." She knelt on the window seat to see out.

"Two men coming in," she announced.

Clara swung round. It was true, the horsemen were trotting up the gravelled drive, heading round to the stables. She shrank back from the window.

"Oh my! It's your Grandfather Reid. I'll find Papa."

Kate smoothed down her pinafore. "I'm coming. He gave us silver sixpences at Christmas."

"No you must stay up here till I send Jane to bring you down."

Kate looked bursting to protest but Clara didn't stop to argue. All of a tremble she ran downstairs. Ridley was in his study.

"Your father's here!"

He leaped up, eyes wide, mouth agape. Instantly composing himself he shrugged his shoulders. "You need not sound so alarmed. Bring him in here and send in some refreshments. I am not afraid of my father."

"He and his man have gone round to the stables."

"Well, he should find Tom there to see to the horses. Stop looking flustered."

Clara ran out again into the passage as George Reid walked in at the back door.

"Well Clara," he greeted her. "I don't need to stand on ceremony here I suppose. I was coming out your way on business."

He was stockier now and grey-haired. His narrow face was hard-lined and not nearly as mobile as his son's. Ridley opened his study door.

"Come in, Father."

"It's time to talk about young Kenneth's future," was his opening greeting and to Clara when she brought a bottle and glasses, "No thank you, too early in the day for wine. I drink coffee mid-morning."

When she carried it in herself he was sitting up very straight in the desk chair so he could look down on his son who had to occupy the armchair by the unlit fire.

"Stuck out here in the country you're cut off from progress," he was saying. "I want young Kenneth trained up to the business. You used to speak of a great dynasty of Reids like the Ridley family. Have you not heard the news that a steam vessel has made a run in fifty-six hours from the Tyne to London? I am going to invest in one of those. There's money to be made. How are you living out here, now you've given up your share in Reid and Sons? I'm putting your brothers in and they are passionate about new inventions. You're not even a true landowner."

Ridley tossed his head, then twisted and turned his neck like a pheasant preening itself.

"I lease my farm from Lord Allendale but I have subtenants and the land is doing well. I have crops as well as sheep and cattle."

"But you can't afford a tutor for your son. He should be sent away to school in a few years. Learn some independence. You have the money I gave you in trust for the children. Use that if you have nothing to spare."

"No, sir, I am teaching Kenneth myself because it is my wish. Who can I trust better than myself to train up my son?"

"For sheep and cattle?" The scorn in George Reid's voice cut like a knife. Clara's hands shook as she poured the coffee. "What's got into you, Ridley?" he went on. "You yourself were after steamboats when the boy was born."

Clara watched Ridley push out his lips and draw a deep breath. What would he say to that?

"I admit it, sir. I was floundering, looking for a new invention. I was on edge. A baby was expected but I dared not count on the family I longed for. Birth is a dangerous business. And then we were blessed with a fine boy and girl. Now I could be the father I wanted to be, not a bully –" George Reid started at the word but Ridley pressed on – "and I can guide and nurture them. I am content. You will not believe how wise little Kenneth is and how lovely our little Kate has grown."

Clara edged the coffee towards her father-in-law with a quivering hand. His face was very red and his eyes flaring.

"Are you calling *me* a bully, sir?" he was demanding.

Ridley had got up in his excitement and was tapping his hand on the mantel shelf. "It seemed so to me when I was young. There was no question of my opposing you. Mother took us on picnics into the country and I loved to see fields and woods, but to live there, work there, when I had to go into the coal business, was denied me. But when the twins came I knew that was our destiny – to bring them up in the natural world, in health of body and mind. Clara loves the country too, don't you, my dear?"

"Oh yes." It had to be said with enthusiasm or he would be frowning at her, but where were her town friends or the pleasure of shops close by or the gentle walk to take tea with her mother in Brandling Village on the leafy edge of town?

George Reid just managed to notice her and the coffee cup at his elbow before he glared up at Ridley now he was standing pugnaciously before him.

"You say there was no question of you opposing me? Should there be? Do you not expect obedience from *your* son? Is not the father the head of the household, the ultimate authority?"

Oh dear, thought Clara. Does he not know how often Anne acts alone and keeps her own counsel? But she was curious to hear how Ridley would reply. He was smiling and confident.

"Sir, my children are five years old. Of course they must learn obedience and I expect good progress in lessons, especially from Kenneth. But I assure you I never bully them. I talk, I explain, I reason. I will not crush their spirits. When Kenneth approaches maturity, if he has special talents and a strong urge towards some lawful and honourable employment I will be the encourager, the promoter, the father he can love as well as respect." He was now gazing through the window as if he saw this vision of the perfect father-son relationship in the clear blue sky out there.

His father tossed off his coffee and set down the cup.

"So if Kenneth wishes to join his uncles in Reid and Sons you will pat him on the back and say, 'You have my blessing.' Eh?"

Ridley brought his eyes back from the distant future and gulped. "If his heart was truly in it . . ."

There was a tap at the door and Jane popped her head round. "The twins is to have their dinner soon and I thought they might see their grandfather before they mess themselves up."

Ridley looked relieved at the interruption, Clara thought, but he said, "Jane, they should not mess themselves at dinner time now they are five, but they may come in if they are clean and tidy."

From the shuffling and little squeals of excitement Clara knew they were outside. She looked at her father-in-law for approval and saw him composing his features from severe to bland.

The children came in hand in hand and stood before him saying in unison, "Good morning, Grandfather Reid."

"Humph." He was unable to stop himself from smiling. "They're not so alike now. Kenneth's hair is darker and his eyes brown. I always said he favours my side of the family. You work at your books, young sir?" Kenneth nodded. "Speak up then."

"Yes sir. I can read, sir."

Kate put on her radiant smile. "I can read better."

"Can you now? Well, don't boast, young lady."

Kenneth pursed up his lips and Clara was afraid he was going to cry.

"They are *both* ahead of the children at the village school," she said.

Ridley said emphatically, "So you can go back and tell Mother all is well."

"Oh I will." George Reid felt in his pocket and produced a small leather purse. From it he extracted two silver sixpences. "Now you two, I believe you each have a money box. Now there is a big sum to add to it. Each of those is worth *six* pennies."

He placed them in the palms they held out and their fingers closed on them.

"Thank you, Grandpapa," said Kate and dropped the sweetest little curtsey.

Kenneth, watching sidelong, repeated the words and copied the gesture.

"Get him into trousers," cried George, "so he can bow like a gentleman."

Clara blushed. "Oh we were planning to, as soon as he's five."

"Will I be a man then?" Kenneth asked. "Because when I'm a man

I'm going to marry Kate."

Kate giggled and looked boldly up into her grandfather's face. "We went to Hexham market yesterday and there was a wedding in the abbey and we watched the bride and groom come out and all the people in their fine clothes."

"Oh dear yes," said Clara. "They've been talking about it ever since." So little happens, she thought. It's lessons, dinner, a country walk. The same day after day.

George Reid got up. "Well, you can't marry your sister, my boy. I must be getting on my way."

"But you'll stay and eat with us?" Clara watched Kenneth's face starting to crumple at the prohibition.

"Thank you but I've been invited to friends in the country."

Ridley put on his sour look. "I thought you despised the country."

Clara mentally wrung her hands. Why will he always alienate his father?

But George Reid was chuckling to himself. He clapped Ridley on the shoulder. "Ah my boy, wealth opens doors to the aristocracy these days. Your father is a sought after figure. Well, if young Kenneth here has an eye for industry as he grows up I know you'll not keep him from Reid and Sons if that is your philosophy. And I can see this pert little girl breaking a few hearts later on. I told your mother I'd drop by to see how you were all faring. She'll be paying you a visit in the summer I've no doubt. Goodbye my dear." He actually gave Clara a peck on the cheek, patted the children's heads and let himself out of the back door.

Clara was relieved to see him go. She had been holding herself tightly together. She retreated to the small front parlour and flopped into the rocking-chair.

Kenneth trailed after her, tears running down his face. "Why can't I marry Kate when I grow up? I wouldn't know who else to marry."

Clara rocked herself, laughing.

Ridley came back in from checking that Tom had rubbed the horses down properly and his father's man had had a drink of ale and some of Jane's scones.

"Go and get your dinner you two and then I'll hear your lessons." They trotted off, Kenneth wiping his hand across his eyes, Kate still giggling.

"What do you make of that?" Ridley said to Clara. "I'll wager he's getting some lord to invest money in a new venture with steamboats. How dare he walk in here and tell me how to bring up my own son? Put Kenneth into the business indeed. He only came to crow because he thinks we're struggling."

"We're not struggling, are we? I haven't spent any money on clothes for myself since we came here."

"No and you have plenty for country life. We live simply from choice. I have been doing the accounts and they are very satisfactory." He sat down opposite her. "Now tell me, is it true that Kate reads more fluently than Kenneth? Or was it just a naughty boast on her part for I cannot let that pass. She was not at all in awe of her grandfather, was she?"

"She is not in awe of anyone I fear. She is very quick and clever and knows it too well."

"That must be curbed."

But I doubt if *you* will do it, Clara thought. If *I* scold her for refusing to go to bed she finds you and with her pretty dimples wins another half hour. When her demands are outrageous you explain why in grown-up language. She loves your long words and the time you spend with her. She doesn't have tantrums with her father.

Out loud she said, "Well Ridley, perhaps you can make her do her copybook over again for she dashed at it this morning. Kenneth is very dogged. A thing must be right before he stops work on it."

"Ah that is a good quality. I was like that myself as a child."

"Well, give him more praise. You spoke to your father of encouraging him. I sometimes find him crying alone in the schoolroom as he copies pages of words or figures. Kate seems to absorb things by accident. Should they not go to school or have a tutor as they get older? You and I can't teach them music or painting and maybe there are new ways of teaching that are easier for them than all this copying out."

Clara stopped, out of breath. Ridley was looking at her with lowering eyes.

"Has my father undermined me in your sight as our children's teacher? Did we not agree that no influences but ours should taint our precious children?"

Clara shrank lower in the chair. He had often said this but she didn't recall agreeing to it. Of course, she reminded herself, I was too lazy as a girl to learn much. I never practised scales on the piano. I was hopeless with my needle and my pencils. Mother never pushed me and Father only wanted me to look pretty and talk nicely. What can I do for the twins but read to them and try to make them behave? Jane can teach Kate more skills than I and she obeys her more readily than she does me.

She lifted her face with a tentative smile. "I'm sure you're right, dear."

Ridley looked satisfied.

It had a profound effect on Kenneth being put into breeches. He began to strut like Tom the groom. He followed him about and wanted to help with the horses. Clara delighted in watching him. She had a boy now. Ridley seemed pleased too but there was no let up in the learning tasks he imposed on him. He was not going to have Kenneth behind Kate in anything.

Anne Reid came to see them in the summer. Of recent years she had not brought Ida Stokoe. Perhaps, Clara thought, it is mother who shuns *her* company. She finds it impossible to put Anne into any category of comfortable matron.

Ridley disliked his mother's influence on the twins. She always wanted to see them playing with other children. This summer of eighteen-twenty-four she said she would stay two nights and on the first morning without a word to anyone she walked over to Tom's cottage and brought back his three little ones to play at Allenbrae. What was worse she brought Bet with her to carry the baby. At four, three and one and a half Tom and Bet's children had never been to the big house but it was the sight of Bet, with the baby on her hip and an impertinent grin on her face, that shocked Clara. Ridley was out somewhere on the farm. Fortunately the day was fine and warm and the back lawn dry and recently cut. Clara hoped she could make them go away after an hour's play before he came back to drink coffee with his mother.

Kenneth and Kate were overjoyed to see them. Bet set baby Billy down beside them and taking a hand each the twins ran him down the slope with his little legs barely skimming the grass. The other two, Elsie and Jack, ended up rolling down as they tried to keep pace. All five children squealed with delight.

Clara settled her mother-in-law on the stone bench on the terrace, where Jane had set out cushions for them, and sat down by her wondering what to do about Bet. But Bet just sat herself on the grass at the top of the slope, looking quite at home there with her hands clasped round her knees.

Anne peered at Clara from under the brim of her straw hat. "So this has never happened before and the family are barely half a mile away?"

"Well, Tom is our groom you know," Clara whispered.

"And do you think your two mind that?"

"The way they talk you know. Ridley won't think it very refined."

"My boy is an ass."

Clara couldn't think of a reply to that.

Bet looked round. "Going to be hot, ladies. I'll get a drink at the pump." And she was up onto her feet in a moment and heading round to the side of the house.

Anne was chuckling. "Does it worry you, my dear, that she makes herself so at home? But she has been with you since you left Leith. She lived here till she and Tom married. She's still very young but what of her previous life? Once she had learnt English surely you asked her of her background? She lost her own child. That was all you ever told me and she was glad to come with you perhaps because of straightened circumstances. Were you never curious about her?"

Clara felt on dangerous ground. "No, she was just needed – for the feeding."

"Perhaps you resented her for being able to do that?"

It was spoken lightly with a smile but Clara was frightened. A picture flew into her brain and she grew hot.

"I can see his little face. He sucked at me and it wouldn't come. He was so cross. It upset me." Tears rose to her eyes now.

Anne was contrite. "Oh my dear, I should never have raised the matter. I can see you are not comfortable with Bet and I'm sorry I brought her. Here she is back again, cool and refreshed. Let's just enjoy the children."

The baby fell down and howled. Bet grabbed him, gave him a rough cuddle and set him on his feet. Kenneth and Kate took charge of him again.

"We'll be Papa and Mamma and this is our baby," Kate announced.

Jack and Elsie ran up. "He's *our* baby. *We* want to play."

"You can be our older children," Kate told them. "We are one family and we'll go down to the bottom of the lawn and have our dinner there. I'll collect plates."

She began scouring the flower bed for pieces of slate. Several slates had blown off the roof in winter gales and she knew where they had been swept.

"A child with great imagination," Anne commented. "Ah but what is she getting now?" Kate had laid five places in a circle and was gathering leaves and flowers and snapping off some short lengths of twigs.

"Meat and salad," she announced beginning to share them out on the plates.

"The little ones will eat them." Anne got up, descended the terrace steps and walked down the lawn.

Bet grinned round at Clara. "Ours eats all sorts but they've never ailed owt."

Clara saw Anne kneel down on the grass to be at the children's level and she began to supervise the party without protest from Kate. Clara felt too hot and lazy to join them, but next moment she wished she had. Bet got up and came and stood before her.

"You know, Mistress, I never told Tom the babies weren't yours.

He still believes they were born while he and Master were on the steamboat."

Clara's mouth fell open. The ground seemed to shift beneath her. Bet was giving her a long challenging stare. Her throat felt constricted but she must find words. The only words that came out were a passionate protest.

"Of course they're ours."

"Well, I guess it feels like that now but you and I know different, don't we?"

Clara looked helplessly round. Her mother-in-law was happily engrossed with the children. Ridley was not in sight. Jane wouldn't be bringing out a tray of drinks for another half hour or more. Sarah was in the kitchen preparing vegetables for the dinner that would be served later. In terror she lifted her eyes to Bet.

"I don't know – what do you mean – why are you saying this?"

"You seem to mind folks knowing. Can't see why myself. You've give the babes a home when they had nowt. But I reckons if you mind that much it must be worth your while to buy my silence."

"Buy! Buy? Is that not called blackmail?"

"Don't matter what it's called. Three children take a lot of feeding and what you pays Tom doesn't go far enough."

Clara flapped her hands about. "I'll speak to my husband."

"Well, you can do that an' all but I need a bit myself."

"I don't have anything of my own. I can't believe you mean this."

"You have some pretty bits o' jewellery. There's a foreign pedlar comes to Hexham market once in a while. He buys as well as sells. He'd give me something for them garnets you used to wear."

"Garnets! Mr Reid gave me them. I haven't worn them lately. The catch is stiff. Bet, please, you must go away. This is not right." She looked down the lawn again. "Take the children and go. I don't want Mr Reid to find you here."

"We're not good enough eh? You wouldn't have them bairns if I hadn't fetched 'em from Stroma and fed them for you."

She was speaking low and fiercely but Clara was frantic for her to stop.

"I'll get the garnets. Sit down where you were. And then you must go."

She fled into the house and panted up the stairs. At her bedroom door she met Jane descending from the schoolroom.

"Whatever's up?" Jane said. "You look that hot and bothered. *I've* been tidying up there and it's a real furnace under the roof."

"It *is* a hot day. You'd better take a tray out to Mrs Reid. Something cool. That's all I came to say. Well, in a few minutes. Bet must go first"

"Bet? What's *she* doing here?"

"Oh Mrs Reid fetched her with the children to play with the twins but Mr Reid won't like it. I'm just getting my fan to cool myself."

Jane raised her speaking eyebrows as Clara darted into her bedroom and rummaged in her jewellery box. She heard Jane going downstairs chuckling to herself.

The colour of the garnets leapt out at her and she snatched them up, wrapped them in a handkerchief and scuttled from the room.

When she stepped out of the door onto the terrace the heat engulfed her. Bet looked round and jumped up at once.

The handkerchief was passed. Bet lifted a corner, saw what was there, grinned and dropped them into her tie-on pocket.

"You won't ever ever do such a thing again," Clara muttered, and then her eye fell on Ridley approaching across the pasture to the gate at the corner of the wall. "Oh he's here. Mr Reid is here."

"Well, he'll not scold his mother, will he?" Bet's eyes were scornful.

Ridley had already looked over the wall and seen the 'picnic' in progress and Clara knew he must have seen her with Bet on the terrace. Every stiff inch of him showed his disapproval.

"Do not be fretting, Mistress." Bet pranced down the slope. "Morning, sir." And to Anne, "We'll be away now, Ma'am, if you don't mind."

Clara saw Bet give Anne her arm to help her to her feet.

"My old bones." She was laughing. "Well, I hoped they could have a real picnic down here. Perhaps another time."

"Baby's hot and fretting. Wants his Mammy's milk." Bet heaved him onto her hip and Clara had a moment's horror that she would pop out one of her large breasts and offer it there and then. Her other two children were protesting at going away but it was evident that she stood no nonsense from them.

Ridley who had spoken not a word held the gate open for the little group and closed it after them.

"That," Clara heard him say to his mother, "is not to happen again. Was it Clara's doing to invite them?"

"No, mine. I fetched them without Clara's knowledge and I think it mighty cruel to let those wee ones go away without a drink on a day like this." She gathered up her skirts and walked up the slope and the terrace steps and sank down on the bench just as Jane emerged from the door with the tray.

She took a long drink of the cordial and declared, "To make up for the curtailed picnic I shall take the twins into Hexham in my carriage after dinner."

Ridley frowned. "I wished to supervise Tom cleaning out the byre."

"I wasn't asking *you* to come," his mother said. "I shall find James and tell him to have the carriage ready at two o'clock. I'm a little warm here in the full sun." She walked round to the stables.

Ridley ground his teeth. "That was mighty imperious. Of course you will go with her this afternoon."

"Oh no, please. It's too hot." Clara was so shaken by the incident with Bet that she longed only to lie down on her bed.

"You will go with her. After this morning I can't trust her at all. If she wishes to buy them some new clothes before she goes home tomorrow I have no objection. Make sure they are plain and neat, that's all. And what was Bet saying to you on the terrace? Did you give her something? I thought I saw –"

Clara's knees were shaking. She flapped a hand before her face. "Oh, just a handkerchief. She was wet. She had been to the pump for a drink."

"Very well. Why are you in such a state?"

"Your mother. She makes me nervous."

"She'll be gone tomorrow. I want none of the grandparents here but I suppose we can't forbid them. I notice your sister is not concerned to visit her goddaughter."

"You didn't want her or your cousin to interfere with the children, you said."

"I did, and I commend your sister for her absence. It just seems odd – as devout as she always reckons she is."

"She is not at ease with children I believe. Not like your mother."

"Huh!" he growled.

It was an uncomfortable afternoon for Clara. Anne insisted on leaving the carriage at the coaching in and walking to the green space behind the abbey where they found a bench in the shade while the twins ran about in joyous freedom.

Anne admonished her then. "Can you not get him to see that the little village school would be good for them? It is less than a mile from you. As they grow older they could both go to schools in Newcastle."

"There is a grammar school for boys in Hexham," Clara murmured, "but Ridley is fearful of contamination as he calls it. And he remembers being bullied at school and beaten sometimes for no fault of his own."

Anne drew a long sigh at that. "True, my dear. He was a solemn little boy. I fear George and I were not very successful in dealing with our eldest child."

"You and Mr Reid are so different," Clara ventured to say. She had often been curious to know how they had met and married.

Anne smiled. "I was eighteen and a green girl but he saw I would mature well like good wine. My parents said he would be successful and arranged it all. I was flattered by him, but his views have become more rigid and mine more wild and radical. You will have to learn to manage Ridley, my dear, but it won't be easy."

Clara made herself giggle or she would have dissolved into tears.

Next day Anne spent time with the children in the schoolroom before she left. When Ridley realised Clara had not been there too he shook his head in exasperation.

"What subversive rubbish has she been putting into their heads?"

"Oh Ridley, they are only *five*. She won't have been talking of politics. It was all innocent fun yesterday."

"They came back very dirty and she bought no new clothes."

Clara watched with relief as Anne's carriage drove away. The daily routine would close in again. There was safety in that. And then she remembered Bet Moray. There would always be a stabbing fear that she had not heard the last from Bet.

14

At twenty-three Rory-Beag was in love. He had been in love many times since he was sixteen but they had been fantasies at a distance. Any girl with a dainty figure and smiling face caught his eye in chapel or walking past the carpenter's shop. But he knew he could never possess one because none would ever come near him.

This one was different. Flora talked to him and though she couldn't yet read his replies she was not afraid of him. She was not beautiful. In fact she was marked with small-pox from which her family had died. This made a strong bond with Rory-Beag and she was a refugee from another wave of clearances which drew her closer still.

Beathag had died just after Christmas in 1831. "I'll be away afore the New Year comes in," she had said and she was right. Rory-Beag and the minister had struggled on through the winter without her and now it was April. There was more to do in the vegetable plot and also for Diarmad, the carpenter, as the local folk looked to their houses and their furniture and their wooden vessels in the lengthening days. There were not enough hours in the day for Rory-Beag to help keep house for the minister and continue with his great work in the leather-bound book. This had now run into a second volume. It was taking a long time as he remembered everything that had happened to him and it was hard to leave anything out. He had reached the point when the minister sat by his box bed and spoke the first words of their acquaintance. After that the Reverend Josiah had shared his story. He was eager to write it but had not touched his pencil for many days.

And now, suddenly, Flora had come into their lives and he was in love.

Everyone in Canisbay knew the Reverend Josiah was without

a housekeeper so it was not surprising that Flora, wandering half-starved into Canisbay village, should be told "If you're looking for work, lassie, there's the minister at the Manse wanting a housekeeper. Can you cook and clean?"

She claimed she was seventeen years old and had looked after her young brother and sister till the small pox had claimed them. So she was sent round to the Manse with the warning "Mind, you'll find Rory-Beag, the carpenter's mate, lives there too. He has the face of a monster and his speech is nothing but roaring but he's harmless enough."

All this Flora herself told Rory-Beag outright. "I'd have gone where the devil himself was living for a square meal," she said, "but now I find you so kind and gentle I don't mind your looks at all. You have beautiful smiling eyes."

Never in his life had a young girl spoken to him directly, much less paid him a compliment. In the four days that the minister with his usual charity had housed and fed her – for she was near fainting away when she reached his door – Rory-Beag had decided she was his girl for life.

He wrote on the slate for the minister, '*Please keep her. I showed her the wash house and she knew what to do.*'

"I would like to give her a trial," the minister said. "She has suffered terribly if all she says is true. Left alone she had no way to pay the rent and was turned out along with the last of the Sutherland crofts. She would like to stay and says she'll go in the attic room for you are too big to be up there and should have Beathag's old room."

Rory-Beag was now a well-read man of twenty-three and knew that a young man and a young woman under the same roof might make people talk. He wanted to write that Flora had a lovely nature and he would marry her and make all things well but Reverend Josiah would say, "It is far too soon for that yet."

Seeing a young woman up close, living for four days in the same house with her had also set his imagination working on Mary Gunn. She must be thirteen and no doubt well fed and dressed in silks and satins, not homespun rags. Perhaps she had as much bosom as he could see on Flora and might even be as tall. Her father, Alistair Gunn, was a tall man. Flora was slight and skinny but even in four days her face had grown plumper and her eyes brightened. The pot marks on her forehead were not so noticeable either because she had washed her hair and coaxed it to hang over them in fluffy curls. The minister had told her to take anything in Beathag's closet and she had altered a black skirt and bodice to fit. When she moved in these clothes Rory-Beag was excited and wanted to put his arms round her. In a few years young men would be eyeing Mary Gunn too. The thought made him uncomfortable. It had been his duty to look after his babies and he hadn't been able to do it.

"Do you still think of those babies?" the Reverend Josiah had asked him on the day when he had read the Story of Angus up to the time of the wreck.

Rory-Beag wrote on the slate. "*Every day. I wonder what they look like. I wonder if they are happy.*"

But now Rory-Beag longed to write that he still wanted to trace Mary and Roderick and at the same time to keep Flora here in the Manse. Only the two things could never be compatible. If Flora was his wife he would have to stay at her side for as long as he lived. If she could read his story she might understand why he had to know the fate of the only other survivors of the wreck but she couldn't read. Of course he must teach her or be without any means of communicating properly with her but it might take a long time, especially as she only spoke Gaelic and he had written his story in English.

There was so much he wanted to say that couldn't be expressed in a few words on a slate. Life was becoming complicated and troublesome. Emotions were involved which he barely understood himself. It had been so simple going to work and learning skill with wood so that Diarmad had once told the minister "Rory-Beag is better than I now at the intricate work." That had been one of the proudest moments of his life. He had begun to earn enough too to give the minister something for his keep. He never bought anything for himself except the occasional garment as he grew bigger so he was saving every penny he could in a tin box under his attic bed for his next attempt to trace

Mary and Roderick. As the years had passed he knew he could no longer hope that the aged minister would accompany him to Leith but he trusted that when his story was perfectly written he could show it to an educated person like the Sheriff of Thurso who would know how to put about the sort of advertisement that the minister had once mentioned to him or send him with a letter to Leith to pick up the trail there.

But now here was Flora and he was in a turmoil about her. *She likes me*, he wrote on the slate for the minister. *I love her very much. Please keep her.*

The Reverend Josiah looked at him in alarm when he was shown these words.

"You have known her four days. She is only just regaining her strength and is grateful at being rescued from poverty but we know nothing of her character. If I gave her a trial as my housekeeper you are not to get impulsive ideas about her. I suggest you ask Diarmad to let you share his little house behind the shop for a week or two while I see if she can work well and be trustworthy."

Rory-Beag was struck with sorrow and showed it in his eyes.

"Nay, I am not angry with you, dear boy. You have known few people with any degree of intimacy since you grew to manhood. You read of social life only in books. Pray write Diarmad a note and he will give you a straight answer. Let me just see of what metal our new acquaintance is and then you shall come back to me."

Rory-Beag knew he must obey without question. It would be hard though not to come home every day to the Manse where he had lived for more than half his life. It would be hard to think of Flora cooking and cleaning and washing without him to help her lift things and without her smile when their eyes met. She had a thin solemn face in repose but he could bring out that funny crooked half-smile as she cocked her head on one side and seemed to be assessing him, not critically but appreciatively. She didn't recoil from his smile as others did. She saw it in his eyes where he knew from his rare glances at the mirror he could make it shine so radiantly that the rest of his face didn't matter.

Well, he would go to Diarmad's till the minister called him back and told him Flora was a capable housekeeper. Then he could marry her without delay. After that, he told himself, I will know a woman as a man should and love her faithfully for the rest of my days. The minister can tell her my story until she is able to read and then she will understand about Mary and Roderick. She is too sweet-natured to be jealous of my longing to hear news of them. Oh if I could set eyes on them that would make me the happiest man on earth! But Flora and I can make it our quest together and if it can be done without leaving the Manse God will have blest us indeed.

In this hopeful mood he trotted along to the carpenter's shop with his knapsack and the leather-bound book and wrote his request on the slate they kept in the shop for jobs and prices.

Diarmad nodded and then added his few words. "Ay, the Reverend's trying out the lassie. You're best awa' till she's used to you about the place."

Rory-Beag smiled to himself. No one could believe that Flora would fall in love with him but he knew it had already happened. Had she not said he was kind and gentle and had beautiful eyes? What else could that mean?

He set about the first task of the day with a light heart.

15

Anne Reid looked up from her scrambled egg. "You know what's happening today, George?"

Peter and Martin, who liked to come down in their dressing-gowns, had already finished their breakfast and gone to get ready for work.

George was reading *The Times* and just grunted. When she continued to fix her eyes on him he glanced up as far as her plate and curled his lips at the fluffy yellow pile on her plate.

"How you can eat that whipped up rubbish instead of a decent plate of bacon, egg and mushrooms like this I don't know."

"I said you know what's happening today, don't you? May the fifteenth, eighteen thirty-two."

"For God's sake, woman, I know what year it is and a bad one it's been so far. Cholera in the winter, food shortages, riots and now a miners' strike on our hands. If you're going to tell me of another of your political meetings I don't want to hear it." He slapped The Times. "Earl Grey has resigned after the Lords reduced his precious Reform Bill to nothing, the Duke of Northumberland has received threats against his life for criticising the Bill and they've even threatened the Bishop of Durham too."

"*He* should know better than to oppose a very reasonable Bill."

George chose not to notice this remark. "And people have written to *The Times* saying taxes should be withheld till the Bill goes through. Is the country becoming utterly lawless?"

"No doubt you will say so when I tell you there's to be a protest meeting on the Spital Field today. Surely you have read the handbills all over town urging Lord Grey's supporters to go. I thought of strolling over there to see what's going on."

"Strolling over there! You'll do nothing of the sort. I must go into the office or I'd keep off the streets myself. There's a restless, rebellious spirit abroad. Look at that society formed last year – the Northern Political Union! Some of my own miners joined it. I'll wager that's what's stirred them up to this strike."

"And many business and professional men lead it."

"Ay, all Whigs of course. Look, politics is not for women. Stay at home and mind the house." He finished off his breakfast in silence and in quarter of an hour he took his hat and cane and, accompanied by his sons, set off to his office in the town.

Anne watched them go. She hoped the boys were not absorbing their father's die-hard philosophy. Ridley's shoots of radicalism – carrying a banner on the Town Moor – had withered before they could flower. Farming had gone through some bad years lately and she wondered if this was why Kenneth at thirteen had still not been sent to school. Was Ridley still afraid of contamination or was he too proud to use his father's money? Unlike Ida she was not inclined to worry but the thought of that little family closed in on themselves depressed her spirits.

Well, she was not going to stay at home herself. An hour after her men-folk had left she went upstairs to put on her hat and ask her maid to accompany her for a little walk. As they came down she was surprised to see Royce their butler at the front door scolding someone outside.

"No beggars I say. Master won't have 'em at the back either. So off you go."

She called out, "Let me see, Royce. I like to know the story."

Royce moved his portly bulk aside, heavy with disapproval.

She looked at the figure on the doorstep, from the worn boots upwards to the breeches and short coat, grey with road dust, but not ragged.

"Grandmother," said the figure.

She lifted her eyes to the grubby face and dark curls under the farm worker's hat. "Dear God, it's Kenneth." He produced a guilty grin. "Royce, the clothes brush if you please. This is Mr Ridley's boy."

Royce muttered under his breath, "Not recognisable in that state." He fetched the clothes brush. "We'll have this on the flower beds. The doorstep and paths have been swept this morning."

Kenneth stood meekly till Royce was satisfied he was fit to ascend into Anne's arms held out to him.

"You are alone? How have you come? Is anything wrong at home?"

"No, I walked. That's all."

"Walked? It's twenty-five miles! Royce, refreshments please. We'll go in the small parlour. Rachel, you can take my cloak and hat. We won't be going out now."

She sent him to wash his face and hands and then sat him down in the small parlour adjoining the front door and gazed at him with happy astonishment.

"I've stopped you going out, Grandmother. I'm sorry."

"It's no matter. I'll read about it in the papers. I was going to walk over to the Spital Fields where there's a big meeting. A petition may go to the king to bring back Lord Grey. But what's that to you? Tell me what's brought you here, dear child. Nay, you are not a child any more. How you've grown since I saw you last!"

He was indeed a substantial shape perched there on her sofa cushion all pent up with excitement. His voice had deepened too. He said, "I'd like to go to the meeting when I've had a drink and eaten something. That's partly why I came."

"What! You heard about it in your remote corner of Hexhamshire!"

"Oh no, we don't hear anything. Father's not interested in the papers but I make Mother buy copies when we're in the town. I want to know what's going on."

The parlour maid brought in a tray and looked curiously at Kenneth before slipping out again. He took a long drink and proceeded to attack the ham and eggs.

Anne watched him for a moment, then sat forward in her chair, shaking her head. "Let me understand this, Kenneth. You left home, I suppose, at first light to walk all this way to find out what's happening in parliament and the country?"

He said with his mouth full, "No, I just had to get out. Kate and I, we're being suffocated. Well, that's how *she* puts it. She wanted to come." He swallowed and met Anne's gaze. "She *begged* to come. She was quite cross. But I told her if *she* stayed the parents wouldn't be worried. She's mighty good at managing Father."

Anne was intrigued but she felt guilty too. I have only glimpsed their lives, she reproached herself. Sweet Jesus, I pray for them every night, my grandchildren, but I didn't know – day after day – what went on between my glimpses. 'Suffocated' is a fearful word but maybe only too apt.

She put her head on one side and watched him eat. His tone was matter-of-fact but there was that pent-up excitement in him, almost joy, that shone in those eyes, so much darker than Ridley's now, as he met hers over forkful after forkful of food.

"What you say makes me sad, Kenneth, yet you look happy."

"Well," he said, "I did it. I walked to Newcastle to find you and I did. Here I am. I did it all on my own. I was alone all the way."

"Ah, indeed. You made a resolution and you carried it out, without help. That is a very big thing. I'm proud of you."

"And not angry at my running away from home?"

"Well, *have* you run away? I thought you'd come to visit your grandparents. Are you not expecting to go back?"

"Would you be angry if I didn't go back? I thought to myself Grandmother Reid is different from everyone else."

She laughed. "I won't be angry but I might be more proud of you if you stayed for a visit and then I took you home and we talked things out with your father. Is it just your *father* doing the suffocating?"

"Well, Mother has to obey him. She says that's the way it is in a marriage."

She laughed again. This was an amazing conversation to be having with this boy she didn't really know at all who had suddenly dropped into her life. "I'm afraid you caught *me* about to disobey your grandfather. He said I was not to stir out today because of the rioting people in the streets."

"I didn't see any rioting people. There were crowds heading in one direction. I had to ask my way and a man said, 'You don't want to go to Brandling Village. Rich people live there.' I suppose I look like a country boy." He ate up the last morsel of bread. "You could tell Grandfather it was your *duty* to take me to the meeting."

"He would say I was filling you with rebellious thoughts."

"Yes, it's odd. He doesn't like change and Father too just wants us to live in his cocoon away from the world. But when the harvest was bad and poor folk were starving Father said Mother must sell her jewellery to help them. She said she already had but he didn't like her doing it without telling him. It has to be *his* little world."

Anne said, "I am glad his conscience is still active for the poor but this great meeting is not just about poverty but about the Bill in Parliament to extend the vote."

He jumped up. "Let's go and see it, Grandmamma."

"It is quite some way and you have walked so far!"

"I'm rested now and feel fresh."

"But your poor feet!"

"These boots are old and comfortable. I could pretend I was your servant."

"You shall be my handsome escort and I will leave Rachel behind."

She considered him. He must already be as tall as his father and his face was square-jawed where Ridley's was narrow with twitching muscles that revealed his passing emotions. You, Kenneth, are still very young, she thought, as she called for her cape and hat again, but if you are given the freedom you crave you may become a solid, determined man, with passions yes, but with command of yourself. I must play my part here, but wisely. He has had enough of being manipulated.

They set out and he held his arm for her like a gentleman though she, big woman that she was, exceeded him in height.

At the gate he said, "I should walk a step behind if I'm your footman."

"Well you are not my footman and I am very proud to be walking with my handsome grandson. And what a strong, sturdy arm it is."

"I chop the logs or carry the coals for the fire when Tom is busy."

"But that's not a suffocating sort of life. I would have enjoyed such work but I wasn't allowed – as a girl – and we had too many servants which can seriously limit one's activities."

He was thoughtful for a few minutes. "I can see it might. Kate is even more hemmed in than I though she sometimes sneaks out and hitches up her skirts and rubs down the horses. But at my age boys are at school. Father works hard at teaching me but it's so – well, dull. I'd like to be at a boarding school. I'd miss Kate of course."

Anne wondered what it was like to be a twin. "When you were smaller I thought you might resent Kate because she is so quick –"

He looked up sharply. "And I'm slow and plodding?"

"Nonsense. She is like quicksilver but too impulsive so she makes mistakes. You like to take your time and make perfect whatever you are doing."

He considered this. "Humph, she's usually right but so sweet-natured I can't be jealous of her. Only I want to live on my own for a while and have friends and see the world. Are we nearly there? I have a blister on my heel and it's hurting."

"I'm not surprised you've got blisters. Not far now. We can take a cab home."

"Father would call that extravagant but I guess you and Grandfather are rich."

She smiled. "He gave your father money in trust for you and Kate. He wouldn't mind some being used for your schooling now if your father needed it."

"I didn't know there was money in trust for us. Father keeps that sort of thing secret. He wants no one interfering. We are a family. Why should we need others? He admits Tom, Jane and Sarah are useful and the farm hands but he's got rid of Foster the Farm Manager. He says he can manage the farm himself now – only I heard one of the hands say you can't have a coal man turn farmer. It's against nature."

"Ah but your father's heart was not in coal. As a boy he loved visits to the country. He wrote pastoral poems but when he showed one to your grandfather he was mighty scornful. And he was bullied at school. Maybe that's why he wants to spare you and Kate. He's a dreamer, a romantic. I can tell you he fell wondrously in love with your mother but he was wretched when no children came quickly. But now he is happy. He has fathered two fine young people." Anne's inner doubts caught up with her as she said it. But whatever the truth of it fatherhood had certainly changed Ridley. "I say this, Kenneth, so that you may better understand him. Well, here we are at Spital Fields. Look at the crowds. It's a fine thing for Lord Grey's Reform Bill."

"Why? What will it do?"

"Much good I trust. Give more men a chance to vote, make sense of the constituencies that send members to Parliament and stop all bribery and corruption."

"No one could disagree with that."

"They are frightened of change. The Duke of Wellington who did so well on the battlefield fears an upheaval in the country in peacetime. Look there, Kenneth!"

A platform had been erected at one end of the grassed area. A few gentlemen in top hats were seated on it and some sort of order was being kept as different people demanded the right to speak. A small man with a loud hailer was yelling that never again should Newcastle Freemen be able to sell their votes for half a guinea.

Anne pointed to men with cudgels on the alert near the platform and sprinkled among the crowd.

"They are Special Constables and look, those horsemen on the edge of the crowd are the Volunteer Corps of Cavalry formed after the last big protest meeting. Your father was in the main procession then and carried a banner. It was the year of your birth before you moved to Hexhamshire. Has he not told you proudly of that?"

"Once, but when I said I'd like to do that he sort of closed up."

Anne was sorry. Ridley's mind is sick, she thought. He daren't let the boy go.

But now she began looking about her in some anxiety. "Those men have cut great staves from trees. If they try to drive off the horses things might turn ugly. This is not like that last one. If the authorities would only stay away there would be no provocation. Men are looking for a fight and the sight of a uniform is all they need."

"It's quite exciting, isn't it?"

"Yes, but I loathe violence. The crowds are swelling all the time and many have come straight from the public houses. Perhaps we ought to take you and your blistered feet home. I must write a note to your parents that you are safe and well. I can send Rachel and it will go on the early mail tomorrow to Hexham."

"Kate will tell them where I've gone."

"But the hazards of the journey – on foot! I should have written at once as soon as you appeared – *that* was a shock and Royce wasn't too pleased." Kenneth giggled. "Ah but when your grandfather finds you here he will be for sending you straight back in the carriage."

"I don't want to go back." He looked about at the crowds. "This is living!"

One of the cavalry came trotting up, reining in his horse at a safe distance from them. "Madam and young sir, I'd advise you to go home. A band of striking miners is approaching from the town. They have taken drink and look an ugly mob."

A man with a scarred face and a stave in his hand broke from the crowd.

"Who are you calling ugly? I got this down the mine when a rock fell from the roof." He pointed to a livid mark across his forehead and, twisting the stave in his hand, he whirled it in the air within a foot of the horse's nose. The horse reared up and pranced sideways towards Anne and Kenneth, the rider struggling to control him.

Anne jumped backwards and losing her balance on the rough grass sat down heavily. Kenneth squealed, "Grandmother!" The man dropped his stave and ran to help her while the horseman called out to one of the constables, "Arrest that man!"

With Kenneth's help Anne was on her feet in a moment and looking round for her hat which had fallen off. The scarred miner picked it up and handed it to her.

"Nay, Ma'am, I didn't see you. I didn't mean *you* no harm."

Two constables came up and seized his arms.

"Pray let him go," Anne said but the yeoman called out. "Take him away. He was endangering life and limb."

A grin split the man's dirty face. "I'll get a meal in the jail, lady.

The bairns had my porridge this morning." And he went with them meekly.

"*Now*, Ma'am, will you and the lad go home," the horseman said. "They could earn money for their families if they were at work. No need to be sorry for them."

Anne adjusted her hat and took Kenneth's arm but she couldn't help turning and retorting. "If they earned a proper wage they wouldn't strike. Come Kenneth!"

She strode away while the horseman, whose mount was standing quietly now, seemed to be thinking up a retort.

Kenneth peered into her face when they were clear of the crowds. "Are you sure you're all right, Grandmamma?"

"Perfectly."

"Could that miner be one of Grandfather Reid's men?"

"Indeed he could."

"Well, I'd rather he raised his men's wages than paid for my schooling."

She gave him one of her broad smiles and squeezed his arm.

Back at the leafy house in Brandling Village she wrote a quick note to her son, simply saying Kenneth was fit and well and she would like him to stay for a week or two since he had so kindly paid them an unexpected visit, but she had not yet spoken with his grandfather. She would write again tomorrow. Rachel was sent to the post-house and Kenneth demolished another large meal.

Later when Anne heard George's voice in the hall she and Kenneth were in the drawing-room upstairs looking over pamphlets of the Northern Reform Society.

She collected them up and slid them under her work box. "I never lie to him but I do not provoke him unnecessarily."

Kenneth laughed. "Kate invented that same strategy with Father."

"Very well, but remember if your grandfather asks whether we went out today and where, we tell him the truth and take the consequences."

George strode into the room and Kenneth leapt to his feet.

"Ha, Royce said you'd come."

"I'm sorry, Grandfather."

"Sorry! Why be sorry? I understand you *walked* here. I shake your hand, boy. I feared you were a namby-pamby lad tied to mother's apron strings and father's boot-laces. So you have come to train up in the business like your uncles. Come in you two and congratulate your nephew."

Peter and Martin walked in, Peter imposing and serious, Martin a joker.

Anne saw Kenneth's look of alarm. Ah, she thought, he fears he has run away to a new slavery and that these sons are bonded to their father as he is to his.

"Hello, young Ken," Martin said. "Tired of the country eh?"

Peter said, "You'll have start as office boy you know."

"No, I just want to go away to school. *You* did."

It was more words than Anne remembered him ever saying to his uncles. She thought, those twenty-five miles have transformed the boy. I wonder what effect they have had on my poor Ridley. I never imagined George would be so impressed with Kenneth's long walk that he would forget he had been a naughty rebel.

George remembered it by next day but the brief scolding he gave Kenneth showed how little sympathy he had for the grieving parents at home in Allenbrae.

"We'll have to send you home, you know, but while you're here I shall show you all my business. I not only mine coal, I oversee the selling and the distribution. You can tell your father when you go back that my steam transports are paying for themselves several times over and making money for the wise investors. He's a dreamer, your father. No head for business."

"I should like to see all that," Kenneth said, "but I hope sir, you'll persuade him I need to go to school."

"I'm training Peter to be in charge of the mines and Martin the steamboats but there'll be more work on the finances as we grow. Are you good with figures, lad?"

"I'd like to be better."

"Well, we'll have to see about school for you. Peter and Martin came back keen to get their heads down and learn what real life means."

Anne heard all this with some dismay and, cornering Kenneth on her own later, she told him, "Pray do not commit yourself at this stage of your life to working for him. Make no promises you might regret."

"No, I shan't, Grandmother. But if it's his money that pays for my schooling I would be under an obligation and I don't like the mines since I saw the man with the scar and heard he had had no breakfast. I wanted to ask Grandfather about the strike but I was afraid it might make him angry."

"You are a wise boy. We'll see what your father says when he replies to my letter."

16

Allenbrae had been a sad place for Kate since her father and mother had woken up to find Kenneth not in the house. Her speedy reassurance that he had only gone to Newcastle on foot to visit their grandparents was not as comforting as she had hoped. To her dismay she heard both her parents sobbing in their bedroom. Indeed her father was actually howling aloud. Even when Grandmother's letter came next day to say Kenneth was none the worse for the adventure Kate was shocked at the desolation in her father's face.

When he had read the letter he turned on her, "How could he *want* to go? He has thrown all our love and care back in our faces. My mother says he longs to go to school and spread his wings. What in heaven's name can he mean by that?"

She went round the table to him. They were sitting after their midday meal, Sarah having already cleared away before the post-boy arrived. Beyond the glass doors to the garden there was a mild May day and Kate longed to be out in it. But she was grieved at his sorrow and his failure to understand other people.

"Dearest Father, baby birds leave their nests as soon as they can fly."

"But I never want you or Kenneth to go away. You are ours. You belong to us. There is no need for you to go away."

She gave him her most dimpled roguish smile, the one that never failed to make him laugh and hug and kiss her. "What about when I meet a handsome young farmer and he comes to you and asks for my hand?"

He gasped as if she had punched him in the stomach. "Oh no, I could not bear that."

Clara leant forward. "My dear, of course Kate will marry when she is grown-up and so I hope will Kenneth but we are a long way from thinking of such things."

Ridley clasped his head in his hands. "I would not have to think of anything so upsetting, but that Kenneth has taken himself off *now*." The word came out as a shout and Kate started back. Her dimpled smile had, for the first time, failed to console him.

Then her father reached a hand to her. "My little girl, my darling. Did I startle you? Tell me now, what am I to do about this brother of yours? I'm sure my father will scold him and send him home but he will also remind me of something I asserted vehemently when Kenneth was only five. I said if there was something Kenneth very much yearned to do and it was not unreasonable I would encourage him."

Clara blurted out, "School is not unreasonable."

"I daresay. It is the way of the world. I suffered it. Maybe if he tries it he will wish to come home. What do you think, Kate? You share all his thoughts."

"Not as much as we did when we were younger but of course that's right, Father. You should let him go."

"Reward his ill behaviour? Send him where he will come under other influences that may be evil ones?"

"He has to learn about life," Clara put in.

"Mother's right." Kate went back to her with a genuine smile, not coquettish but loving. Mother has a hard time of it, she thought, and needs help.

Her father's face crumpled in dismay. "Learn about life? Is there not life here? I should go to Newcastle at once and demand of him why he has done this terrible thing? But I cannot leave the animals. I am torn in two."

"You have farm hands," Clara said. "Besides, your mother said they would bring him back in a week or two. You can talk to him then. You will be calmer. There will be a letter tomorrow from your father."

"I fear he will grab the boy for the coal business."

Kate shook her head. "Kenneth won't be grabbed. He's as stubborn as a mule deep inside. If he goes away I'll miss him very much but when he's spread his wings he'll come back."

She watched the furrows on her father's brow deepen. He shook his head several times and then, as if to forestall more weeping, abruptly rose and walked out to the farm.

Kate sighed and looked at her mother. "*You* don't seem to mind it so much?"

Her mother spread her hands. "What can *I* do? Things happen and I have to let them. It will be wretched if Kenneth goes away but there's never anything *I* can do."

"You spoke up for him."

"I couldn't stop it – your father stifling him – all those lessons. So much copying out. I was often sorry for him."

"I have them too."

"But you never seem troubled by them."

"I hate them. I want them to stop. There's a lady in Hexham who gives singing lessons. I've seen the sign in her window. I'd like to go to her."

"Oh Kate, not now." Then her hands flopped by her side and she wept. "It's all going wrong. I fear we are being punished. I don't know where it will end."

Kate watched her with sudden distaste, a bulging figure slumped in her chair, the picture of helplessness. Pity, which came readily to Kate in the face of grief, was almost snuffed out. She was thinking, Father and Mother are strangers. I am growing up. My mind dwells on young men. Kenneth is growing up and escaping. The family is breaking apart. Mother says 'Punished.' Punished for what, I wonder.

She left her mother sitting and went out to the stables and talked to the horses.

News reached Hexham in the second week of June that the king had created several Whig peers and the Reform Bill was passed. The country went mad with joy. Even in conservative Hexham a grand dinner was arranged to mark the occasion. Ridley received an invitation for himself and Mrs Reid and politely declined.

Clara begged to go but he said, "We are in mourning till Kenneth is home. Nor do we know these people and I am not so sure the Bill is cause for rejoicing."

Clara thought, I care nothing for the Bill but we will make no acquaintances if we never accept invitations. Then a letter came from her mother which cheered her.

'After his visit to the Reid family Kenneth has stayed with us for three nights and we will bring him home. Pray let us stay a few days. Newcastle is lighting great bonfires on the Town Moor and there is so much bustle going on that I need the peace and quiet of the countryside.'

"Grandparents, grandparents!" muttered Ridley. "I suppose your sister is coming too and where we can bed them all I don't know."

"Adelaide is *not* coming," Clara said. "Mother writes that she has a little cold. Are you not happy that Kenneth is coming home? Someone had to bring him."

"He walked *away* from us alone. So desperate to escape he needed no one's help with a conveyance. Now he is under other influences as I feared."

"But good ones. Oh Ridley be happy again. Life is nothing when you're sad."

"I await the outcome. That is all I can say."

They watched from the nursery window with Kate when the carriage was expected. And it was Kate's young eyes that first spotted the driver's hat as it broke the line of the road coming up the hill from the direction of Hexham.

"It is, it is!" she shrieked. "Oh it seems an age that Kenneth has been away. Will he have changed do you think?"

"Why it's not even a month," Clara cried.

"It's long enough." Ridley withdrew from the window. "I will not go out. You may greet your parents but send Kenneth to me in my study."

Kate ran after him. "You are not going to beat him, are you?"

Ridley turned round on the stairs. Clara saw the look of horror on his face.

"Beat him! Beat my son!"

He glared so fiercely at Kate that she shrank back. Then he turned and walked down to his study and went in and shut the door.

Kate looked round at Clara. "Sometimes I feel I don't know Father at all."

Clara spread her hands. "We must go down. Your grandparents will think him odd but I can't help that."

The sound of the carriage wheels could be heard turning in at the gates as they reached the hallway. Jane was already opening the front door. She grinned round at them, her eyebrows active. "So the young master's back again. We'll all be happy."

It was Kenneth who jumped down first and then remembered to turn and give his Grandmother Ida a hand. She was all smiles under the huge brim of her hat and came towards them on Kenneth's arm. Clara laughed at the sight of her stout father, descending last with the help of the footman. The shoulders of his coat were padded, his stock was up round his ears and his trousers strapped under the instep. She had seen pictures in the papers of London fashions and if he's trying to be dandified, she thought, he has hardly the figure for it. But she was happy to see them and the sight of Kenneth, in new clothes and with hair neatly trimmed, filled her with joyful pride.

Kate ran towards him, giving a little bob to her grandparents before pulling him away and hugging him hard. His embrace for her is just as fervent, Clara thought, while his approach to *me* is with a sheepish smile and a wary look around.

"Where's Father?"

"You're to go to him in his study," she whispered, "but oh I'm so thankful to have you back. Well, Mother." She kissed her. "You'll be wanting a dish of tea I warrant. Father, how are you?"

"Shaken about on that dreadful road after we left Hexham." He looked at her very pointedly. "Well, girl, I see you are with child again."

Clara felt the blood rush up her face. "What, no oh no."

"Well, you are just the way you looked when you and Ridley went off on your travels and came back with these two."

Ida snapped, "Nonsense, Henry. Clara's put on a little weight but it's in quite different places." She put a protective arm round Clara. "Men have no notion of these things, my pet. Yes, I need that tea, the dust was terrible. I see dear Kate is bonnier than ever," and she stopped to take her hands and give her a peck on the cheek.

Clara, shocked by her father's remark, was thankful that Ridley had not been by to hear it.

"Where's Ridley then?" asked her mother, looking about.

Kenneth squared his shoulders. "I have to beard the lion in his den."

Henry Stokoe pushed after him. "*I* want to speak with your father."

He grabbed Kenneth's arm to check him and his own bulk was first through the door to the study. Clara, fearing an eruption, called to Kate to look after Ida and followed them in, saying, "No, Father, Ridley wanted Kenneth alone."

Ridley had risen in astonished indignation behind his desk but Henry Stokoe was not deterred. He held out his hand in the most genial manner. Ridley ignored it.

"Ridley, it's good to see you. Now before you scold the lad for his little escapade I want you to know he's a good boy, loves and respects you and his mother as he ought. Now I gave you a thousand pounds when he and Kate were born and you've had nothing since so it's time for some more." He reached into his waistcoat pocket and produced a paper. "There's my banker's draft for five hundred for the boy and Kate will get the same when she needs a dowry for I can see that won't be many years hence. What do you say, man?"

Clara, for whom this was a total surprise, watched the struggles on Ridley's face. The sight of the bank draft held out to him left him with his mouth agape and deep creases of bewilderment between his eyes. He was bereft of words which gave Kenneth a chance to rush in.

"Father, believe me, I had no idea Grandfather was going to do this. I came as you requested and I wish to say I was sorry for causing you a moment's anxiety."

Ridley held up one hand and made a silencing motion with it. He had not shifted his eyes from the bank draft. Clara, nodding her head, was making smiling faces at him to accept it. He lifted his eyes to her and at last found his voice.

"Sir" – he switched his gaze reluctantly to her father – "it is most handsome of you but I cannot take it. The manner of your breaking in here when I wished to speak privately to my son quite astonished me. I see you meant to forestall what I might say with this extraordinary offer. I assure you Kenneth and I were to sit down quietly together and talk over what he did. This is still my wish but it will now be postponed. Pray put up that paper and I will make my proper greetings to you and your lady."

He began to move round his desk but Henry Stokoe's large paunch was between him and the door. Clara saw her father wag the paper under his nose.

"By the Lord, you're a rum fellow, Ridley. There's nothing extraordinary in a gentleman laying out a little money for his grandson. I wouldn't do it if I hadn't got it to spare. Of course you want to talk to the boy. If we can stop tonight so Ida doesn't have to be on the road again which knocks her up a bit we'll leave you in peace tomorrow. So there you are, take it, man."

Ridley put his finger-tips towards it as if it were a snake that might bite. "You mean this comes without *conditions*? You are leaving me to decide how it is spent?"

Henry Stokoe threw back his head with a chuckle. "It's not for you to buy a prize bull – it's for the boy, but he's too young to have his hands on it now. If you lay it out for his progress to manhood as you think fit that will make me a happy man."

Ridley seemed to have been holding his breath and now he let it out slowly. He took the bank draft, laid it on the desk and very precisely placed a paperweight over it. Then he turned to his father-in-law and positively wrung his hand. Clara thought he was near tears.

"Sir, I am deeply ashamed. I have been discourteous. I thank you from the bottom of my heart. It is a noble gesture and utterly appropriate from a kind grandfather. Kenneth," he upbraided the boy, "what have you to say?"

Kenneth, startled and bewildered, Clara could tell, by the whole scene, looked at his grandfather. "Oh Grandfather, I'm mighty grateful. Thank you very much sir."

Somehow, jostling benevolently, they all got themselves out of the study and made their way to join Kate and Ida in the small parlour where tea was being served.

There Ridley surprised Clara by inviting her parents to stay the few days they had originally planned. Afterwards he told her, "I was rude to your father. A shocking example to Kenneth. I see that I cannot keep other people at bay though it *kill* me with shame and grief. I will have my interview with Kenneth as soon as they've gone."

For the rest of their stay he behaved with excessive politeness.

When their carriage had rattled away and Kenneth was closeted in the study with Ridley Clara tried to mend a tear in one of Kate's dresses to keep her thoughts from fear of the outcome, but her stitches puckered up the gingham and in despair she set it aside for Jane to finish and lay back listening for the study door opening. She was half-asleep when Kenneth walked into the parlour and threw himself into a chair opposite her.

"It was heart-rending, Mother. Father couldn't understand at all why I would ever want to leave him. Did I not love him? Had he not taught me all I know? Was he not willing to continue to teach me? I couldn't tell him I longed to meet with *other* minds. I could only beg to be sent to school, far enough to board there but not too far because I *do* love him. I couldn't believe it when after half an hour he jumped up and cried out, 'Well go, go. I must endure it. I am no tyrant." I embraced him then and he wept. But he sat down and took pen and paper and wrote 'To the headmaster of Durham School.'" Then he said, "That is about the distance you require eh?" and he wrote the rest, asking for a place for me in September. So, the deed is done!"

He finished on a note of triumph and leapt up and pranced round the room.

Clara broke down sobbing. "And do you not think that *I* will be grief-stricken too, and Kate who has been your constant companion since birth." Saying these words she sobbed louder. It *was* punishment as she had feared. God was taking away one of the two who had been the innocent cause of deceit for thirteen years.

He stopped in front of her. "Oh come, Mother. Don't take on so. Boys go away to school all the time. The uncles enjoyed it even if Father didn't. I want to learn so much. Grandfather Reid said he'd have me in his business after a couple of years of school but I saw what that would be like – at a desk, calculating profits. He showed me his office and took me to watch the coal barges loaded on the Tyne. That only made me long to travel. I could see great merchant ships down river heading out to far away places."

Clara snorted through her tears. "Durham is far enough. What does your father know of the school there?"

"He said he had read that it was founded in the fourteen hundreds so it must be a noble establishment. But look, Mother, I think you'd better go and comfort him. I'll find Kate and tell her the news. She's in the stables. She goes there sometimes to talk to the horses and then I'll go look at the atlas in the schoolroom and see just where Durham is." He bounded out of the room, leaving Clara exhausted by his high spirits.

She heaved herself to her feet. Ridley had not noticed lately how much she was comforting herself with sweetmeats but if her father had thought she was with child she must be careful. Jane had remarked how quickly her cakes and pastries were vanishing from the larder while Kenneth was away. "So I won't be blaming *him* now," her eyebrows told Clara. And he'll be away from September to Christmas, she thought as she dragged herself down the hallway to the study door, oppressed by the thought of Ridley weeping behind it.

Before she reached it an urgent knocking came on the back door. "Oh what now," she muttered. Opening it she found Tom in a state of distress. Dear God, had a horse kicked Kate?

"Why Tom, what is it?"

He shook his head. His tousled hair looked as if he had been running his fingers through it in anguish. "Oh Mistress, it's Bet. She's left me. She's walked out on me and the bairns. What am I to do?"

A terrible feeling of relief swamped her for a moment. Kate was all right and if Bet was gone there would be no more blackmail. She had nothing of value left to give Bet. She had lied to Ridley that she had sold her jewels for the poor and she had told Bet only lately that there was nothing more. Was that a coincidence? Relief gave way to fear. Had Bet gone off to tell the secret somewhere?

She looked up at Tom. "Where has she gone? Why? Oh goodness, you'd better come in."

"She left a note. I only just found it. Here it is. I can't rightly read it all."

He stepped in and held it out to Clara just as Ridley opened his study door and looked round. His eyes were red, Clara saw, but he managed a stern, steady voice.

"What's happened? I heard excited voices."

"Oh Ridley, Bet has left Tom and the children. He's brought her note."

Ridley took it from her and beckoned them into the study and closed the door.

"Sit down, Tom."

"I should be riding after her, sir. But there's the bairns and I don't know – does it say where they've gone?"

"They!" Clara squeaked, while Ridley held the paper to the window.

"It's that Italian tinker." Tom ground his teeth on the words. "I know it."

"Tinker!" cried Clara but Ridley held up his hand. "I will read it to you, Tom. Sit down. You are shaking." Tom sank onto the hard-backed chair against the wall. "She has headed this at eight o'clock this morning. You were here in the stables before that."

"And not been back till now, sir. I've spent too many hours about the farm. Bet always said that. I'll need more time for my own family now and how we are to live I know not. Elsie said her mother went shopping hours ago and they wondered why she was so long. And now she's not coming back at all!"

Ridley struggled to read the words. Clara could see he was moved. *"Tom, I'm sorry but Luigi wants me and life with him will be much more exciting. I put up with the bairns while they were small but they're old enough now. Elsie can manage."*

"She's only twelve," Tom broke in. "Oh sir, Bet wasn't a bad mother. She got impatient with them but I thought she loved them in her way. Does she hint where they've gone? Her writing's scrawly and my reading's not so good. Damn him to hell if you'll pardon me, sir, ma'am."

Ridley stepped over to him and laid a hand on his shoulder.

"No, she only adds, *'Don't try to follow because we'll be far away and I am not coming back. I want a new life. Bet.'*"

Clara wept at the misery in Tom's face and for the jewels that had allowed Bet and her tinker to vanish anywhere they liked. But surely it meant Bet no longer cared about the secret.

"Ridley," she said suddenly. "Here is something Kate can do now Kenneth is going to school. She can help Elsie look after Jack and Billy."

"Missy Kate is but a lass herself," Tom said. "I wondered if *you* might keep an eye on them, Ma'am, from time to time. I know it's a terrible thing to ask."

"Oh but I will and I'll send Jane over too."

"Ay, Jane is a mighty capable woman," Tom said and then his voice broke and he cried out, "I'm so ashamed. If a man cannot keep his wife what use is he?"

Ridley's face echoed Tom's distress. This was another blow to his once-contented world. He managed a nod in Clara's direction. "As Mrs Reid says we will do all we can. Nay, man, the shame is not yours. You were a good husband to Bet and I fear she didn't deserve you. The children are alone. You must go back to them and explain it as best you can. Would you like Mrs Reid to come with you?"

Clara looked alarmed and her expression must have been plain to Tom.

"Nay, sir, I must do it myself. I'll go and take my troubles away."

He got up and walked out as Kate was coming in at the back door from the stables.

"*There* you are, Tom. I think Petal has a sore foot – Why, what's up?" He had brushed past her and made off on the path to his cottage.

"Bet's left him," Clara said.

"What!" Kate swung round and looked after his running figure.

Ridley came forward and took his daughter's arm. "There is evil abroad, my child. I am distressed that you should have to know of such things. The devil – in the shape of that Italian tinker who haunts the markets – has beguiled Bet and she has fallen into the gravest sin that can possess a woman. She has quit her husband's home and given herself to another man."

"Oh!"

Clara thought, Kate looks more excited than shocked. She is young and has read novels from the circulating library – unknown to her father of course – and this is her first experience of such drama unfolding among people in her own life.

"I thought you might help Elsie sometimes with the two younger ones," she said, but Ridley intervened at once.

"Kate is far too young. She would be exposed to situations she is quite unused to and unprepared for."

"No, Mother is right." Kate glared at her father with defiant eyes. "You have been driven to set Kenneth free, Father, and now it is my turn. If we never meet situations in life how will we ever learn to deal with them?"

Ridley gazed back at her with his hurt, bewildered look and instantly Kate's face dimpled and her sweetest pleading smile appeared.

"Dear Father, please let me read stories to the poor motherless children. I would surely take no harm and would it not be a kindness in God's sight?"

Without waiting for a reply she reached up and gave him a hug and a kiss on his cheek and skipped out of the room. Clara could see he was lost at once. Kate's occupation was secured. Maybe she would not herself have to visit the cottage. She would send Jane in the morning to see what state the place was in. At least Bet had gone from their lives and the secret still lurking in the bottom of her reticule was safe.

She looked up at Ridley. "Changes have to come, you know. You were so restless when you were younger. You *wanted* things to change."

He sank down on the upright chair by the wall and dropped his head on his hands. "Yes, but not now, not now when I had achieved the perfect life."

How can it be perfect built on a lie, she thought. It was never perfect for *me* but at least he was happy strutting about his land and keeping the children close and believing he was raising them to perfection. Now I see he is going to be miserable and I can do nothing to help him.

She left him sitting there and drifted into the kitchen where Jane and Sarah had their heads together discussing Tom. Nothing that happened ever escaped Jane.

"Is there any of that cake left that you made for the company? I could fancy a slice," was all she could bring herself to say and she took it to the small front parlour to eat it alone.

17

The Reverend Josiah came in person to the carpenter's shop on a serene day in early June when the Pentland Firth sparkled in the sunlight and the green of the long back of Stroma Island was so bright it hurt the eyes.

Rory-Beag paused with the chisel in his hand. Was this the summons at last?

"Well, Angus" – the minister was still the only person who used his baptismal name – "Flora has moved her few possessions up to the attic and scoured Beathag's room till it gleams. Your desk and stool are there and there will be no more stooping for you. I am teaching her to read but she is happier with her hands busy. She has cleaned and mended every scrap of linen in the house and though her cooking is not wonderful it suffices. We are ready for your return unless you prefer to stay with Diarmad."

Rory-Beag pointed to himself and then the minister.

"You'll come home tonight?" He nodded. He had been attached to his little room in the roof space but it was true that his broad shoulders constantly brushed the sloping sides.

Diarmad looked up from his bench and asked the minister, "You're suited with the lassie then?"

"I'd be better with an older woman who won't leave to be wed but she'll serve for the present."

Rory-Beag smiled to himself. Didn't the minister realise she wouldn't need to leave to find a husband? But he must remember that Reverend Josiah had always counselled patience. Patience learning to read. Patience seeking the babies. Now he must be patient in winning Flora's hand in marriage though he was quite sure in his own heart that she already loved him.

So he waited through the summer, eagerly offering his help to her whenever she might need it and treasuring up the things she said to him. "Eh, you are strong, Angus." She used his name now. "You have such capable hands." "I love your smiling eyes." "You must be so clever to have written your life story." But she asked little about it, only wanting to talk of her own family and all they had suffered. The minister said it was good for her to speak of these things so that she could share her grief and Rory-Beag often wept when she told how the small pox had carried them off and she only had survived.

Once, dry-eyed herself, she kissed his forehead as she rose to bring their evening drink of tea. "You are such a kind soul. Angus."

His only disappointment was that she didn't try to learn English and only seemed concerned to know how to write down enough Gaelic words to run errands to the wee store for the minister. She was clever in the garden, having cared for the vegetable patch her family had maintained on their croft. This meant he had time in the evenings after work to finish his story up to the unsuccessful journey to Carlisle. He gave it to the minister but he couldn't read it aloud to Flora. One day, when we are married, I will write it all in Gaelic for her, he told himself and decided he had been patient long enough and the time to be united to her had come.

But how to tell her? Writing it on the slate in Gaelic seemed unromantic and her reading was still poor. Conveying it through the minister would be worse. He had read novels – the minister allowed the novels of the great Samuel Richardson on his study shelves because he said they portrayed good and evil so plainly – and they had impressed Rory-Beag with the nobility and purity of women and the wickedness of those who ill-treated them. The physical act was sacred and must be sanctioned only in holy matrimony and that should be the fruit of pure love. So he must show Flora that he loved her and she would understand that she was to be his wife.

He chose a day of wind and rain at the beginning of September when they had closed the shutters early and he had built up a good fire in the parlour and she had brought in the candles to light from it.

He waited while she set them on the table and had turned to go out again. He barred her way with a great smile on his face and his arms outstretched.

She laughed. "Now then, Angus! What are you up to?"

He made his arms enfold her and draw her closer. She resisted but he knew that was right. She was pure and would guard her treasure till she understood his honourable intentions. He bent his head towards her trying to make love shine from his eyes into hers. He was sure he must be making his purpose plain but she pulled her head away. This was not going well.

"Stop that, Angus, or I'll call the minister."

His lips, which had never met properly because of his misshapen jaw, itched to kiss her. That was the next step but it was as impossible as saying the words he longed to say: "Flora, will you marry me?"

He drew back and gave a wrenching sigh. Then he caught sight of a notepad on the mantel with a pencil beside it. These were scattered about the house so he could scrawl quick notes to the minister. Urgently gesturing her to stay, for she was making for the door now with a frowning face, he wrote in Gaelic the word 'Bean', wife, and held it up to her, beaming again and pointing from himself to her.

"Bean!" She repeated it with a great laugh. "Oh Angus, you poor thing." Now she was shaking her head, still laughing and, plucking open the door, she called, "Reverend, will you come here."

He was only in his study with the door ajar and he came hurrying through, pleased to see by her merriment that nothing serious had happened.

"What is so amusing then?" he was saying till he saw Rory-Beag's face and heard her say, "It's Angus. He wants me to wed him. Well," still chuckling, "I *think* that's what he wants."

Rory-Beag nodded vigorously. Once she had grasped it properly she must stop laughing. Or was it joy and relief that he had finally proposed? He didn't know and the suspense was like daggers.

"I think he wanted to kiss me," she said. "Imagine that!"

The Reverend Josiah held up his hand. "Nay, say no more, girl. I see in his eyes that he means it in good faith. You know him to be a man of noble character. He is the soul of honesty. This is no joke, Flora. You must answer him truly and kindly."

"But how can he think anyone would want to marry *him*? It's against nature."

She stuck her hands on her hips and looked at the minister with genuine astonishment.

Rory-Beag could see that plain in her eyes. A spasm, like a convulsion, shook him to the core. One moment he had been sure she was his for the asking. The only question had been how best to achieve it. Now like a powerful blow to his solar plexus he knew the thought should never have crossed his mind. He was not a human being. That was the beginning and end of it.

The minister was nearly weeping. "Flora, say nothing more till I have spoken alone with you. Go to the kitchen I beg you." She shrugged her shoulders and went. "Angus, my son, sit ye down. I can see you are stunned."

Rory-Beag remained standing. He began to shake his head. He held up his hands and made sideways movements as if to stop more speech. He stepped towards the minister and putting his hands on his bent shoulders lowered him firmly into his usual seat, the rocking chair to the right of the fire. Then he laid one finger on his lips and left the room. He went into his own room, Beathag's old room which was on the ground floor, and closing the door he locked it.

In a few minutes, as he expected, the minister came knocking on the door, begging him to come out.

"Flora was only startled. She didn't know what she was saying. She has always been fond of you but says marriage had never occurred to her. She's sorry if she has hurt your feelings –"

Rory-Beag made the shouting noise which the minister would recognise as "Go away." Immediately he regretted it and picking up one of his notepads he wrote, "Please go away. Flora spoke God's truth. Let me alone a while. All is well with me."

This he pushed under the door as the minister was still begging him to come out. There was a silence as he would be reading it and then an anxious, "I'll leave you for now but you would not make away with yourself? That would be a sin. You are a good man."

On the next scrap of paper he wrote, "I will not."

When he had pushed that under the door he heard the minister's footsteps retreating to the kitchen. From there, Rory-Beag could hear, he took Flora into the parlour where their voices would not be overheard.

Rory-Beag sat down on the bed with a sigh of relief. He didn't need to hear any more. He could imagine the whole tenor of their conversation. It was irrelevant now.

He began to speak words plainly in his mind. Lord, I have come to my senses. You have shown me in the clearest way that I have deluded myself. You have made me incomplete and I am not to fight it. I can never be a husband. I can never have children. To have supposed so for a moment has made me a laughing-stock. I saw love where there was only pity. Oh Angus, she said, you poor thing. The minister may scold her for being cruel but she was not cruel. She was honest.

He sat still, a thing he rarely did, for another half hour, wrestling with his new knowledge, trampling down tiny shoots of self-pity till there was nothing left.

Then he rose with a smile on his face and began to pack his knapsack, talking to himself all the time. I can never have children of my own, he told himself, but I still have my babies. They will always be my children and in my memory is locked all that they need to be told of their parents and their birth. It is their right and I have neglected too long the doing of it. This time with God's help I will succeed. He has shut me off from a foolish road I had thought to travel and now He will open the way to what He has always entrusted to me as my life's work. Why else was I saved from the wreck with those two tiny infants?

He took from his chest of drawers the cloth bag in which he kept his best shirt and neck-cloth. Leaving these in the drawer he placed in the bag the two volumes of his book and a purse containing all his saved money. It would be heavy but he would slot his belt through the handles of the bag and push it round so it sat on his hip where it would be hidden by his coat and he could always feel it. This time, he thought, I can be well equipped. I will wind round my neck the scarf Beathag knitted for me and this I can pull up over the lower half of my face. I am a big man not a ragged child. The scarf may make people believe I have a bad throat and that is why I am holding out a paper for them to read. I can speak courteously with my eyes.

When he had assembled what he needed he heard a tap on the door. "Angus, I am retiring to bed. Will you come out and wish me goodnight?"

He wrote "Good night, dear kind, reverend friend and good night to Flora. All is well with me." and passed it under the door.

He heard the minister say, "God bless you then and goodnight."

Then he lay on his bed and slept for exactly six hours, waking when the first glimmer of light showed in the east.

Ten minutes later, leaving his door locked, he climbed out of his window and sniffed the wondrous fresh air that the storm had left. He pushed the casement shut behind him and with a huge grin on his face began walking again to Helmsdale where he could pay for a passage to Leith.

He would stand on the very spot where the babies had been brought ashore and it would be given to him where he had to go next.

18

Passing through the streets of new houses built in a grid pattern Rory-Beag reached the harbour front at Helmsdale and gazed in astonishment at the mass of boats in the harbour. The fishing fleet must have come in at first light and with the catch already unloaded men were hosing down the decks.

It was a good omen, Rory Beag thought, that the first person he recognised was Calum MacNeill. He hailed him with his familiar roaring noise and Calum looked up from his scrubbing and gave a great grin of delight.

"Is it Rory-Beag then? Bye, it must be nigh on ten years since you were by this way."

As it was obviously a fishing boat he was scrubbing Rory-Beag pointed to it and looked about for the neat lines of *Seagull* with raised eye-brows.

Calum was quick to understand him. "Nay, you won't find *Seagull* any more. Old Mrs Mackay died and left her to Ewen who was always her favourite. He sold her for there wasn't the money in hiring her out now the stage coach runs to Wick and Aberdeen. He bought this and with the new harbour built the fishing is prospering."

Rory-Beag understood that Calum now worked for Ewen. Ewen had been the one who could read so he wondered if there was any point in writing down questions for Calum. There seemed to be no chance of a sea passage to Leith but perhaps he could do it by the stage coach. He made a clicking sound and mimed a galloping horse, turning to look at the largest inn he could see up the main street.

Calum laughed. "You've done well for yourself, eh Rory-Beag? Is it the stage you're asking for? Where are you heading this time? Did you find those babies at Carlisle?"

Rory-Beag shook his head with sad eyes.

"Are you still after finding them? Are you for trying Leith where they were last seen?"

Rory-Beag nodded with delight.

"The stage comes through at ten. It'll be several stages as far as Leith. Are you in the money then?"

Rory-Beag slapped his hip and then feeling under his coat he drew out a few coins and handed them to Calum.

"What's this? *I* don't want your money, man."

Rory-Beag made signs pointing from Calum to himself trying to explain it was what he owed him from ten years ago.

Calum recalled it at last. "Nay, that was a gift to a starving lad. You'll need it for your travels. I can tell you what that hotel was like where the babies was took in but it may not be there now o' course. I mind it was a tall narrow house between others even taller, just the word 'Hotel' in the pane o' glass above the front door." He scratched his head, trying to remember. "There was five or six steps up to it and a mounting block under the left hand window. Look for the stone bollards along the sea wall for the moorings and cross the paving from there. I hope you find it but you'd best go book your place in the coach now and good luck to ye."

Rory-Beag took the coins back with his best smiling grin, saluted his friend and made his way to the coaching inn, warm from this encounter and the September sunshine. He must keep his coat on to protect his wealth but this time he was certain his mission was blessed.

The ruse with his scarf worked well. He made little coughing noises and pointed to his chest. People assumed he had no voice and left him out of their conversations at the inn and on the coach when the journey began. It took three days to make his way to Leith and he felt like a rich nobleman until he realised how fast his savings were diminishing. But his triumph at standing at last on the waterfront at Leith swallowed up any anxiety. He was here and it was here that those babies had been brought ashore thirteen years and more ago.

Of course Leith must have changed. There were steam vessels in plenty loading with goods of all sorts and along the waterfront huge warehouses. He stopped by a chandler's store and saw that one way led to busy docks while stretching the other way was a row of motley buildings with different roof heights and the signs of shipping offices in their windows. On the quayside were lines of bollards so he crossed over and began to study each building for stone steps and a mounting block on the left.

Dark clouds drooped low over the leaden water and it began to rain but he was so intent on his quest he hardly noticed it. Then a couple brushed past him, the woman putting up an umbrella and squeaking about saving her precious hat. It was indeed an elaborate hat perched on copious fair curls but it was the man who startled Rory-Beag. He had black ringlets emerging under his hat, an olive complexion and curly whiskers. He must be from foreign parts, Rory-Beag thought. This place is a hub of world trade. I am excited but I mustn't be distracted.

His big strides brought him up with the couple who had paused to look closely at the buildings as he was doing. The woman gave a shriek and burst into a run.

"There it is. That is the very place. And there" – she pointed towards one of the bollards – "is where they set down my box and I sat on it."

Rory-Beag looked up at the building she had reached. She was standing at the foot of stone steps. The house was tall and narrow but lower than the two towering either side. He couldn't see a mounting block because her figure and umbrella obscured it but above the door which stood open was a glass pane bearing the word 'Hotel.'

The Lord has led me to it, he marvelled, and strangely these people too are looking for it and she at least has been here before. The woman closed her umbrella and ran up and vanished inside. The man followed and Rory-Beag saw the mounting block under the left-hand window. Two pots of geraniums stood on it. Perhaps few people came on horseback now.

His heart pounding, he climbed the steps and entered the hallway where a porter was listening to the woman's excited request for a room.

"Yes, Madam, the first floor front has sitting room, bedroom and dressing-room. That will suit, Madam, Sir? This other gentleman is not of your party?"

The woman looked round. Rory-Beag had his scarf well pulled up. She seemed momentarily alarmed but hid it by shaking her head and laughing.

"I think he just followed us in out of the rain. Our portmanteau is at the Edinburgh staging inn."

"Name of Manzini," the foreign man said.

"It will be sent for at once." A stout woman had emerged from a door beside the stair. "Let me show you the rooms. I will be with you in a moment, sir," she threw out at Rory-Beag. "Were you wanting a room or just some refreshment?"

He nodded, his eyes smiling at her. She raised her eyebrows, shrugged her shoulders, and lumbered up the stairs ahead of the couple. The porter had already disappeared out of the back premises presumably to take a barrow to the inn.

They will think me a poor creature to travel only with a knapsack, Rory-Beag thought, but that's of no consequence. Everyone bustles about so in these busy places. It is not at all like the pace of Canisbay. I wonder how I will fare with my inquiries by pencil and paper and manage not to frighten them with my face. But I am here and thirteen years ago last May my babies were here. I will not be afraid.

He stood patiently in the hall till the stout woman came trundling down again. She was about fifty, he thought, and could easily have been here thirteen years ago whereas the porter was a mere youth.

"Well sir, is it a room you're wanting?" she said.

He made a growly noise in his throat and nodded, keeping his hand over his scarf so it wouldn't slip.

She looked him up and down doubtfully. "It'll have to be the second floor back."

He made his eyes keep smiling and nodded again.

"Lost your voice, have you?"

He nodded some more. She looked up the stairs and sighed. "Adam'll take you up when he gets back." She pointed to a room to the right of the front door where he could see some tables and chairs and a worn sofa under the window. "I serve a supper in there at seven o'clock. D'you want anything before then."

Rory-Beag reckoned that despite the dark sky it was only mid-afternoon. He could have eaten a banquet but he smiled and shook his head. She looked about to see if he had any luggage. He slipped the knapsack from his back, careful to turn away as he did so, and then it occurred to him that he might write an inquiry to her now.

He pointed to the room to indicate he would like to sit down while he waited and she preceded him in and put a few lumps of coal on the small fire in the hearth. He installed himself with a notebook on the nearest table while she did so and had it open at the right place when she hung up the fire tongs and turned to leave him.

He caught her arm and pointed to the page he had prepared before leaving the Manse.

"Eh, what's this?" She peered at the words. They read, 'Were you here thirteen years ago?' "What's that to you?" she said. "Who *are* you?"

He turned the page and pointed to another sentence. 'I am seeking long lost friends. They were here thirteen years ago in May. They had two newly born babies with them. Do you remember?'

"No I don't and you won't find anyone who will. I'm Mrs Duncan. I own this place. Mr Brodie that had it then died three year back. He'd been ill and it was in a poor way. My late husband bought it and we worked night and day to put it right but that killed him and I've been keeping it going since, best I could. What staff I've got we brought in so there ain't anyone was here that long ago. Do you still want to stay? I think I can hear Adam back now." There was a noise of a trunk being dragged along the passage.

Rory-Beag looked at the rain streaming down the window. He felt knocked flat by her news but he nodded and put away his notebook and stood up.

She called, "Adam!" and the youth looked in at the door. "When you get that trunk up to the first floor front go on and show this gentleman the second floor back."

Adam looked doubtfully at the trunk. "It's mighty heavy. I wheeled it on the barrow from the inn."

Rory-Beag stepped into the hall and snorted a little noise which in his head said "Let me." But to make it clear he laid his knapsack in Adam's hands and picking up the trunk by its handle he stooped and hoisted it onto his back. He could feel the scarf slipping down below his chin but with head bowed he moved ahead of Adam and clambered up.

"Gracious me!" he could hear Mrs Duncan exclaiming below. "He's strong and no mistake."

He concentrated on trying not to bang the plaster pillars he saw ahead as the stairs turned right. Adam squeezed by him at the top.

"This way sir. Thank you very much sir."

Mr Manzini of the curly whiskers opened the door of what was evidently their sitting-room and said, "Carry it to there, my good man."

His lady was holding open the door of the dressing-room. She had discarded her hat onto a chest of drawers and was gesturing him to lay the trunk down in the centre of the floor. Rory-Beag saw it would be impossible to lower it and keep his face hidden as he straightened up. He expected a shriek of horror and it came.

"Oh God, Luigi, look at his face!"

He pulled up his scarf at once, bowed and tried to back out, but she reached up and pulled it down. Luigi was in the doorway and his eyes opened wide.

"Ah! He in the wars! Jaw shot to pieces, poor man. Downstairs he follow us in. I not know he work here." And he put his hand in his coat pocket and held out a sixpence.

Rory-Beag shook his head and the boy Adam, hovering at the sitting-room door, called out, "Nay, sir. He's a gentleman staying here. Your trunk was too heavy for me up the stairs."

Luigi took back the sixpence with a flourishing gesture and bowed low. "I humbly beg pardon, sir. Pray accept hearty thanks instead."

With flamboyant waving of his hands he escorted Rory-Beag back to the landing. Adam was looking up at him curiously but his face was now covered and he didn't think the boy had seen it. Let them think it was a war wound if they wanted. He looked about for the next stair up.

Adam paused by the Manzinis' door first. "Please sir, ma'am. There'll be supper in the dining parlour downstairs at seven or you can have it served in your room if you wish."

Luigi looked at his lady. "My love, I think we go down and I pleased if this gentleman allow me purchase supper for him also – repay kindness."

Rory-Beag saw her look up at her man. "You do love grand gestures." She spoke it softly with a giggle but Rory-Beag's sharp ears caught the words. He bowed smiling to the man and nodded his head in acceptance. He wasn't going to turn down a free meal though his heart was heavy with disappointment at the failure of his mission. Then he followed Adam through a door to a narrower stair and the second floor back that had been assigned to him.

The view from the small window here crushed his spirits still further. It was all vertical lines, the backs of tall buildings crowded together, slits of windows, dark wells of grime and rubbish in between, spattered with the relentless rods of rain. He thought of the wide skies of Caithness, the low green land sparsely dotted with clusters of white houses, the vast ocean in all its moods, the long horizontal lines of the Orkney Islands and Stroma floating between. Had he done a great wrong in coming here after all? Would the Reverend Josiah be fearing that Flora's rebuff had driven him to make away with himself despite his note. He had left no word where he was going for he was afraid the minister would try to follow.

Not possessing a watch he went downstairs at last, his stomach telling him several hours must have passed. The hands of the grandfather clock in the hallway pointed to six o'clock. No one was about. At least the view of the harbour with ships coming and going and a few people scurrying along the waterfront offered something to watch. At quarter to seven a girl in a mob cap and grubby apron hurried in and flung a linen tablecloth on the largest of the tables and laid three places. Rory-Beag had chosen to sit at a small table by the window with one chair to it. He didn't want to be obliged to eat with the Manzinis. His eating was not a pretty sight. Although the husband had been sympathetic in his flourishing way the wife had been abrupt and rude when she pulled down his scarf. He had thought them a lady and gentleman when they first hurried past outside. Now he was not so sure. She spoke English with a coarse accent and he with a foreign one. Yet they must be well-to-do if they could afford a suite of rooms. Was that where his precious babies had been taken when they were carried up those stairs to the rich couple who took them away with them?

He beckoned the girl to bring his plate and cutlery over to his little table. She shrugged her shoulders, took a napkin from the pocket of her apron, wiped his table roughly and then spread out the napkin which barely covered it and banged down the pewter plate, knife, fork and spoon on top. She did peer at his face – no doubt she had been told something – but he kept his scarf up round it.

At a few minutes to seven he heard the voices of the Manzinis on the stairs.

The woman was saying, "No, it does *not* always rain in Scotland. I have agreed to go to Italy for the winter but I had a hankering to see Stroma again and see it I will."

Rory-Beag sat up. Stroma! Had he heard aright? Could he ask her? Stroma featured prominently in his story of the wreck but he was reluctant to give that precious book into the hands of strangers. He had it by him in the bag fastened to his belt. He had left the knapsack upstairs but armed himself with the small notebook and pencil so that he could communicate if he had to. For the moment he thought he would content himself with listening to their conversation.

They strolled in and saw the table laid for two.

Manzini made enveloping motions with both arms in his direction. "Come, sir, join us."

Rory-Beag shook his head, smiling his thanks.

"Leave him be," Mrs Manzini said. "*I* don't want to see him eating. What dishes will there be, I wonder."

Mrs Duncan came trotting in with a pan containing a hunk of boiled beef, some small potatoes, chopped turnips and leaves of kale. There was to be no choice.

"Will you have beer or tea to drink?" she asked.

"Have you no wine?" Manzini asked.

"I can send the boy down the cellar to see what there is."

"If he bring five or six bottles I choose the best."

Rory-Beag wrote the word 'tea' on his notebook and held it for her to read. At the Manse tea had become the drink of choice. It was not cheap but it was all over the highlands these days and the minister, who had no strong drink in the house, offered tea to anyone who called. She brought the tea-kettle and shortly after Adam came with some bottles of wine in a basket. This occupied Manzini for the next few minutes and Rory-Beag despaired of the conversation ever returning to a visit to Stroma.

He cut up his beef and vegetables as small as he could which was the only way he could eat since he had few teeth that would meet for chewing. Despite what she had said he knew Mrs Manzini was covertly watching him whenever he half turned to look. There was an expression of suspicion on her face as well as disgust.

At last Manzini said, lowering his voice, "You know, my love, we get no good fortune in your wild places. You say the people are poor like the mice of the church. You see Leith now and we find the hotel. Is that not enough?"

She laughed. "It's exciting to be a grand lady in the same rooms where I had to sleep in the dressing-room but my childhood was on Stroma and the early years were happy. Anyway we have booked passage on the steam packet for Thurso in the morning. It's all settled."

Steam packet for Thurso! Rory Beag had not known of such a thing. He could return the same way. It would be nothing for him to walk from Thurso to Canisbay and bring joy to the minister. But should he give up so soon? This woman was young still but had been here before, perhaps while it was under Brodie's management. If she had been a child then it was likely she would have slept in the dressing-room.

Could he ask her how long it was since she was here? He had laid down his knife and fork to pick up his pencil when she said, "I'd like to see how the kitchen has changed in thirteen years. That's where I ate my meals that time."

Thirteen years! It was the very year he was interested in. But her husband said, "You here only one night. Not many meals. I hope better than this one."

"I ate what I was given. They spoke no Gaelic and I spoke no English. But I was only eighteen and always hungry. All food was delicious then."

Manzini drank off the wine in his glass and filled it up again.

She took a few sips from hers and grinned at him over the top of it.

"I remember how thirsty I was then."

"You feeding two babies," he said.

Two babies! Light broke out all round Rory-Beag like a sudden blooming of the Northern Lights on his horizon.

He leapt to his feet, overturning his chair. His scarf fell off. The Manzinis exclaimed in alarm.

He pointed at the woman. "You are Bet Moray," he cried, except it was a horrible roar that came out.

"Are you ill?" Manzini was on his feet.

His lady had retreated to the door. "He's mad."

Rory Beag made flapping gestures before his face, trying to calm them. Oh for speech to express this amazing revelation. He clasped his hands together in prayer, his eyes pleading for them not to be alarmed. He picked up his chair. He sat down on it. He made soothing downward gestures and stayed perfectly still.

There was no intervention from servants at the noise. They must be behind closed doors in the kitchen at the end of the passage.

Manzini took his wife's arm and brought her back. "He quiet again. Was it something in food? Did he choke?"

"He pointed at me and made that dreadful noise."

Rory-Beag was now writing on his notepad.

"He want to explain. He try to tell us something," Manzini said.

He wrote the four words he had tried to shout and folded the paper. His hand trembled as he passed it over, pointing to the woman so they would know it was for her. Her fingers quivered as she took it, opened it and read it.

"No," she screamed and closed it at once. Then with a look of terror handed it to Manzini to read.

He read it and stared. "So, he recognise you, my sweet, what so dreadful?"

"But I've never seen him before. Could I have forgotten that face? What does he want with me?"

Rory-Beag was writing again, several sentences. 'Forgive me for frightening you. I was excited. I have been seeking the babies all my life. I saved them from the sea, those two you say you fed. Pray tell me news of them.'

This was handed over and the couple studied it together, Rory-Beag watching every flicker of their expressions. Manzini remained curious but calm, Bet wary and suspicious. She looked at him, biting her lip, shrinking back on her seat, her fair brows knit together.

At last she spoke in a husky small voice. "They told me a boy survived the wreck. Some said 'devil boy', 'monster boy'. They didn't want the children to look at him. God in heaven, was that you?"

Rory-Beag clapped his hands and beamed at her and tapped his chest. He was in ecstasy. God had flung open wide the door to his babies. God had brought the very woman to whom they owed their lives here to meet him. It was no coincidence of time and place. It must be God's work.

Manzini was cheerfully lifting his shoulders and spreading out his hands.

"You see, my love. He is not threat. He happy to meet you. Why, man, you not in the wars then? You damage in the shipwreck. You here often looking for news of those children?"

Rory-Beag tried to convey answers to these questions in nods and shakes. It was too difficult. Instead he began to write again and presently handed over another page. He had written, 'Where did you go with the babies? What are the names of the people who adopted them and where do they live?'

Now Bet studied Luigi's face with warning eyes. He shrugged his shoulders again. She shook her head vehemently. Then she demanded of Rory-Beag, "What's your name and where do you live?"

Rory-Beag was pleased to answer. It was only fair that he should explain himself properly and win her trust.

He wrote his nickname and his baptismal name and that he lived with the Reverend Josiah Mackenzie at the Manse at Canisbay. He earned his living as a carpenter.

He studied Bet as she read this. She pointed to the minister's name. "He's the one asked me to feed the babies or they would die. And sent me to Leith with that fat old boat owner whose name I forget." She looked up at Rory-Beag and keeping her hand squeezed over Luigi's she said, "So your proper name is Angus. Well, I'll tell you, Angus, I fed the babies till they were weaned and then I had nothing more to do with them. I can't tell you more than that. We stayed in rooms in Edinburgh and then the family went away and I lost touch with them."

Rory-Beag, shifting his gaze from her to Manzini, sensed the man's ill-concealed surprise at her words. It was obvious to him. She was lying.

He wrote again, "Tell me their name, please, and where they went."

But it was at this moment that Mrs Duncan came back bearing an apple tart and a jug of cream, the little maid following with three china bowls.

In the bustle of the removal of the dinner plates and the setting down of these Rory-Beag could see there was a whispered dispute going on between Bet and Luigi over her response to his enquiries. Several times she mouthed, "How can I?" and kept shaking her head and when the woman and the maid had gone out she lowered her eyes and concentrated on eating.

Luigi passed the jug over after they had lavishly helped themselves.

"My wife not want to remember that time, Mr Angus. She unhappy then and no family. Now she have me and all is well."

This was patent nonsense, Rory-Beag told himself. Bet Moray, or Manzini, had come deliberately to see this place and even to go as far as Stroma to share parts of her old life with her new husband. I will not be denied now, he resolved.

But Bet ate up quickly and laid down her spoon and rose to her feet. "Come, Luigi, we will go up now." Luigi held up his wineglass to show he was still drinking. "Bring the bottle and glasses, then. Come along. I'm tired."

Luigi rose, grinning at Rory-Beag who had risen too and was holding out his notebook again. Noises of protest and pleading came from him but Bet pulled on her husband's arm and positively dragged him from the room.

They are staying here, Rory-Beag consoled himself. But if she has not told me by tomorrow I will sail with them to Thurso and ask Reverend Josiah to speak to them on Stroma where they will not be able to run away from him because it is an island.

So resolved, he finished every scrap of the apple tart and cream and poured himself the last of the tea in the tea-kettle.

When he went upstairs he paused on the first floor landing. He hadn't told Bet yet that the babies she had fed were not twins. This he must do. Taking courage he knocked at their door.

Manzini's voice called, "Who is it?"

He made what sound he could in reply.

"No, please go away, Mr Angus. We rest now."

He tried the door but it was locked.

Her voice screeched out, "Go away. We have nothing more to say to you."

I'll put a note under the door, he decided, and went upstairs by the light of a brazier on the wall. In his room he found Adam lighting two candles.

"I can set a fire, sir, if you wish it, sir."

He shook his head. He would get into the bed and write his note and then sleep. They had had no fires in bedrooms in the Manse before October.

The boy went, keeping his eyes turned away. The scarf had slipped to round his neck, Rory-Beag realised.

Now he removed his boots, slid under the covers and sat up against the wooden bed-head to write. When he was satisfied that he had said all he wanted to he folded the paper and crept down in his stockings and slipped it under their door.

He had written, 'I need to tell you that the babies you fed were not twins but of different parents who all died. That is why I wish to have the name and address of the family who adopted them so that I can inform them of this. If you have not seen them for a long time I am certain you can give me some information which will help me to trace them. I will not trouble you or your husband again if you will help me with this.'

Satisfied he went to bed and was asleep almost at once.

Sunshine woke him up. When he went down to seek breakfast he was surprised to see the door of the first floor front sitting-room standing open and the little maid sweeping up inside.

He expected to see the Manzinis in the dining-parlour but it was empty except for Adam laying a fire in the grate. Not sure if the boy could read he was taking his notebook from his pocket when Mrs Duncan bustled in saying, "I heard you come down. There's porridge made and I have a ham hanging and plenty of eggs."

He pointed to the main table and raised his eyebrows, looking about him.

"Huh," she grunted. "They was away hours ago, crept out without a word to a soul. They left money on the table but I don't reckon it covered what they owed. He'd left a note too saying it included pay for Mr Angus's supper last night. I take it that's you, sir? And there's a letter for you too."

Rory-Beag's devastation at their vanishing turned to hope as she fished in her pocket and pulled out a crumpled folded paper. He was eager to read it at once but she said, "Say what you'll have then."

Distractedly he started to write it down.

"Shall we say everything," she asked with the first suspicion of a grin he had seen on her face.

He nodded and she went out again.

He sat down at the small table by the window as Adam blew on the kindling and a few flames shot up.

Spreading out the sheet of paper he saw it was written in a flourishing style but unevenly as in haste.

'*Mr Angus, my wife believe you knew we come here and so you spy on us. I not think it. You innocent and unfortunate. I not met family of babies but I know are alive and happy and wealthy. My wife say not need to know history. Better not. Let them alone, she say. She not know I write this. L.M*'

Rory-Beag looked out at the sparkling scene of colour and activity that was the port of Leith in sunshine. For him the day had darkened as the door to his babies had again slammed shut. Bet Moray had been a bad girl as Martha had told him on Stroma all those years ago and she was still bad. She told lies. She feared discovery of something and had run away to escape.

He watched a steam boat puff its way out of the harbour. What! Could that be the one for Thurso? Were they aboard it?

Mrs Duncan came in with a bowl of porridge as Adam went out with his hearth brush and bucket. Rory-Beag wrote on his notebook 'For Thurso' and pointed urgently to the ship.

"Nay," she said. "That one goes in an hour."

'Where would I go to book passage?' he wrote.

"The shipping office four doors down. If you've the money Adam would go for you while you have your breakfast."

He nodded vigorously. He had no notion what it would cost but when she had set down the porridge and gone out to fetch the boy back he fished inside his coat and drew out a handful of coins. She came back with Adam and a dish of ham and eggs.

Seeing the money on the table she picked out some and gave orders to Adam who ran off with it. Rory-Beag tucked into the food. He must eat though hope was at a low ebb. The Manzinis couldn't know that he had heard them speak of Thurso. They had left the hotel to avoid him and must be somewhere waiting for the hour to leave. He would approach the dock carefully and hope not to be seen till they were under way and then he would get to work on her again. Surely he could show her she had nothing to fear from him whatever sins she had committed. Luigi was a good man. Luigi was kind to have written the note even though it said so little. Mrs Duncan was kind to send Adam to book his passage. One silly frightened young woman in this world of helpful people was not going to come between him and his goal.

When he had well fed he paid Mrs Duncan what she asked for his room and breakfast.

She said, "That Italian man didna leave enough but I'll no charge for the supper for you carried his trunk up." She added, "They must ha' carried it down themselves in the early hours but I wear ear plugs so I don't hear the racket o' the boats and the last trump wouldna wake Adam and the girl. Leastways you've been no trouble and I'm sorry for whatever happened to your face. Adam will show you where the steam packet's berthed."

He shook her hand warmly, hoisted his knapsack on his back and left.

When they reached the gangplank to the steam-packet he had his hat pulled down and his scarf up and looked warily about him. The Manzinis were nowhere to be seen. They might already be on board. He gave Adam a sixpence and realised he had only a few shillings left. That was of no consequence. If the good Lord squeezed open that door again he would find out all he wanted to know and be home in the Manse very soon with the ability to write a letter to the babies' family and perhaps win their permission to come and visit them. To see Mary and Roderick, alive, happy and wealthy! Rory-Beag's heart gave a skip of glee as he boarded the ship.

The ship emitted screams and hisses which made him cover his ears but the wheeling away of the gangplank and the casting off of ropes and much shouting proceeded in the normal way. When they were well out in the harbour he walked round from end to end, went down into what was called the saloon and found no sign of the Manzinis. He wrote in his notebook and carried a sheet of paper to one of the ship's officers.

"I expected to meet Mr and Mrs Manzini on this ship." He went through the show of having lost his voice.

"No sir," the man said, "they cancelled early this morning."

Rory-Beag walked to the stern of the boat and looked back at the wake they were leaving behind, his eyes following the line of it till it was lost in the shimmer of the sun on the water. That was all the ripple he had made in Leith. He was returning with nothing achieved. Perhaps if he had not left so impulsively he would have been able to ask all over Leith at staging inns and ship's offices and hotels and picked up the trail of Luigi and Bet. They were distinctive enough, a dark be-whiskered ringletted Italian and a fair-haired girl with a big straw hat and flowered gown. But the chance had gone now. They were probably on their way heading for Italy. Bet had abandoned the idea of Stroma because she knew her past was lurking there for her and she would meet the old minister and be asked a thousand questions. Luigi would have his way that the wild places were no good for them and he, Rory-Beag, had spent his savings for nothing. Or would Luigi get the message to Mary and Roderick? It was not likely.

Tears were running down his cheeks. God had used Bet Moray to tell him what the minister had said before: he was not to pursue his babies. He was to leave them alone because they were well and happy and could live very comfortably without the interference of Rory-Beag.

He spoke the lesson in his head in plain words. I am not to marry Flora or any woman. I am not to find Mary and Roderick. I am to work for Diarmad patiently in the sight of God. There is no reason to write another word of my life story.

He began to fish under his coat for the two black leather books to fling them into the waves but when he had them in his hands and felt their soft, sleek surfaces he couldn't do it. The dear minister had paid good money for them. He slipped them back into the bag, drew his coat round him again and continued in a sad daze to watch the sparkling wake flowing away into the distance.

19

Allenbrae
Hexhamshire
October 29th 1832
Dear Kenneth,

    I am pleased to see from your last letter that you are still happy at school and even more pleased that you are 'missing me horribly' because I am you. At least you have a host of boys to talk to while I have Father and Mother. There are a thousand things I could say to you which I cannot possibly say to them.

    Here is one of them. Please do not be shocked.

    As you know I am spending as much time as I dare – Father doesn't realise how much – at Tom's cottage. The boys are at school so I am teaching Elsie to read in between the washing, cleaning and cooking and we often sing together as we work. She has the sweetest voice and yesterday she taught me a haunting Gaelic song which she says her mother sang to them.

    Now it's the strangest thing, Kenneth, but that Gaelic song made me go all over goose-pimples when I heard it. I told her, 'That echoes in my heart' and she looked at me very oddly and seemed about to say something and then compressed her lips. I asked her where her mother learnt it and she said, 'On an island where she grew up.' Elsie believes she might have been homesick for Stroma as the place is called. I found out from the big Atlas in the schoolroom that it lies off the very north coast of Scotland. Mother has always said they hired Bet in Leith where we were born. But why would a girl from such a distant island come to be living there? Elsie said she didn't know but again I thought she was holding something back.

    That was when the horrid thought struck me that we might be Bet's children and Bet was sent away by her family in disgrace to give birth and have us adopted. Elsie could have been told this by her mother or has guessed. I suppose babies can hear tunes in the womb so maybe Bet sang to me then.

I did ask Tom about the day when he and Father returned from the steamboat trip and found the babies had been born. He's still sore and angry about Bet and hadn't much to say, just that she was already in the hotel and as she had no English then he couldn't talk to her. He learnt much later that she had had a child who died and that's why she could feed us. Of course Father and Mother would require her silence if they didn't want to tell us the truth.

Oh Kenneth, am I being fanciful? Why have Father and Mother not had more children? There are families round here who have one a year. I could ask Jane but I'm afraid if it's true she would tell the parents my suspicions and I couldn't bear the upheaval. You'll be home at Christmas and Grandmother Reid has invited us all. I could ask her about our parentage but I suppose she only knows what they told her. If you tell me I'm being silly I'll believe you. I have too much imagination and no one to talk to.

Jane comes with me to Tom's cottage sometimes and gives Elsie cookery lessons. Sarah came and 'bottomed' the place as the locals say but Mother has only been once and didn't do anything but hug the children and cry a little which only embarrassed them I'm afraid. Did you know that Jane is seventy? She told me the other day how she tried to teach Mother cooking and sewing as a little girl but she would never apply herself. Well, that's Mother isn't it? I only realised recently how lazy she is and rather helpless. She's getting fatter too but it's not a baby. Do you remember when Grandfather Stokoe brought you home he thought she was with child? He said she looked as she had when she and Father went to Scotland and we were born. Mother was quite upset but Grandmother Ida brushed it aside. Was Mother upset because she was frightened the secret would come out?

I daren't approach Father. I have caught him grinding his teeth and demanding, 'Why, why did Kenneth go off like that?' You should send a personal letter just for him. He was hurt that you only sent your duty to him and Mother at the foot of your last letter to me.

Continued next day. We had a snow shower early this morning and something weird happened. I don't know if it's connected with my horrid suspicion but they found a small folded paper pushed under the front door. I don't know what it said but Father was raging in his office and Mother was sobbing. I begged to know what was the matter and Mother gasped out that Father said the letter must be the devil's work because the snow had stopped yet there were no footprints. I pointed out that it could have been still snowing when the messenger left it. Wasn't that obvious? But I could hear Father in his office crying out that it was sent by the Father of Lies.

I won't post this yet. I will see how they are tomorrow. The snow has already melted.

Continued two days later. Father ceremoniously burnt the letter in the office fireplace and I saw him bury the ashes outside. He laughed and told me he had put paid to the devil for good and I could tell Mother all was well.

Continued next day. He saw me writing this letter and asked if it was for you. I said yes and prayed hard that he wouldn't demand to see it. All he did was fix his eyes on me and then he said, 'He is coming home for Christmas? Nothing can stop him now?' I said of course you were and he went quietly out to his precious animals and has been peaceful ever since. Mother will only say, 'He gets odd notions, your father. Don't go telling Kenneth in your letter.' Well, I'm certainly not changing this now so I will send it anyway. You may think my imagination over-active but all this happened as I have written it. I heard Jane say to Sarah, 'Just one of the Master's little tantrums.' Nothing ruffles Jane.

I must stop to catch the post boy. Pray don't let this worry you. Father is very tender with me and protective of your ever loving sister,

Kate.

Kenneth wrote back quickly and suggested that the mysterious note had been left by someone demanding money, perhaps for an imagined trespass of Father's animals which would be certain to enrage Father with his hatred of lies. As for her suspicions about the other matter they seemed to arise from a song and he couldn't help feeling that was a peculiarly feminine response.

This made her cross, especially as he went on to write at some length about school and his own feelings.

'There is not much serious teaching here and I am not acquiring social graces but I get on with the other lads as I am bigger and stronger than most of my age. The other day I beat a fifteen year-old who was bullying our crowd. It was a fair fight and one of the masters watched to make sure we didn't kill each other. Don't tell the parents or Grandmother Reid. She doesn't like violence. But here you have to be able to stand up for yourself. I suppose girls don't have to worry about things like that.

I admit I think about girls a great deal now which is bothersome. The older boys here go into the town and meet street women and boast about it. Those that don't are looked down on. I don't want to do that. Did you know that you can catch horrid diseases from them? Anyway I know it's wrong. I shall keep myself for a future wife.

You told me in one of your letters that you are reading Jane Austen's novels and starting to think about young men. I didn't like to hear that but I suppose it's all right if it stays at thinking. What a pity we can't marry each other! I remember saying that when we were five and you and Mother laughed but I still think it sometimes. I can't imagine meeting anyone that would suit me better.

I can hear you laughing when you read that.' No, she thought, that's sweet. 'Well, go ahead and laugh. You need laughter at home. I don't read Jane Austen but I do take books on history and philosophy from the library and they make me think!

I have learnt about the coal industry too which I can show off to the uncles and Grandfather at Christmas. A group of us skipped school to go and see how the green country is being eaten up by mine after mine between here and the coast as engineers learn how to break through tough rocks and dig deeper and deeper. Does Father realise how the world is changing? Does he know about the plan to build a railway line all the way from Newcastle to Carlisle? It will go through Hexham and should make farming more prosperous in the Tyne valley.

Well, Kate, I hope this rambling letter won't put you off writing back to me. I love to get your letters however fanciful your imagination. I suppose Tom never hears from Bet. I wonder if she went back to her remote island or is in Italy with her tinker, I long to travel. I live and dream of doing that, but will always remain your affectionate brother,

Kenneth.'

It was not quite the letter of anxious concern for herself that she had been hoping for but there had been no consequences from the mysterious message and her father was unnaturally exuberant until she mentioned the railway to him when all he said was "It had better not pass through *my* land."

Elsie gave her no more odd looks. She had her hands full managing Jack and Billy. They are surely not my half brothers, Kate told herself, and longed for Kenneth to be home. He would bring his common sense and his zest for life into her narrow world. She pictured his sturdy frame, his bright brown eyes, curly hair and cheerful grin. Her arms ached to embrace him as she had done when he returned from his escape to Newcastle. She remembered how tightly he had held her then. He was a great deal more real than Mr Knightly and Mr Darcy with whom she fancied herself in love. The more she longed for Christmas the more slowly the days passed.

20

Rory-Beag thought the minister was not as warm and delighted at his return as he had been the last time he had gone in search of the babies. He embraced him on the doorstep and drew him in out of the rain which had been incessant since the steamship had docked at Thurso. Walking all the way Rory-Beag had tried to focus his thoughts on the joy he would see on the Reverend Josiah's face, but when they were standing together in the parlour the minister looked him up and down with a solemn shake of the head.

"I am mighty relieved to see you, Angus, but when will you stop giving me frights at your disappearances? Where did you go? You locked your door and I had nearly broken it down when I bethought me to walk round the house and look in the window."

Rory-Beag hung his head in shame. But before he could write a reply Flora came into the parlour hearing his heavy footsteps. She looked at him doubtfully with her lips pursed up and eyebrows raised. He wondered why he had ever supposed she loved him or why he had thought he wanted to marry her.

She said, "I am glad you are home, Angus."

The Reverend Josiah looked from one to the other.

"Well, can you two live in the same house now or will you be happier at Diarmad's, Angus? He said to me yesterday, 'I'll have him back if he turns up again' which was generous since you deserted him so suddenly. Work is waiting there."

Rory-Beag, nearly weeping, picked up the pad of paper that lay on the book shelf. First he wrote of his sorrow at causing them distress.

When he showed this to the minister his manner changed and tears stood in his eyes too. "Come, take off your wet coat and sit close to the fire. When did you last eat or drink? Flora, fetch something I beg you."

She took Rory-Beag's coat and hat and went out.

Then he sat down opposite the minister and as his breeches steamed he wrote on the notepad, 'I was wrong. I am never to marry. I am never to have children and now I know I am never to find the babies. God dangled hope before me for I found Bet Moray in Leith but she fled me, telling me nothing and I am no wiser where my babies are except that they are well and happy and wealthy. I wrote down a message that they are not twins nor even brother and sister but I know not if that word will ever reach their family. Old Martha told me Bet was no good and she was right. And now I have spent my savings for nothing and I fear God punished me for my folly.' He handed this over to the minister who read it with astonishment.

"As soon as you are warm and rested you must write more fully how this meeting with Bet Moray came about. But as for your comments about the Almighty I should warn you that we mortals are not to put thoughts and motives into the mind of God. His ways are mysterious and it is often not till the end of our days that we can understand His dealings with us. Have I not always counselled patience?"

Rory-Beag nodded vigorously.

"Well, if you had not been impatient after the unfortunate rebuff you suffered from Flora you might have advanced your purposes in quite a different way."

Rory-Beag put his head on one side and opened his eyes wide.

"Yes, we had a reporter from a newspaper here in Canisbay. He was a good young man who wanted to write a piece about the latest clearances. He had heard how some from Sutherland and even the Hebridean Islands had travelled into Caithness to find work. Someone in the village told them a young woman was working at the Manse and he came to see me and asked very courteously if he could speak with her. Flora was willing for her story to be told and I sat with them while he wrote it down since she did not well understand his very fine educated English and he knew only a few words of Gaelic. When he had her story he promised to send a copy of the paper where he hopes it will be printed. I offered him refreshment and while he ate a hearty meal I told him a little about you and how you had written your own tale of the clearing of Glen Kildonan and a disastrous wreck that followed and would it not make a fine story for his newspaper to publish? If only you had been here I would have shown him your book and explained how you wished to contact the family who adopted the only other survivors of the wreck. Do you see what an opportunity was lost by your hasty vanishing?"

Rory-Beag banged his hands on the side of his head and grimaced in shame and despair. Will you never learn, boy, he admonished himself? Will you not consult with wise heads before you rush into acting for yourself?

He scrawled on the next sheet of paper, 'I am a worm and no man. I bite the dust.' He held this out and the minister shook his head, smiling. Rory-Beag withdrew it and wrote, 'Will the reporter come back again?'

"Ah that I cannot say. He only stayed a few days in the area. If I had known how soon you would be back I would have begged him to remain longer but I feared it might be months, or worse, that I might never see you again or know what had happened to you. I did look in your room but, as I expected, you had taken your book with you. I have been on my knees praying for your safe-keeping and that you would not be hurt for ever by what happened in this room."

Rory-Beag was thinking how he could express his feelings about that when Flora pushed open the door with her foot and brought in a tray with a steaming dish of a mutton chop and vegetables and a mug of tea.

She set it down on the small table before Rory-Beag and looked at him very fixedly with her hands on her hips.

"Am I forgiven, Angus? I always liked you but not for a husband. Can you bear to have me here? It's *your* home and 'tis I should go if it don't suit."

Rory-Beag felt tears start to his eyes again. She was a good girl, not pretty like that horrid Bet Moray, but shapely now and tempting to a man's eyes but women were not for him and he had been wrong ever to think it.

He gave her his widest grin and made his eyes smile despite their moisture. Then he pointed to the tray and nodded his delight and picked up his knife and fork and set to work.

The Reverend Josiah looked up at her from his rocking-chair. "I think our household is restored, my dear, and all is well."

She nodded and went dancing out.

Next day Rory-Beag strode along to the carpenter's shop on a day of fresh moving air clearing the smell of wet grass and sucking up the puddles along the track.

Diarmad looked up and pointed to a table with a broken leg. "They're wanting that back the day."

Rory-Beag set to work at once and the feel of the smooth wood was good in his hands.

21

On a misty day in April 1834 when the little family at Allenbrae was at breakfast Kate watched her father opening a letter from Grandfather Reid. His expression was doom-laden.

"I hope he's not proposing a visit here." He glanced down it and raised his eyebrows. "No, he and Mother wish to host a party for the twins' fifteenth birthday. Well, it is not a suggestion but a command. It's hard to see how we can refuse."

Kate cocked her head at him with her twinkly smile. "It's a delightful idea."

She saw beyond the French window that the mist was becoming luminous. That was how she felt about turning fifteen. Fifteen was womanhood. A glowing wondrous haze would engulf her. She let the parental dialogue flow past her.

Her mother said, "Think of the money it will save us, Ridley."

"I was not planning a party so it saves us nothing. Instead we will have the trouble of a drive to Newcastle and livery charges for the horses and carriage, for Mother will certainly insist on us staying for more than one night."

"Well, it will be a change for Tom. He likes driving the carriage. It will do him good to have a few days away from his children. We can leave Sarah to help Elsie and of course I must have Jane. And Kenneth will have to ask for a day off school so we will see him in mid-term for a change. Will that not please you?"

Kate's attention was caught at the mention of her brother.

"He has chosen his path," was all her father would say.

 Her mother pleaded, "He is still our son."

"Of course he is. Bone of our bone, flesh of our flesh."

The words struck Kate. He had used them before and they

sounded significant in the context of her suspicions about Bet Moray, not totally put to sleep by Kenneth's rebuff and the fun he had made of her that first Christmas holiday.

"I shall be pleased to see Kenneth," he said now and the arrangements for the birthday celebrations went ahead.

To Kate's delight Clara asked Jane's advice about a new dress for her. Jane was enthusiastic. "It'll be a joy to dress a lovely figure like yours. We'll go to that new exclusive ladies' draper just opened in Hexham. She calls herself Madame de Voisin though she's no more French than I am, but she has books of patterns and will order and make-up anything we choose for my old eyes won't see to do fine stitches now, mores the pity."

Kate had never had such attention. Madame de Voisin called her the 'très belle' young lady. When the close-fitting dress in delphinium blue with white lace edging was tried on she was entranced with herself. Jane brushed out her hair. "It glows like the sun on a doe's back" she said, and it became imperative that new shoes were bought too.

Her father was shocked at the cost till her saw her dressed on the afternoon of the party. Then it was, "My beautiful daughter! Oh Clara, what we have produced!"

Kate thought she saw tears in his eyes and ran to hug him.

When Kenneth arrived a little late from Durham he too gazed at her with an expression of awe which made her want to laugh. She looked at his dusty school trousers which were decidedly too short for him.

"I hope *you* have brought something better to wear for the party."

He grinned down at himself. "I walked. I thought Uncle Martin could lend me a suit with a fine fancy waistcoat." Uncle Martin could and Kenneth was soon washed and attired as well as any of the gentlemen. Now Kate stood back and admired *him*. He was man-sized now. His hair had darkened to a deep chestnut, his features well formed with a strong jaw. He looked older than fifteen. An excited shiver ran through her. This was a handsome youth but she feared he was no longer the twin who had been her second self in their childhood.

She looked at the other men in the room. Her uncles whom she had thought good-looking had the narrow Reid face with more regular features than her father, but their complexions were sallow like his and their hair a nondescript brown. Beside them Kenneth was high-coloured and his eyes sparkled from the morning's exercise. He was a different breed and all her doubts flooded back. She watched the reaction of the Stokoe grandparents as they came into the drawing room where the guests were assembling.

Ida cried out, "Just look at these young people, Henry. What a sight they are! Kenneth is much handsomer than his father."

She whipped her hand over her mouth but Kate saw her father was at the other side of the room listening to Grandfather Reid holding forth on colliery railways.

Grandmother Reid was close by however and nodded her agreement.

"Fifteen years ago in this very room when we first saw those two fair little babes we could not have imagined they would grow into such fine young people – and not at all alike any longer!"

"Why no, they aren't," Clara said, "but of course I was just such a slim fair girl at Kate's age, wasn't I, Mother?"

"Oh, exactly, my dear."

No, Kate thought, you were golden fair, Grandmother Ida has always said, and the shape of our faces is quite different. We are beings set apart. At this moment I wish I could whisk away to a magical world with Kenneth.

When the guests had all arrived she noticed a tall, slender young man with delicate features who momentarily drew her eyes from Kenneth. She knew he was Arthur Herrington, the son of Grandmother Reid's doctor and at medical school himself. Grandmother Reid brought him over to them and Kate heard Kenneth mutter, "Bother, I won't know what to say to him."

He approached with an air of confidence and Kate responded with questions about his studies. "Is it true you have to cut up human bodies?"

"Yes, indeed," he said. "For how else would we understand what we are all like under the skin?"

"I don't think my sister wishes to talk about such things," Kenneth put in.

"On the contrary," she said, wanting to giggle, "I asked Dr Herrington the question."

The young man smiled. "I am afraid I am not entitled to be called Doctor yet, Miss Reid, but I have to admit I find it very pleasant coming from one so charming."

Kate, feeling Kenneth quiver, cast him an understanding glance. It tickled her to think he would like to punch Arthur Herrington for his boldness.

After supper the carpet was rolled back for dancing and Herrington tried to monopolise her, though Grandfather Reid demanded a dance from the 'birthday lady' and Peter and Martin claimed that their lovely niece must give them the pleasure too. Kate's head spun. This was a scene from Jane Austen. She had 'come out' and a young gentleman was paying her marked attention. Then she noticed Kenneth stubbornly not dancing. She heard him telling their father that it was not one of the skills they were teaching him at school. Their father seemed pleased. Kate heard him say, "I myself have no sense of rhythm and you have inherited that deficiency from me. For farming it is an unnecessary accomplishment and I trust that will be your life's work."

She was whirled away in the dance but when she came round the room again they were still standing together and she heard her father say quite loudly, "I would not stand in your way. I am happy to tell the world I love my son and that is what I have resolved – not to stand in his way."

She saw Kenneth turn towards him, flushed and wide-eyed. "I say, Father, that's mighty decent of you."

Kate bubbled with happiness. Everything could be perfect now. The family that had seemed fractured was complete again.

The last dance was over and Arthur Herrington was helping himself to a drink from Royce the butler. Kate felt Grandmother Ida pluck her arm.

"You could do worse, my dear. The wife of a society doctor is well placed. I am thinking of changing to his father as our medical man. Your Grandmother Reid thinks very highly of him."

The word 'wife' set Kate's ears tingling. At fifteen she had come within that sphere of possibility. She was not prepared to think of it yet but it was exciting.

George Reid was not in favour of late nights. He was too eager to be up and at the office in the morning so the party closed at eleven and throughout the house candles were extinguished by midnight.

Next morning Kate was still blissfully asleep when she heard Kenneth's voice at her bedside.

"I'm going now, Kate. Wake up. I need to speak to you before I go."

She kept her eyes shut though she felt there was sunlight behind the curtains. She was fighting to stay asleep but she managed to mumble, "Why? You're only going back to school."

"As it happens I'm not."

She opened one eye and saw his face was very solemn. She gave a large yawn and rolled over to face him. "You know I hate you being away but I've had to get used to it. I was having a lovely dream."

"Not about that pale stick, Arthur, I hope."

She sat up. "He is not a stick and he's an excellent dancer."

"Huh! I hope you're not going to do anything as disgusting as fall in love with him."

"Not before you're home for the summer I expect."

He sat down on the bed. "That's just it. I'm not coming home for the summer. That's what I came to tell you. We never had a chance to talk yesterday."

She frowned and shook her head, still fuzzy with sleep. She remembered everything had been perfect yesterday and now it seemed he was about to spoil it.

"I'm going travelling with my friend, Jackson, starting today. We've booked passage to London as a first step on the steam vessel *Hylton Jolliffe* and it leaves the Tyne this morning."

"It's still term time and what do you mean by 'a first step'. Is this what Father was talking about last night? When he said he wouldn't stand in your way?"

Kenneth made an impatient gesture. "Oh no no, he thought I might want to go to University but I don't. He was in a good mood which makes it all the harder but my plans are settled and if he means he won't stand in my way over *anything* well, that's all right, isn't it?"

Kate pushed both hands into her hair and lifted swathes of it.

"You'll drive me mad. What plans?"

"Well, after a look around London we'll sign on to a merchant vessel and sail the world." He stopped and assessed her expression to see how she took this.

"I suppose you are jesting," she said.

"Not at all. I always told you I wanted to see the world."

"But you're a schoolboy!"

"Not any longer. The school is quite disorganised and parents are beginning to take their sons away and I don't want Father or the grandparents to get wind of that and kick up a fuss so I'll just slip off and send them letters from wherever I am so they don't worry about me. I'll learn a deal more about the world and life and come back a tougher character I hope."

She clasped her hands in front of her mouth and bit on her thumbs. She was now very wide awake. "I believe you are absolutely serious."

"Of course I am. But mind, don't tell them till after the ship's sailed."

She withdrew one hand and shook her fist under his nose. "Oh, no, no. You're not going to do that to me again. I won't be the one left to calm the tempest."

"It won't be like that – if Father meant it last night. I was really touched. First time in my life that he's talked to me as a human being not as a parcel belonging to him, and to tell you the truth it made me wonder about my plans but I'm going ahead. Jackson will be waiting for me on the quay."

He took out his pocket watch and checked the time.

"And what about Mother?" Kate said in an icy tone.

"She's all right if Father's all right."

"She loves you, you heartless boy. *I* love you. How do you think we will all endure not knowing where you are and what dangers you may be facing? How long do you propose to stay away?"

"Not above two years."

"Two years! That's an eternity."

"I'll still only be seventeen. That's a good age to start a profession and it may be that I won't want to do anything but farm. I told Father that and he seemed happy. He's young enough still to carry on himself."

"And what about *me*? Suppose I wanted to come too? What would you say?"

"I'd say it wouldn't do at all. Merchant vessels don't allow women except the captain's wife or visits from wives and sweethearts when they're in dock and then I believe it's a very bawdy business, not fit for a young lady." He rubbed his chin and crinkled his nose in a way he had when he was thinking. "I'd like to have a look at young women, at arm's length you know, because the trouble is I've never seen any as beautiful as you who have character as well. I'll be holding in my head the vision of you in that dress last night and there's never going to be anyone to equal it."

She determined not to be moved by this. "With your plans you won't meet any young women."

"I said 'to look at', like when we put into port. Foreign ones maybe but you'll still beat them all." He stood up. "I'll have to say goodbye now, Sis."

She reached up and threw her arms round his neck and clung on. "You can't! This isn't really going to happen. You don't know how it's been for me since you went to school. You're the other half of me. I know what you're thinking and feeling and you know me and I have no one else close to me to talk to."

He stood there comically scratching his head. "But you didn't know I was planning this. We're separate people."

"Do letters reach you?" she broke in. "How do you send any?"

"When we put in to a port. It's quite civilised nowadays. Letters roam about all over the world. I promise faithfully I'll keep in touch with you. Now I must go. Hugh has my baggage at the shipping office."

"Hugh?"

"My friend Jackson. He knows I'll tell *you*. You won't betray me, will you, Kate?"

She shivered in her cotton nightdress. How dare he have a friend who would have all his company! He *couldn't* walk out of the room and disappear for two years. In a moment she could rouse the house and there would be a great rumpus and the adults' combined efforts might stop him going. But she would be cutting herself off, driving a wedge between them for ever. She could feel his stubborn determination. He was edging towards the door. He must be away before Grandfather was up and Father too, a restless sleeper, who never lay longer than seven.

She made a sweeping gesture of dismissal with both hands. "I think you are mad. I think I must be mad."

He flashed her an excited grin, softly opened the door and was gone.

She had made no promise but she knew he trusted her and that trust was a flame inside her melting the cold anger that she should be feeling. His love, his trust, his sweet words of admiration would sustain her through the storm that would follow. She could hear herself explaining to her father that Kenneth had a companion, young men were expected to travel and he was only proposing to do it in a humbler way and at no expense to anyone else. Two years was not a long time and if he said two years then that was exactly what he meant.

She listened for any sound of his departure but it was a solid house, carpeted in thick Wilton. For a second the urge to leap up and run after him and hold him back had almost propelled her out of bed, scantily clothed as she was, but she held herself in, pulled the covers up round her and buried her face in her pillow and sobbed.

When Jane came in at nine o'clock to see if she was awake it became obvious that she had no need to say anything at all. Everyone was prepared for Kenneth to have left early for school.

Grandmother Reid said, "He took his leave last night and gave me hearty thanks for a delightful party when I'm perfectly certain he didn't enjoy anything except the food."

Kate wondered uneasily when suspicions would be awakened. Her mother would send a letter after a week but surely the school would first inquire where he was? Could they be so disorganised that they didn't even notice? Kate trembled at the prospect of admitting she had known his plans all the time but their father had so ingrained in them the evils of lying that she knew she would have to confess.

22

Nothing had come from the school and they were back at home when the post brought a letter in Kenneth's handwriting. She took it to her father in such a state of fear and excitement that he cried out, "What ails you, child? Clara, look how our Kate's colour has flown."

Her mother came almost at a run from the front parlour to his study door.

"My precious! Are you ill?"

Kate held out the letter. "It's from Kenneth."

"So he has written first. Most dutiful," her father said. "But what has set you a-shaking, girl? Have you a fever?"

She struggled to be calm and lay the letter in her father's hand and smile and make as if to walk away.

"Nay, stay and hear it," he said and sat down at his desk leaving the armchair for Clara and the hard-backed one by the wall for Kate. He seemed satisfied that her colour was returning and she wedged her hands in her lap to stop them trembling.

"A passing faint," her mother said. "Young girls, you know, Ridley. She is well now."

He slit the seal and ran his eyes over the page.

"What! What is this? He is not in Durham at all. Why, he is on board a ship! He is about to sail for the West Indies!"

Clara struggled from her chair and looked over his shoulder. "Oh no, he must be playing with us. This is some kind of jest."

Kate buried her face in her hands as if she could make herself invisible. Her father reared up and pulled her hands away.

"You knew. You knew what he was planning. He tells you everything."

She looked up with her most pathetic face. "May I see what he has written?"

Her mother's large round face was hanging over her too. "*Did* you know? Oh Kate. That's why you were so agitated. You knew it was to come out. He has run away to sea and we will never see him again. He will be taken by pirates or drowned."

She sank back into the armchair and broke into hysterical weeping.

Kate was more alarmed by the intensity of her father's glare. There was fury in it but even as she looked the mask of anger dissolved into one of horror. He let the letter drop into her lap and clutched the corner of his desk.

"There are evil forces at work here." The words came through clenched teeth.

Kate watched him, frightened at his pallor and burning eyes. This was not what she had prepared for. Reasoned arguments about young men and travel could do nothing about this. She got to her feet, laid the letter on the desk and put her hands out to him fearing he might fall.

"I have to speak to your mother," he whispered. "Take the letter and go. But keep it safe. There is evidence in it. I must have it back."

She picked it up, longing to look at the words. At the door she said, "Don't be upset, Father. He promised to come back in two years."

He shook his head; his eyes seemed to be staring at something fearful.

"Ah so he says but can he if the devil has him? I must speak to your mother."

Kate ran all the way up to the old playroom and spread out Kenneth's letter on the window-seat. It was brief and to the point. He and Jackson had signed on a ship that was short-handed, bound for the West Indies. It would be a great adventure. He loved his family and asked forgiveness and promised to return in two years. Nowhere did he say that Kate knew his plans.

Kate perched on the window seat. How could she account for her father's reaction? Anger and grief of course but not these strange words. She gazed down the gravelled drive to the rough road that led back to Hexham. She hated mysteries and just for the moment she hated Kenneth for plunging her into this one.

"Is our family mad?" she said aloud. "Why can't we be like ordinary people?"

The image of Arthur Herrington came into her mind, neutral in colour, conventional in manner, and on a predictable path to a safe respected profession. It was, briefly, a comfortable image.

Clara, left with Ridley in his office, lifted her eyes to his distorted face.

"What are you saying? Don't look like that, my dearest. You frighten me."

She could see him making an effort to control himself. "Have you forgotten that paper that came under the door? I burnt it but it is not so easy to annihilate the devil. Sinister forces are at work to destroy our happiness. The devil is the Father of Lies. That paper came after Kenneth was removed from us for the first time. Only as far as Durham and he returned to us periodically. But now – can you not see? He has been moved hundreds of miles away. The next stage will be his death."

Clara gave a little scream. "No, Ridley no. It is not the devil. It is our punishment. Is it not the hand of God? I fear it *is* the hand of God, using evil people. Kenneth has been lured away because we have pretended all these years –"

Ridley leapt up and put his hands over her mouth. "Now *you* are lying. There is no pretence. They are ours." She tried to bite his fingers. He drew them away, staring her down with eyes like fire. "You *know* they are ours. That beautiful girl who was with us just now we made her together. We gave her life."

Clara was afraid to shake her head. She murmured, "Yes yes, I know they are ours. We have been father and mother to them fifteen years." She squirmed under him, leaning over her. She put up a hand to his chest but he gripped her wrists.

She remembered plainly what the mysterious note had said '*Your 'twins' have different parents. They should be told.*' Was Ridley supposing the writer had lured Kenneth away because they had done nothing about his warning letter? She had feared another blackmail threat like Bet's from someone who knew the truth but nothing had been heard since.

"All I can do," he breathed, still leaning over her, "is pray that the devil who has our son in his power will be prevented from driving him to his death. He has entered into him as the devils did whom our Lord cast out. This is what devils do. This one seized our boy just when his soul was striving towards goodness and duty. You saw Kenneth on his birthday. Kate too. They were like a god and goddess for beauty. I was enraptured, looking at them. Our children. And that night the devil struck and put wild thoughts into the boy's mind and swept him from us."

Clara's hands were going numb. He was still gripping her wrists like a vice. She tried to wriggle away and he stepped back, bumped the desk and sat down on it, but he was up again at once.

"We must save Kate. She is reading her brother's letter. We must see she is not infected too." He opened the door and Jane scuttled away to the kitchen, calling over her shoulder, "I'm just making a dish of tea."

"We never have tea now," Ridley said. "She was listening at the door. We are beset with evil in our own house."

"Jane likes to listen at doors but *she* would never betray us."

He stopped and stared at her. "Betray. There is nothing to betray. Clara, sometimes you talk in riddles. My concern now is to save Kate from evil forces."

They were mounting the stairs, Clara panting with the effort. Ridley seemed able to leap up them. He is driven by madness, she thought. I am in the hands of a madman. I have to break out of this somehow.

Kate was not in her bedroom.

"She is in the schoolroom or she has gone out," she said, pausing on the landing but Ridley was already taking the attic stair in his stride.

Kate must have heard them. She came to the top of the stair. "I'm sorry, Father. I was just coming back with Kenneth's letter."

Clara, struggling up several stairs below, saw him turn Kate by the shoulder and propel her back into the room. When she reached it she found them sitting on the worn sofa and Ridley with the letter back in his hand pointing to the words.

"He told you this the night before?"

"No, in the morning, very early."

"Ah, so I thought. The devil tempted him to this in the night. Did Kenneth appear to you to be possessed?"

Clara stumbled over to the window seat and lowered herself. She must intervene. Kate should not be put through such questioning. But Kate was very cool and collected now.

"Father, Kenneth had laid his plans already. His box was taken to the shipping office by his friend before he walked from Durham to Newcastle for the party. He walked to save money for his adventure. He has had this in mind for a while. Look at his letter. Nothing could be plainer. He knows what he is doing. We don't like it but there is no sinister meaning behind it."

Ridley looked momentarily shaken by her calm tone but then his body suddenly convulsed. He cried out, "*You*, you were possessed or why did you let him go? You could have stopped this madness. But he entered into you too. This cold reason is all of a piece with his deceitful ways."

Clara got to her feet. "No, Ridley, you will not say these things to our dear Kate. She kept silent because Kenneth asked her to. I will not blame her though my heart is breaking for the loss of my boy. He is too innocent to know the dangers he will face and she knew nothing but to please him." She squashed down beside Kate and folding her in her arms began to sob.

Ridley rose at once and paced about the room but when he saw Kate in tears too he rushed out and slammed the door. They could hear him stamping all the way down the stairs to the hallway and then the study door banged and silence followed.

"What will he do, my darling?" Clara said. "Is he going mad?"

Kate shook her head. "No, Mother. He has clung onto us both so hard that now Kenneth has broken away it's upset his balance. Let's give him a little time and be very sweet and loving to him and that will prop him up and he'll recover."

"Yes, yes, you are so good at that." Clara thankfully choked back what she had been on the point of saying: 'Don't fret about him. He is not your father.' It was like stepping away from the edge of a precipice. I am so weak, she thought. I nearly plunged over and that would have been the end of everything.

Her breath was coming fast and Kate still had her arms round her. She was peering anxiously into her face. "Mother, are you all right?"

"As well as I can be with my boy at the other side of the world. Oh Kate, *you* won't go away too? What if that Arthur Herrington asks you to marry him?"

Kate giggled and it was a joy to see her dimples. "He can't till he's made doctor and I'm sure Kenneth will be home before that. He called him a pale stick."

Clara managed a smile too.

"Your Grandmother Stokoe told me it might come to a match but, oh my precious, not for a long time – though if I could ever be a grandmother myself – !" She gave a long sigh as she thought of the turmoil that life with Ridley would bring to the intervening years.

She struggled out of the sagging sofa and Kate jumped up too.

"My precious, we must go down to your father," Clara said.

23

It was a momentous day when Diarmad had his accident. Rory-Beag was in the front shop and didn't see him let fall a screwdriver from his limp hand. He took up a saw, not sure what he was doing, and his foot slipped on the screwdriver which rolled back beneath him. He fell forward and the saw in his right hand severed the tops of three fingers on his left.

Rory-Beag's attention was caught by a stranger who had just walked up smiling. This was so unusual that Rory Beag was taken aback. Should he know this man? He was sure he didn't and yet the man was not shocked by his face. He did not hear the throaty gasp from the back shop as the man held out his hand in greeting. But it was at that moment that Diarmad cried in a thin wail, "Angus!"

Rory-Beag made a flustered gesture to the man and took two steps back to see what had happened. Diarmad, his face grey under his cloud of white hair, was sitting back on his haunches with his mutilated hand held up and blood soaking into the sawdust. Rory-Beag uttered a great cry of horror.

Diarmad looked up at him. "I'm finished, lad. I should have stopped before I got old and careless." And then he fainted away.

"Poor old man!" a cultivated voice said in English and Rory-Beag saw that the stranger had followed him in. He had already taken from his pocket a large white handkerchief.

"We must bind his hand tight to stem the blood. Have you more clean cloths?" He was bending down and doing it as he spoke. Rory-Beag ran into the back premises where Diarmad had his kitchen. There was a drawer in the table where Diarmad had once shown him the best linen tablecloth which his mother had passed down to him and which had never been used. He grabbed it and tore strips from it and came back to the stranger who was on his knees cradling Diarmad's head and shoulders in his arms. The handkerchief was already more red than white.

"Tie that tight round his wrist. I believe that will cut off the blood vessels. Is there a doctor in Canisbay?"

Rory-Beag was busy with the linen strips. He shook his head.

"I forgot," the man said. "You can't speak. We will do the best we can. Has he a bed on the premises?"

Rory-Beag nodded as he bound and knotted several strips very tight round Diarmad's wrist. Then he picked up the saw and screw driver and laid them on the workbench. What had Diarmad been trying to do?

He took him up and carried him through to the box bed in the wall of his living space. The stranger held up the damaged hand as they went and when the old man was laid down he propped that arm against the wall. Diarmad opened his eyes.

"Don't be bothering with me, Angus. I'd rather just slip away. Is yon man a doctor? I'm not seeing rightly. It's dim in here or am I going? If I can't work I'd rather die. You can have the place and the work, Rory-Beag." He closed his eyes and a smile briefly played about his lips, a rare thing with Diarmad.

"His hand will turn cold and blue," the stranger said. "You have stopped the blood altogether." Rory-Beag looked at him with distress in his eyes. "No, it is good for the moment, but I fear we are losing him. Perhaps some kind of seizure before the accident caused him to fall." He laid his finger tips against a pulse in Diarmad's neck. "He says he will slip away and he is doing just that. He is not your father is he?"

Rory-Beag shook his head. He couldn't explain that he looked on Diarmad as a father. He had reverenced him even when he had overtaken him in skill. He had declined in recent months. The Reverent Josiah had suggested he should hang up his tools and he had just shaken his head and said nothing.

Watching the old man's face Rory-Beag thought it would be best if he did die now. He would not wish to live on mutilated. The stranger was not a doctor but he knew the poor hand would die if it had no blood and Diarmad would die if all his blood flowed away before medical help could come. Diarmad had run his course in this life and the little smile seemed to show that he was happy to go to his Maker. All the same when the head flopped sideways on the pillow and Rory-Beag, who had seen death so many times, knew that the soul had flown away, he gave a great howl of sorrow and turned his face from the stranger and struck his forehead against the wall.

The man put a hand on his shoulder and murmured words of comfort. Rory-Beag's mind was at once aware of him as someone who had seemed to know him. He had said, "I forgot you can't talk." How could he forget what he could not know?

The man was fiddling with Rory-Beag's knots at Diarmad's wrist. He loosened them. "We'll leave the hand wrapped and propped up but the blood flow will cease. Will you lock up the shop and we can go and tell the minister what has happened? Do you wish to be addressed as Rory-Beag or Angus? The old man used both to you, I heard him."

Rory-Beag shrugged his shoulders and spread out his hands. This man knew the Reverend Josiah so the mystery was explained. Still gulping with grief and shock at the suddenness of it all he drew the coverlet over Diarmad's face and took down the big key which was never used and followed the stranger through to the shop. There were shutters that could be closed and bolted from inside and an outer door to lock. If anyone passing from the village saw the place all shut up like this they would know what had happened. Rory-Beag turned the key and tried not to think that Diarmad had said it was all for him now.

The stranger began to walk in the direction of the Manse. He seemed to have no baggage. Rory-Beag assessed him. A man in his thirties perhaps with modest side whiskers and plainly dressed in a good broadcloth coat. The white linen showing at his wrists was spattered with Diarmad's blood.

When he turned his face to speak it was warm with sympathy. "I am truly sorry this happened just when I was going to unfold the purpose of my visit. That can wait until we have broken this sad news to the Reverend Mackenzie."

The minister was sitting on the garden bench outside his front door evidently expecting them for he rose at once exclaiming, "So you have met Mr Hunter, Angus. Has he told you his mission?" Then he seemed to register their solemn faces. "You are not aggrieved that I sent him to you, Rory-Beag?" The minister alternated the names too. When he was moved the pet-name came out.

Mr Hunter explained what had happened.

Reverend Josiah shook his head. "Ah poor old Diarmad. He was older than I and has been looking sickly. I fear it was his heart gave out with the shock. I'll send Flora to Mistress Lang to see to the laying-out but we must not delay you, Mr Hunter. Come into my study, Angus, and I will show you what this gentleman has brought me and what he would like to do."

Rory-Beag followed him in, wondering. He was handed a newspaper and read a headline, *The Sad Tale of a Highland Orphan*. Casting his eyes over it he saw it was the story of Flora. This must be the reporter whose coming he had missed because of his foolish journey to Leith. That seemed an age ago but London was a long way away. This gentleman must have been very anxious to show the minister the paper in person. He had made a great journey to do it.

The minister was smiling at him very pointedly.

"He wants to read *your* history, Angus. I told him the outline on his last visit and described your phenomenal memory. He says he knows a publisher who is eager to have your diary and has already decided on a title for it, *The Memory of Rory-Beag*. I have explained to Mr Hunter that your baptismal name is Angus but he believes Rory-Beag is much more eye-catching."

The reporter, standing in the doorway of the study, smiled. "It is indeed. I am afraid that is how we sell newspapers by catching the reader's eye and if this young man's work is published as a book the bookseller will only have to display it on his counter or shelves for it to be quickly noticed. I will see that a subtitle concerning a fearful wreck is also printed boldly on the cover. People love to read of disasters, especially at sea."

Rory-Beag stood very stiff and quiet. This was something he was not ready to consider. He could not dismiss so easily from his mind the sight of Diarmad with his stumps of fingers spurting blood. As the reporter spoke he struggled to imagine his precious diary exposed to public view in the same way, not just the facts but his thoughts and emotions, all that his poor mouth could never frame in words, spouting forth from a printed page.

Mr Hunter looked at him, stroking his whiskers and seeming to appreciate his hesitation. "If you allow me to take it with me I will treat it with great care and send it back with a published copy."

Now Rory-Beag was shocked. Take it with him! Was he being asked to let it out of his sight? The precious diary was in two volumes now and he was adding to the second part anything that happened in his present uneventful life. The death of Diarmad would go in, painted in word pictures with all that passed through his own mind as he fetched the linen and bound up the wrist and marvelled at the behaviour of the stranger.

Then the Reverend Josiah said, "Maybe it will lead to the discovery of the babies' identity."

Rory-Beag's face and eyes lit up. He looked at Mr Hunter who was nodding.

"I think a separate advertisement could be published with the book, something like a placard to hang on newsstands and booksellers' walls. That would catch attention before anyone had a chance to read the book. If you'll allow me I will scribble something down while I am here and you can approve it yourself."

Rory-Beag clapped his hands.

The minister said, "Mr Hunter, we can give you Angus's bed if you would stay here the night rather than return to the inn. Angus sleeps sound anywhere. The parlour floor would have been luxury to him in the days when he was a wandering waif."

Rory-Beag nodded with his happy grin. Then he picked up the notepad and pencil that were always ready on the minister's desk and began to write.

"Please make a placard but I don't think I can let my diary go."

Mr Hunter read this and plucked doubtfully at his whiskers. "It is the young man's own words the publisher wants. Will you allow me to read it while I am here? I am used to working fast and if I could transcribe verbatim the key events and maybe summarise in between – ?" He stopped and smiled since Rory-Beag was nodding vigorously.

The minister said, "That would be a great labour but if you are willing –?"

"Let me start at once."

"But you have had no refreshment."

The minister found Flora and gave her his orders for dinner, but told her to run first to the village for the woman who would lay out Diarmad. Rory-Beag gave her the key to the carpenter's shop and then went to his room to fetch the beautiful black leather volumes of his diary.

Mr Hunter settled himself at the minister's desk and looked at the closely written pages with some dismay, but he began reading at once and Rory-Beag with a strange feeling in his stomach crept out and left him alone.

Mr Hunter stayed three nights and by the end had filled a notebook and prepared a separate page to be printed as a placard. It was headed *Where are my Babies?*

Rory-Beag read it with awe.

'Rory-Beag, a carpenter in the village of Canisbay on the north coast of Scotland, is seeking news of the babies he has not seen since the day he saved their lives sixteen years ago. The sloop, Gannet, was wrecked in a storm in the North Sea. This brave boy, only eleven years of age, placed the babies in a barrel and committed it to the waves. By the Providence of God it was washed ashore on the Island of Stroma in the Pentland Firth. He and the babies were the only survivors.

Rory-Beag has been unable to speak from birth. Unknown to him the babies were taken to Leith, the port of Edinburgh, and, it is understood, adopted by an English couple who were mistakenly informed that they were twins.

Somewhere, probably in England, are a young man and a young lady born two days apart in May 1819 to different parents from the township of Glen Kildonan in Caithness. The tragic families had hoped to emigrate to

Canada following the seizure of their homes for sheep farming.

In his book, The Memory of Rory-Beag, shortly to be published, this young man has written the remarkable story of his life before and since the wreck. Now he pleads for anyone who can shed light on the whereabouts of 'his' babies to be in touch with the address below.

At the bottom of the page Mark Hunter had put the address of a newspaper in London. He explained that it would be easier to contact than remote Canisbay.

"Be assured I will come in person if I hear any news at all."

"Should you not reproduce the message left in the barrel with the babies?" the minister asked.

"I would but unfortunately it helped to reinforce the idea that they were twins. Rory-Beag includes it in his book of course in the original Gaelic and his English translation. But you see the placard must be short and simple or no one will read it."

"Is that why you have made no reference to Angus here finding Bet Moray who was wet nurse to the babies?"

"Yes. From what I read in the diary it seems likely she is in Italy now with her husband. She was uncooperative and has probably done nothing to let her former employers know what Rory-Beag told her in his note. I think the date of May 1819 and the location – Leith – are the factors that will prompt a discovery when this receives widespread attention."

The Reverend Josiah's furry eyebrows were very active, Rory-Beag noticed.

"Permit me to ask how you will give it publicity? We know not where in the whole of England these two young people are – if they are indeed in England."

"I will see that the wording on the placard goes into all the London papers as an advertisement. As you know London papers are sent all over the country. We will also advertise the book as soon as it is in print. I trust you are content for my edited version of your book to be given to the publisher, Rory-Beag? Your memory is extraordinary. The detail was so profuse that I had to leave some out. I would give you my notes to read but most of them are in my own shorthand."

Rory-Beag was still in a state of humble amazement that something at last was happening that might lead to the discovery of 'his babies'. The name by which he had been known so long would be in newspapers all around the country. A book with his story in would appear in bookshops. It wouldn't be every word he had written himself but this clever man who worked in London for a great newspaper had sat at dear Josiah's desk here in this corner of Scotland and read all about him for three whole days and made pages of notes which he would carry away in that fine leather case that stood by his chair.

Mr Hunter said again, "If you are content I must be making my way south tomorrow. I will negotiate terms with the publisher of course and I thank you, dear sir," to the minister "for your generous hospitality. So you are happy, Angus?"

Rory-Beag nodded solemnly, then he wrote on his notepad, 'Don't need money. Very happy.' Then he crossed it out and wrote 'Sad for Diarmad. I loved him.'

The next day Mark Hunter with his precious case of documents was conveyed by hired carriage to Thurso from where he intended to take ship for London.

At dinner which they all took together in the kitchen Flora said, "Well, you'll be famous too now, Angus. He should pay you well. He gave me a golden guinea for my story in the newspaper. People everywhere will be buying your book."

Rory-Beag wrote down, '*If he finds my babies it will be reward enough.*' Then he looked at the clock and added '*After Diarmad's funeral I will reopen his shop. I want to work to earn my living. I wrote because God does not allow me to speak.*'

The minister wiped his mouth on his napkin and stood up. "You are right, Angus, I will go and make ready and we will lay Diarmad to rest. He is for eternity now and we still have to look at clocks. Flora, you'll have some refreshments ready in case anyone comes here rather than the public house in the village."

"I know where I'd go," Flora said with a grin. Rory-Beag knew she liked her ale but kept it hidden from the minister's sight. "Don't you fret, Reverend, I was up at dawn and baked cakes and bannocks."

"You are a good lass," said the Reverend Josiah and Rory-Beag rose too to go and put on his best black coat. He would weep for Diarmad but inside was a blaze of hope that after all God did mean him to find his babies. Patience was what he had to learn. Always patience.

24

Allenbrae,
Hexham
June 1836
Dearest Kenneth,

    Why are you not home now? We have had our seventeenth birthday. You promised! Your last letter was from Barbados but I suppose you knew nothing of the ways of merchant ships when you made your promise so I will try to forgive you.

    But today you missed great excitement in the Tyne valley – the extension of the railway to Carlisle. Mother and I and Tom's family were on the platform at Hexham Station. The trains were late coming and it rained so the passengers looked comical sitting in the wooden carriages with their umbrellas up. A band played and all the school children cheered. Father stayed with his beasts to comfort them but I do not believe they could hear three miles away. I was told there were many mishaps going and coming back from Carlisle but we are now joined almost sea to sea. A great day!

    But now I must urge you again to be home soon. If I am not careful I will find myself married to Arthur Herrington. He is very persistent and the family seem to think it is a good match. He's sweet-tempered and defers to me in everything, but oh Kenneth I find this very cloying. It's like watching Mamma eating her sweetmeats. She keeps returning to them, remembering their soft sugary taste but after a while she will put one back on the plate half-eaten. Even for her they have become too much. I wonder if that's how it will be if I marry Arthur.

    Mother is getting even fatter and Papa is getting thinner. He seems to be eaten up by hidden worries but there have been no more Satanic letters that I have heard of! He doesn't want me to marry but he says 'She will not be far away. Arthur will take over the practice and stay in Newcastle'. Only he looks wretched when he says it.

I try to keep happy with Tom's children. I took Elsie to the singing teacher in Hexham and now she entertains the gentry and Tom is pleased with her earnings. Jack is helping on the farm and Billy still goes reluctantly to school. Tom and Father spend many hours with the animals and that's when they are both most contented.

You make light of the harsh conditions at sea and describe the ports you call at in such vivid language and sound so cheerful that your letters are a joy to read. I cannot imagine how you can write in the noisy cramped quarters below deck.

I am so glad you mention that you and Hugh Jackson skylark together. I think Father at last believes he is an ordinary boy not a demonic spirit. After your last letter he said, 'Maybe I still have a son.'

You said your ship was picking up a cargo of spices before sailing for home but can you not volunteer for another ship that is coming direct to England.

I do long for you to be here. I feel incomplete without you.

Write again if you can and delight your sad sister

Kate

January 1837

Dearest Kenneth,

No more letters have come from you. Perhaps they have gone astray. You did say in your last that you were likely to be calling at Gibraltar for some repairs on the way home so I will send this there. It is now two and a half years since you went away. In May we will be eighteen. You must, must be home by then.

We had a pleasant Christmas at Grandmother Reid's which seems to have become a tradition now. We all took a trip into the centre of Newcastle to see some of the new streets, particularly a very handsome one they are renaming Grey Street after the great Earl Grey who has his seat in the county at Howick Hall.

There was actually some political talk among the family as a result of this outing. Grandmother Reid spoke warmly of Lord Grey's work but regretted that the reform bill has only gone a small way towards what she called universal suffrage. I know she believes every adult in the country, even women, should have a vote. Grandmother Stokoe squealed out, 'I'm sure I do not want a vote. I wouldn't at all know what to do with it.' There was some laughter but Grandfather Reid said, "There you are, Anne, that is how ninety-nine out of a hundred women would respond if you tried to drag them into politics.' Father was nodding gravely but I don't think he had been listening. Mother seeing him nodding agreed that she didn't understand anything about government and I wanted to get up and scream that it was our duty to understand it but Arthur was sitting beside me and I knew he wouldn't like me to. That was cowardly wasn't it? If you had been beside me I think I would have done it. You must have so much courage to do what you've done.

Arthur wants us to be engaged and everyone talks of our future together as if it were a settled thing. I tell him I will give him an answer on my eighteenth birthday which is quite soon enough.

Continued next day. I made a strange discovery today. Oh Kenneth I do need you. Why are you not here so I could tell you about it face to face? I write not knowing when or if ever you will receive it.

Mother had a dizzy moment coming down the stairs. She sat down on the bottom step and I ran for her smelling salts. Her reticule was in the small front parlour as usual but in my haste I picked it up by the underside and upturned it. The smelling salts fell out and I took them to her and Jane looked after her while I went back to gather all her little treasures together. I thought I had everything and gave her back the reticule and she soon felt better. But going back to the parlour I noticed something half under the skirts of the sofa. (She had it done up lately with a flowery chintz) I picked the thing up and saw it was a little book with embossed flowers on the cover. I looked in and found it was a diary for 1819 the year we were born. I know it was wrong but I looked quickly in May and found it was all a blank after that. I wanted to read what went before but I heard Mother crying out for me. I did turn to the end to see if anything had been written later and there was a page of a foreign language in Mother's writing. All I could tell was that there were some names, two with capital A's, but Mother sounded so agitated that I had to run to her and I found it was indeed the diary she was worried about. She snatched it from me and pushed it right down to the bottom and gave a huge sigh of relief.

I couldn't ask her about it then. I just couldn't. But what does it mean? More and more I think there was something strange to do with our birth. If it is not that Bet was our mother there is something else they are hiding. Oh Kenneth please come home. I daren't ask Father anything. He is so on edge unless he is talking about the farm and how the animals are. He has bursts of passionate affection for me when he grips me by the arms and hugs me close and says 'My beloved daughter, bone of my bone and flesh of my flesh.' He reiterates this expression many times.

Continued later. I have asked Jane. Well! I managed to get her to my bedroom on the pretext of asking her advice about my ball dress. Did she think it was too tight now? She said it would do very well but then I sat her down and said 'Jane, I want you to describe the day Kenneth and I were born.' You know what a solid face she has but she was startled I could tell. 'What a funny thing to ask!' says she. 'You know how babies are born. You and Kenneth were born like any other twins, Kenneth first and then you.' And she got up abruptly and left the room. I know she went and talked to Mother because Mother looked very red-eyed later but Father was out in the fields and nothing was said to him. He was cheerful in the evening and said he believed all our ewes are in lamb which will be good revenue come summer.

Elsie won't talk about her mother any more. I tried. She can be rather a dour, secretive girl except when she's singing and then she's like an angel. I feel sure she and Jane are hiding something from me but I must bide my time because I will do nothing without you. This concerns us both so I will watch and wait, only please do not delay. I need you here. My heart aches for you. It doesn't for Arthur though it is very pleasant and comfortable to be so loved. He is sure I will have him which makes me feel guilty that I only like him. I know he would be a steady and devoted husband and I wouldn't have this unsettling home life I have at present. I send this to Gibraltar and pray that you receive it safely.

God keep you safe and bring you quickly home to your loving sister,
Kate

When Kenneth received this his ship was indeed undergoing

repairs in Gibraltar. As he read it his heart ached for Kate. He wanted desperately to be in her presence. He could see her in his mind's eye on his last evening when she had looked so ravishing and in the morning when she had been so sweetly tousled and half asleep till she had realised what he was planning and all her passionate nature had burst out.

When he had got safely away on board ship he knew her total loyalty had prevailed and she had not betrayed him. That made him ashamed that he had been unable to keep his promise to be home for his seventeenth birthday. They were in the Caribbean and chugging from island to island. Seeing another ship bound for England he had told Hugh he would stow away on board and then beg permission to work his passage if he were discovered. Hugh had determined to join him. He was homesick too but their plan had gone wrong. They hid in the hold where a box of pepper had been spilt and their sneezes led to discovery before the ship sailed. They were sent back to their own ship and received a beating each. This he had not revealed in his next letter home, the one that had apparently gone astray.

Now he knew they would be sailing from Gibraltar next day and he would be home for their eighteenth birthday. Then he would do his best to stop Kate engaging herself to that stick Arthur. What! She only *liked* him. That would not do at all. As he read and reread the letter his impatience to be home grew unbearably. He had done as he said and observed many attractive young women on his travels but none matched Kate. He would put a stop to all this nonsense that was upsetting her.

He and Hugh had not been allowed ashore at Gibraltar. They were set to scrubbing decks which was a never-ending task because of the swarms of seagulls overhead. He had ceased to hear the incessant squawking and screaming and was remembering instead the sound of larks high above the Allenbrae farmlands while the muted colours of Northumbrian stone and the soft blue of distant hills soothed his sight. He was weary of the glare of sun on the dazzling sea and the pink and white houses clustered among black rocks.

Hugh came over to him with a clutch of papers in his hands.

"Someone who's been ashore brought these old English newspapers. I rescued what I could from the cook who was going to light his stove with them."

The deck steamed and with no sign of the Master or First Mate they sat with their backs to the bulwark and browsed through them.

Presently Hugh said, "You were born in May 1819 in Leith, weren't you, Ken? Here's a piece about twins rescued from the wreck of a ship called *Gannet* – oh no that was on an island off the north of Scotland and they were not twins at all. Odd, the date jumped out at me and the word Leith. They were *taken* to Leith that's all."

He was going to chuck it aside but Kenneth stretched out his hand for it. "Let me see." He read it carefully and felt the hair lifting on his head. Kate had found out that Bet had been born on an island in the far north. Was it Stroma? It might have been. And an English couple was believed to have adopted the babies in Leith. How many English couples were in Leith in May 1819? Dozens perhaps but how many were having babies? But these babies were *not* twins.

He sat very still, swallowing hard. He was beginning to read it again when a hand came over his shoulder and snatched the paper away.

"Get scrubbing, Reid." The hand screwed up the paper and tossed it overboard.

Kenneth leapt up. "Oh no, that was important." He saw it land among the slime and filth of the harbour. For a second he wanted to leap after it but it was quickly saturated and would be unreadable. Two words in the opening sentence he had just been looking at again stayed in his mind. 'A carpenter in Canisbay.'

He would write that down, not now, because he was already on his hands and knees scrubbing, but he repeated the words in his head. The one who had the clue to this was a carpenter in Canisbay. Where was Canisbay? It must be in Scotland.

He crawled nearer to Hugh who was hard at work again too.

"Where is Canisbay?"

"No idea. You weren't thinking that had anything to do with you, surely? You and Kate are twins."

Are we? he wondered. We are nothing like each other. But that paper said not even brother and sister? Why did Kate feel haunted by a Gaelic song Elsie sang? Gaelic! What does that look like written down? What language was that in Mother's old diary? It was nothing Kate recognised. Was it Gaelic? And why was Mother so frightened? Why had she kept it all these years but never written a word since?

His head pounded with all that Kate had written and with what he had gleaned over the years from the grandparents and Aunt Adelaide. No one had known Mother was expecting a baby when they went on their travels to Scotland. Twins had come as a joyful surprise after six barren years and there had been no more children after that.

He slapped the brush on the deck in his frustration. That damned paper. Has it set a fanciful train of guesses in my head or could it be all true? How can I live in this uncertainty till I get home? My God, could Kate not be my sister after all? That would be a terrible blow. I love her. She and I –

His hand stayed. His sweating body froze. I could marry her. Dear God in heaven! She must not marry Arthur Herrington. I must write and stop her.

A kick landed on his ribs.

He jumped up. "I need to write a letter."

The bo'sun grinned. "Who to?"

"Home, my sister."

"We sail at dawn. If you're leaving us at London docks you can be home as quick as the mail. One of these days we'll be travelling on railroads they tell me at twenty miles an hour!" He threw back his shaggy head and laughed. "Is it so urgent to tell your sister what you read in an old newspaper?"

Kenneth looked down at the wet deck and shook his head. He would have loved to knock the bo'sun over the side but he held himself together and said no more.

Hugh was curious that night when they lay in their hammocks one above the other but Kenneth kept his counsel. Too many ears in the other hammocks might be listening. Sleep was impossible. His thoughts rushed down one avenue after another plunging him into fury at the possibility that he and Kate had been told lies for eighteen years. He crushed that down only to torment himself that the wretched paper was nothing at all to do with him and he was pounding his brain unnecessarily.

"For God's sake," came Hugh's voice, "keep still, man. I can't sleep a wink under all your wriggling."

25

Kenneth descended from the train at Hexham Station with the smell of smoke in his nose and a mush of smuts and rain on his hat. He wiped his face and the handkerchief was smeared with black. It was his first train ride after a combination of coach and horseback from London. A railway all the way from London was being built, he was told, but would take several more years. They will have to install covered wagons for all passengers, he decided, not just the first class or people will prefer the stage coach. He left his sea-chest at the ticket office to be fetched later.

He was here and only three miles of a by-road lay between him and home. He would walk it despite the rain. There was not a penny left in his pocket. The exigencies of the journey had kept thought at bay but as he climbed the steep hill into the town the nearness of the encounter with the family came forcibly upon him. They would know he was on the way home but not the day he would arrive.

He emerged onto the market place where the lucky stallholders under the Shambles were keeping dry. It was market day. Would Father be down on the fields next to the river with some of his beasts for sale? How should he greet him? *Is* he our father? As he passed through to the south side of the town and began the climb up the Allendale Road he found it hard to imagine that the family awaiting him might not be connected to him by birth. Beloved Kate not his sister? I pray God she has not married Arthur Herrington, that's all! He repeated these words as he walked. If she had she would not be at home. Her home would be somewhere in Newcastle. His strides grew longer and faster. He must cover the ground. He must devour these remaining minutes that lay between him and discovery.

Clear of the town he found himself in the landscape of soft grey-greens and blues, veiled with rain, that he had often longed for in the glaring tropics. He put out his tongue on which he could still taste smoke and licked in the wet.

It was late April and there were lambs in the fields huddled close to their mothers. I hope Father's ewes have all lambed, he thought, for he will be in a good mood. And there it was again. Father. Mother. Fat flopping Mother would weep with joy to see him, he knew that well enough. He must not destroy happiness, not at once. But oh to hold Kate in his arms and see the delight in her eyes!

He noticed the rain had stopped. There was a line of brightness in the northern sky and he could see the gentle blue outline of the Cheviot Hills. Whether or not it held his own family, this was home and he thanked God he was here.

As he breasted the last slope the outline of Allenbrae came into view, a big solid shape of grey stone, unmistakeably a farmhouse. As he drew near he could see a new cattle byre at the far side of it. The front gate had been repaired and was closed. The gravel drive was shiny from the rain. He clicked open the gate and looked up at the window of the schoolroom.

A frantic arm waved and vanished. In a moment the front door would open and Kate would come running out. She *was* here. Thank God for that. He braced himself, his breath coming fast. He heard her voice screeching his name through the house. He heard her footsteps and the door was flung back.

She stood there, arms wide, her breasts heaving, unable to speak.

He took two paces forward and she leapt down the step and they were in each other's arms. He was holding her in a way he knew he had never held her before. He pressed his lips to hers. Oh she was a woman indeed, no girl any more. He panted and she withdrew from him. Her eyes were streaming but she was trying to laugh, trying to laugh off his extravagant embrace.

"I don't believe it," she said several times. "You are truly here."

And then he saw Father and Mother in the square hallway, clutching each other and sobbing, struggling to approach him, supporting each other as if the strength of their emotion was too great to bear.

Kate took his hand and led him in. With almost hysterical laughter she told them, "He's very wet."

Father came towards him first, his eyes probing him intently. "My son at last, my son always and for ever." He gripped both his hands in his. "You are well, hale and hearty, in body, soul and spirit?" His voice lifted at the end as if there was a question mark attached to the last state.

"I am, sir, in all respects. I certainly thank God for my safe homecoming and beg forgiveness if I have distressed you and Mother." He reached out an arm to embrace his mother who had come close, wanting to feel and then hug him.

She sobbed on his shoulder. "Oh what a man he is now! The size of him, the muscles of him! And so wet! Oh we will get him dry by the kitchen fire. Jane has not heard. She is deaf now, poor thing. And Sarah went to the cottage where wee Billy has the croup. Come, come to the warmth, my precious boy."

Kenneth was made to sit down by the kitchen hearth where he steamed gently. Jane, delighted to be roused up to feed a hungry man, produced slices of beef and bread and butter and set some eggs to boil. Kate ran to the kitchen garden for some radishes and leaves off the young lettuces. A great pot of coffee was made and they all partook of it while sitting ranged the other side of the table watching him eat.

This is my family, Kenneth thought. They love me. What can I say?

It was, however, astonishing how quickly he adapted to being at home and they to having him. Tom willingly took the horse and cart and drove into Hexham for his box from the station, saying only, "Eh Master Kenneth it's good to have you back. The master's fretted himself terribly while you've been away."

The box was unpacked and the few trophies from the West Indies handed out. A thousand questions were asked and answered. He learnt that Kate was holding to her promise to give Arthur Herrington his answer on her eighteenth birthday. "He's a sweet young man," their mother said. "Steady and reliable," said their father, "but I insist we hold onto her for a long time." Kate seemed not to want to talk about it which he took as a good sign.

He was shown round the new byre and a lambing shed he had not noticed beyond that. He walked over to Tom's cottage to greet Sarah and the children with a few small gifts. Little Billy sent himself into a paroxysm of coughing by jumping up and down with glee over his tiny wooden elephant.

Kenneth walked back through the wet fields and had to dry himself again. By the time they all sat round the fire in the small front parlour in the evening Kenneth couldn't believe he had only arrived home that morning. He had been told there were clean sheets on his bed, a warming pan inside it and a fire lit in the room though he protested that he could sleep anywhere, out in the byre with the cows if necessary. When it was time for candles to be lit downstairs Kate uncurled from the fireside rug and gave him a meaningful glance.

"I'm quite exhausted with all you've told us," she said. "Sleep well."

He gave her a few minutes and then protested that his eyelids too were drooping. Leaving the parents to sit a little longer he ran up to the first landing and found Kate in her nightdress and bed-gown peeping round her bedroom door.

"I knew you'd come. We must talk without them. You have a fire."

"Yes, good, come in."

His old bedroom at the back was small and now very cosy. He drew her to the wide window seat set in the thickness of the wall and for a few moments they enjoyed silent companionship as they watched the last light fade from the fields.

When it was fully dark they got up so he could close the shutters. "Well, I'm home," he said drawing her down again. "You wanted me badly in your last letter."

"I did and do," she said at once. "Oh you don't know how much I do. I have been trying so hard to find out more about the mysterious page in Mother's diary. I wanted to look at it again when she was asleep but she has taken it from her reticule and hidden it somewhere else. But now I believe the language is Gaelic."

"Ah!" He felt his heart beat quickening. "Gaelic."

"Yes, when I was helping Elsie spring-clean their cottage we came across a printed song at the back of a drawer. 'Mother couldn't read much,' she said, 'but this is the one she sang to us most often.' The words had the look of the words on the diary page. So I asked her if that was Gaelic writing and she said it was."

Kenneth put the question he was longing to ask. "Do you remember the name of the island Elsie said her mother came from?"

"Yes, Stroma."

He nodded, his lips compressed with excitement.

"Why?" she asked. "What do you know? Do you know something more?"

"If it's true," he said solemnly, "and I'm beginning to think it's too much of a coincidence *not* to be true, then you are not my sister."

"What!" She leapt to her feet. "I don't want that. What are you saying? How could that be?"

She looked quite distraught. He regretted at once that he had blurted it out in that way. "No, please, please, Kate, sit down again. Listen to this." And he began to tell her about the advertisement in the newspaper.

"Show it to me, show it to me," she exclaimed.

"I can't, it's in Gibraltar harbour." He told her what had happened and as much of the writing as he could remember. "But I can list the clues that set me on this train of thought and now you confirm the Isle of Stroma."

She broke in, "No, this is all too sudden. I need to take it slowly. I need to set it down so I can look at the words. We must put together what I know and what you know. Have you pen and paper here?"

"Everything has been put away. The room has been repapered I see, but here" – he got up and opened the drawer of his small desk – "here we are." He lit two candles from the fire and she sat down at the desk.

She took the pad of paper and a pencil. Pen and ink was too much trouble and the ink would surely be dried up. She drew a line down the middle of the page and headed the first column, 'FACTS'. Then she said, "Bet is certainly not our mother. You've told me it said in the newspaper that on a date in May 1819 two babies were saved from a wreck off the Island of Stroma. The ship was called *Gannet*. That's a fact. Our wet nurse hired by our parents came from Stroma. That's another. We have been told we were born in May 1819." She was writing as she spoke. "Those facts could be coincidences of course."

"But those babies were taken to Leith where they were adopted by an English couple. Our parents were an English couple in Leith at that time."

"Yes, a fact *and* a possible coincidence but no proof. Now we know that Mother, with great anxiety, has kept hidden a record of something in the Gaelic language. She copied it down from somewhere for it was in her writing and it dates from May 1819. We know that language is spoken in the highlands and islands of Scotland. Those are also facts." She wrote them down and looked up with her forehead puckered. "What happened to the original document I wonder? Was it a record of births? It contained names beginning with A and I think there was one with a capital G. *Gannet*?" She clenched her fists in frustration. "We *must* try to find Mother's copy. Perhaps Elsie could translate it. Ah Elsie! Those odd looks when I asked if her mother told her about our birth in Leith. I'll swear she knows or guesses something. But Tom didn't think it odd that Mother had given birth to twins while he and Father were on the steamboat. He supposed Father thought the birth was not imminent or he would not have gone. And the grandparents and Aunt Adelaide never suspected anything. Did you never think how odd that was? They said they accepted it was a secret to spare them disappointment in case Mother miscarried."

Kenneth shrugged his shoulders. "When I was younger I never thought much about *that*. It's rather more a feminine concern. But there are no *facts* there. You could call it all speculation or suspicion." She nodded and headed the second column "Suspicious Happenings" and wrote them all down.

"Now," he said, "I'm afraid we have to note some of the other information I remember from the newspaper. The uncomfortable facts. The advertisement said the babies in the wreck were born to two different parents from Glen Kildonan and so were not twins nor even brother and sister."

She bit her lip. "That is a fact about *them*. But surely it destroys the case that *we* are those babes. We have always *known* we were twins."

"Kate, look at us! We are nothing alike at all and we are certainly nothing like our parents."

"I grant that," she said, "but suppose they did adopt us they would *know* we were twins, wouldn't they?" Then she clasped her hand over her mouth. "You are thinking if they set out to deceive everyone that the babies were their own they would have to *pretend* they were twins because they were the same age. Oh Kenneth, have they, have we lived a lie all these years?"

Kenneth recalled one crucial fact in the advertisement that he had not yet mentioned to Kate. "Oh they have lied all right but on *that* matter they may not have known the truth. I must tell you what the paper said: the only other person saved from the wreck was a boy of eleven who had been unable to speak from birth. He was the only person who knew the babies' origin."

She stared round at him on the window seat, open-mouthed. "What! Has he spoken miraculously now?"

"No, but the press got hold of the story, I don't know how. I was rereading the paper when the bo'sun snatched it away. But this man – he must be about thirty now – has *written* an account of it and it is to be published. Maybe it already is. I never noticed the date on the newspaper. There were words at the foot of the page about contacting someone in London. I know not what it said, but I do remember – for I wrote it down quickly in my pocket book – that the dumb man is a carpenter in Canisbay and he wants to trace the babies, '*his* babies' for it was he who saved their lives."

"Oh Kenneth," she came to sit by him, her eyes shining, "where is Canisbay?"

He put his arm round her. "We'll find it in the atlas. You looked for and found Stroma."

She jumped up again. "Of course, that battered old atlas. It's still in the schoolroom in the attic."

He pulled her down. "Not now. The attic stair creaks. We must look in the morning. Let's not perplex our minds with that now."

"But we may not be brother and sister! And you are telling me that our so-called parents may not even know the answer. This will drive me mad."

Kenneth grieved for her. He upbraided himself. I have had days and nights, he realised, to grow accustomed to the idea that she might not be my sister. I saw her on the doorstep as a woman and for a second I held her as such. "No, Kate," he said aloud, "I should never have let you begin to think that way. We are still in doubt. Set down more under your heading of 'Suspicions.' You wrote of Father's odd behaviour. What was the mysterious note in the snow?"

She went back to the desk, biting the end of the pencil. "I'll try. Well, there have been many strange things but that I never discovered except he thought it the devil's work. Did you notice how he asked you today if your soul and spirit were as healthy as your body? Oh you don't know how hard it has been to keep him rational. He keeps repeating, 'bone of my bone and flesh of my flesh' and Mother tells people how like I am to her when she was young." When she had written that she laid down the pencil and looked at him with wide eyes. "That will have to do for tonight but oh Kenneth, if only they hadn't lied to us I think I could bear it if we really were adopted. But not to be your sister –"

"We don't know. Don't think of that yet. We will always be close." He got up and lifting her from the stool held her tight. "Let me just say that if I have learnt one thing by going away it is that no one could ever be more precious to me than you are."

"Oh!" She released herself from his grasp and stood looking wonderingly into his eyes. They were astonishing words from a brother.

He clasped her hands. "We're tired. Let's go to bed. We have more to discover, and a decision to make as to when – if ever – we confront the parents directly."

She nodded, took one of the candles and stepped quickly to the door. There she paused. "I dread the thought of that," she said in a whisper. "They were happy tonight but they will have gone to bed now. Goodnight Kenneth."

She was gone and it seemed a sudden ending. His arms were

empty of her. She had taken her notes away with her and all at once it was as if nothing remained of the momentous subject they had been discussing. His head buzzed as he prepared himself for bed. How could he possibly sleep? But when he got between the sheets the warmth and comfort of the bed, so far beyond anything he had known for three years, enfolded him. He was asleep at once and slept till morning.

Kate was tempted to creep to the attic for the atlas but no, she thought, that must wait till the morning. Kenneth and I will study it together as we did when we were little children trying to please Father. We were brother and sister, she repeated to herself. How can that stop?

Standing at her bedroom window and watching the moon struggle through ragged clouds, she pondered Kenneth words. I ought to feel like that about Arthur Herrington. I am expected to put the love of my life before any member of my family. I don't feel like that. I can't imagine I ever would. Oh Kenneth, how am I to live not knowing what *you* are to me? I would like to tear the truth out of Mother. I have known for years there was something hidden and I had to endure it without you. It is a joy to have you here now but this is a strange shock! Can it be that God put that newspaper in your way to end confusion or confound us more?

She shivered and wrapping her bed-gown more closely round her she crept into her bed and snuggled down. Ridley decreed no fires in bedrooms after Easter. He had a strong Spartan streak which poor self-indulgent Clara found a great trial. Thinking of her mother Kate recalled how she had used the words "we are punished" when Kenneth went away. That was something else to add under the heading 'suspicion.'

The candle was still alight on her bedside cabinet. She sat up and wrote, 'Mother believes they are being punished for something. What?'

She blew out the candle and lay down. Yes, she thought, it is Father who is preventing Mother from telling the truth. I must not be cruel to Mother. It is Father who will have to be confronted and

I can only pray that the telling will give him relief. Kenneth said 'if ever we confront them direct.' 'if ever?' No, it must be done soon for all our sakes.

She lay, stiff and straight, determined not to weep. Uncertainty, she realised was a form of torment but if Kenneth, who had suffered it from that moment in Gibraltar, could endure it stoically, so would she. Sleep, however, would not come.

26

On Rory-Beag's shop counter below the window which usually stood open he kept a little bell which gave a pleasant tinkling sound that he could always hear in the back room even if he was sawing.

It rang now on a late April morning with a steady drizzle falling. The voice of Malcolm the post-boy called, "Parcel for you, Rory-Beag."

There were a few men called Angus in the village so the appellation 'Rory-Beag the carpenter' had retained its familiarity.

He came through and looked at the big square package on the counter. It was evidently a box made of stiff board with the direction written on 'To Angus known as Rory-Beag, Carpenter at Canisbay in the County of Sutherland. It was the first time he had ever received anything in the post. He tested the weight. It was heavy. He cut the cords round it and opened it up, not having any idea what it could be. There was a fine paper wrapping inside covering something in dark red leather. He began carefully peeling it back. Gradually he exposed in gold letters a title, 'The Memory of Rory-Beag.' Underneath were the words in smaller letters 'The Amazing Chronicle of a Shipwreck and its Aftermath by a Survivor.'

A great whoop of joyful astonishment came from him. He capered about the shop. He looked up and down the road to see if anyone was in sight with whom he could share his joy. A figure came into view from the direction of the Manse. It was Flora with her shopping basket. She would be going to see if the boats were in so she could buy fish for dinner. He flung wide the shop door and danced into the road waving his arms. He was calling out, "Flora, Flora, come and see" but they were wild roaring sounds.

She broke into a run. Perhaps she believed he was in trouble from an accident like Diarmad's but she knew his facial expressions and soon realised he was laughing and joyous.

"Why, whatever is it?" she panted as she came up.

He drew her in out of the rain and pointed to the parcel. She turned back the paper and stared awestruck. How thankful he was that he and the minister between them had taught her to read a little.

"It's your great work," she murmured. "That Mr Hunter's really done it at last. My gracious, how many copies have they sent you?" He had not even taken one out but now, wiping his hands on his apron, he gently withdrew the top copy and felt carefully inside the box. He held up both hands spread.

"Ten copies!" she gasped. "My, what must they cost, so handsome as they are!" She pushed her hands inside her cloak to dry them. "May I hold one?" He gladly handed one over and she opened it up, marvelling at the scrolled title page and a woodcut of a ship in towering waves. She looked further on. "Eh it is all here! What they call a preface, how it came to be written and the name of a London publisher. Why you are a great man, Rory-Beag. I thought I was famous when they printed my story in a newspaper but this is different. You are a true writer yourself. These will be in every bookshop in the land. And I can call you my friend." She laid the book reverently on the counter and gave him a deep curtsey.

He shook his head, unable to stop grinning and lifted her up.

"I'll tell the whole village," she cried and, grabbing her basket, she raced off.

Rory-Beag stood and looked after her and then opened up the first copy he had taken out. An official-looking paper headed 'Contract' he laid aside and found below a letter from 'Your sincere friend Mark Hunter'. It told him there had been interest roused by the poster and newspaper advertisement though no responses yet as to the identity of the babies. But he had great hopes 'that the book, ten copies of which I enclose, will attract much attention among the reading public of whom I am certain the English couple who brought up the children can be numbered.'

Rory-Beag tried not to let a sense of disappointment cloud his delight. He was tempted to shut up shop to go and tell the Reverend Josiah but he had a chair to mend for the harbour master who would certainly send for it before the end of the day.

The wind was getting up and the rain was beginning to blow in onto the counter. He slid the two books back into the box and carried it through to the kitchen table. Work must not be neglected.

He had not been more than fifteen minutes at work before he heard voices outside and his little bell ringing. He put down his chisel and went through to the front shop where he found a crowd already pushing its way in. Voices clamoured. "Show us your books Rory-Beag." "You'll be giving up work now you're a wealthy writer." "Will you finish repairing my table leg before you shut up shop?"

He looked at the grubby wet state of them and made frantic negative gestures. Holding up his hands to stop them coming any further he went and fetched one book, carrying it in a piece of clean cloth and holding it up for all to see. They gaped at the crimson leather and the gold letters but those that could read wanted to reach for it. He took it back into the kitchen and closed the door, putting his big bulk against it. Then he picked up the chalk which lay on the hollow rim of his big slate and wrote, '*Always carpenter.*' He grinned round at them and was surprised to see angry faces.

"The swine in London are going to cheat him because he's a poor dumb man."

"We'll write to the Earl of Sutherland. We'll see you get justice, Rory-Beag."

He laughed and wrote, '*I have a contract. London people good, but I love my work.*' They cheered him then and he wanted to give out a copy each but not until they had washed their hands. No, there were not enough and he must keep one for the minister and one for the school which the teacher could read to the children and of course when he found his babies he would give them each a copy. All he wanted now was to carry the books home to a safe place where he could sit and devour them.

He wrote on the slate, "Work to do" and made friendly shooing motions.

Reluctantly they began to disperse, talking among themselves. "Fancy Canisbay having a real author." "Some of us could put money together and buy a copy to pass round." Their eyes lingered on him as he returned to work. "Who would have thought to look at him that he could write a book!"

Flora came by with her fish, the rain blew away and splashes of sunlight lit up the colours in the wood under his hands.

"Will I tell the Reverend what's happened?" she asked, as if she had not already told the whole world. He nodded. He would come home as soon as the chair had been collected. He must use the daylight hours for his reading.

When the time came and the minister had handled the books with loving care and they had eaten their fish, they both sat down in the study and began to read.

Soon Rory-Beag was making grunts of surprise. The minister looked up at him and said, "You are thinking Mr Hunter has been free with your text."

Rory-Beag wrote on the slate, '*It begins when I was little, not with the babies.*'

"He has put your life in chronological order. The poster stated the baby facts. He has distorted nothing just left out some of your mass of detail. His name does not appear anywhere. You can be happy, Angus. You are a published author and I am very proud of you."

Rory-Beag drew a long happy breath and read on.

27

Kate, rising early from a night of fitful sleep, found her father in the kitchen pouring himself tea. Aware of her presence he concluded the delicate operation, saying as he did so, "Well, my Kate, did not God rejoice over the return of the prodigal son?" She could think of no appropriate reply so he swung round with a great smile on his face and for the first time in years she saw no tension in his body.

"We must have a celebration of your brother's homecoming. We have never had a family party at Allenbrae. We will have one next week." Now he looked at her a little curiously. "Are you not delighted? What is this? You look as if you have not slept. I on the contrary slept soundly."

She tried to laugh it off. "It must have been the excitement."

He poured another cup and handed it to her. "Drink that. It is very refreshing in the morning. I will go and see if any lambs have been born in the night. Tom may be there already. He is a good man is Tom. Your mother is still asleep and Kenneth too after his travels. Tell them my plan when they come down. Jane used to be early but she is getting old and Sarah slept at the cottage to keep an eye on the child Billy. She will be here soon but we can manage breakfast very well ourselves. I will need to bring in help though if we have a party." He gave her a swift hug and kiss, tossed off his own cup of tea and went out.

Kate said under her breath, you may act the normal father as much as you like, but you will not turn Kenneth and me from our quest. She took her cup and ran lightly upstairs, pausing to listen at Kenneth's door. There was no sound so she continued to the attic, too impatient now to wait for him. The stair squeaked but waked nobody.

She set her cup down on the old stained and scratched nursery table and looked round the shelves. Yes, there was the atlas next to a pile of 'Moral Tales for the Young.' Containing her excitement she drank off her tea first and then drew the big clumsy book out and spread it open on the table where there was already a paper marking the place.

The last time she had used it was when she had looked for the Island of Stroma. Canisbay should be in the same area, she reasoned, and presumably at the seaside.

Tracing with her finger the mainland coast opposite Stroma she squealed with excitement. There it was, Canisbay, in small print, suggesting it was no more than a village. She wanted to run down and wake Kenneth, but Canisbay was for the future. Leaving the page marked she closed the atlas and returned it to the shelf. First they must replace doubt with certainty and how could they attain that without destroying the new harmony of home? She had never seen her father so at ease with himself. If she challenged him now there could be no party next week. She went to the window where she had often sat lately praying for Kenneth to come. Now he had come and all this turmoil in her brain was the result.

It was nearly an hour before he and their mother and Jane were all up and in the kitchen for breakfast. Kate told them about the idea of a family party and their father came in, bright and windblown, just as they were all discussing it.

"Oh dear," their mother was saying, "won't the family want another one next month for the birthday? We can't have two."

Ridley laughed. "I'm sure my parents will want to host that as they did the twins' fifteenth. No, this is to be *our* celebration. We have our boy back, never to disappear again." He slapped Kenneth on the shoulder. "Eh, son?"

Kenneth made a rueful face. "I'm not *planning* to disappear, sir."

They ate breakfast and Ridley demanded that Kenneth come out with him to see three new lambs.

"I'd like to see them too," Kate said, desperate to have time with Kenneth.

So they went and looked at the lambs, already up on their legs and fighting for their mother's teats. Kate watched them with strange pangs of longing to know who truly had been her own mother. She suggested she and Kenneth could walk over to Tom's cottage to see if Billy was better.

"Tom's already told me he is," their father said. "You took the children little presents yesterday." It seemed he wanted Kenneth by his side all day but presently he remembered he must go indoors and write to the grandparents and godparents to invite them to the party. "And of course you will want Arthur Herrington and his parents, I suppose, Kate, though I have no wish to hasten a liaison there."

"No," she said, "if there is to be a party on our eighteenth birthday I am sure Grandfather and Grandmother Reid will invite them."

Their father chuckled. "Ah yes, that is the day you are to give him your answer. I have a suspicion you have not made up your mind yet. Well, I care not how long you keep him waiting. I have both my children at home with me which is how it should be." He strode off with exaggeratedly long steps which with his small stature looked a little ridiculous.

Immediately Kate grabbed Kenneth's arm. "I looked in the atlas while you were still asleep and found Canisbay. It's on the north coast of Scotland, near Stroma Island."

"Good, but we won't be needing that information for a while. We can do nothing about that business now till after next week."

"Why not? I can't live in uncertainty that long."

"But he's in such a good mood."

They were walking across the fields without any particular sense of direction. Kate stood still and faced Kenneth. "*You* have not lived at home with him for years. I've been thinking about it and I believe a gathering of the family would be an excellent time to confront him. If Mother is upset she will have her own mother to comfort her and her father who makes light of everything. Besides we'll have the wisdom of Grandmother Reid. I'd like that."

Kenneth frowned. "It would be mighty embarrassing. There'll be servants about. Father will ask the grandparents to bring some of their own to help serve."

"Their presence may restrain Father. No, it must come to a head and before then I shall see if I can get something out of Elsie and Jane and if Mother goes to town to order provisions I shall search their room for that paper."

"You're really set on this aren't you?"

"Do you not want to know who our parents are and whether we are brother and sister?"

"Of course I do but it doesn't seem quite so urgent when I find you are not as enthusiastic about Arthur Herrington as I feared you might be."

She wanted to say, "What has that to do with it?" but she was not ready to bring such thoughts into the open. Since his kiss on the doorstep they hovered dangerously on the edge of her mind. All she could say in a sharp reply was, "Don't you suppose *Arthur* might want to know who I am?" And she turned and began to walk in the direction of Tom's cottage. He ran after her.

"So what are you going to do?"

"Tell Elsie what you saw in the paper."

"I'll come too but she mustn't speak of it till we're ready. Can you trust her?"

"If *you* wrest a promise from her she'll keep it. She almost worships you. You didn't notice yesterday but she never took her eyes off you."

They found Elsie alone since Billy had been sent to school and Jack was somewhere in the woodland fetching kindling for their fire. She was very grubby from clearing a fall of soot that had come down the kitchen chimney and her efforts to wipe her face when she saw them at the back door only made it worse.

"What d'you want, Kate? I'm all in a mess. Don't you come in Master Kenneth and get it on your boots."

Kate grinned to herself at 'Master Kenneth.' She and Elsie had had no ceremony themselves during the years since Bet had disappeared.

Kenneth came in anyway saying, "We need to talk to you, Elsie, and I'll help you clear up at the same time. Give me that pan and brush and you sit down a minute and listen to what Kate has to say."

Elsie's mouth hung open but he took the things from her and

pushed her down onto a kitchen chair. Kate sat opposite her and began at once.

"Elsie, I think you've always known from your mother that our parents didn't tell us everything about the day we were born."

"Oh Kate," she cried in alarm, "not *that* again. You've asked me before –"

Kenneth looked round from the hearth. "We know more now. I've seen a newspaper report. You've got to tell us what you know."

"How could there be newspaper reports after all this time?"

"Never mind that. Rumours are in the air."

"Oh dear, it's not that message that got sent to Mr Reid a while ago is it? I never opened it. I made Jack take it at first light so no one would see him but it started snowing. I was afraid if he left footprints it 'ud be known where it came from but he said the snow kept falling and covered them up. Our Mam's letter said not to say who'd sent it. She said she didn't agree with sending it but Luigi had insisted."

Kate had not expected this. "Elsie, I didn't know you'd heard from your mother since she went away? You never told me."

"She said not to. And I kept it from Father. She's calling herself Madame Manzini now she's gone to Italy, pretending she married that Luigi. She did write that she still loved us and hoped we were doing all right." And to Kate's distress Elsie burst into tears.

What she had said though was crucial. The message that had upset their parents came from Luigi Manzini. Kate looked at Kenneth who nodded round at her. But what had Luigi said? Was it blackmail? If so it seemed it had never been followed up. At least, she thought, I can show Father it was not supernatural.

"Elsie," she said, "don't cry. I knew Father had a message that bothered him but it was some time ago. What we want now is to get to the truth. Did your mother ever tell you that we were adopted? There I've said it out loud and you must tell us."

Elsie nodded several times but could only produce a whispered 'Yes.'

Kenneth went outside with his shovelful of soot and filled the sack that stood by the wall. When he came back in he met Kate's eyes and saw the same shock and relief in his. The word had been spoken. What would follow was still hidden.

Kate handed Elsie her handkerchief. "Thank you for telling us."

Elsie dried the mixture of soot and tears on her cheeks and looked pleadingly at Kate. "You won't let on I told you? My father doesn't know. Only Jane and my Mam knew and the people in the hotel in Leith."

"We've heard from another source. You'll never be in trouble for saying it, Elsie. And did your mother say we were not twins at all?"

Now Elsie's eyes widened with astonishment. "Oh no, she always said you was twins. Saved from a shipwreck. I don't remember the name of the ship."

Kate felt her throat contracting. "Was it *Gannet*?"

"Ay. It was a seabird. I think it was *Gannet*."

Kenneth broke in. "We'll leave it there, Elsie. You've only confirmed what we already suspected. Nothing more will be said that need bother you. Don't mention this to anyone. If you hear it talked about it has come to us another way and you'll know we have not attributed it to you. There, I've cleared the soot but I'm sure you will clean up further."

"Oh but you shouldn't have, Master Kenneth. Look there's a bucket of fresh water from the pump. You'd better wash before you go. I am ashamed I can't give you a hot drink till Jack comes back with kindling for the fire."

While Kenneth washed his hands Elsie looked pitifully at Kate. "I never wanted anything hid between us you know but Mam said if the master didn't want it known it wasn't her place to tell only she didn't see why they minded. It amused her I think that our father believed what he was told. As for the message Jack took maybe –if she'd told that horrid Luigi – he thought he could make money from it."

"Maybe it doesn't matter now." Kate wanted to hug her but she shrank back.

"Don't now, Kate, you'll mark your dress." She looked at Kenneth with adoration. "Go now while you're clean and I'll not say you've been here at all."

She almost shooed them out.

They were silent as they walked back by the field path. Kate was saying over and over in her head, who are our parents? I need, I need to know.

At last Kenneth spoke. "Well, Father and Mother didn't lie about us being twins. They were told so and believed it."

Kate turned her face to him, biting her lip. "They are *not* our father and mother and if that paper was right we are not brother and sister either. Our world has fallen apart. I am wandering in a great desert from which every landmark has been removed and I know not which way to go."

"Oh Kate." He took her in his arms. "We've got each other. Nothing can ever separate *us*."

She gazed into his eyes. She felt the strength of his arms. She couldn't breathe.

"No." She pulled away. "I can't. No. Not now." She broke into a run. She had to do something, find certainty somewhere. When she was nearly at the gate into the back garden she looked back and saw him coming slowly by the edge of the cattle pasture. Had she hurt him? Oh she didn't want to do that but she must find her own way out of the desert.

She ran up the sloping lawn and into the dining-room by the French windows. Jane was there drawing out a leaf of the table.

She looked up, her eyebrows imperious. "You tell me, Kate. Can we sit twelve in comfort without the other leaf? The master says four grandparents, two uncles, your Aunt Adelaide and Kenneth's godfather and the four of you. It's an odd business for he's never wanted to entertain all the years since he married your mother."

Kate stepped up to the table and leaning her hands on it hissed at Jane, "But she's not my mother, is she and he's not my father and you've always known it and never said."

Jane cupped one hand over her ear. "What? What are you saying?"

"You heard me, Jane."

"Well, who's told you that? Have you been over to the cottage? I didn't know Elsie knew."

"It's nothing to do with Elsie. Kenneth found it out when he was away. Why did you let Mother pretend? She's always listened to you."

Jane shook her head like a horse with an uncomfortable bit and bridle.

"Nay, *I'll* not be blamed. The master took on so about it. He got that he believed it himself. I went along with it for the sake of his sanity. What difference does it make? They've been father and mother to you."

"What difference! I *had* a father and a mother and I want to know who they were and all about them."

"You'll not learn that from anyone. *I* don't know. A big rough ship owner fetched that Bet Moray with the babies and said there was no one left of friends or family for the ones that hadn't been in the wreck had all gone off to Canada. Just these twin babes were left with no one to take care of 'em. *That's* how you got a family. And now Kenneth's had the sense to stop gallivanting about the world everything can settle down again."

"So you believe we are twins?"

"What else would two newborn babes be? I can't think where Kenneth could have found anything out after all these years. Has he been up in the far north where the wreck happened?"

"No. It doesn't matter how. He's heard things. Jane, do you know where Mother keeps that little diary she had a long time ago with a jewelled clasp? It used to be in her reticule but it's not now."

"What do you think I am? I don't go prying into your mother's things."

She slid the leaf of the table back into its place. "We don't need it yet but I reckon one leaf will do. Now you stop worrying and fretting and accept that you've got parents that's brought you up and done right by you and leave well alone. I don't want no upsets in my old age." And she hobbled out of the room on her arthritic legs and went into the kitchen where Kate could hear her scolding Sarah for letting the broth boil over on the fire.

Kate was contrite. She had been harsh with Jane which was quite contrary to her usual nature. She had broken away from Kenneth too. But she was still driven by a longing to find her mother's diary. She looked in the small parlour but Mother was not there. She went back to the kitchen.

"Where's Mother?" she asked Jane.

"Why the Master drove her into town to take his letters to the station so they would go quickly and then they were to buy her a new gown at Madame de Voisin."

"Mother a new gown! Well!"

"Oh ay, I know, everything's changed since the young master came home." She gave Kate a pointed look.

"Yes, I'm sorry, Jane." She kissed the wrinkled face and hurried out, closing the kitchen door behind her. She heard the French windows click and Kenneth came through the dining-room into the hallway. He looked at her warily so she ran to him and grabbed his hand. "Father and Mother are both out. We must search their room."

"Oh, the diary?" She nodded and they bounded up the stairs.

The best bedroom looked down the front drive and boasted a four poster bed, a wedding present from the Reids. Kate began pulling out drawer after drawer of the tall chest standing against the wall next to the bed. As befitted the best bedroom there was a small dressing-room off it and Kenneth began to rummage in there.

After a few fruitless minutes Kate said, "It won't be anywhere obvious, like a drawer or cupboard. She wouldn't want Father to find it. That was why it was in her reticule. He abhorred the clutter of things in there. So where else might he *not* look?"

"Her bookshelf? He is not interested in her novel reading."

Kate agreed and began to peer among the books to see if it was hidden between any of them. Kenneth came round and lifted out the fattest and heaviest which was a volume of Richardson's *Pamela*.

"Kate! Look!" Behind it flat against the back of the bookshelf was a small book with embossed flowers and a jewelled clasp. He held it up.

"That's it. Oh let me see."

She took it and opened to the back page. There were the Gaelic words.

"Thank God. Oh Kenneth, here is the date 1819 and that must

be the Gaelic for May and there are the names I saw beginning with A – Alistair Gunn and Annie something, not Gunn. Can these be our parents? And look, the word '*Gannet*', the name of the boat. And there is Annie again. What can it be saying?"

"You'll have to copy it out and put the book back."

Kate took the notepad of 'Facts' and 'Suspicious happenings' out of her pocket.

"I will, I will but see first how the diary is blank after our supposed birthday in May. Before that it reads, 'Ridley is enthusiastic about steamboats. He has taken Tom on an excursion to Bo'ness. I decided not to go. They are noisy and smelly. Jane will keep me company,' And then it stops and she hasn't written another word."

Kenneth went to the window and looked to the road. "We'll hear the carriage but pray start copying. You write more quickly and much neater than I."

Resting the notepad on the bedside table she turned to a clean page and copied the words, commenting as she wrote, "But there are only these two names and that scrawl in the middle which may be a signature. It can't be a record of the passengers on the boat. No, of course!" She looked up at him, pencil poised. "These are the babies' names. And the surnames *are* different. That must be it. They are *our* names. You are Alistair and I am Annie. Grandmother Reid's name! *She'll* be pleased."

She felt her eyes filling with tears. Am I truly called Annie? But she went on writing till it was done. Kenneth took the diary from her and placed it exactly where it had been and lifted Volume I of *Pamela* in front. He looked round to make sure all was tidy as before, then took her hand and led her out of the room.

"We don't know anything for sure yet, Kate. *I'm* not ready to take on a new identity. Do you really think Elsie will be able to translate it?"

"I don't know. Oh Kenneth I'm sorry I left you so abruptly. I had to do something. I had to find this."

"Do you feel less lost and alone?"

"I don't know. I'm bewildered, but it's good with you beside me.

Only I've got to know who I am. I've got to know the whole truth and it keeps eluding us. Let's go back to Elsie now."

Elsie had washed the hearth and every surface in the kitchen. Jack had been back and made a fire and gone out again and she was sitting at the scrubbed table with a hunk of bread and cheese and the tea-kettle bubbling on the hearth. She was surprised to see them but pleased at the state of the room.

"Don't let us interrupt you," Kate said, "but can you look at that and tell us if you know what it means." She laid the notebook on the table.

"Oh my! It's so long since Mam went and she didn't talk Gaelic to us very much and I didn't hardly ever see it written down, just in a few songs."

"Try. Are any of the words 'baby'?"

"I think that is 'to marry' for it comes in a song I knew and 'an diugh' is 'today'. It might be saying this Alistair is marrying Annie on that day in May."

"I thought they must be the babies' names."

"Eh I don't know. That's *Gannet,* the name of the ship and that says the town of Helmsdale."

"What is this below the scrawl?"

"That's the word for 'marry' again and that last word 'daoine' means 'men' I think. You see Gaelic sounds different from the way it's written. My Mam could never have spelt it right for she couldn't read till she worked for your family and then it was English she learnt off my father. She knew the words of the songs though."

Kenneth picked up the notepad. "Don't worry about it. Thank you for trying."

She looked up at him, quite distressed. "I wish I could help more."

Kate's frustration had deepened. If Elsie was right the document now appeared to be the record of a marriage. Captains of ships, she had read, could marry people, but one couple only was named. Perhaps she or Kenneth was illegitimate and the parents had been trying to put that right when they were in peril of their lives. But the fact was she was no nearer being sure of anything. The paper Kenneth had read was snatched from him. His recollection was that it stated they had different parents. Had he read it correctly?

They thanked Elsie again and left her to her modest meal.

As they walked back Kenneth said, "We have moved at least one coincidence to the status of fact. We *are* the babies from the wreck."

"Oh yes, *Jane* confirmed that. But *she* believes we are twins."

"We have to go to Canisbay and talk to the dumb man."

She stood still, quivering with excitement. "Let's go at once."

He laughed. "We couldn't get there and back before the party and I haven't a penny for the journey. I couldn't ask Father if he still has some of the trust money."

She stamped her foot. "I save the allowance Father gives me. There might be enough. And if we went away there wouldn't be a party, would there?"

He shook his head. "I would feel wicked doing a vanishing act again. No, I have been thinking that maybe it *is* a good idea to use the family gathering to tell them we know we're adopted. I would be expected to make a little speech, thanking them for coming and Father and Mother for arranging it, and perhaps an apology for the way I went off. Then I could express our gratitude to our parents for saving us from the fate that would certainly have been ours if they hadn't taken us in. I suppose we would have been handed over to a charity that looked after orphans and ended up scrubbing floors in a workhouse."

"Oh Kenneth, you're right. I hadn't thought of that at all."

He laughed again. "I go more slowly than you but it gives time for my mind to weigh things up."

She felt suddenly happier. "We are very different, aren't we?" She clutched his arm and her feet pranced beside his more measured tread. Inside she was thinking, I need firmness and steadiness. Arthur follows my every whim. Oh if I could know that this solid man I am holding onto is *not* my brother? Could I ever forget he was? I *must* know. The suspense is fearful.

All the same, her excitement soared and the wilderness panic lifted.

They went back into the house, found that the carriage had returned and her mother was impatient to show her the new gown for the party.

"You really must tell me, my sweetie, if it makes me look stout."

28

The first carriage to arrive was the Stokoes', and Kate, stepping out to meet them with her mother and father, was astonished to see Arthur Herrington descend first and hold out his hand to Aunt Adelaide and then Grandmother Ida. There was no sign of Grandfather Stokoe.

Aunt Adelaide was the first to greet them. "Father's laid low with the gout, sister," she told Clara, "but Mother said we must have a man so we've brought *him*." She jerked her finger at Arthur who had given his arm to Ida and was progressing across the gravel at her halting pace.

"Bother!" muttered Kate and her father standing beside her chuckled. "You don't want to marry him?" He actually put an arm round her waist and gave her a squeeze. "That's my girl. Stay with your loving father."

She gritted her teeth and said nothing. Kenneth, the other side of their mother, had his eye on her. He lifted his brows with a little half smile and then they were engulfed in the ceremony of polite greetings.

Arthur, nervous and blushing, came to her side. "Dear Kate, do not be angry with me for coming. I die for the sight of you and when Mrs Stokoe sent to me that your grandfather could not possibly recover and they needed –"

"I know, I know. I expect she's still afraid of highwaymen. This is the nineteenth century. You could all have come by train."

"You are not cross with me? You know I have passed all my examinations and can practise medicine with my father? He will set us up in such a charming little house next to his that is available to rent after the summer. We can be married in the autumn." He was murmuring all this as they walked in and went up the stairs to the seldom-used drawing room above the dining-room and overlooking the garden and the fields. It was a sparkling April day of intermittent sun and showers. Kate wished she could be walking down through the fields to the wooded valley that lay hidden from their sight.

Royce, the Reids' butler, who had been sent ahead with their cook and two maids by train the day before, was ready to hand round drinks. He had been very put out, Kate noticed, by the family's country habit of going out to welcome their guests. He had evidently expected to announce the arrivals as they mounted the stairs but his gravity remained unshaken. Arthur received from him two glasses of wine and continued to appropriate her company by ensconcing her on the corner sofa and bending affectionately over her as she sipped her wine.

Compelled to answer him she said, "I have promised you an answer on my eighteenth birthday. I will keep my promise." What difference, she wondered, will Kenneth's speech make to Arthur's proposal? Will he still want to marry the daughter of unknown peasants from a highland glen, perhaps born out of wedlock too? Will his family want me living next door in that charming little house?

The Reids arrived and Cousin Cuthbert from Durham who had travelled by train as an experiment and was talking very loudly about how unpleasant it was. Kate watched Kenneth circulating among the guests. He was acting the gentleman very well but she felt inclined to laugh.

The amusement died when she looked at her mother trying so hard to do everything right and very much in awe of Royce and the starched maids. Then she observed how her father was astonishing everyone, especially the Reid grandparents and uncles with his good humour, almost amounting to hilarity. Neither of them knew that an earthquake would shortly erupt beneath them. She was aware too that Jane had taken to her bed for the duration of the party. She had told Clara, "You don't need my ugly old face around when you've got such smart help." But Kate wondered if she sensed that the eruption might be about to happen and preferred not to be there.

What if Kenneth's courage fails him at the last moment, she asked herself. Will all this bonhomie be too much for him? It was I who first suggested such a public unveiling. Will I be able to step in if he loses heart for it? Everyone thinks I am sweet as sugar and spice but there is steel in me. I can build up anger thinking how Father and Mother have lied to us over the years. I could do it now, but I know Kenneth is waiting till everyone is well fed and wined. I will be patient.

"Pray allow me to bring you another glass," murmured Arthur at her ear and she realised he had been telling her about the 'charming little house' which had a gazebo in the garden and a stable for his horse.

She stood up, "No thank you, Arthur, I never have more than one. If you will excuse me I must speak with my Grandmother Reid. I have scarce exchanged two words with her yet and I am very fond of her."

"Of course. Let me escort you across the room and pay my own compliments to her. She is as you say, a very special lady who performs many compassionate works among the poor of Newcastle."

There was no shaking him off. Grandmother Reid greeted them both warmly.

"Kenneth looks robust after his adventures. I see a maturity in him that was lacking before. I always thought he would make a tough man with a good heart. Oaks grow slow and steady and he is of the oak species I believe."

"And Kate is a perfect flower, is she not?" Arthur said. "A sweet rose."

"Roses are prickly," Kate retorted and Grandmother Reid laughed.

Grandfather Reid sitting the other side of Grandmother beckoned Kenneth over.

"Well, lad, there is still room for you in the coal business you know. Your uncles are in no hurry to settle down and I need a grandson to secure the future of Reid and Sons. I know why you left Durham School. I made inquiries and learnt that it is in a sorry state at present. You should have told us and we could have put you in somewhere else but I suppose you reckon you learnt more of life on your travels. Well, there's no better way to learn the coal trade than study it from inside."

"I think I am more inclined to farming, sir, but I have a piece of business to attend to first."

"Farming! Huh! And I hope the piece of business is not a woman. You are too young to be entangled with that sort of thing." He glanced at Kate and Arthur. "It's all right for your sister. Dr Herrington is settled in his profession."

"It is not a woman, sir. Ah, I believe Royce wishes to say they are ready downstairs."

Royce cleared his throat. "Ladies and gentlemen, dinner is served."

Grandfather Reid got up, grunting. "My joints are getting stiff. Ridley should have a more commodious place where the sitting and eating are on one floor." He put his hand on Kenneth's shoulder. "You won't make money in farming, boy, that's certain, unless you own great estates like Lord Allendale."

The company descended to the dining-room where Kate saw that both leaves of the table were out which made more space to show off the best cutlery and china but squeezed her father, at the head of the table, against the glass cabinet behind him.

Aunt Adelaide and Cousin Cuthbert from Durham had been placed next to each other and he recounted his train journey to her in detail although she said at the outset that she would never trust herself to those terrible engines. Kenneth sat between the two grandmothers and Kate between Arthur and Grandfather Reid who, when he was not talking about coal, threw out remarks which appeared to assume that their engagement was a settled thing. Arthur did nothing to contradict this and Kate tried but was talked down by George Reid who liked the sound of no voice but his own.

Thinking of what was to come she was not hungry. There were too many courses which she was not used to and she kept looking across the table to catch Kenneth's eye and draw courage from his cheerful grin.

At last the final dishes were cleared away and the servants had withdrawn.

Her father, cautiously because of the tight space, stood up to address the company.

"Dear friends, we do not follow city ways here in the country and I am not asking the ladies to run away so that we men can indulge ourselves with port."

"Shame!" cried his brother Martin. "That's the best time at a party."

There was uneasy laughter. Everyone knew Ridley's puritanical habits and George Reid frowned his youngest son down very heavily.

Ridley ignored the interruption. "I only want to say that we are celebrating the return of our son Kenneth who has given three years of his life to travelling the world and undergoing much hardship with great stoicism. I did not sanction his going which seemed to be prompted by strange influences which he knew not how to combat, but I believe, with the help of Almighty God and our own prayers for his spiritual well-being, he has mastered them and come home in a quiet spirit of submission to his mother and myself."

Kate glanced at Kenneth's reddening face. His fists were clenched together and he was staring down at the table.

Their father went on, "He has told me that the prosperity of Allenbrae Farm is the goal of his life and I need hardly say that this delights me mightily and I now feel that the son we were so proud to bring into the world is all that we hoped for." He looked at Kate. "And I will not leave out the daughter who has given us joy all her life and whom I hope to keep here a while longer. In any event her mother and I would trust that we would never lose her altogether. She and her brother are bone of our bone and flesh of our flesh and that will always be the case. We will love and cherish them as long as we live upon this earth. In a few weeks they will be eighteen but though their birthday has not yet arrived we will drink their healths. Pray raise your glasses to Kenneth and Kate."

Kate would have loved to leap up and run from the room. But what was to come had to happen and had to be endured. If Kenneth did not speak she would do it herself. She kept her hands tightly clasped between her knees, her head low. The drinking and clapping subsided and she heard with a sudden quickening of her heartbeat the scraping of Kenneth's chair on the floor as he stood up to reply.

"Thank you all." His voice came out thin and hoarse and he cleared his throat.

At once Cousin Cuthbert cried out, "Don't be nervous, lad. You sound just as I did when I gave my first sermon."

There was a general laugh and Kate saw it gave Kenneth a chance to swallow and square his shoulders and look round at all the faces.

"Thank you all for coming and Father and Mother for deciding to hold a celebration for anything as unimportant as my return. I grant that I went off a boy and I hope I returned a man. I don't think I was impelled by anything stranger than a longing for travel and adventure" – Kate saw their father shaking his head – "but I learnt to endure pain and discomfort and gained a knowledge of men –"

"And women I wager," Martin chuckled. Kate was sure he was tipsy.

"Not women," Kenneth said sternly. "Please don't interrupt, Uncle Martin, I have something important to say."

"That's put you in your place," Peter muttered.

Kenneth drew a deep breath. "I won't say any more about my travels. You've all asked me and I've answered most of your questions as well as I could but now I must thank Father for the good things he has said about me and especially about Kate who deserves much more praise than I and then I want to thank him and Mother for bringing us up and caring for us all these years."

It's coming now, Kate thought, and hid her face in her hands.

Kenneth paused for a second and then brought out in a rush, "They couldn't have done more for us if they had been our real parents so Kate and I owe them our eternal gratitude." He sat down.

Exclamation marks hung in the air for half a second.

"*What* did he say?" roared George Reid.

Kate dropped her hands to look from her mother to her father. Both appeared stunned. Everyone else was exchanging puzzled looks and murmuring questions.

Kate felt compelled to break in with a slightly hysterical laugh. "Didn't you all realise a long time ago that we were adopted?"

At the word her mother screamed and her father leapt to his feet, shoving his chair backward so that it fell against the cabinet and shattered the glass. Several ladies shrieked at this but Ridley Reid seemed completely unaware of it. He was pointing at Kenneth with a rigid arm and accusing finger.

"The devil has *not* left him. The father of lies still has hold of him."

His mother stood up and said in a level voice, "You are bleeding, Ridley. A piece of glass has grazed your forehead." She looked round the table. "I don't think this news is a surprise. I have long suspected it. The twins are nothing like the Reids or the Stokoes."

Aunt Adelaide said in a clear voice, "*I* never believed Clara had them herself. She's barren."

Ida Stokoe was fanning herself furiously. "Clara, it's not true! You *told* me."

Clara half rose but slumped back again. "I can't talk about it, Mother. Ridley's hurt."

He had put one of the napkins to his head and was looking at the bloodstain in bewilderment. Everyone was getting to their feet now. Kate, only two places away, slipped behind Grandfather Reid who was shouting, "Is it true? When were you told, boy?"

Going to her father she took his arm.

"Come to the kitchen and I'll wash the blood. Mind where you put your feet. I'll send one of the maids to sweep up the glass."

"Sensible girl," Grandmother Reid said.

"What glass? What glass?" Ridley was looking into Kate's eyes as if he didn't know where he was. She drew him out of the room and found Sarah at the door.

"I'm sorry, Miss Kate, but Mr Royce told me to see what had happened."

"Father's chair fell against the cabinet. Can you fetch a brush and shovel and sweep it up before anyone walks in it? Put the big pieces in a bucket but take care."

Sarah scampered to do her bidding and Kate, leading her father, announced to the curious servants who were washing up, "An unfortunate accident. Perhaps, Mr Royce, you would be so kind as to go to the dining-room and advise our guests to leave the table at the window end and go up to the drawing-room. I'm sure someone could be spared to serve tea up there as soon as possible."

He bowed. "Tea in the drawing-room is already laid out and the kettle will be sent up directly." He went over to the dining-room door and Kate heard him saying, "All will be well in a moment, ladies and gentlemen, but pray do not try to come round this end of the table. I beg you to make your way up to the drawing-room where tea will be served."

Royce's presence silenced the intense gabbling that had been going on and a subdued company took to the stairs in silence only to break out in talk when they realised the drawing-room was momentarily empty of servants.

Kate had found a clean cloth and washed away the trickle of blood on her father's head and saw the wound was no more than a scratch. "Keep that in your hand," she said, "and if you feel it start to run down again just dab it. It's not deep enough to warrant a bandage. Shall we go back to the drawing-room?"

"But what happened?" He was holding her arm as if he couldn't stand upright without help.

"Jane was right," she said. "Jane thought one leaf of the table would be enough. The people would have been a little squashed but your chair would not have been so close to the glass cabinet. Fortunately no one else was near enough to be hurt."

"The cabinet is broken? What a pity! We have had it all our lives. Yes, I must go back to my guests."

As she led him into the hall he looked through the dining-room door at the clearing-up operations in progress.

"Dear me!" He paused to speak to the maids. "Mind you get every speck up."

Then he addressed himself to the stairs, turning to Kate as he took hold of the banister. "We had finished dinner, I hope. Were there not speeches?"

"Oh yes, all done. It was when you were getting up the chair fell back."

They reached the drawing-room door which stood open and as they went in the buzz of conversation died.

It was George Reid who stepped forward and grabbed Ridley's other arm.

"You're all right then? I thought heaven was dropping vengeance from the skies. Well, the boy's been telling us how he came to find out and it's such a strange story it must be true. But what in heaven's name did you think you were doing? If you and Clara couldn't have children did you think the family would be angry if you adopted some? We're not monsters but we don't like deception."

Kate peered at her father's face. Bewilderment was giving way to a dark fury in his eyes. He pulled away from them both and drew himself up, a small firework about to explode. His head jerked towards her.

"I knew there was something said. You tried to bamboozle me. So the devil has been at work in here." Now his glance swept round them all like a scythe and lighted on Kenneth standing behind Clara's chair. Kate saw that she was flopped with her head down and her hands covering her ears.

"Have they believed your lies?" Ridley screeched at Kenneth. "It is what I feared. First you run from me to Newcastle, then to Durham and then to the uttermost parts of the earth and now, finally you are trying to cut yourself away for ever. And I thought you were cured. I was so happy. Why did I bring together our friends and family but to rejoice with me over the son I had lost and found again?" He paused for breath. "You had better all go home."

"Is it convenient for tea to be served now, sir?"

Kate saw that Royce had accompanied the girl with the tea-kettle.

"Set it down," she told him. "We'll serve it ourselves."

He bowed and withdrew without a flicker of expression on his bland face. The girl, though, was round-eyed and open-mouthed. Kate shut the door firmly behind them.

Grandmother Reid rose from her chair and sailed across the room like a galleon. "Enough of this, Ridley. Clara has confirmed that the twins were adopted and that you have all but persuaded yourself that they are your own. Accept Kenneth's words of gratitude for their upbringing and start a new life on a sound basis of truth and openness."

Ridley looked up at his mother. "They *are* our own. I lifted two naked newborn babes from her and laid them on her breast. I can see it now."

Clara screamed out, "Don't listen to him. He put me through hell. He has put me through hell all these years. I never wanted lies."

Kate yearned to run to her but she saw Kenneth bend over the back of her chair and take hold of her hands and squeeze them. "We'll start afresh with you, Mother. We understand. We know you've loved us all these years."

Aunt Adelaide who hadn't sat down yet remarked to Cousin Cuthbert, "You see what happens when women do what men tell them? Disaster all round. We are the ones with commonsense."

"I dispute that, Madame," he retorted, "but all I want to know is where the babies came from. I couldn't make out what Kenneth was saying about a newspaper report."

Arthur Herrington was making his way round to Kate. "*I* don't care where they came from," he told everyone. "Kate is still Kate. My dearest, it makes no difference to my feelings at all."

Ridley had left go of her and was jerking his head from one to other as the remarks flew about.

"Why are you believing their lies?" he burst out. "Jane was there. Jane knows. Where is Jane?"

The door opened behind Kate. Jane, wrapped in a woolly bed-gown stood in the doorway. She stuck out her jaw at her master.

"I couldn't help hearing all the commotion. So you want me to back you up, Mr Reid, is that it? Well it's no good. The game's up. I knew the young folks were getting suspicious a while ago and now it's out. The babes came quite by chance. Mrs Reid saw them in the street, brought ashore in a basket from a ship. Bet Moray, the young woman with them was feeding one openly so Mrs Reid kindly told me to fetch her up to our hotel room so she could do it in private."

Kate saw her father shaking his head in disbelief. He broke into cries of "No, no, never, none of that."

Jane went on addressing the company. "Then I fetched up the ship owner who had brought the babes. He said they were saved from a wreck and had no family left. He had a paper about them which he gave Mr Reid." She turned suddenly on him in the midst of his protests. "What did you do with that paper eh?"

Ridley thrust his hands through his hair. "Paper! There was no paper. I burnt it."

There was a general exclamation and Jane laughed in his face.

Kate suddenly knew this had gone on long enough. She seized his arm again.

"Come away, Father. You've admitted it. And don't worry about burning the paper. It has been copied and we know how to learn more about our true parentage."

She almost dragged him to the door as he broke into hysterical sobs. Jane stepped aside but jerked her head at Clara, her eyebrows telling her to come too.

Kate said to the company, "Please stay. I am taking Father to bed. I know this has been very distressing for you all but pray partake of the tea and comfort Mother. Kenneth, you can pour out."

"Nay," said Jane. "You stay, Kate. Clara, pet, you come with me. You're in a right state yourself and I can give you both a soothing draught that'll calm you down."

Kate saw her mother begin to struggle out of her chair. She was moaning, "I can't face him. He'll be so angry with me. I did copy it. Oh goodness, you must have seen it, Kate. Was that how – oh dear. He'll never forgive me."

Kate was amazed at the way Jane took them both under her wing like distressed children. She seemed rejuvenated by their helplessness, hustling them across the landing to the door of their bedroom. She had always been the solid presence in the background but now she was the power in the house. Kate was thankful as she saw all three disappear into the room and the door close upon them.

"Jane was always a treasure!" cried Grandmother Ida. "*I* couldn't soothe Clara. She was too ashamed of the lies she told me. Eh, those letters sent from Edinburgh! Henry took in all that nonsense but I couldn't believe I wouldn't have known my own girl was having a baby, two babies at that! And then she was churched if you please, when they came home with them. Henry's not going to like it when I tell him." She shook her fist at George and Anne Reid. "Your son's had her terrified. That's what it was. I wish I'd never let her marry him."

"Now you're being silly, Mother," Adelaide said. "Stop talking and drink this tea." Kenneth was taking cups round on a tray and begging everyone to settle down.

Kate went to help him. "Well, it's done," she whispered, "and you see the madness Mother and I have sometimes had to face. I don't know if he'll ever recover, but thank God for Jane."

Grandmother Reid took a cup as the tray reached her. "I am so glad this thing has come to light. I believe I have always known and I only regret I didn't challenge Ridley at the beginning before it became a thing entrenched in his mind."

Beside her, George growled, "I don't like them not being our grandchildren. We don't know who they are now."

"To me they will always be my grandchildren," Anne Reid said. "As dear as my own sons. Yes," she added, looking pointedly at Peter and Martin, "I will still love Ridley. He didn't want to be a coal owner. He had a dream of a country paradise with children playing about his knees and this has been his way of achieving it."

George got to his feet. "*I'm* not going to be blamed for his madness. And I don't want any tea either. Peter, go and find Royce and tell him to see the carriages brought round. The best thing we can all do is go home."

Peter nodded and went out. Martin, who had managed to finish off the last of the wine, was nodding in his chair.

Kenneth looked round at them all. Kate saw tears had come into his eyes when Anne Reid had spoken of their father. "I trust you can all be our family still. I intend to take steps to find our true identity but we never want to lose all of you." Kate heard the hint of a sob in his voice.

Grandmother Reid said, "*Is* there more you can do? I thought the clues were at the bottom of Gibraltar harbour."

"There are some more lines of inquiry open and I promise to tell you anything I find out."

Teacups were set down and there was an unspoken agreement that no effort would be made to say a farewell to the host and hostess. A general surge downstairs began and found Royce and the maids lined up in the hallway with coats and shawls.

Arthur Herrington tried to snatch a kiss from Kate but she avoided him. "You will hear from me," she promised. "I have to know who I am first."

He shook his head in desperation. "My Kate, always."

She gave all the rest loving hugs and when the door finally closed on them all, she put her back to it and glared at Kenneth. "What was that about *you* taking steps to find our true identity? We do it together. We go to Canisbay."

"I thought of trying to obtain this book the carpenter fellow wrote."

"No no, let us go to the source direct. Do you not want to meet the man who saved our lives?"

"I do, I do, but can we? I have no money."

"I have my savings and Father told me only yesterday that there is still trust money from the grandfathers. Yours was not all spent on schooling."

"And yours is for your dowry."

"Only the Stokoe money was for that and I may never need it. We must go to Canisbay. I feel it calling me." He stroked his chin. It was a gesture she knew he had picked up from Ridley.

"I wonder if we did right. It was mighty unpleasant."

"Oh Kenneth, when a limb's gangrenous a surgeon cuts it off. It hurts but it has to be done. I pray it will be like that for him."

Jane came down the stairs. "Well, they are asleep in each other's arms. I had a hunch you were planning this, Kenneth. Tell me tomorrow how you found out." She gave a sigh which turned into a yawn. "Maybe it's for the best. I'm for my bed too. I'm keeping out of the kitchen while the troops are still there."

Kate gave her a hug. "Jane, you are a miracle worker."

"Nay, pet, a good dose of laudanum in their mug of chocolate. Goodnight."

She headed back up the stairs.

"Can I have a hug too?" Kenneth said.

29

Two weeks later Kenneth and Kate stood on the quayside in Newcastle waiting for the steam packet.

Clara had pleaded, "It was this time of year that you babies encountered the great storm."

Kenneth said, "But we are going by steamboat – immune to wind and waves."

Now Kate saw the packet arriving and was surprised at its modest size. It was smaller than the big sailing ships she could see moored further downstream. Kenneth had pointed them out. "I sailed on one like that to the West Indies." He is a seasoned traveller, she thought, and I have been nowhere.

The baggage had been carried aboard and the passengers were now pressing forward. Kenneth took her hand as they crossed the gangplank. She looked down and could see the Tyne slapping its burden of coal dust against the stone wall. Every new sight, even this, filled her with excitement and a shiver of apprehension.

When they were underway and heading down river amid a clutter of shipping, she seized his arm. "You can have no notion how strange and bewildering everything is to me. But for you – merely voyaging up the coast of Britain!"

He looked down at her with a smile that lit his whole face. "We are on the way to our goal. Our journey is sanctioned by all the family. And I have you with me."

His answer delighted her but she couldn't help saying, "You have not *Father's* sanction. He told you the trust money was for *his own* children. If we claimed to be his we couldn't have it."

"Yes, but he relented when the good old grandfathers wrote that we must."

She mused on this while her eyes darted hither and thither, taking in the huge warehouses, the cranes and the ever widening river as they approached the sea.

"He didn't relent, Kenneth. He couldn't fight it, that's all. He became cold and silent but Mother is still afraid of his anger. I wanted to clear up everything before we left but she said, 'Don't mention the note. He'd be angry with Jack for bringing it.' She is sure it was Bet's doing, resuming the blackmail she had to endure but she daren't tell him about that either. Did you hear the exact wording of the note?"

"Yes, simply 'The twins have different parents. They should be told.'"

"Different! From each other?"

"No, she took it to mean different from *them*. That we should know we were adopted. It didn't contain any threat. I don't think it was blackmail. Perhaps Luigi felt that now we were growing up Bet should have made sure we knew. Italians are fierce about heredity I believe."

"Are they?" She gazed up at him, their surroundings momentarily forgotten. "Oh Kenneth, what if it meant 'different from each other'."

"Ah that is why I wasn't going to tell you what it said. It only adds to your 'wilderness' feeling."

She fell silent as they passed a huge four master where the sailors were on exercise furling and unfurling the sails. The activity compelled her to look. She was aghast. "How can they do that – so high up?"

"You get used to it."

"You did that?"

"The captain made everyone do it."

She was silent again.

"Kenneth," she said at last, "I don't want any more puzzles. I only want to live in the here and now but I can't help fearing for Mother. He has been so strange the last two weeks, avoiding us, walking wildly over the fields and when you cornered him in the lambing shed about the money – short snapping anger. He was better when he saw us packing up, as if he wanted us to go."

"Both Grandmothers invited her to stay with them but she clings to her duty to him. She told me so through her tears in her last goodbyes."

"Poor Mother, she has indeed stood by him." She broke off to exclaim, "Oh look at that mass of black rocks. What a fearful sight!"

"They are the Black Middens. Many a good ship has been wrecked on them."

"Oh Kenneth, we *will* be safe, won't we? Are we nearly at the open sea?"

He pointed to the smiling sky and calm water. "Conditions are perfect."

"Then I shall just stand here and hold the rail and take in the wonder of being at sea and not talk any more. We can do nothing now about the folk at home."

"As long as you stay forward of the funnel you will smell only the salt air. I will take a turn about the ship and come back to you."

It was nearly an hour before he returned and then he came with quick, excited steps. "Kate, have you the Gaelic paper handy or is it packed in our baggage?"

She drew it from the reticule she carried on her arm. "Why? Take care it doesn't blow away. The wind is rising."

"Don't be alarmed. There is always more breeze on the open sea. I have found a Scotsman who understands Gaelic. I got into conversation with him and he is willing to translate it for us."

"Oh!" Her heart raced. "I'll come with you."

The gentleman, large and be-whiskered, was in the saloon where most of the passengers had gathered. He took the paper and screwed a monocle into his eye.

"It is a statement of a marriage in May 1819 performed by the captain of a sloop, *Gannet,* of Helmsdale, between Alistair Gunn and Annie something."

"That was smudged in the original," Kenneth said.

"I see. And that I presume is the captain's signature but is also indecipherable. This part below must be by the man Gunn. It says 'I married Annie to bring up our children lawfully before God and men.'" He chuckled. "It sounds as if he is putting something right that he should have done earlier."

"Thank you. We are very grateful," Kate said, taking back the paper and turning abruptly away. She fumbled her way to the saloon door again and opened it only to be engulfed by the smoke from the stack. She drew back in and found Kenneth had followed her.

"Let's sit down here." He pointed to the wooden bench that went round the walls of the saloon. "You are upset by this."

"Elsie was right about a marriage. There is only one couple mentioned and one set of children."

"Suggesting we *are* brother and sister. That bothers you?" His eyes were searching hers.

She tried to answer steadily. "I am not Annie Something." Her lip trembled. "I didn't want more confusion. You were sure you knew what that newspaper said?"

"I *am* sure."

"But as the ship foundered could the paper have dropped in the barrel with us by mistake. Perhaps it doesn't apply to us at all."

He took off his hat and scratched his head. "It's true we know not how many passengers were on board, but the dumb man said the babies were of different parentage. Oh Kate, we will find out soon. We must contain ourselves till we reach Canisbay. Do what you said before. Enjoy the here and now."

She nodded and turned her head to look from the window at the distant Northumberland coast. It was green and low-lying but on the horizon were humps of blue hills. "Are those not the Cheviots we see from our back windows?"

Kenneth looked. "Yes indeed and see there, this nearer land is the Holy Island of Lindisfarne. We will enter Scottish waters in the next hour or so."

"Oh this is wonderful. I will be patient and savour every moment."

"You are not missing Arthur Herrington?"

"Who?" she said.

30

Rory-Beag was having a dripping day. Rain was streaming down the shop window and there was a constant plop-plop from a leak in the workroom roof. When the sound of that changed he knew the bucket was full and he must go and empty it in the tin bath in the kitchen. But there were tears too dropping on the *owl he was c*arving for Flora as a door stopper. When she hung out the washing the *wind* would bang the back door. This was to be a surprise for her. His mind though was taken up with the visit of the doctor to the Reverend Josiah which would be taking place this very minute. He didn't need any doctor to tell him that the minister was dying. His breathing had been shallow and laboured for many days.

He is happy, Rory-Beag kept telling himself. At turned eighty he is ready to go to his Maker but I cannot bear to lose him. Eighteen years ago I saw the young and healthy die around me but I was a boy and had seen so many disasters I was inured to them. Now I have had long peaceful years of communication with a friend who had the patience to read my replies. I cannot see that it will ever happen again and I will be so alone. Another minister will come to the Manse with his wife or his own housekeeper. *Flora will* marry Malcolm *the post-boy and I will be utterly bereft. I will have to come and* live here as Diarmad did and I should be thankful that I have a home and the means to live. But the loneliness . . .

A tear dropped on the hollow he had chiselled out for one of the owl's eyes and winked sadly at him. He wip*ed it away, smoothed out both the eye hollows* and became aware that *the plop-plop had cease*d. He looked up at the crack from which the drip had come and saw brightness behind it. A sunbeam fell across the workshop floor turning the grains of sawdust to flecks of gold. He walked through to the shop and opened the window and wiped the counter. The clouds were splitting to reveal a long streak of blue. Was God telling him to cease moaning on his own account or was this a sign that He had called the minister's soul and opened heaven to receive it?

He must run to the Manse and see. He had flung down his chisel when he checked himself. Be patient, the minister always said. Do not be impulsive. Finish the owl and take it to Flora. It will cheer her if she is in a house of death.

So he dabbed a little glu*e in each eye socket and reached for the beads* he had ready for the eyes. Just dipping them on one side in the glue he pressed them in, then set it upright on the iron stand into which he had already screwed it so that it would be heavy enough for its purpose. He stood back and decided it was a happy owl. As he did so he heard the bell on his shop counter ring. Bother. He didn't want a customer now. He wanted to go to the Manse.

Walking through to the shop he could make out two figures, male and female, but the light dazzled him so that he didn't lift his eyes but covered the lower part of his face with his hand as he always did when strangers appeared. Judging by their clothes they were strangers.

The woman spoke. "Are you Rory-Beag?"

He nodded. Someone in the village must have directed them to him.

"Well, Rory-Beag" – her voice was gentle – "we are glad to meet you Rory-Beag because we think we are your babies."

Babies! His whole body convulsed. The word always stabbed him with longing and the pain of dashed hopes. But what else had she said? He lifted his eyes now and tried to focus them on her face. He stared. He had died and gone to heaven with the minister. She was there smiling that little half smile he loved. He reached his hands to touch her and she met them with her own and grasping them began to sing in a sweet voice an old Gaelic song. In his head he uttered the word, "Mary," but it came out a grunt.

She said, "Do you know that song? Do you recognise me, Rory-Beag?"

He repeated the word, "Mary."

"I am afraid we have startled you," she said.

Steam was rising from the wet earth and light and warmth shed all round them. He must be in heaven but the grip of her hands was palpable.

The man said, "The fact is we saw a poster and heard you had written a book. That's why we've come."

Now Rory-Beag looked at the man for the first time. He was the same height as himself. He could look into his eyes which were brown, his hair was brown, his jaw square, his mouth smiling. Roderick Matheson.

He looked back at Mary. The man's words had set his brain whirring.

Here were two young people, yes they could easily be eighteen. They spoke English yet she had sung a Gaelic song. They were in fine English dress.

He drew his hands away and grabbed the slate which always rested against the side of the counter. Stubs of chalk were scattered along the groove. His fingers fumbled to get hold of one. To write he had to grip the wrist of his right hand with his left so he could control the chalk. He managed to scrawl, "Am I dreaming?"

They said together, "No, you are not dreaming." The girl added, "We are the babies you saved in the barrel. Did my mother sing that song to me?"

He switched his gaze to her. He knew his jaw had dropped but his eyes were as smiling as he could make them. This was not Mary, but Mary-Beag. Little Mary and this was Roderick-Beag. Little Roderick.

His arms flew in the air. He capered about. "My babies have come to me. My babies have found me." Words poured through his head and came out in a babble of sound.

Through the noise Roderick said, "Do you think we could come inside, Rory-Beag?"

He grabbed at the door and yanked it open. He pulled them inside and fell to hugging them. Oh Little Mary was a delight to have in his arms.

She said, "You seemed to know me, Rory-Beag. Did you see my mother in me? Was it Annie?"

He stepped back and shook his head hard. Roderick handed him the slate.

"You are Mary," he wrote. "You are so like her. Yes, she sang that song. And you are Roderick."

They looked at each other and said with wonder the other's name.

"Mary!"

"Roderick!"

Then they turned to Rory-Beag and asked with one thought, "Were we baptised?"

He nodded happily. Then he pointed to Roderick and wrote, 'Father and mother Roderick and Annie Matheson.' He pointed to Mary 'Alistair and Mary Gunn.'

Then a strange thing happened. The two of them went into a sort of ecstasy, hugging and kissing each other. Rory-Beag's head jerked from one to the other.

They stopped and beamed at him. "We are not twins? Not brother and sister?"

He shook his head back and forth laughing heartily. It was astonishing but very pleasing that they were not upset. But of course he must give them his book and they would understand everything. The books were not here. They were at the Manse.

And that was when it came home to him that he had completely forgotten about the Reverend Josiah, dead or dying. He could feel the laughter shrivel away out of his face. They looked at him, alarmed.

He picked up a rag and wiped the slate. 'We must go to Manse. Minister ill. I live there.' He flung off his apron and reached for his coat hanging on a peg in the workroom. Now they could see through to the table where the owl stood.

"Oh isn't he splendid!" cried Mary.

Rory-Beag picked it up and wrapped it in a clean cloth and tucked it under his arm and hustled them in front of him out of the shop. He wouldn't stop to lock it up. The key hadn't been used since the day Diarmad had died. He was just beginning to realise the urgency of getting to the Manse to tell Josiah the babies had come. Oh how happy that would make him if only he was still alive!

He began to run, calling over his shoulder, "Follow me." Only a roar came out but they seemed to understand and came running after him too. My babies are following, he said in his head. To think of it, I have my babies. God has sent them to me. Blessed be God!

He stopped when they reached the Manse and they came up hardly panting. They were healthy young things. He was proud of them. He set down the owl, still wrapped up, by the house wall. There would be time for that later. Now he put his finger to his lips and approached the front door which was never locked. It creaked when he opened it and Flora came running to see who it was.

"Oh," she said in the Gaelic that came easier to her than English, "it's you, Angus. The doctor gave him something to soothe his cough and he's had a sleep. Why, who are these people? He's not *up to visitors.*"

He saw that Roderick and Mary were hesitating outside. He beckoned them in, but Mary had seen Flora's indignant looks. She said, "We'll wait here," and indicated the bench where so often Rory-Beag had sat when the sun was out, writing his book.

He shook his head, and pointed desperately from them to Flora. There was no time for writing down.

Mary understood his gesture to mean 'explain yourselves to her.' She said, "You know Rory-Beag wrote a book?"

Flora's English was equal to that. "Course I do."

"We are the babies he saved from the wreck. We came to find him."

Flora's eyes opened wide. Then she giggled, "You have grown! Please go in there," pointing to the parlour. She lapsed into Gaelic. "I'll see if the Reverend's fit to hear the news. Angus, just you wait a minute." She peeped in at *the door of the minister's study where the desk had been removed and his bed set up when h*e stopped being able to climb the stairs.

He heard her say, "Angus is here to see how you are. He's very excited. A young lady and gentleman have come and they say they are his babies. Can he come in if he calms down a little?"

Rory-Beag made downward soothing motions with his hands to show how calm he was. Then the weak voice croaked, "Let him bring them in. I want to see them."

Rory-Beag clasped his face in his hands to quell his excitement and beckoned his babies who were still just behind him. Then he opened the door wider and waved them in with a flourish. The bed filled half the room so they had to stand quite close and he could tell they were concerned and embarrassed. He was used to Josiah's pinched, parchment face but to them it must seem very shocking. But the Reverend Josiah held out a hand to them.

"Roderick Matheson and Mary Gunn. Am I pleased to see you!"

"Oh sir," Mary said, "we wouldn't have intruded on you for the world but Rory-Beag, Angus we should call him, insisted."

And Roderick said, "We haven't even the honour of knowing your name sir, but that you are the minister here."

"Josiah Mackenzie at your service, my dears. I wish I could be up and welcoming you properly. Was it the poster or his book that found you?"

"We haven't seen his book yet, reverend sir," Mary said. "Kenneth did have a glimpse of a newspaper advertisement and we also saw a copy of the paper that was in the barrel. We have a thousand questions to ask Rory – Angus, but we have left our baggage at the hotel in Canisbay where we will stay for a while and we can get to know Angus at his workplace. We will not intrude on you any longer now."

Rory-Beag was surprised at the name Kenneth till he remembered they had only known they were Roderick and Mary for about half an hour.

"We should introduce ourselves," Roderick said. "We are called Kenneth and Kate Reid at home."

"And where is home?" the minister asked.

"We live on a farm in Northumberland near the town of Hexham."

Rory-Beag was listening to all this in rapt amazement. His babies had grown into fine, kind-hearted young people and they were here in the Manse speaking with the dear minister who was not coughing and actually looked better than he had for some days. Could there be greater happiness in the world than he felt now?

Josiah was already asking the questions he was longing to ask. From their answers he learnt that they had not been told they were adopted but many things had made them suspect it. They were not too surprised now to find they were not twins, nor even brother and sister. They scarcely resembled each other and their parents not at all. What they most wanted to understand was why the paper in the barrel said Alastair Gunn had married Annie Matheson.

The minister was looking weary now. "You must read Angus's book."

Rory-Beag didn't wait to see them take their leave of him. He rushed into his room and snatched up two copies of the crimson leather printed books which he had always hoped to give to 'his babies'. Then he remembered that Mark Hunter had rearranged the sequence so that the printed version began with his own first memories of his parents' home. No, Roderick and Mary must see first his own diary where the answer to their question appeared quite quickly. He extracted the first volume in the beautiful black leather cover from the special drawer where he always kept it. Tonight he would have the joy of writing into the second volume a description of the coming of 'his babies' to his carpenter's shop.

Flora had shown them into the parlour and gone to make tea for them.

He went in and opened the book before their eyes and pointed to the words.

'Roderick Matheson was married to Annie. He died in October 1818.

Annie had a baby boy baptised Roderick in May 1819, the day before the clearing of Glen Kildonan.

Alastair Gunn was married to Mary Munro. She had a baby girl the day after the clearing. They were all on the sloop Gannet sailing to Thurso.

Mary died. Captain James Mackay baptised the baby Mary.

He married Alastair Gunn to Annie Matheson.

Annie died. Alastair died. The Captain died.

The babies were put in a barrel and lived.

I swam ashore and know all this is true.'

He watched them reading. How young and painstaking was his round writing!

They exchanged looks. "You are two days older than I," she said, "but it's still not clear why my father married your mother in the middle of a storm."

Rory-Beag picked up one of his notepads and wrote 'Please take the book to the hotel. I will be at work early tomorrow if you want to see me.'

"We *will* want to see you," Mary said. "Tell me, this is handwritten, but we learnt you had a book published?"

He nodded hard and ran to his room and fetched the crimson-backed, gold-lettered volumes: 'The Memory of Rory-Beag.'

They took them reverently and his happiness was complete.

Flora came in with the tray of tea with home-made bannocks and oatcakes.

"Ay," she said in English when she saw them admiring the books, "he big author now."

He wrote on his notepad, "*Journalist make my diary into book. Easy for you to read in print.*"

"May we take both?" Roderick asked. "The printed and your own? We'll bring them back of course."

More joyful nods but he pointed to the crimson books and wrote, "*Yours to keep.*"

While they were eating Flora fetched the newspaper in which her story had been told and showed it to them.

"You are famous too," Roderick said and she giggled.

When they got up to take their leave, Rory-Beag accompanied them to the door and could hardly bear to let them out of his sight. Would they come back to him at work next day? If they went would he be able to believe they had truly been here. He longed to tell them their coming was a miracle. Tonight he would write in the pages of his diary how it had happened in the midst of rain and tears, with heaven opening and light falling all round them. He would show it them tomorrow.

They turned and waved as they walked away from the Manse and his legs longed to run after them so that he could point across the sea to Stroma. If they stayed a while they could take a boat and visit Stroma. Oh if only he could pour out in spoken words to them all that was in his heart.

Flora had come to the door too and pointed to the cloth-wrapped parcel by the wall. "Who brought that?"

He leapt out and brought it to her, pulling off the cloth.

"Oh, you made it? For me?" She took it from him. "It's heavy!" He led her to the back door and pointed. "I see! To hold it open! He's beautiful." She set it down and gave him a kiss. This was joy upon joys.

He went back to peep in at the minister. His eyes opened and he said, "Your hopes are fulfilled, my son. I am ready to depart in peace."

Rory-Beag flung himself down by the bed and grasped the cold, knobbly hands as if he could keep him here by force.

He was still there on his knees half an hour later when Flora found him fast asleep from the emotional exhaustion of the day, his head flopped on the bedcover and his hands slackly resting on the minister's which were now truly cold.

31

Kenneth and Kate sat reading by the hearth in the inn parlour, so engrossed they didn't even look up when the landlord came in to put more peats on the fire.

When the evening light was too dim for reading he brought candles and they were dragged back to the present and looked at each other with tearful, wondering eyes. He made up the fire again and went out without speaking. They had already found his English was very limited.

When they were alone again Kate said, "Oh Kenneth, Rory-Beag writes with such love for my parents and your mother too that I feel I have got to know them all. He has written down every word spoken on that doomed ship. What a memory! But now I am missing them so much. I wish they could have been our parents. They were not at all like the Reids. I suppose we would have been brought up in Canada. How strange! I don't think I can read any more. I must go to bed." She closed the black book in which Rory-Beag had told first in emotional detail the whole story of the babies' brief lives up to the discovery of them in the barrel. "That man is all heart, Kenneth. He has loved and longed for us from the moment we were taken away from him in the arms of strangers till we appeared today at his carpenter's shop. Did you see in his eyes, above the wretched deformity of his face, the intensity of his joy?"

Kenneth nodded and stood up, the red book open in his hand. "This account begins from his earliest memories of his own parents and I've reached the point where he starts life with the minister. It's all in the first person but I can tell where the editor has used his own words to summarise. Print is easier to read but I look forward to reading that one."

Kate was so charged with inward weeping that she wondered he could sound so calm. "Are you not devastated reading about your parents?"

His eyes darkened and his jaw clenched. "Don't. I've been trying not to let anger get hold of me. They were both cruelly done to death. I didn't expect that. Drowned in a storm yes but no, not the way it happened. I'd rather read the rest of Rory-Beag's own story. He seems to bear no bitterness despite everything."

Kate picked up one of the candles. "Yes, but Kenneth, what about the marriage between my father and your mother? We can see now that it happened for a future in Canada. But does it make us half-brother and sister?"

He picked up the other candle and they made their way between the huddled chairs to the room door while he thought about his answer. "I say no because we still have different parents and the marriage – if we can call it that – was performed a few minutes before the death of both so was never consummated. With a villain like Jamie Mackay gabbling a few words it was a mockery of a marriage anyway."

She nodded and began to mount the stairs. They had asked for and been given separate rooms under the eaves with nothing in either but a bed, a wash stand and a few hooks in the deal panelling where they might hang some clothes.

Some light still came through the tiny windows. She thought of her mother great with child crowded with the rest in the attic room of Robert Mackay. I was that child, she kept telling herself, and the wailing baby that disturbed their sleep was Kenneth. How will I sleep now with my mind so full?

"Goodnight," she said.

Kenneth seemed taken aback at the abruptness of it but replied "Well, yes, goodnight, sleep well." He went into his room but now his thoughts rushed on to the logical end of his answer to Kate's question. Ever since the night in Gibraltar he had stopped thinking of Kate as a sister. During his travels he had held in his mind the images of her in the blue ball dress and in her nightgown when he had said goodbye. On his return the embrace on the doorstep had roused his passion. During the weeks at home and all the way here on board ship he desired her, body and soul. He loved her as he had never done as a brother. But what was her true state of mind? She had seemed to rejoice with him when Rory-Beag revealed they were not related but was she ready to shed all sisterly feelings? She had cast aside Arthur Herrington but was that on his account or because she never really loved Arthur?

I must proceed very slowly with her, he told himself, taking off his coat and flinging it on the bed. She is taken up with the past just now while I want to think solely of the future.

Only a little warmth from the afternoon sunshine had found its way into these upper rooms. He changed into his nightshirt and slid under the covers lying flat on his back and trying not to shiver in a bed that felt slightly damp. He was unsatisfied. He and Kate had sat silent a long time reading but not shared their thoughts to any depths. Their parting had been too sudden. It wouldn't do. He jumped up and put his coat round his shoulders and crept out and tapped on her door, calling out softly, "Are you asleep?"

"No," came her voice and he thrilled at the sound of it.

He went in, reminding himself – proceed slowly, nothing of the future yet.

"I can't sleep," he said, "can you?"

She was in her nightgown, half sitting up on the pillows, her hair down round her shoulders. The one candle set in a bracket on the wooden bed-head lit up the curve of her breasts. He felt a surge of passion so great he had to sit on the end of the bed and clutch his arms round his chest.

"No," she said. "If you want to talk about it all I don't mind."

"Only one thing really." His voice came out thick. His resolve to move slowly flew out of the window. "I need to know. If we're not brother and sister then can we be husband and wife?"

She stared for several seconds, mouth and eyes open. "Oh Kenneth."

Then she began shaking her head and his heart sank, but it was only to say, "No, not Kenneth, Roderick." She put out her hand towards him. He shuffled closer and her hand caressed his arm while he held himself in, waiting. "You are Roderick. I am Mary. Roderick and Mary have been parted since we came out of the barrel. We were only reunited yesterday."

He managed to croak out, "So what are you saying?"

"I need time to get into Mary's skin."

"And then?"

"Yes, Roderick and Mary can marry."

He flung open his arms and clasped her and she held him close, her head on his shoulder and wept.

He didn't try to kiss her. He had vowed to proceed slowly and the pace of her response was robbing him of breath. He couldn't help it. He began to sob too. They clung together till at last her chest heaved and she murmured, "This was meant to be."

They drew apart and looked at each other. Her mind as always rushed ahead of his and she said, "What will they say when we go home?"

"It doesn't matter."

"We must tell no one at first. We must take our time. We shouldn't live in the same house. We must plan a home of our own. I will be Mary Gunn and you will be Roderick Matheson for at least two more years. Perhaps we will tell Rory-Beag."

She laughed and her face was dimpled and radiant as he loved to see it. He thought, I have bumbled slowly and ponderously to this point and she has made the leap like a flash of lightning.

He stood up. "I'll have to tear myself away. It's too hard being so close, clad as we are. I love you, love you, Kate. I love you." He was at the door looking back at her when she said, "No, no, no. *Not* Kate. *Mary.*"

He nodded solemnly. "Mary," and went quickly out.

In the morning, a pearly morning, all that May ought to be, they couldn't wait to go to the carpenter's shop but when they approached it they saw the shutters closed and a notice hanging outside.

The Reverend Josiah Mackenzie has died. Inquirers please come to the

Manse.'

They looked at each other. Are we inquirers? They decided they were and walked on, their joy in each other a little dimmed at the thought of Rory-Beag's grief.

He opened the door to them with what they now knew to be his happy grin. He held up his slate on which he had written, *Josiah is with God. He is happy. We must all be happy.'*

Flora, though, had red eyes as she waved them into the sitting room.

"Funeral," she said, and held up three fingers.

"In three days' time?"

She nodded.

"We will stay for it."

"Men only," she said, nodding again and managing a smile.

They learnt that women did not attend a graveside but could share in feasting afterwards.

It was a strange time. Everyone in the district seemed to know that Roderick and Mary, Rory-Beag's babies, had arrived in the shape of the young, handsome English couple. People who had copies of his book brought them to the inn and wanted them to sign their names in them. Their landlord made brave attempts at English and furnished their rooms with a small table each and a stool. They spent time at the Manse in the evenings telling Rory-Beag about themselves and Allenbrae and how Bet Moray had married Tom and then left him for Luigi and how Luigi had tried to send word to their father about their birth. Rory-Beag was glad to hear it.

'Bet Moray bad girl,' he wrote, *'Luigi honourable man.'* They smiled at this.

After the minister's funeral Kate sat down to write to Arthur Herrington. "He must be told before my eighteenth birthday. I promised. I will only say I am sorry but I cannot return his love. He'll recover."

"*I* wouldn't," Kenneth said.

She looked up with a crinkled forehead. "Don't make it any harder to write. I can't bear to hurt people's feelings."

The letter was very short and was despatched with longer ones from them both to the Reid parents as they had begun to call them. They said they had discovered all they could of their birth parents and would now like to be called Roderick and Mary as those were their baptismal names. Kenneth wrote that he wanted to work on the farm with Ridley and live at Allenbrae while Kate wrote separately to Grandmother Reid and hoped to have a stay with her for a while to savour town life.

After they had taken a boat trip to Stroma Kate also wrote to Elsie describing the island where her mother was born and the way of life of the people there.

Rory-Beag came with them and for the first time since his boyhood he stood on the shore where the waves had flung him. He pointed to the great craggy cliff where *Gannet* was smashed and the shelving pebble shore where the barrel had rolled in. He was so overcome by the memory that he had to hold both of them in a passionate embrace as if he could not bear ever to lose them again.

Kate said to Kenneth later, "If we go home in another few days how will he bear it? Can we possibly take him back with us? He has lost his one dear friend."

"But his work? The people here will lose their carpenter and could he ever settle in an English town or village when he has known only this wild open landscape of Caithness with the sea and islands?"

"But we've each finished both the books," she said, "and know of the journeys he made to find 'his babies.' He cannot lose them again. Let's ask him."

Rory-Beag had transferred his few possessions to the two rooms Diarmad had used at the back of the shop. The Kirk authorities were alerted to the need for a new minister at Canisbay and Flora and Malcolm the post-boy had named the date of their wedding.

Rory-Beag saw Roderick and Mary approaching early on a day of fierce wind. They were battling against it, pushed this way and that, clutching their hats.

As they came up he opened his door and pulled them inside. They were laughing with the effort. Oh how he loved them!

He shepherded them into the kitchen and sat them down and began to get together some kindling to raise a fire in the hearth but they shook their heads.

"We've come with an idea," Roderick began. Mary was looking at him with her glowing smile. It seemed full of meaning today. He sensed something important was about to be said. He sat down on the hearth seat and leant forward, all agog.

"We will have to go home soon," Roderick said and Rory-Beag's heart plummeted. "Would you consider coming with us?"

He shot off the seat, banging his head on the corner of the chimney breast. He capered about the kitchen clutching his head and laughing.

Mary put out a hand towards him and he drew her onto her feet and danced round the cramped space with her till they were both dizzy and had to sit down again.

"I think he's pleased," she said.

Roderick turned his chair towards him. "We are speaking of a permanent move to England where you could still practise as a carpenter. Could you bear that?"

Rory-Beag nodded vigorously.

"We have to tell you that Mary and I hope to be married in two years' time."

He leapt up, banged his head again and clapped his hands. His babies marrying, that was a miracle!

"But meanwhile," Roderick went on, "we will have to find you somewhere to live till Mary and I can offer you a home with us."

He nodded slowly, then went into the back room where he had a box of his treasures and brought out a paper which he showed them. It was a bank draft from his publisher for fifteen guineas.

He grabbed one of his notepads and wrote, *"Pay for journey and rent shop?"*

Mary exclaimed, "They are selling your book! You have two professions – author and carpenter." She looked at Roderick. "We'll visit the newspaper offices in Newcastle and tell them you have come.

We'll write reviews of your book and it will be in all the shops. The mayor will interview you. Mark Hunter will come from London and write another story for his paper that you have found your babies."

Rory-Beag could hardly contain his excitement. But then he clasped his poor chin and wrote, '*Not good at interviews. Don't want to be famous. Just live and work not too far from you.*'

"You shall live *with* us," cried Mary, "when we have our own home. If God blesses us you will play with our babies."

Ah! Babies! Babies! Rory-Beag sang in his head. This time I will be patient and God may let me see them grow up. He hindered me when I sought Roderick and Mary in my own time. But then He sent them to me and they are here, their blessed selves. Dear Reverent Josiah, I believe I am learning.

He sank his big frame to his knees and tears of thankfulness ran down his face.

They joined him one on either side, their arms across his shoulders, holding him.

Epilogue

June 1839

All the ladies of the family are seated on the terrace at Allenbrae while the men have walked over to see the progress made on Roderick and Mary's future home. A heat haze lies over the fields and the hum of bees is in the air.

Clara speaks up. "Surely, Mary, Roderick hasn't asked Angus to be best man – in the *Abbey* where the county people go? I screamed when I first saw him."

Anne Reid says, "My dear, who else could he possibly ask? Angus is his best friend. He wouldn't be alive if it wasn't for Angus. And they have shared a cottage for two whole years while turning it into a fine home with the labour almost entirely of their own hands."

"But he can't speak."

"He has written a speech which Ridley will read at the wedding feast. Is that not another reason for him to play a prominent part? He has transformed my son from a nervous irrational being into a man I am proud of. I still marvel how he did it."

Adelaide looks up. She has given Mary a wide lace border and is showing her how to sew it on her veil. "*I* know how he did it. Ridley's study door was open just now and I saw he had a framed text on the wall. Well, I like texts so I went in and read it. But it wasn't a Bible text. It was headed, '*Angus's answer to my question 'How are you so happy and yet so afflicted?*' Below it read, '*God always gives the afflicted an opportunity to do good. You and Mrs Reid were afflicted with childlessness but you did a good work. You made a loving home for two orphans.*'

Clara clasps her head in her hands. "*I* told him the same thing in

Leith twenty years ago. There's no disgrace in adopting, I said. But he never listened to me. It was his pride! Yes, that was knocked clean out of him by Angus's joy when the twins brought him home."

Mary giggles. "You'll have to stop saying 'the twins' when we're married."

Grandmother Ida throws up her hands. "Eh, Kate, I don't think I'll ever understand how you can marry your brother."

Adelaide snaps, "Mother, you've had two years to get used to calling her Mary. I've accepted I'm not her godmother any more but I'm happy to give her this bridal lace. *I'll* never wear it now so *she* might as well have it."

Mary says, "I'm very grateful, Aunt, and I'm happy for you to be godmother still. The lace is beautiful." She holds it up. "There! My stitches are not as fine as yours but I don't think anyone will notice."

Footsteps crunch on the gravel and male voices are heard.

"Hide the veil," squeals Clara. "It's unlucky if he sees it before the day."

Four men appear. Roderick and Angus, bronzed and hardened from labour, Ridley, looking sprightly, and Grandfather Reid, wizened and walking with a stick. Peter and Martin are in Newcastle minding the business and Henry Stokoe has been dead a year, leaving Ida in distress and confusion.

George Reid sits down with a grunt. "I'd say that was a good mile walk but worth the effort. From a two up, two down cottage it's now a fine dwelling, worthy of my grandchildren. Yes, Ridley, I'm still calling them that whatever you say."

Ridley folds his arms across his chest. "*I* say we will have new neighbours on the estate next week, Mr and Mrs Matheson. My farm manager, Roderick Matheson, is marrying a Miss Mary Gunn."

His mother laughs. "Ridley, you ever flew from one extreme to the other. But now tell us, Roderick, have you thought of a new name for the place?"

"If Mary agrees – I thought as we came along – what about Stroma House?"

Angus leaps in the air and nods wildly.

Mary, hiding the veil in the folds of her skirt, says, "Yes, please. I'll never forget standing on that shore and picturing the barrel rolling in. I could imagine myself bouncing inside with Roderick and dear Angus here running along the shore with his legs all dripping blood to see if we were still alive."

Ida lifts her head. "Who's dripping blood?"

Anne Reid pats her hand. "No one, dear. Go to sleep."

Angus, who always has a notepad hung round his neck with a pencil on a string writes, "*Can I help get the meal?*"

Everybody laughs. He is always hungry.

Mary jumps up. "Elsie has everything laid out on the dining-table – a cold collation."

Ida frowns again. "Elsie? What happened to Jane?"

"Jane died last winter. She was seventy-seven."

"My poor Henry was only seventy-two."

Anne Reid helps her to her feet. "No talk of death. We are here to settle the final arrangements for the wedding of these dear young souls. Let us go in and feast."

Ida bumbles after her. "I don't know how it is. I always thought they were twins. What happened to Arthur Herrington?"

Mary smiles. "He found a nice, comfortable wife, Grandmamma."

"Oh yes. I've met her, but isn't *he* your *brother*?" She points at Roderick.

Roderick slips his arm round Mary's waist. "Husband sounds better to me. My darling, what are you clasping rolled up there?"

"Sh! it's my veil. You're not to see it before the day." She pops it on her chair and sits on it.

When they are all sitting down Ida looks across the table at the two of them sitting together and exchanging the looks of lovers.

"I don't know." She shakes her head. "You *used* to be twins."

Angus chuckles. He will record that in Volume Three of 'The Memory of Rory-Beag', already filled, page after page, with hard work, happiness and laughter.